THE HAPPENING

VERED EHSANI

Copyright © 2021 by Sterling & Stone

All rights reserved.

No part of this book may be reproduced in any form or by any electronic or mechanical means, including information storage and retrieval systems, without written permission from the author, except for the use of brief quotations in a book review.

The authors greatly appreciate you taking the time to read our work. Please consider leaving a review wherever you bought the book, or telling your friends about it, to help us spread the word.

Thank you for supporting our work.

THE HAPPENING

Chapter One

"This is what happens when you follow a white elephant into the rabbit hole," Jamaal told Abe once it was all over.

Abe tutted. "My dear cousin, don't you mean follow the white *rabbit* down the rabbit hole?"

"Nope. It was definitely a white elephant."

But on Monday morning? Jamaal wasn't thinking about white elephants or rabbits, or the destruction of the world as he knew it. The morning started the way almost every Monday started: *with war.*

He focused on the battle raging around him, and on not getting killed. Especially the *not getting killed* part.

"Surviving would be nice," he muttered.

Surviving was less likely by the gunshot. Thick smoke curled across the ceiling of his team's last refuge. Their warehouse hiding place was so derelict, even the horned rats didn't want it. The enemy was going to take it at any moment. So much for a safe haven.

A nerve-grating shriek scraped at his psyche, followed by wordless pleading. Who — or what — was being tortured out there? The sounds gnawed at his ears, plucked his spine like a guitar string. Good thing the crashing bombs blotted out the most gruesome noises.

Jamaal shouldered his portable cannon and rested it on the edge of a windowpane. Shattered glass ornamented his view. "Got my sights on the sniper," he whispered into his comm.

"Abe that," Abe said.

"Why can't you follow the rules, and say *Roger that*?"

"What rules? It's war," Abe shouted over an explosion. A bronze airship crumpled to the ground.

"Don't complain when you die first."

"Abe that."

A metallic T. Rex crashed through the far end of the warehouse. It belched flames through silver-spiked fangs. Fire swallowed the remaining members of their team. Their charred stumps crunched under the beast's claws.

"Great. Now what're we gonna do?"

"What we're *not* going to do is panic," Abe said. "Do you have eyes on the cyborg?"

"Nope. I swear she's a serial killer." Jamaal checked his ammo. He was almost out.

"I beg to differ. Serial killers use axes or chainsaws or—"

"Sporks?"

"I suppose, if you're planning on scooping out eyeballs. The point is to use anything to increase the blood and gore. She's an assassin."

"Bad enough."

"I see her. Crazy Eyed Cyborg's on your nine o'clock!"

"Jamaal, exit the warehouse on your three o'clock," his Placer ordered. Her words were clear, crisp despite the armageddon around him.

"I'm on it, Abe." Jamaal ignored Sarah's efforts to send him *away* from the battle. She was always trying to save him. "Cyborg's not gonna kill me today."

"Famous last words," Abe said.

"I mean it."

"Let's get at it, then."

"Okay, I—"

"Jamaal, where're you going?" Abe shuffled to his side. "I said your *nine* o'clock, not your six o'clock. How are we related?"

Jamaal cursed while squatting. He turned around, squinting through the smoke and dust. "Maybe my six o'clock is your nine o'clock. You ever think about that?"

"Ladies, can we please focus?" a woman's voice cut through Abe and the roar of battle.

Sadly, the voice didn't belong to Sarah. She would've said something sweet, like, "Please exit Hell's Fury, Jamaal, or else you'll die. And I will be heartbroken if that happens."

Okay, her heart wouldn't really break, because she didn't have one. But she'd pretend. That counted for something, right?

This other voice ... His personal nemesis. Always trying to impale him with one of her swords. Glaring at him with her glowing red eye.

"Whatever, Crazy Eyed," Jamaal said. "I'm ready to die, but not today!"

The cyborg burst through the warehouse's flimsy wall, leaving a gaping hole behind her.

She raised her arm — the one with a small machine gun attached to the end — and grinned. "Got news for you, Jam Boy."

"Retreat, Jamaal! I'm saving myself, but it's not too late

for you. Although it probably is." Abe disappeared into the shadow-filled chaos outside the warehouse.

Abe was right. It was too late for Jamaal. The cyborg squeezed a round of miniature bombs into his chest. Before they hit, he thanked the gods of hAPPn he wasn't wearing a sensory suit. Especially one of those newer models. The updated S-Suits were crazy sensitive. He would've felt every bomb.

The force of their impact tossed him outside. He landed on a pile of scorched something. Best not to look too closely.

"Jamaal, your mother is summoning you," his Placer murmured.

He rolled off of the pile and onto the battlefield. His insides oozed outside. "I'm kinda busy, Sarah. Take a message."

He reached for his lifebelt. He was pretty sure he had one more life left for this level of Hell's Fury. Otherwise, he'd have to borrow one from Abe. Again. Like he wasn't already in serious debt to his cousin. How did Abe always manage to *not* get shot?

"She's rather insistent, Jamaal." Sarah's smooth, calm voice invited him to leave the disaster that was his life at the moment. "She says breakfast is ready."

"Well, I'm not! I need to finish the level. I'll beat the cyborg this time."

"Based on your previous history in Hell's Fury, a victory over Crazy Eyed Cyborg is highly unlikely, Jamaal."

"Thanks for the encouragement, Sarah. You're supposed to be on my side."

"I am. Your mother is still summoning you."

"She can wait."

The cyborg stood over him, grinning. She tapped the

golden medallion hanging around her thick neck. "Look who won ... again!"

He blinked moisture away from his eyes. Sweat, not tears. The Caligula Medallion — the key to victory in Hell's Fury — winked at him. He raised his forearm and gave her the finger.

"That's not gonna save you, Jam Boy," said Crazy Eyed Cyborg. She yanked off the machine gun, then fitted the stub with a laser cannon blaster. "I'm gonna smear you like a condiment. Are you wearing an S-Suit?"

"No."

"Too bad for me. Because the blaster? That would've hurt like a—"

"Jamaal, she's marching down the stairs," Sarah said. "She'll arrive at your door in approximately 3.2 seconds."

"I love it when you talk numbers," Jamaal grunted, and reached for a plasma gun. It wouldn't save his life, but it would definitely put a few dents in the cyborg's armor. That'd set her back a few cybercoins. Teach her not to underestimate him.

More importantly, she always wore an S-Suit while in hAPPn.

Prepare for sensory overload, he thought with a grin.

"Say hi to your mama for me." Crazy Eyed Cyborg aimed her cannon blaster.

"Right after I say hi to yours."

They pulled their triggers in unison. Jamaal didn't get to see the impact of his feeble, Hail Mary effort. Bright white light bloomed before him. He groaned and yanked off his wraparound Shaids in reflex.

He glanced around his bedroom, rubbing his eyes. He almost expected to see a cyborg standing in the corner. Arm cannon lifted, aiming at his head. She always went for the most brutal, messiest shots.

A loud rapping alerted him right before his mom flung open the door.

"Mama-i!"

"Jamaal Shirazi, I'm calling you, and I'm calling you, and now I'm up and down the stairs. It's breakfast." She gestured at his bare legs. "Put on some clothes."

"What are these?" He patted his shorts.

"Dirty laundry. Upstairs in one minute. Dressed!"

He glanced down at his Shaids. He hadn't logged off yet, so Crazy Eyed Cyborg and Abe had heard the entire interaction. He could hear them through the Shaids' small speakers: Abe laughing like a hyena, snorting and howling, the cyborg shouting something about *mama's boy*.

"Whatever." He slipped the Shaids back onto his face.

The battle was over. Bodies were strewn across the landscape. Only Abe and Crazy Eyed Cyborg were left standing. Still laughing, they dodged around burned-out vehicles, taking shots at each other.

"Placer," Jamaal said.

"Yes, Jamaal."

"Exit Hell's Fury. Log out."

The battlefield dissolved in a shower of fiery pixels. When the smoke cleared, he was standing under his welcome arch. His personalized menu floated to one side, the names of his three perfect-fit Places, his e-Trax work-Place, and his favorite public sites listed in alphabetical order.

And the archway in front of him, granting entrance to the world of hAPPn.

He glanced up at the top of the archway where three words were engraved in the stone blocks: *Here For Truth*.

"More like here for fun." Jamaal glanced at his menu, figuring he had at least a couple more minutes before

Mama-i threatened to drag him up the stairs. "Placer, log in. Enter Geo Rocks Place."

"Logging in. Entering Geo Rocks," Sarah said.

He popped into the public area of Geo Rocks. His other Places — Geeks Rule, and Metals & Mud — were definitely a lot more fun, but weren't work-related. And his supervisor liked to see him spend his time wisely, so he ended up visiting Geo Rocks more often. Besides, it was a great Place to network and get geology-related news.

The public area was a crystal cavern. Stalagmites and stalactites glowed into life as he glided past them. Videos streamed across their surfaces, everything from adverts to fun facts. Great for school kids and tourists, but not his thing.

He entered the members-only cave, then ducked down a side chute into the news stream. Headlines floated like visible currents around him. They bobbed into view long enough for him to decide if he wanted to read them. He let most of them float downstream.

An article swished around his avatar. A new rare earth metal discovered in Kenya. Headlines promised the metal was the key for the next generation of energy storage. Big news, if it was true.

He reeled it in closer, wondering if e-Trax had registered the claim yet. Or had someone leaked the story before the company announcement? He didn't have time to read the article, but snagged a copy in his net for later.

Another headline swam by and grabbed his attention, only because it was closer to home: *Eco-War Now's leader arrested for vandalizing Vancouver's industry monument.*

He flicked the headline away, as if being in the same digital space could contaminate him. What a bunch of green necks. Always getting into trouble. It seemed Eco-War Now was constantly involved in angry, ignorant protests against progress, and violent skirmishes with the police.

"Get a real job," he muttered as the headline drowned under a steady stream of other news.

Everyone knew the members of green neck Places were a bunch of unemployed bums who lived in their parents' basements.

Sure, Jamaal also lived in his mom's basement, but the similarities ended there. He was gainfully employed as a lead geologist for one of the biggest geology companies in North America. And he had to live with his mom. Vancouver was crazy expensive for anyone earning less than a billionaire. Lucky for him, his mom wasn't in any hurry to kick him out. One of the perks of Persian culture, he guessed.

He skimmed a few more headlines.

"Jamaal, your mother is summoning you again."

"Thanks, Sarah. Guess we can't avoid it anymore. Send me alerts for any work-related meetings," he ordered. "See you soon. Log out."

"I'll be waiting, Jamaal. Logging out."

Jamaal was still grinning when he removed the Shaids and tossed them onto his workstation.

When he trudged upstairs in sweatpants and a T-shirt, his mom clucked disapprovingly but waved at him to sit. Abe was already there. His cousin had been living in their house ever since his move to Vancouver.

"Ey, baba! What is more important than breakfast?" Mama-i muttered and pushed way too much food onto his plate.

"Lunch?"

"Sitting with your family, that's what!"

Jamaal didn't bother arguing. She'd only complain he

was too skinny. Three cooked meals a day, and she still insisted he never ate enough.

"Mama-i, that's enough! Thanks." He pulled out his Doodad and scrolled through the notifications. Jamaal had abandoned his phone, laptop and every other smart device after buying a Doodad. He didn't need any other device after that.

"And turn those off." Mama-i jabbed a finger at his Doodad, sitting on the table next to his plate. "You spend too much time on it. Too much! What do you think, Abe?"

"Absolutely," Abe agreed while scanning the notifications on his own Doodad.

Jamaal kicked Abe's chair. What a traitor. "Come on, Mama-i. I've got to keep up-to-date. Work starts in a few minutes."

"You are not a heart doctor. Your sister, though. Now she has a reason. A real doctor. Can you imagine?"

Abe smirked. "Let the boy eat, auntie."

"I wish he eats. Look at him! You think I don't feed him, the way he looks."

"Apart from dressing like a slob, he's fat ... I mean, fine," Abe said.

"I'm deciding what's fine. Don't you dare."

Jamaal's hand froze on the way to his Doodad, a string of new notifications floating across the screen. "Mama-i, seriously."

"Rules, Jamaal-joon. Rules! How are you going to meet a nice Persian girl if you are always inside that thing?"

Abe snickered. "And so it begins."

"How do you know I'm not meeting nice Persian girls in hAPPn?" Jamaal asked.

"Are you?"

"No."

"Do they cook real food in there?"

"No, but—"

"Then why do you spend so much time in it?"

"Not everything revolves around food, Mama-i."

"Ey, baba! You don't eat for a few days, and then see what you say."

Jamaal snuck a peek at his Doodad. "You have membership in a Place or two, right? Something about Persian cooking."

Mama-i huffed. "I do more than cook."

"True. You talk about cooking, and eating."

"Let's not forget the nice Persian girls," Abe said.

Jamaal pointed at Abe. "Why don't you tell him to get off his Doodad?"

"Snitches end in ditches, Jam Boy," Abe said.

"There's more to life than hAPPn." Mama-i stared over her teacup at him, silently daring him to argue.

Jamaal stole another glance at his Doodad. "Not really. Everything happens in hAPPn. Work, entertainment. You're basically missing out on life if you're not in it."

Abe clapped Jamaal's back. "That sounds like a company slogan."

Jamaal shrugged and focused on eating as fast as possible. He was going to be late. Again. Being late for work could cost him some cybercoin.

He'd built up a decent account, thanks to his frequent interactions in his Places. He was at Level 3 Intermediary membership in Geo Rocks and in Geeks Rule, and Level 2 Basic membership in Metals & Mud. He only had to invite another twenty more people, and he'd jump up another level. But he still didn't have enough cybercoins for the bubble bike he wanted.

"Jamaal-joon, I heard about a new Place," Mama-i said.

"Already at my limit," Jamaal said.

"It's a dating Place for Persians."

"I logged out for this?" Jamaal groaned.

"Good for you, auntie," Abe said. "It's about time. You should absolutely start dating—"

"Not for me!" Mama-i wagged a finger at Jamaal. "I am only looking for very *especial* girls. I want you to be happy."

"I am happy."

Mama-i made a disgusted noise. "I mean happily *married*."

"Are we finished yet?"

"No. I met Mrs. Vahabzadeh last week. Her two daughters graduated from doctor school."

"Medical school, Mama-i."

"Very smart. Pretty. Good family. Very especial."

"Mama-i, the word is *special*. No one says *especial*."

"Don't you want your children to grow up with their cousins? Rana is having her second. At this rate—"

A notification beeped on his Doodad, at the same time. Abe's too. A general invite from the CEO of e-Trax. Everyone was being summoned for an emergency company meeting. No excuses. Attendance was mandatory.

"We're saved by the bell, dear cousin," Abe said. "Although it looks like a fire alarm rather than a bell."

Jamaal read the message. "What does *she* want? And what could be so important?"

"There's a fire?" Mama-i asked.

"One can only hope," Abe said.

"Gotta run, Mama-i." Jamaal gave his mother a kiss on the cheek. "See you inside, Abe."

"Don't forget to feed the cat!"

"This is why you should have a digital cat," he said to Mama-i on his way to the kitchen. "It can feed itself."

"That cat is especial. It keeps me in the real world."

"Reality's overrated." Jamaal quickly opened a can of cat food and dumped it into a bowl.

He had better things to do, like get to work on time. And after that? Find a way to destroy Crazy Eyed Cyborg.

Chapter Two

Eva Taylor woke up without any premonition that a three-headed elephant was about to trample over her carefully organized life.

Instead, she smiled at the sunshine pooling on the floor near her bed. A chiming *ding* notified her of another message. She didn't have to look at her Doodad to know what it was about.

She stretched her arms and sighed. "Chief Growth Engineer." She said her new title slowly, tasting each word like a piece of dark chocolate from her favorite brand, the one with cocoa nibs and blueberries. "Sure sounds better than Assistant Growth Engineer."

Talk about a terrible acronym. Her staff had referred to her as AGE Eva. But Chief Growth Engineer? There was no acronym at that level. Not at hAPPening. The company behind the most successful social media app in the history of apps referred to its top management as *Chiefs*. And her new position as Chief Growth Engineer was arguably the second-most important job just behind the CEO.

And I made it, Eva thought as she admired the bedroom.

They'd bought the house shortly after she'd been promoted to Assistant. Theo had freaked out the entire week before they signed the purchase agreement.

"This is huge," he'd said while pacing the kitchen of their two-bedroom apartment. "I mean, really, *really* huge. Do you realize what we're doing?"

"We're buying a house, Theo," she'd said, rubbing away her smile. "Not a mansion."

"Might as well be, for what we're paying. The mortgage. It's like that sword from Rossi's English homework …" He snapped his fingers. "What was it called?"

"The Sword of Damocles."

"Which hung by a thread—"

"To be specific, it hung by a single hair of a horse's tail over a king's throne. Do you see any horses around here, Theo?"

"Forget the horsehair. This house, the mortgage, it's a sword over our necks. We promised we wouldn't go into debt. We'd be comfortable. Live within our means. But this—"

"Are you kidding, Theo? We scrimped and saved to get here. We finally did it! We're not exactly earning minimum wage anymore. Besides, I need a dedicated office, now that I'm Assistant Growth Engineer, and you …"

She'd wrapped her arms around his neck. "You, my talented man, deserve your own workspace. Our living room looks like a laundromat lost its war with a paint factory. Rossi has to do her homework at the kitchen counter. And I'm scrunched up in a corner of our bedroom."

"I know. I get it. But this is big."

She'd grabbed Theo's shaking hands. "Yes. It is. And so

are we. We can do this. Our careers are taking off. We can afford it, so why not?"

Theo had half a dozen arguments. But in the end, he'd agreed. They almost always saw eye to eye eventually. It was one of the reasons she adored him. They never fought. Not the way other couples did. Sure, they had disagreements. Who didn't? But they never lasted long. By moving day, he'd taken the lead in organizing and decorating their new home.

Eva rolled onto her side and stared out the floor-to-ceiling window. The view was stunning. It should be. They'd paid for it when they'd moved into one of Seattle's most expensive neighborhoods. Almost every room had a beautiful view. She had her own office now. Theo had a workshop where he could toss paint without worrying about staining any furniture or laundry. And Rossi …

Eva tried not to frown. She was still convinced that the move was good for them all. Rossi no longer had to sit on one edge of the kitchen counter to do her homework. Her bedroom boasted a study nook, a walk-in closet, and a private balcony. But despite these perks, nothing seemed to make her daughter happy lately.

"Teens. It's just a phase," she'd told Theo, and hoped it was true.

Eva stretched out an arm and snagged her Doodad as another *ding* alerted her to more notifications.

She scrolled through the mostly congratulatory messages, pausing when she saw one from Marsha White, Chief of the Advert Department.

Good job. I guess you're the obvious choice since the CEO has firsthand experience with your talents.

Eva snorted. Typical Marsha. Congratulating her while she slid the knife into her back.

The applicant list was supposed to be confidential, but

Eva had heard the rumors. Marsha had also applied for the position. hAPPening's Growth Department was widely viewed as the most exciting, innovative and essential department. It's where everything happened.

Sure, Advert generated massive revenue for the company. But Growth was responsible for enrolling more members, increasing membership in hAPPn's various Places, and encouraging those members to spend more time inside the app. Without the audience, there was no revenue from advertising or from affiliate sales.

Even the sales of hAPPening's wraparound, 3D-enabled Shaids — the most popular side product they had yet created — relied directly on the work done by Growth. And as its Chief, she was next in line as CEO. Eva felt sorry for the Advert staff; it was going to be a rough day for them.

"Sore loser," Eva said, still making her way through the more positive congratulatory messages. There was one from hAPPening's CEO Jackson Rustle.

Super thrilled you're Chief Growth! We're going to spend more time together! Wink, wink.

Eva laughed softly at Jack's flirtatious undertone. At least he was a harmless flirt. More of a tease than anything else. He'd never crossed the line while maintaining an informal professionalism with his staff. He'd been madly in love once, or so said the rumor, and got his heart crushed when the woman had dumped him. Eva found it hard to visualize him being madly in love with anything but himself, and the bottom line. But hey, miracles happened, right?

Another message from him: *Remember. World domination, baby!*

That made her smile. When Eva had been promoted to Assistant Growth Engineer a year ago, Jack had invited her to meet him for a one-on-one in his online office — a glass cube immersed in an ocean, surrounded by very lifelike sea creatures of all shapes, sizes and colors.

"Like the view, Ms. Taylor?" he'd asked, waving at a dolphin swimming by overhead.

She had to stare straight ahead. Vertigo did weird things to her head when she risked a glimpse at the clear glass floor. They were floating over a coral reef. Sure, it was all a digital creation, a collection of cleverly designed pixels. The glass wouldn't crack beneath her weight. She wouldn't drown in this replica of an ocean.

But a part of her brain begged to differ, and her vision furiously blurred at the edges.

She'd focused on his bright blue eyes, using them as an anchor to some semblance of reality. "It's ... different."

"This has always been the goal, Eve. You're okay with a first-name basis, right?"

"Of course, but it's Eva. And what's the goal? A fish tank office under an ocean?"

"No. I mean, yes. Of course. Because who doesn't want the corner office, when every corner overlooks this majestic creation?" Jack chuckled while admiring the view. A school of neon green fish flashed all around them before disappearing into the coral jungle.

"Then what—"

"I mean the perfect app. One app to rule them all."

"That sounds familiar."

"A cultural reference. And not the point. hAPPening has achieved what no other social media company has done before."

"Record profit?"

"World domination."

"Domination?" Eva's eyebrows crept up her forehead, while a shark three times her size drifted toward the office.

"Did I say domination? Ha-ha! I mean *penetration*. We have world penetration. But when you think about it, that amounts to pretty much the same thing. You know what the second-largest social media platform is?"

Eva nodded. She knew. She'd heard the promotional speeches before.

"At their height, the second-place platform, our so-called rivals, had just over two billion users. Know how many members we have so far? Three billion, and climbing. We'll be at four by this time next year, Eve. Four billion!"

"It's Eva."

Jack had grinned, winked and moved the conversation into strategy and his vision for her new job. It was the first of a number of meetings between them. He'd been right about the numbers, as usual. hAPPn now had almost four billion members.

Some of hAPPening's employees — those who didn't know Jack as well as she did — joked that if this were a Jurassic Park movie, he'd be the first one to be painfully ripped apart by a pack of velociraptors. While he could get on her nerves, her boss did have some good qualities, like being a reliable and fair-minded leader.

So let's hope we don't invent dinosaurs, then, she thought.

Ding! Another message popped onto her screen.

Breakfast ready. Pancakes! Come get it, chief.

Eva's smile widened. Count on Theo to use any excuse for a pancake breakfast.

She paused on her way downstairs to again admire the view. It was spectacular at any hour, but during sunrise and sunset the rays turned the lake into a gleaming basin of silver. The sky turned crimson and gold that not even Theo's oil paints could rival.

Gorgeous house. Check. Loving husband. Check. Awesome career. Check. Snotty child. Double check.

They even had a dog, albeit a digital one inside hAPPn. No way was she going to have a real puppy mess up her hardwood floors and the Persian carpets.

"The Chief has arrived," Theo said as she entered the kitchen. "You were talking to yourself again, by the way."

"Good morning to you, too. And I was talking to my Placer."

"Right. Forgot about the Placer effect."

Eva smiled. "hAPPn has trained us well."

"To walk around talking to ourselves like crazy people."

"Were we ever sane?"

"Probably not. Please don't do it in public."

"No promises."

Rossi was already sitting at the table. She clapped. "Finally. Can we eat now?"

"Smells great," Eva said, glancing again at her Doodad and yet another notification. "Unbelievable." She lifted the device to show Theo the latest breaking news.

A glance, then, "It'll pass. It always does."

"They should arrest the whole lot of them," Eva said. "I hope the protests don't convince the judge to let her out of jail."

"Dad, the pancakes," Rossi said and slid her Doodad on the table.

"Coming. What happened to *innocent before proven guilty*?"

Eva gave Theo a knowing look. "You really think Eco Warrior is innocent? The board is this close to shutting down her Place." She held up a thumb and finger, almost pressing them together.

Theo shrugged and tossed the last pancake onto the serving plate. "Has Eco-War Now broken any laws?"

"Not yet. But with a leader like that, it's only a matter of time."

Rossi groaned and turned on her Doodad. "Self-digesting over here."

Eva glanced at Theo, who sighed and said, "Rossi, you know the rules. No devices at the table."

"You guys are taking too long. And I'm playing with Fluffy."

Eva sat across from Rossi and almost wished she'd said no to digital pets as well. When she'd first purchased Fluffy, Eva thought this was the perfect pet. An online, designer dog. No fuss, no muss. They didn't have to find a dog walker or sitter when they went on vacation. She didn't have to worry about her valuable Persian carpets being chewed up, or peed on, or worse.

Only one problem. Rossi took her pet responsibilities extremely seriously. She was always online, playing with the digital mutt. Training it. Even grooming it. Who knew a collection of animated pixels needed to be groomed?

"I'm sure Fluffy can wait until after breakfast," Theo said.

"You guys took too long, and now I have to catch up."

"With what?"

"We're going to enter hAPPn's Best Pet competition. We're definitely going to win."

"That's great, Rossi," Eva said, trying to generate enthusiasm for an event about imaginary pets. The Chief Growth Engineer in her cheered.

Rossi's lips twitched upward into an almost-smile before falling into a frown. "Anyway, the more I groom and train Fluffy, the more points we get. So, you know."

"Again, the dog can wait until after breakfast." Theo set a platter of pancakes down on the table.

"Maybe if I had a *real* dog, I wouldn't have to be online as much."

Great. Eva looked at the wall clock. *The never-ending puppy argument.*

"You barely have time to do your homework." Theo flipped a pancake onto Rossi's plate. *Thunk.* "Never mind looking after a living creature."

"I can make time. I do it for Fluffy. So—"

"You really think you have time to take it for walks?" Theo asked. "House train it. Clean its messes. Feed it."

"Yes. I promise!"

Eva shook her head.

"What your mother said." Theo raised the maple syrup, studying the bottle like an art piece instead of a condiment. "The house is chaotic enough. Mom's about to start a new job. You're at a new school. We've got a lot going on. And adding a real dog into the mix? That's one too many new things."

"Whatever," Rossi said.

"You'd think that private school would've done more for your vocabulary." Theo's tone was mild, almost jovial, but a tiny knot had colonized the space between his eyebrows.

"So not fair," Rossi muttered. "Everyone in my class has an offline pet *and* an online one."

"Everyone? Is that literal or metaphorical?"

Rossi scowled. "*Everyone.*"

"Okay, enough." Eva held up her hands. "I'm sure we can consider a real dog one day. Just not right now. Now, guess what one of the perks of my new job is?"

Rossi rolled her eyes and pulled the Doodad closer. "At least I don't have my Shaids on."

"We can book the company lodge for holidays," Eva

said. "That'll be great. Right, Rossi? You can go jet skiing, sailing—"

"Get bitten by mosquitoes and catch Zika virus," Rossi said.

"There's no Zika here," Theo said.

"Anyway, that's just *one* of the benefits."

Theo patted her hand. "That's great, Eva."

But the knot between his eyebrows, and the twitch at the edge of his jaw, reminded Eva of Theo's warning when she first told him she was on the shortlist for the job: "That's great, Eva, but be careful. The view from the top isn't always majestic landscapes and sunsets."

Chapter Three

"Girl, stop chasing that elephant!"

Moja had never heard David Ojil shout before. The way the old park ranger said *girl* let her know just how much trouble she was in. Assuming she survived. But his tough act cracked when his voice warbled at the end.

Not that she blamed him. Running after a young male elephant armed only with a German rifle manufactured a half-century ago wasn't the wisest decision — definitely outside Kenya Wildlife Service protocols.

But this isn't any elephant.

Moja quickened her pace. Thick branches slapped at her thighs. Tangled vines snagged at her arms as she pumped them faster.

Just another day at work.

She caught a glimpse of the elephant's backside.

The walkie-talkie at her belt screeched loudly as Ojil continued to plead with her. "On your father's grave, Moja. You! You will be the death of me. You hear? My death! If that elephant tramples you—"

She lowered the volume to a muted whisper without

slowing. Even still, Ojil's panic surrounded her like a cloud of gnats, blocking out the whistles and hoots of tropical birds. But it didn't stop her.

Flashes of mottled pink and brown hide appeared in the small gaps between leaves and large tree trunks.

"Baby Moja," Moja gasped, mentally urging the elephant to slow down, to let her help him. Just as she'd once done several years ago when he was a baby orphan, cast aside by the cruelty of poaching and the harshness of the Kenyan wilderness.

But the albino elephant charged through the forest, oblivious to her voice. Pain urged him on.

Ojil was right. She hadn't seen Baby Moja in a few years. He might not remember her. In his current state, he might not care.

Instead of slowing down, instead of listening to reason and the frantic voice of her fellow park ranger, Moja started jogging. The undergrowth between old trees thinned when she reached the elephant's path. Broken branches carpeted the ground, cracked by heavy feet. Now she could run.

"—Foolish, crazy ... can't believe I recommended you ... this post needs mature ... dangerous!" Ojil's words crackled with static.

He was right. Running after a wild, hurt beast weighing several tons ...

Definitely foolhardy, and dangerous, and everything else he was currently shouting.

But this was her Baby Moja. She had faith in the elephant's ability to remember, and to recognize her. She had more faith in the elephant than she did in most of her fellow humans.

Didn't we learn that lesson well enough?

She pushed the thought away. Bitter memories threatened to slow her down, drag her backward, stop her from reaching her elephant and saving him again.

She trotted into a small clearing. Tall grass and short shrubs replaced trees. The park rangers had created a salt lick next to a watering hole. Baby Moja had finally stopped his blind charge and stood next to the water, his trunk slashing the air and ears flapping.

"Hey, big fella," she cooed, approaching from an angle that would allow him to see her clearly. Sneaking up on an elephant ... now *that* was crazy.

The albino's skin appeared more pink than usual under the direct glare of the equatorial sun. Normally, Baby Moja knew well enough to stay inside the protective shade of the trees, only venturing out when the sun was low on the horizon. But pain had a way of obliterating logic. Another fact Moja could appreciate.

"You and me, Baby Moja," she said, the Swahili words naturally rhyming with each other.

The elephant's ears flapped hard against his sides.

"You and me, we know these things. We know the pain that drives out thought, and invites the demons. But I'm here now. I'm here, and I will never let them hurt you again."

"Oh, Moja," Ojil's voice hissed in the static caused by the walkie-talkie. "You! Are you alive? You better be. And if you're not ... That's what happens when you don't respect your elders."

Without taking her eyes off the elephant, she pulled up her walkie-talkie and spoke softly into the speaker. "Still breathing. Not trampled yet. I'm at the salt lick."

"Oh, oh. Don't move. Don't do anything stupid like ... like approach that elephant! That one, he's not a baby anymore. He's a young male. Unpredictable, dangerous, can't be trusted—"

"Are we still talking about elephants?"

"Oh, yes. Not funny. You stay in the forest. You wait for me. Okay?"

She clicked off the walkie-talkie and slid it into its holster. Distraction was the last thing she needed. And the last thing Baby Moja needed was to hear the voice of a man. After all, it was a man who'd set the snare trap now encircling the elephant's trunk.

Thin wire bit into skin. Rivulets of blood streaked down, plopping onto the dry ground around the pond, staining the salt dark pink.

Moja knelt and lay her rifle on the ground, breaking about half a dozen park regulations. But this was her baby. He'd never hurt her. He—

"You crazy?" Ojil huffed as he pulled her back and behind one of the giant trees near the edge of the forest. "Oh, you want to lose your job? Or be transferred? You know how I argued for you to get this post? They wanted to give it to a senior ranger, not one fresh out of school. But I reminded them about your father, how he helped create this park, and—"

Moja shrugged away from Ojil. "I'm fine."

The old ranger's wrinkles created a map of life across his face. The race through the jungle had crumpled the map and deepened his lines. "It's not fine. We follow the rules. Isn't it? We'll call in rangers from another station, tranquilize him. Yes?"

"There's no time. It'll take at least a few hours for them to get here. By then, he could be anywhere."

Ojil sighed, wiped a sleeve across the map, smoothing it out. "Oh. There're many albino elephants around here, then? No! Him, he's the only one, isn't it? And he has a tracking chip. We'll find him."

"It's hurting him."

Baby Moja waved his trunk, his ears now smooth against his sides. Ojil kept talking, but Moja had blocked his voice. She studied the wire around the elephant's trunk.

It was designed to catch antelope, not elephants. But somehow, Baby Moja had triggered the trap. The wire was now compressed around his trunk. Not enough to do any serious damage right now, but it could definitely lead to infection if left unattended.

Why had she stayed away so long? Maybe if she'd come back earlier, she could've protected her elephant, found the trap before he did. What if the poachers succeeded next time in killing him or another animal? Questions collected in her stomach, a heavy sludge sloshing upward along with bile.

"I should never have left," Moja said.

"Oh, you are correct. You should've stayed at the station, called in for help."

"I mean Kenya."

Ojil paused, pushed off his wide-brimmed hat, rubbed his bristly scalp. "Hmmm. You had to. Isn't it?"

He was right, again. At the time, she felt she had no choice but to go. Because some ideas were too big to ignore. Some creations begged for a creator, and she'd heeded the call.

But now, she silently cursed the world of ideas. They'd led her down a false path, lured her in, seduced her with their promise of changing the world. And where had it led her?

"Four hours," Ojil said. "The other rangers? Them, they can be here in four hours."

She glanced at the old man. "He can't wait that long."

"He can't, or you can't?"

"Both."

Ojil scratched his chin. Re-positioned the rifle hanging

off one shoulder. Settled his hat back on his head. "You, you're like my daughter."

Moja smiled. "You're going to remind me how you held me when I was a baby. How you helped change my diapers. Aren't you?"

"Oh, yes," Ojil said and nodded several times. "That is how it is. I held you when you were a baby, and now I'm an old man."

"You were always an old man."

"Hmmm. Have you lost your respect as well as your manners? This is what happens when we send our young ones to foreign lands." Ojil clucked in disgust. "Me, I'm telling you, we wait."

"Okay, uncle," Moja said.

"He's not a baby anymore. He's a wild thing. Big enough to hurt you."

"Understood. You wait here." She slipped around the other side of the tree and was halfway across the clearing before Ojil shouted wordlessly after her.

"Stay there, uncle," Moja ordered, ignoring his hiss of protest.

The elephant studied her. He shifted from side to side, then waved his trunk.

"That's right, Baby Moja." Moja waved her arm in an S, mimicking his trunk. "You remember me. It hasn't been that long, has it?"

"Your father, you know what he'd say?" Ojil said softly.

"I'm sure you can tell me."

"Animals are not pets."

Her father's voice whispered up through the memories. The two of them pulling a starving albino baby out of a sinkhole. Father telling her the little elephant probably wouldn't survive the night. It had been abandoned for too long. Maybe its mother had been killed by poachers. Or chased off.

It didn't matter. The baby would die. And if by some miracle, it didn't? An albino's chances of surviving in the wild were barely there.

"I can save it," Moja pleaded, her arms gripping the tiny baby, holding it upright despite its weakness.

"And if you can?" Father asked. "Look at its skin."

"It can live with us."

"It's not a dog."

"It can live in the forest. After I save it."

Ojil laughed and slapped Father on the back. "Oh, she is your daughter."

"And after I'm gone, she'll be your niece," Father said. "Okay, it's all yours, my daughter. Don't cry if it dies."

She'd named the elephant Baby Moja. Baby One. Her first wild animal rescue. After that, everyone jokingly referred to her as Mama Moja. It had become her name, a constant reminder of the connection between her and her elephant.

"I didn't give up on you then," she whispered and reached out a hand. "And I'm not giving up on you now."

The elephant was close enough to trample her before Ojil could do anything to help. He could swat her with a trunk that was as muscular as a weightlifter's thigh. But instead, Baby Moja stretched out his injured trunk and tapped her hand.

"That's right," she said, tears mingling with the dust on her cheeks. "High five. Who's my Baby Moja?"

The elephant snuffled, then pressed closer. He was too big to lean against her, and he seemed to understand that. Instead, he placed his trunk over her shoulder. The snare was now at her eye level.

"Moja," Ojil said. "Are you sure?"

She stroked the trunk with both hands, slowly reaching up to the location of the snare. The elephant watched her, unmoving, his ears relaxed, motionless against his sides.

"Don't worry," she said. "It's going to be okay. Just like before. Everything is going to be like it was. Before."

She'd loosened the snare's ugly wire enough to slide it down his trunk, then leaned against him. She marveled how once upon a time he'd needed her support to stand.

"It's going to be okay," Moja promised.

In that moment, as her elephant supported her, she allowed herself to believe it.

Chapter Four

"Stupid cat," Jamaal grumbled as he yanked on his Shaids. "Now I'm gonna be late. Who's late for an online meeting?"

That was easy. He was. It wasn't the first time, and the cat couldn't always be blamed.

He settled back into his chair and flicked on the Shaids. A bright red warning flashed before his eyes: *Is life hAPP-ning without you?*

"Not anymore. Log in," he ordered.

"Logging in," his Placer's voice tickled his ears, soothing him.

Too bad Sarah wasn't a nice Persian girl he could bring home to meet Mama-i. He'd once made the mistake of telling Abe how Sarah was the perfect woman. Abe had subjected him to weeks of mocking references to the upcoming nuptials, the first ever between man and … whatever Sarah was.

His welcome arch materialized in front of him. Roughly hewn stones made up the circular base and archway. A copy of the entrance to the ancient, haunted Castle

Caligula in Hell's Fury, where the Caligula Medallion was hidden.

"One of these days, Crazy Eyed," he vowed. "We will find it before you do."

His menu floated to the right of his avatar, glimmering silver and black text. Standing next to the menu was Sarah's avatar. She was dressed as a flight attendant today. A very pretty flight attendant.

He flicked a finger, and his Shaids picked up the motion. "Entrance, e-Trax workPlace."

"e-Trax workPlace, opening now," Sarah said.

A shimmering silvery mist appeared within the archway. Stepping forward, he popped into the e-Trax lobby.

Several 3D holographic ads bobbed around him, declaring e-Trax's purpose for existing: a power company specializing in highly efficient, cheap, clean, next-generation energy packs. And not just for e-motorcycles and electric cars. e-Trax's goal for the year was to commercialize their newest energy pack. A portable power station with enough juice to light up a small city. It was already close to achieving that goal, and then some.

"Jamaal Shirazi, employee number X3257."

"Accepted," replied a gender-neutral voice. "Welcome to your workPlace, Jamaal Shirazi."

The public face of e-Trax dissolved as he selected the meeting hall from the workPlace menu. He popped into his preassigned location and found just about everyone else already there.

"This must be a new record for lateness," Leah Chan said. "It's not as if you can use traffic as an excuse, Mr. Shirazi."

He glanced to his left. His supervisor shook her head, making a point of turning away from him. She was wearing her favorite mood digitalizer — an angel perched on one shoulder, and a devil on the other. The angel ignored him, while the devil stuck its tongue out.

"The cat. I had to—"

"Sure. Blame it on the feline. Nice. I've sent you more core samples from the new site. Message me your analysis by end of day. Unless the cat eats your homework." Ms. Chan faded from view, and reappeared at the front of the hall, closest to the stage where all of the middle and top management stood.

"I see your day has begun as per usual," Abe said. "Your ability to land in trouble continues to astound me."

"Hey, I tried."

Abe shook his head. Their avatars remained standing side by side, waiting for the CEO to launch the meeting. "And therein lies the problem. You really don't try. Or rather, you are content to remain mediocre. In an office of geeks, you out-geek us all."

"Says the lawyer," Jamaal said.

"It's a good thing one of us is. I'll be the one to defend you in court if she fires you."

"Good to know."

"Try to restrain your gratitude."

Jamaal stared at the back of Ms. Chan's head. "You think she'd really fire me?"

"Now aren't you glad you have a lawyer for a cousin?"

"More like a nuisance."

"The finest, most talented lawyer available, I might add."

"Awesome."

Jamaal glanced down at his inner forearm where a replica of his Doodad was imprinted into his skin. Notifications kept streaming across the surface. Mostly from Geo Rocks, but a few from Geeks Rule, and the new Place he'd recently joined, Metals & Mud. Nothing of interest, except for the reference to the rare earth metal. Plus another reminder from the CEO to show up for the companywide, emergency meeting.

Jamaal said, "Guess when you're that important, you don't have to show up on time."

"Add that to the things you'll never know," Abe replied. "Are you going to this year's Sustainable Resource Extraction Convention?"

Jamaal shrugged. "Yeah, of course. I heard the CEO's attending offline. That would be kinda cool to be there for the live action."

"I'm surprised to hear you say that, cousin."

"Why?"

"Why would you want to physically interact with the unbathed masses at an offline event?"

"Good point. Anyway, I don't have the time or budget to go live, so yeah. Online it is. Should be good enough. They're mirroring all of the exhibits and presentations in the online convention hall."

"An excellent decision."

"Any idea what this is about?" Jamaal didn't really care. He was being paid to stand around and wait. Worked for him.

Abe straightened his tie. "I've had no word from Legal. Maybe they're going to give us raises?"

They scoffed in unison. Yeah, that was a joke. e-Trax giving out an impromptu, midyear raise was about as rare as a rare earth metal. Maybe rarer.

"Does your mom ask you about Persian girls?" Jamaal asked, not because he was particularly interested, but because this was getting boring. Maybe he could pop out for a quick game of backgammon with Sarah.

"She's not into women. She's definitely hetero."

"That's not what I meant."

Abe grinned. "They leave me to my own devices. Jealous?"

"Sure, *Badi-u-llah*."

Abe grimaced. Jamaal didn't blame him. What had Abe's parents been thinking, giving their kid a name that was guaranteed to raise red flags and "random" security checks at every airport in the Western world? No one wanted that headache.

"Did you receive the invite for the party tonight?"

Jamaal twisted his forearm, glanced down at the built-in Doodad, and scrolled through the notifications. He accepted an invite to a round of Quickie Quiz scheduled during the morning break. "Nope."

"I didn't think you would. It's from an ex-colleague of mine. It's over at the new Mars Place."

Jamaal whistled. "They're hosting the party there? That must've cost them a lotta cybercoin."

"I'm sure."

"You going?"

"Sadly, I will have to decline. My supervisor wouldn't approve. It's times like these I wish I had an incognocoin."

Jamaal glanced around the room, wondering if Ms. Chan would notice him leave. "Come on, Abe. A magical coin letting you go anywhere in hAPPn, completely incognito? Those things don't exist. That's right up there with urban legends like … like Prime Placer."

"Don't mock what you don't know. Prime Placer is real, as are incognocoins."

Jamaal looked at Abe's avatar. A mirror image of his cousin, down to the thick unibrow scrunched up over his big nose. Per e-Trax regulations, all employees had to use mirror image avatars at work. Something about security, offline meetings and blah blah blah. The avatars were the latest models, and accurately reflected the body language and expressions of their owners.

"You're serious? You actually believe in all that?" Jamaal asked. "Like for real, Abe? Did the Tooth Fairy tell you all about it? Or did you get a message from Santa Claus?"

"The Prime Placer exists."

"Right. Let me guess. One day they will return. Like a digital messiah."

"Oh, ye of little faith."

Jamaal snorted. "Whatever. But the incognocoin? If it does exist, it costs a small fortune. And who needs it?"

"I can imagine all sorts of people who need it, or at least could put it to good use. Anyone who wants to explore hAPPn outside of their three Places—"

"Why would they? I have three, and I seriously can't keep up with everything. Three's the limit for a reason. More than that?" He shook his head, staring at the stage. A shimmer of gold was starting to dribble down from above.

"My dear Jamaal, grow some curiosity."

"How about you grow up and stop believing in fairytales?"

The shimmering intensified, and the background chatter settled into a restless anticipation. Trumpets blared from all corners. Then the e-Trax CEO strode across the platform under a cascade of gold. Her high heels looked lethal, sharp enough to stab someone with. A golden lion almost as tall as the CEO kept pace by her side as she took the stage.

Jamaal squinted out of habit, even though eyesight was perfect inside hAPPn. No glasses in here. "Cool. A golden lion. That must've cost a bundle of cybercoins."

"I'm sure it did," Abe said as people clapped sporadically around them. "Which it shouldn't, by the way. It's a digital creation. It uses the same amount of data as a large dog or a pony, and those don't cost that much at all."

Jamaal shrugged, tired of Abe's argumentative mood. "Someone had to design it. So someone has to pay for it."

An older man in front of them turned around. Jamaal recognized him as a fellow Geo Rocks member. "I heard it's a metal lion that breathes fire."

"A metal lion!" Jamaal whistled. "Crazy expensive, then. Not that she can't afford it."

"It makes no sense," Abe said. "It's still digital, and therefore shouldn't cost that much at all."

"Give it up," Jamaal said.

CEO Danielle Rodriguez raised her arms. The lion sat beside her, belching out a puff of flames as it settled onto the floor.

The audience cheered and clapped.

"What a showoff," Abe muttered, just loud enough for Jamaal to hear.

"Fellow members of e-Trax." The CEO's voice came from all around them, amplified by whatever software was being used to generate the meeting hall. "It's a good day to be engineers and geologists."

An appreciative cheer rolled through the room.

She nodded. "It's an even better day to be a member of the e-Trax workPlace."

The collective cheer blossomed into a deafening roar. She let it hang around them before again holding up her arms.

"It's like she's the Messiah," Abe said.

"Stop talking, before she *pops* you out of here," Jamaal said. It wouldn't be the first time. Abe had always been the troublemaker between the two of them, and sometimes he went too far.

"I'm filled with pride at our history when I think of our

accomplishments," Rodriguez continued. "But when I think of what our future can be, I'm filled with unbridled excitement. Today more so than ever. You may have seen headlines in your news streams about a new rare earth metal. What hasn't been announced yet is which company laid claim to the deposit first."

She allowed a breathless silence to settle across the crowd.

"I'm delighted to announce that e-Trax discovered and claimed the single largest, near-surface deposit of EA-L029 in the world."

There was a fraction of a moment of awed silence before the meeting hall erupted into shouts, cheers and clapping. Even Abe let his bored expression slip, and clapped his hands slowly.

"I suppose our employee shares will receive a big boost from this one," Abe said as if to justify his interest.

Jamaal grinned. It might even be enough for him to buy a bubble bike.

"Tomorrow, we will announce that the near-surface deposit of the rare earth metal nicknamed Lucy has been registered under our company's name. We are going through the application process to begin mining operations in Kenya. Lucy is a perfect material for the next generation of energy storage packs. Our packs will be found in everything, everywhere. One modestly sized pack using Lucy can power a small city. We have never been this close to achieving the ultimate goal for e-Trax: clean, cheap energy for everyone."

More clapping and cheering. The metal lion coughed, releasing a long jet of flames that exploded over the audience before dissolving into red and gold mist.

She raised a hand and waited for silence. "As of today, energy storage is about to get smaller, cheaper, cleaner and more powerful. With this material, we can halve the costs of energy tech, increase power output per kilogram by two hundred percent, and the best part? The biggest deposit is near the surface in a designated wasteland area."

Jamaal whistled and clapped along with his fellow geologists, even though he already knew the details. His team had analyzed the core samples.

Abe frowned at him.

"Near-surface," Jamaal repeated, just in case Abe hadn't heard it.

"I'm a lawyer, Jamaal, not a digger of rocks."

"Near-surface, in an area designated as wasteland? That means we can use strip mining. Not even Eco-War Now can protest."

The CEO was nodding at the audience, as if overhearing every one of their exuberant side discussions. And for all Jamaal knew, maybe she did hear them. The owners of a workPlace could install whatever surveillance systems they wanted. Abe should really stop complaining. If the CEO or their supervisors felt Abe was unhappy about working at e-Trax, Jamaal might get painted with the same brush.

"As some of you have figured out," Rodriguez continued, "near-surface, in a wasteland area, means we can use the cheaper, safer and easier process with the unfortunate name of strip mining." She smiled indulgently as people laughed. "We prefer the term *surface* mining. We've already committed to rehabilitating the land after each strip is mined, thus leaving it not as a wasteland or as a mining dump, but as a viable ecosystem for trees and wildlife. It's a win-win. Easily accessible rare earth metal, better energy technology, cheap and clean power for all, and improved, rehabilitated land."

More clapping, although people had started glancing at

their Doodads. Work was piling up along with the news streams and notifications.

Rodriguez must've noticed as well, because the lion roared. More flames jetted out, dissolving into more red and gold glitter. "And if the mining proposal is approved by the Kenyan government, and we proceed with the project, each employee will receive an additional year-end bonus."

The clapping and cheering resumed in earnest. Everyone congratulated each other at the news. After another metallic roar from the lion, the CEO dismissed them.

Jamal nodded at Abe. "See? It's all good."

Before Abe could give him some conspiracy theory why it wasn't great news to start the week, Jamaal ordered his Placer to send him to his work cubicle.

He popped out of the meeting hall and appeared in his office. He took a minute to appreciate just how awesome the day was, despite the disastrous battle in Hell's Fury. It was a great start to what would surely be an excellent week.

Jamaal had no idea how deeply mistaken he was.

Chapter Five

When Eva slipped on her Shaids and opened up hAPPn, a warning in bright red letters flashed across her view. *Is life hAPPning without you?*

"Not anymore. Log in," she ordered.

She landed on a circular platform made of cedar wood with the same rich color and texture as the hardwood floors in the house. She took a moment to admire the realistic design of her welcome arch.

Maybe not completely realistic. The archway in front of her was made with garnet. Another one of the perks of working and playing in hAPPn. Online reality was limited only by the member's imagination, membership level, and the total in one's cybercoin account.

"Placer, open menu."

"Opening menu," intoned a disembodied, gender-neutral voice. A silver menu appeared to one side of her.

A lot of hAPPn members preferred to give their Placers names and avatars. She'd never chosen the option for herself, but understood perfectly well why many members did.

Studies showed people preferred interacting with something that looked and acted human, even if they knew it was nothing like a real person. The Placer was an incredibly sophisticated, constantly learning and highly adaptive piece of software, but that's *all* it was. Lines of clever code translating into a seemingly endless stream of ones and zeros.

Eva had worked for hAPPening long enough to know what its app's various tools really were. She didn't need the pretense of humanity to use the Placer, even though she'd been one of the leads in designing Placers to be more personal, more human in appearance. Upgraded Placers had increased the engagement of hAPPn members; more engagement meant more revenue. As Chief Growth Engineer, increasing both membership and engagement would be a major focus of her job.

She scrolled through her menu. "Placer, enter the PR room for the hAPPening's workPlace."

"Entering PR room."

The platform and semiprecious archway dissolved, and she popped into the expansive PR room of hAPPening. Other avatars started to populate the space, including journalists from tech-related media outlets.

Marsha White popped into the location next to hers.

Coincidence? I think not. Eva matched Marsha's insincere smile with her own.

Like many workPlaces, hAPPening had a strict policy about employee avatars. They had to be mirror image avatars, exact visual replicas. The board wanted staff to recognize each other if they ever met in the offline world. It was also for security reasons, and because nobody wanted a ten-foot-tall cyborg in the room.

Eva glanced at Marsha. She was pretty sure some people tweaked their images a bit here and there. No way could Marsha's current bust size and waist size coexist in the same body. She looked like a Barbie, or a human wasp, a figure that would require surgery to create, and an anorexic diet to maintain.

Yes, a wasp. That was the perfect description for both Marsha's character and her online physique.

Jack was the last to arrive, of course. She half-expected him to appear on his flying horse. That was his usual choice for grand entrances. Flying horses didn't come cheap. The one he liked to ride into meetings matched the flying unicorn in his signature stamp: gold fur and feathers, silver mane and tail, and an obscenely long ivory horn.

Talk about overkill.

But Jack was using uncharacteristic restraint. His avatar strolled rather than flew onto the stage. A large crocodile waddled behind him. Members of the audience chuckled appreciatively.

Trust Jack to always have some dramatic pet next to him. He'd made it a requirement in his contract: an unlimited number of pets, any design. The croc was one of his personal favorites. It opened its jaws, then snorted out a stream of fireworks.

The audience wasn't a crowd of new members, easily wowed by the wonders populating hAPPn's 3D version. They had enough experience. They'd seen all manner of creatures and impossible environments. Still, the illusion was perfect, and many people instinctively flinched as fireworks exploded overhead.

Jack waved to get everyone's attention, and tapped his throat. His voice boomed across the room when he spoke, digitally magnified in a way no one else was permitted without being on-stage.

"Is life hAPPning without you?"

"Not anymore!" a number of enthusiastic employees shouted back.

The journalists looked bored.

"That's right!" Jack punched the air above him. "If you're here, you are where everything good happens. You can do everything in hAPPn except eat your lunch, and take a dump — and we're working to fix that."

He waited for the friendly groans and laughs to subside.

"Last week I announced the retirement of Pierre Marit, our Chief Growth Engineer. An outstanding member of hAPPening. He was always active in the workPlace, and many other Places." He paused and grinned while several senior colleagues laughed.

"Trust Jack to go too far," Marsha muttered.

Eva kept quiet.

"Today, it's my pleasure and delight to announce our new Chief Growth Engineer. The lady joining the senior management staff — the Chiefs — needs no introduction. She's been a fixture of hAPPening since its early days. A gifted programmer who quickly rose through our ranks. Smart, charming, and almost for sure gunning for my job, it's my pleasure to introduce you to our newest Chief, Eva Taylor."

"Placer, move to stage," Eva murmured.

"Moving to stage."

Her vision blurred at the edges, then Eva was staring not at the stage, but out from its floor. She stood next to Jack, and nodded as the crowd clapped.

"Take it away, number two," Jack said under his breath and winked.

Eva kept her smile bright, and resisted the urge to trip him as he strolled past her.

"Thank you," Eva said as she tapped her throat. "Jack's

always been *so* encouraging. I'm excited at this new opportunity. hAPPn has almost four billion members, and is by far the single largest social media platform. With the increasing preference of many companies to work online, our app provides the perfect solution. Realistic workPlaces, the ability to interact in a meaningful way on the 3D version while still providing for 2D interface, hAPPn has given the world an elegant solution to our modern need for safe, accessible work spaces."

Eva paused to allow for a spattering of polite clapping. "But more than that, we also provide community. Members of hAPPn are assigned a personalized Placer who assists them to find their perfect-fit communities. The app also helps you, members of the press, to find your perfect-fit audiences."

More polite clapping.

Then a reporter raised her hand.

Jack had warned her. "Chiefs are on the frontline, Eva," he'd said when privately informing her of the board's decision to elevate her to Chief. "The press will blame you when something goes wrong. I'm the one they praise when everything goes right. It's not fair, but that's how it is."

Eva knew that wasn't true. Jack got his fair share of heat. But his point was still valid.

The view from the top isn't always majestic landscapes and sunsets.

"Placer, display participant map," Eva muttered under her breath.

A screen appeared in the corner of her vision. Invisible to everyone else, it provided a map of all the avatars with their names and titles.

"Yes," Eva said, pausing to quickly consult the map. "Sofia Morales from World Media."

"When hAPPn was first launched, members could only apply to one Place. Soon after, the limit was raised to three. Why are we still only able to enjoy membership in three Places?"

"Starting off tough today," Jack murmured.

Eva nodded. "One of hAPPn's goals has always been to help our members find communities they'll enjoy. Studies show people are happier with fewer Places, as this allows them to develop deeper, more meaningful relationships."

Definitely the truth, but not the whole truth. It also made it easier for advertisers to deepen their relationships with potential consumers. Jack had insisted that she skip that little detail.

Another hand. Eva used it as an excuse to talk over Ms. Morales' follow-up question. "Yes, Ms. Patty O'Conner of Guns & Steel."

"Could you comment on the recent death of Louie Deaver, the fourteen-year-old boy who became addicted to hAPPn?"

Jack stirred next to her but held his silence. The crocodile shuffled closer to the edge of the stage, jaws creaking open.

Eva allowed her avatar to reflect her frown, indicating she'd heard the question and appreciated the issue. "All new members of hAPPn receive guidelines on healthy use of the app. The vast majority follow them responsibly. Sadly, a few people don't. There will always be those who misuse or abuse the products of any industry or technology. However, it's extremely rare and—"

"Rare but growing," shouted another journalist as he stood.

"Jacob Broznick from Health & Fitness for Nerds," her Placer said.

"Yes, Mr. Broznick."

"Just last month, the number of hospitalizations related to people addicted to hAPPn increased by almost ten percent compared to the previous six months."

The reporter looked at his arm and Eva had to throttle her smile. Checking one's forearm was now an automatic habit for most members. She and her team had designed the software, and were blown away by how quickly the behavior had become commonplace.

"It's a twelve percent increase," Mr. Broznick continued, reading off of his notes. "People who hAPP too much forget everything else. They can get severely dehydrated. Their bodies shut down from lack of sleep and nutrition. In seventeen percent of these cases, intervention came too late, and those members actually died." He looked up at her. "What is hAPPening doing to prevent fogging? How are you helping foggers?"

Eva tried not to flinch, glad that she'd already lowered her avatar's responsiveness, the amount it reflected her physical body's reactions.

Jack's suggestion. "Reporters," he'd said. "Can't live with them, can't live with them. Trust me, Eva. They're the plague. A necessary one, but still. You want to minimize your responsiveness to them. Respond. Don't react."

She cleared her throat, buying a moment to sort her words.

Fogging. Jack hated that term. So did she. A fraction of a percent of members became addicted, but the concept and the related vocabulary had already infiltrated the pop culture lexicon.

Did you get in trouble? You were *fogged up*.

Screwed your best friend's girlfriend? What a *fogger*.

It was a nervous word, and nervous words could chip away at a company's armor. Especially a company like hAPPening which relied on positive perceptions of its primary product.

Leave it to a small group to soil all their hard work. The world would always have addictive personalities, prone to latching on to something. Chemical substances. Obsessive habits. Gambling. And now, excessive use of hAPPn. Eva's team had conducted its own research into the trend. But the results didn't matter. If people deemed the app unsafe or unhealthy, perception would conquer reality.

"Thank you, Mr. Broznick, for highlighting this troubling trend. It's something that we at hAPPening are extremely concerned about. As a start, we've installed alarms to notify a member if they've been using hAPPn for more than four hours straight."

"But is it enough?" Mr. Broznick shouted.

"We're keeping a close eye on it. And let's be fair. hAPPn has saved more lives than any intervention since vaccinations, chlorinated water, and sewage treatment plants. As more people work from home offices, the number of traffic accidents has decreased globally by over twenty percent. Air quality has dramatically improved in most urban settings, resulting in lower asthma and cardiovascular-related diseases. Of course, we'll continue to investigate ways to discourage addictive usage of hAPPn."

Mr. Broznick didn't look completely satisfied, but another reporter stood with a more mainstream question. Less controversial, more in line with her job description.

After a few more queries, Jack finished the PR event and closed the room. Avatars popped out of view, until it was just the two of them remaining.

Jack clapped twice to dissolve the room, then replaced it with an exterior location. "This is one of my favorite views."

"Mine, too."

He and Eva were standing at the edge of a cliff. hAPPn stretched out below them, a giant, interactive map of people and Places. Twinkling lights showed the location of members, blinking in and out as they logged on and off.

Jack rubbed the crocodile's snout before pulling a Smolders cigarette out of one of its nostrils. "Love this world. All the fun without the pain. Want one?"

"No, thanks," Eva said.

"They won't give you cancer in here, you know."

"I'm good."

"Your loss." He snapped his fingers. The crocodile coughed a small flame. Jack lit the end of his cigarette, inhaled, and held the smoke for a moment. "Tough crowd, eh?"

"You did warn me."

"Yeah. Not the best part of the job. But win them over, and they can be allies."

"So did I?"

"I think you did. Don't forget the Meeting of Chiefs is in a few days. Your first one. I'll send you an invite."

"Looking forward to it." Eva sent a silent request to her Placer for a link to her office.

Jack hesitated, frowning at the croc as if the digital creature had pooped on his fancy leather shoes or something. Then he turned to her, a question forming in his eyes. "Eva?"

She decreased her avatar's responsiveness when her body tensed offline. She'd done enough already. He better not—

"Good job," he said and returned his attention to the crocodile. "We'll chat more later, okay?"

"Sure."

She tapped the link, and the view melted into a blur of pixels, before solidifying into her office.

At least he hadn't asked her for anything. The first one hadn't been too big a deal — a small favor, really — but what about the next time?

Problem was, him asking was a matter of *when*, not *if*. Eva couldn't postpone the inevitable, even if she was a Chief.

So what could she possibly tell him?

Chapter Six

Ojil GRUMBLED the entire way back to the Kenya Wildlife Service station.

"Oh, you. You're lucky," he said for the umpteenth time. "So lucky. But luck? Luck only handles so much. It carries only a little weight. And eventually, it collapses. Like a table made of straw. Isn't it?"

"Our cabin roofs are made with straw," Moja said, trying not to laugh. She focused on clearing the vegetation from their path.

"That's thatch. Good for keeping out rain and rats. But you try putting an elephant on it, and it'll fall."

"Why would anyone put an elephant on the roof?"

"Oh. You, you're going to be my death. Or your own. Probably both."

"Probably."

Bird calls filled the silence between them, but it was a comfortable silence. One based on a relationship that started from the day she was born. Ojil had been like a brother to her father, and now he was her family.

"My baby remembered me," Moja said.

Ojil grunted, the only indication he'd heard her.

"He'd never hurt me."

Another grunt. "Him, he's a wild animal. You don't know what he can do."

"I know. But you have to admit. He remembered me."

"If I admit it, you promise to not do that again?"

"No."

"Oh, you." A pause. A sigh. "He remembered."

Laughing, she waved at him to lead the way home.

Home.

It was the first time she'd felt at home in a while. Training to be a ranger had meant moving around between parks and getting trained on the job. Before that, ranger school. And before that …

"How long before you retire?"

Ojil snorted. "You just got here, and now you want to get rid of me?"

"No. I want to make sure you're going to stick around."

"Oh! Really? With you here, your elephant will probably trample me."

"So we're going to be working together for a long time, then."

"Lucky me."

She opened her mouth, but Ojil suddenly stopped. His abrupt motion jolted her into awareness. The sounds of birds had vanished.

He glanced back at Moja, then past her, searching the thick undergrowth.

"Cheetah?" she whispered.

They rarely saw the big cats moving into the thick forest, but it wasn't unheard of. Uhuru National Park bordered a vast savanna connecting other national parks to a migratory route stretching from one end of Kenya to the other, and into Tanzania.

Moja gripped the butt of her rifle. She had no intention of shooting an animal, trusting the loud noise to scare any creature away. But as Father and Ojil liked to remind her, they weren't working with pets. These were wild animals, no matter how familiar they might seem.

Ojil shook his head. "No cats." He glanced skyward.

Moja followed his example and hissed.

A soft buzzing filled the air as a drone floated into view. A camera hung from its base, continuously revolving, a green light blinking.

Ojil's wrinkles withered into a grimace. "We need to inform HQ."

Moja nodded, her expression as grim as Ojil's. It was protocol to inform HQ, but that didn't mean much. By the time anyone who could do anything about the drone arrived, the drone would be long gone.

"Think they have a permit?"

Ojil shook his head, swiveling to keep an eye on the drone. "No permit. No ranger assigned to be with the pilot. We would've heard."

"The pilot must be nearby," Moja said, already directing her attention to the forest around them.

"Hmmm. Maybe."

The drone hovered as the camera scanned the terrain. Moja shouldered her rifle, aiming upward. No permit plus no ranger equaled potential disaster. Enthusiastic photographers often flew their drones too close to the wildlife, stressing the animals, sometimes causing dangerous stampedes.

"It's illegal," she muttered.

Ojil nodded, then jumped as Moja snapped back the safety.

"Moja!"

Her first shot clipped one of the twirling blades. "Who're they going to complain to? They broke the law."

The drone careened to the side, losing altitude. She took better aim with her second shot, demolishing one of the other blades.

A flurry of birds followed each of her shots, but she kept focus on the falling drone.

"The death of me, for sure," Ojil said.

"Come on, old man," she shouted, pushing branches and vines out of their way.

The drone still buzzed and whizzed, but was in no shape for flying, caught in a branch halfway up a tree.

"Oh, if she doesn't kill me, she'll get me arrested," Ojil said.

"No one's going to arrest us. Hold my rifle." Moja tossed her rifle and began to climb the tree.

"And broken bones," Ojil said, holding up his hands. "Broken bones. Cracked skull. Arrested. Trampled by elephants. Maybe I shouldn't have agreed to be your partner. Isn't it?"

"Yes, it is. But too late now."

"Your father, he wasn't this reckless."

"Yes, he was."

"Okay. He was. But only when he was a young man."

"I'm still young enough to be reckless."

"And I'm too old for this."

Moja reached the branch, and knocked the fallen drone free. It landed on the ground with a soft thump.

"You trying to kill me with a drone now?"

"If I wanted you dead, I would've asked Baby Moja to do it for me," she said as she shimmied down the tree. "That way, it would look like an accident."

"Oh, so now, I know your evil plan."

She took back her rifle. "Only the first part."

They kneeled next to the fallen machinery. It was average size for a survey drone. The digital video camera was standard. Nothing fancy.

Moja traced a finger across the broken lens. "You're sure no one recently submitted a request to film in the park?"

Ojil shook his head, and pulled out his Doodad.

"I was right, then. Illegal filming."

"Hmmm. Seems so." He took a photo.

"Maybe a news company? Or a film studio? Someone making wildlife documentaries?"

Ojil frowned.

"Fine. I'll stop with all the theories. You think the town office might know?"

Ojil took another photo, then secured his Doodad in a pocket. "I'll send Moses the photos."

Moja nodded. Moses was the biggest gossip. He seemed to know everyone's business before they did. Not that it was hard to do. Uhuru Town was a tiny place. Everyone knew everyone, and no one owned a drone. Whoever had hired or purchased this one was from outside, and outsiders attracted attention.

"Okay?" Ojil asked.

"Okay. Let's go." Moja picked up the fallen drone. No sense in leaving garbage lying around the park.

The KWS station at the main gate of Uhuru National Park wasn't much to look at. A small office building with a couple of rooms and a storage closet. Four cottages, of which two were occupied. Utilities building covered in solar panels, providing power for the water pump, and electricity.

An old Land Rover squatted near the covered picnic table in the middle of the compound, all surrounded by an electric fence.

Moja tossed the drone onto the picnic table, making a mental note to take it with her into town the next time she went. Not that she planned on going often. Being out here, away from too many people, suited her perfectly.

"Are you going to update the stats on animal sightings?" Ojil asked when she entered the office.

It was their first full day working together. She'd only arrived yesterday, and they still hadn't had time to establish a routine.

Moja nodded and sat in front of a screen.

"It's good to have you here." Ojil slumped at a desk near hers. "Even if you're going to be my death."

"At least you'll die in an interesting way."

He grunted, smiling as he poured them tea. "You've been away too long."

She kept quiet, inputting stats. Apart from her albino elephant, they'd spotted several types of antelope, a small herd of elephants, and a number of parrot species.

"Us, we need good people. We need more rangers."

Moja glanced sideways at him. "How's the poaching?"

He shook his head. "Not so bad. Not how it used to be. But it happens. As we saw."

Moja nodded. They were lucky it had only been a snare. For a smaller animal, that snare would've been a painful death.

"So you missed me?" she asked.

"Oh. Sometimes. You're like my fourth daughter."

"I'm fourth on the list, am I?"

He chuckled. "No. But don't tell my children."

"I bet you say that to all your daughters."

"Hmmm. Will you go back? When you're tired of this quiet life?"

"Never." She stared at the database. It felt like a lifetime ago when she'd made the decision to leave. And now it was time to create a new lifetime, one with a new story, new characters.

Ojil pulled out his Doodad. "What Places are you members of?"

Moja shuddered as another voice asked her the same question.

"What Places are you a member of?" Jack asked, his voice loud in her memory. "That's right. *None* of them. You float through like a ghost, passing over them. You never participate, never belong. You don't realize the sense of community that members develop with each other. Yet you dare judge the effectiveness of limiting the number of Places when you have no idea."

"The walls are too high, Jack," she argued.

"You're being paranoid. We designed it this way for a reason."

"But reasons change. Just as our world changes. So must we."

He shrugged, gave her his cheeky grin, the one she'd always loved. "Why change what's not broken?"

Because it is broken, Jack.

"Moja?"

Ojil's voice pulled her back to the present, and away from memories she wished would evaporate like rainwater puddles at noon on the savanna.

"Sorry, what?"

Ojil gazed at her, the creases on his face soft, each one a loving memory. Moja knew she was in many of them. Her, Father and Ojil.

She returned his smile. She appreciated how he listened intently even when she said nothing. How he let a loud silence pool around them, allowing thoughts to weave together in the absence of noise. And when he finally spoke, it was with compassion, and a deep appreciation for everything she said and didn't say. He was only verbose when lecturing her about chasing wild animals, but he communicated abundantly.

"Your Places," he said.

Moja shook her head and pulled out an antiquated cell phone. "No Places at all. Just the one I physically inhabit."

His eyebrows rose, deepening the wrinkles on his forehead. He rubbed a hand over his stubbled chin. The creases around his dark eyes crinkled as he smiled. "Serious? You still have that? Oh!"

He chuckled, unspoken words flitting around the sound: *You don't have a Doodad? A young person like you, using antiques? And me, an old man, has the latest and greatest technology?*

Moja grinned. "Absolutely."

"That thing, it's from a museum, isn't it?"

"It works just fine, wherever it's from."

"Does it even connect to the internet?"

She laughed at his laughter. "No more than I do. It's all I want. Or need."

"Oh, and I thought I was an old man."

"You are an old man."

"Old but connected! I live in the modern world."

"You'd be amazed how well you can live without a hAPPn account."

Ojil hooted, his laughter filling the office, reminding her of a time when her father had been alive. The three of them would spend days at a time getting lost in forests, camping, fishing, learning first-hand about the world and all its wonders. Before she'd left to create another world with its own wonders, and its own dangers.

She grinned. "And what do you use your hAPPn account for?"

He inhaled deeply. "Hmmm. It's useful."

"How?"

"I use hAPPn for everything. And my Placer? Oh! Like a park ranger for the online jungle. Don't know how I managed without it."

"But you did."

"Barely. It guides me. Has all the answers. Knows what entertainment I'll like most. Sorts my mail. Keeps track of my groceries and medicines. Orders things before I know I need them. And for an old man on his own, that's something."

"You're never on your own."

"You know what I mean. Ever since Agnes …" He paused, cleared his throat, looked away. His hands gripped each other, his fingers squirming together, like worms tossed into a bucket. "I can focus on what I need to focus on."

She nodded, kept quiet. This was the first time he'd mentioned Agnes since the time he'd called to tell her what had happened. Moja wouldn't ask him details about his dead, and he'd observe the same discretion when it came to hers.

He cleared his throat again. "The problem here, it's the bandwidth. Not enough to use the 3D version. Portable boosters are too expensive." He sighed, turned on his Doodad and opened the app.

A message flashed across the screen: *Is life hAPPning without you?*

"Not anymore. Log in," he ordered, then patted the chair next to his. "Hmmm. Now come here, young one, and be modern. See? My menu. I'm a member of Kenya Parks & Nature Place. And look! We made the news."

Ojil's smile was back. The pain summoned at the mention of his dead wife skittered away like a startled gazelle, but it didn't go far.

Moja played along. "Great. Are we famous yet?"

He pulled up an article describing the history of Uhuru National Park, Kenya's youngest park. She glanced at the summary paragraph.

The piece was surprisingly accurate, describing how the park protected a large swathe of old-growth rainforest, as well as an endangered, endemic species of antelope, and a rare bird.

"See?" Ojil held up his Doodad. "All the news I want, in one Place. It's good, isn't it?"

"Imagine that."

Moja returned to her desk and stared at the database. The numbers sat in a row, dark green against silver. They reminded her of the deep green chairs surrounding a large table, all made with digital jade. Walls and floor covered in a silver sheen. The chairs and their occupants blurred as she walked out of the room, her heart breaking as a voice congratulated the new CEO.

If only real hearts could have firewalls around them the way her avatar's heart did—

"Oh! Some more news," Ojil said.

The image of the meeting room vanished. Moja rubbed at her eyes. She could still hear an echo of clapping.

"Moses. He replied. A party of three foreigners tried to rent camping gear. They're planning on camping in the park."

Moja frowned and pushed the past back into a mental file she'd labeled *Never Again*. "But visitors aren't allowed to stay in here overnight."

Ojil just hummed, saying nothing.

Chapter Seven

JAMAAL DIDN'T MEAN for the argument to spiral out of hand, but Abe had that effect on him. Always poking at the truth. Instigating problems. His cousin *was* the devil's advocate. And who needed that hassle?

Abe was already at the dinner table when Jamaal shuffled upstairs. He waited for his cousin to sit before waving a knife at the kitchen and saying, "Jam, my dear man, could you fetch the ketchup?"

But that wasn't why they started arguing.

Mama-i's mouth thinned out and formed a straight line. "Why can't you boys use your own names?"

"Because they're difficult to pronounce, Mama-i," Jamaal said, but he wasn't really paying attention. They'd been through this countless times.

"Ey, baba! How is Jam easier than Jamaal?"

"Because it just is. And Abe's name is even worse. He's called all sorts of weird things."

Mama-i huffed and dumped more rice on his plate, even though he had plenty already. "You might as well call yourself Peanut Butter."

"That makes no sense, Mama-i."

Mama-i clucked her tongue. "It makes sense. Peanut Butter and Jam."

Abe snorted a laugh, almost choking on his mouthful, before glancing at his wrist. He was the only person Jamaal knew who wore an analog watch, or any watch. Most people used their Doodad to keep track of time, or a floating digital clock when online. Abe also insisted on dressing in a business suit, even when no one would see his physical self apart from family. Jamaal once asked about it when Abe made fun of his usual work clothes: jogging pants and a sweatshirt.

"My dear cousin," Abe said in his pompous, courthouse voice. "Of course, one could dress up one's avatar in whatever attire is appropriate for the occasion. But I prefer to dress the part offline as much as online."

"Even when you're sitting in your bedroom?" Jamaal asked, not sure how anyone would make a choice to wear a suit and tie when no one was around to even possibly care.

"It's elementary, my dear young cousin. You see—"

"You're only two months older than me."

"Yet what a world of difference those two months make."

"And you're shorter."

"Only offline."

Jamaal didn't judge Abe for taking advantage of the online perks. He'd tweaked his avatar's arms to add a few extra pounds of muscle. He made a mental note to increase his height.

"Regardless of my physique, I dress in a suit every workday because I dress for success," Abe continued.

"Nice slogan. Did you make it up all by yourself?"

"I did, my befuddled, underdressed Jamaal. I certainly did. And do you know what else I made up on my own?

Success. I'm one of the lead junior lawyers for e-Trax because I'm always dressed in a winning mindset."

"And you got all that by wearing a tie?"

"Finally, the student comprehends. Winners dress like winners. Losers dress like … Well, let me help you pick out your first suit. It'll be good for you. You dress like a bum, Jamaal. There's no swagger without a suit."

Jamaal tugged at his hood strings. "I've got swagger."

"You poor, deluded man."

"I don't need swagger, okay?"

"That's probably true. While you play with rocks, I, dear boy, play with words. And masterfully so, I might add."

"Humble, too," Jamaal said.

"I should hope not. Humility is for pet rocks, Jamaal, not for eagles."

Jamaal wasn't impressed. Sure, Abe always looked like a playboy millionaire. Maybe even a billionaire. But since Jamaal seldom went into the physical office space of e-Trax, he decided comfort was much more important than looking the part when no one was around to see. So he kept his track pants and T-shirts. Let Abe sit in his overly starched dress shirt and business attire.

"Peanut Butter, you forgot the ketchup," Abe said, dragging Jamaal back into the present. "Crazy Eyed Cyborg sends her greetings. At least I don't call you Mama's Boy."

"What's wrong with that?" Mama-i asked.

"Maybe I should move out," Jamaal said.

"And why would you do that?" Abe asked. "Who'd cook for you?"

"I wouldn't mind a break from cooking." Mama-i dumped more stew on their plates.

"Mama-i, enough," Jamaal said. "You love cooking for

us. What would you do if we weren't around?"

"I do other things. Visit friends. Take the cat for a walk. My Placer recommended a new Place. Because it knows my interests better than my own son."

Jamaal shook his head, wondering how he was going to finish all this food. "Another cooking Place?"

"No. I follow environmental news streams as well."

"Really?"

"I do."

"Good for you, Mama-i. Abe, the water."

"You want to know which Place?"

"Yeah, sure. Abe. Water. Now."

"It's Eco-War Now." Mama-i lifted her chin, waiting for his reaction.

"That's the Place your Placer recommended? Those green necks?" Jamaal stared at her in disbelief. "Those guys are into all sorts of funny business, Mama-i. Their protests almost always end up violent. They vandalize—"

"Ey, baba! They're especial."

"Sure are."

"They're not violent. The police are. Tear gas. Guns. That's where the real violence is."

Jamaal groaned. "If my supervisor finds out … Promise me you won't go to any of their protests, okay?"

"They aren't protests. They're sit-ins. They sit peacefully and hold up cards. No violence."

"Tell that to the police," Jamaal said.

Abe yawned. "And in other news streams, how was everyone's day?"

"Awesome." Jamaal talked over his mom before she could spout more nonsense about the green neck terrorists she was thinking of joining. "Hey, Mama-i, e-Trax laid claim on a new deposit. It's going to change the world. Plus end-of-year bonuses. Sweet deal. Right, Abe?"

"I don't know how sweet it is," he replied, straightening his tie.

Jamaal sat back in disbelief. "Has everyone lost their minds? Mama-i jokes about joining a gang of green necks—"

"Not a gang," said Mama-i.

"And you wear a tie to dinner."

Abe gave Jamaal's shirt a pointed look. "You might want to try it one day."

"You heard the boss, Abe. It's all gonna happen. Which means we get an extra end-of-year bonus. What's wrong now?"

Abe patted his mouth delicately with a napkin. "Remember how she said it was in a designated wasteland area?"

"One of the best parts. We won't have to deal with any of those environmental nut cases."

Mama-i tapped her fork on his plate. "Ey, baba! We are *not* nut cases."

"*We?*" Jamaal repeated. "You mean you were serious? You actually joined that Place? It's full of green-necked criminals."

Abe said, "I'm concerned about a source of potentially misleading information."

"Yeah, I know," Jamaal replied. "Mama-i's Placer needs a software update or something. Quit right now, okay, Mama-i?"

"I wasn't referring to your mother's new hobby."

"What're you talking about?" Jamaal asked Abe, poking a spoon at the piled food on his plate.

"After the meeting, I visited one of my Places. A member had shared an image of a recent article. I wasn't able to make a copy, but some of the details didn't add up."

"They're not green-necked," Mama-i muttered and reached for the rice bowl.

"I've had enough, thanks. What article, Abe?"

"It claimed the near-surface deposit isn't in a designated wasteland. It's inside a national park, under an old-growth forest."

Jamaal threw up his hands. "You believe that? Someone's messin' with you, Abe. Of course it's in a wasteland. Otherwise, e-Trax wouldn't be planning on strip mining. And the CEO wouldn't commit to rehabilitating the land."

"Maybe they made a mistake. It's possible. Did you ever think of that?"

"No, Abe. I didn't. Wanna know why? Because I don't listen to people who spout off conspiracy theories and other nonsense. I'm the geologist here, remember? Geo Department was sent copies of the map. And guess what? The deposit is actually inside a *wasteland*. Nothing is there. No parks. No forests. No cute, furry, endangered animals. Just rubble and dirt and land that nobody wants. Nobody except e-Trax. And after they extract Lucy? They're gonna fix up the land."

"It's not a conspiracy theory if it's true."

"Of course that's what all people who believe in conspiracies would say! But they're still conspiracies."

"That happen to be true."

"No."

"But what if—" Abe began.

"What if what? e-Trax would *never* get involved in something that would damage a national park, or be illegal, or … anything. Besides, parks are protected. So why would the Kenyan government let anyone mine the deposit if it was under a park? Oh, I know. They wouldn't. Because there *is no park*. It's a wasteland, Abe. So just drop it, okay?"

Jamaal was huffing by the time he finished.

Abe straightened his tie, then swirled his glass. "Mistakes do occur from time to time, my young cousin. What if e-Trax was provided with an outdated map of Kenya, one that didn't display more recent changes in—"

"It's kinda hard to make that kind of mistake, okay? You're a lawyer. Focus on the contracts and fancy words no one understands except other lawyers. Besides, it's not as if this is the only deposit of Lucy they found. Oh yeah, I bet you didn't know that, right? They found other ones, too."

"Deep-earth deposits," Abe retorted. "That's right, Jam Boy. I actually know about those, because I read the news streams. I also received the company memo. My team was assigned to lead the negotiations."

"Congratulations. So you know if the deposit was really in a park, e-Trax would focus on the deep deposits."

"Only if it had to. Deep mines are expensive, rock digger."

"Then it's a good thing we don't have to dig deep," Jamaal argued.

"I saw what I saw."

"You said it was a photo of an article. Which means you can't see the author's signature stamp to trace it and verify the contents. Besides, why would the CEO insist it's a wasteland area?"

"Mistakes—"

"And if you're so sure, Abe, bring me proof."

"If I find proof, will you raise the issue with the Geo Department?"

That shut him up. The Geo Department's job was to survey territory and make maps of deposits. If there was an issue with the mapping, Jamaal's department was responsible.

"You're not gonna find proof." Jamaal started scooping the rice.

"Scared?"

"No."

"Boys. Too much talking. Not enough eating."

"Then why won't you agree?"

Jamaal almost choked as he swallowed. "And lose my job? The one I actually like?"

"As opposed to …?"

"Go away. Besides, what about the NBA?"

Abe grinned. "I believe you mean NDA. The non-disclosure agreement."

"Yeah. That."

"I'm impressed you remember signing one."

Jamaal sat up straighter. "Sure do."

"Alas, it's true. Legal can sue you for the rest of your miserable life if you break ranks and share e-Trax's corporate secrets."

"Exactly."

"So about my proof."

Jamaal ignored Mama-i's warning look and waved a fork at Abe. "Are you listening to yourself? What about our NDAs, and how we promised to never disclose company secrets and stuff?"

"What about them?"

"We could get sued."

"Only if we share it with someone outside of e-Trax. And why would we, if there's no damaging secret inside the company?"

"Drop it, Abe. That article you read? It's wrong. There's nothing to hide."

Abe held out his hand. "Then you agree?"

"I forgot to feed the cat," Jamaal said, then left the table.

Chapter Eight

"Knock, knock."

Eva jumped and yanked off her Shaids. Theo peered around the door at her.

She laughed, rubbed her eyes and waved him in. "Is it that time already?"

"You mean the time when a human being needs to unplug and consume calories and nutrition in order to continue slaving away at their new, high-powered job? Sure is. It's called dinnertime."

"Wow. Good thing I don't have to eat, then."

"Isn't there a maximum recommended time for using hAPPn without a break?" Theo stood behind her, massaging her shoulders.

Her muscles tensed, before relaxing under his knowing touch. "Something like that. Can I hire you to stand here all day and do this?"

"As long as I can paint on your back."

Eva glanced at one of his hands. It was gripping her shoulder, kneading the exact points where muscles had clenched into a silent scream. His knuckles and fingertips were stained with yellow and orange. "Working on sunsets today?"

"More like an explosion. But let's go with sunsets."

"I'm sure it's going to be brilliant, as usual." Eva closed her screen. She'd almost finished her handover notes for the new Assistant Growth Engineer. Someone else could suffer with the worst acronym for a job title ever. She leaned back and closed her eyes. "Let's just skip dinner."

"Since you already skipped lunch, I'm going to give that a hard no."

"There was lunch?"

He squeezed a bit harder. "You mean you didn't hear the shouting match? You know, the one with your almost teenage daughter. That's usually an indication it's mealtime."

"Maybe we should make her eat in her room." Eva was joking, but it was a tempting proposition.

"They have this thing called boarding schools. Those do the trick."

"You'd miss her."

"Sure. All that teenage angst and sarcasm. The argumentative comments made just to press my buttons. Can't imagine why anyone would ask someone else to look after their kids."

She patted his hand, enjoying his warmth. "What was it this time? Fluffy again?"

"She spends more time with that thing than she does with humans."

"It could be worse."

He leaned into her shoulders, and she almost forgot what their topic was until he murmured, "Enlighten me, please."

"She could be wandering the streets with a gang of drug fiends. At least we know where she is."

"We know where her body is. I'm not sure about her mind."

"It's with Fluffy, a designer pet that doesn't actually exist."

"Tell that to Rossi."

Reluctantly, she twirled her chair around. "It's just a phase, Theo. You know, that thing teenagers go through? I'm sure we did the same, if not worse. At least nowadays, she's at home." She jabbed a thumb upwards, indicating the floor where the bedrooms were located.

Theo shuffled around until he could lean against her desk. "That doesn't mean she's actually safe."

Eva frowned. She was used to hearing these sorts of arguments from anti-hAPPn campaigners. Usually stay-at-home parents who insisted the only way to educate a child was to do so out in the forest or on a farm or something like that. "Where's all this coming from?"

"You mean you're not concerned about the recent report on fogging?"

Eva controlled her expression. She knew she couldn't fool Theo. But at least she could minimize her irritation. "Of course. There's always going to be people who turn every tiny event into a catastrophe. Rossi's safe in hAPPn. We use industry-leading algorithms to protect our members, but particularly minors."

"That's not what I mean, Eva. The announcement by the World Health Organization—"

"The what?" She straightened and waved a hand for him to continue.

"An hour ago. You didn't see it? WHO launched the results of their global report on online living and working. It was posted on my Arts For Life & Health Place."

Eva glanced at her Doodad and did a quick search. Sure enough, the WHO report had made headline news in a few Places. "There's an article from Journal of Facts / Fiction that discredits the study, and they're usually solid when it comes to analyzing scientific data," Eva said with a gust of relief.

"Really? I never saw that article. But I did read the WHO's summary. And it's definitely on the increase."

"What is?"

"Fogging."

She grimaced. That word, two times in one day. "They never asked for our input."

"Who didn't? The World Health Organization, or Journal of Facts / Fiction?"

"The WHO."

"But of course, the journal did."

She narrowed her eyes. "If I didn't know better, I'd say you were edging toward conspiracy theory territory."

Theo gave her his charming half smile. "Hey, I'm just the messenger. You should read the report, Eva. It's more than a minority of addiction-prone crazies who are experiencing the health impacts of fogging. It's a real trend."

"Fine. I'll look into it. We good now?"

"You don't think Rossi's in danger of fogging, do you?"

"Absolutely not. At the very least, we make her eat with us."

"Lucky us. It's just ... We used to be so close. But lately, she's disconnected, distant. And she's *always* criticizing us."

"You mean she's a teenager." Eva laughed. "That's all it is, Theo. She'll get over it. We'll have to buckle down for the next few years, wait it out, and voilà."

He rubbed his chin. There was at least two days of stubble, and the sound of skin scratching against skin made her smile.

The knot forming between his eyebrows didn't. "Not to

sound old-fashioned or anything, but she's only twelve. And it's not like there's a minimum age to join hAPPn."

Eva pushed her chair away from the desk. She'd heard this debate before, as well.

"That's because there doesn't need to be. Underaged members are never totally on their own. The Placers make sure they don't sign up for anything that isn't child-approved and age-appropriate."

"There's a big difference between a digital algorithm, and a human guardian. You can't compare them."

"I'm not. A Placer doesn't sleep. It sees everything the child is doing online, and reports any concerns directly to the parents or guardians who helped open the account. Humans lose focus, get distracted sometimes. A Placer never does."

"You're not worried Rossi spends so much time online?"

"Some of that is for school."

"Sure. *Some*. But a lot of it isn't. In case you haven't heard the latest, she wants us to recycle everything down to the skin we shed in the house. She's joined Green Teens, a Place for young environmental activists."

"That's great! She's showing interest in something meaningful."

Theo hesitated. His gaze became unfocused, and he stared out the window that swallowed their wall.

Eva was tempted to turn around and admire the view, but that might give Theo the wrong impression. He was sensitive about things like that, about body language and positioning. Turning her back on him might make him think she wasn't as interested or concerned about this topic as he was.

She was definitely interested, just not concerned.

Rossi grumbled a lot about her Placer being a digital

babysitter. That was more than enough proof to convince Eva the Placer was doing its job.

"If you're sure," Theo said as he stood, his gaze now focusing back on her.

"Absolutely. But if you want, I can check out Green Teens. Make sure they're not up to any mischief."

Theo looked chagrined. "I already poked my head in there, and Rossi saw me do it. She wasn't impressed."

"She knows the rules. As her parents, we have automatic visitation rights to any Places she joins. So was it a den of sin?"

"Hilarious, Eva. Dinner's in five. Try not to be late. We need to set some sort of an example for our wayward daughter." He sauntered out of the room, and Eva admired the view.

Then she turned to face the window.

Theo was always the worrier between them. He'd worried she'd say no when he asked her out on their first date. When they'd discussed getting married, he was concerned they weren't ready for the commitment. He'd agonized over the pregnancy, about every time she experienced morning sickness. He'd fussed over her food. Was it nutritious enough, organic enough?

She'd almost expected him to faint during the delivery, but he was there the entire time, squeezing her hand, encouraging her. Only after Rossi was safely delivered did he finally collapse into a chair and sob.

He'd fretted about their move to Seattle, then the real estate upgrade. When he cooked, he was anxious about gas fumes entering the house and causing cancers as yet undiscovered.

That was Theo. Always worrying about others, sometimes to his own detriment — and theirs.

But when it came to hAPPn? That was her world.

She'd joined the company in its early days. She'd been actively involved in developing the Placers, and the regulations for underaged members. She knew the system inside out. Without a doubt, Rossi was safe, despite Theo's concerns.

But maybe it wouldn't hurt to pop into Green Teens and check it out. She could even go as an anonymous guest. As a Chief, she could do what Theo couldn't. And Rossi would never know her mother was snooping around.

Her Doodad *dinged* before she could add the to-do. She glanced down, saw Jack's name, and tried not to groan.

His message was marked *urgent* and had an invite link to a private meeting room.

Eva was tempted to ignore it, to pretend she never saw it, and join Theo in the kitchen. It was dinnertime, after all.

Ding!

A new notification appeared on her Doodad. It was as if Jack had seen her hesitate. *Urgent, quick meet. No time to delay.*

"I'll be right back," Eva whispered before she reluctantly logged in, and opened the invite.

Chapter Nine

THE SOFT WHIR of helicopter rotors chased Moja as she ran down the long hallway. Floor and ceiling, walls on either side, all glowing white. She didn't see any lines to indicate tiling. Nor did she slow down to look.

The whirring came closer, just around the corner behind her. Closing in. Except this time, it wasn't a camera hanging from underneath the drone.

Moja lengthened her stride, but the hallway still yawned ahead of her. No doors, no windows, no intersections she could duck into and hide.

Because there was no hiding.

She snuck a glance over her shoulder. The drone glided smoothly around the corner, picking up speed. The green light at its base turned red and began to blink. Slowly, then faster, as it gained on her.

"Jack," she shouted.

"You're being paranoid." His words bounced against the walls, and floor and ceiling, like a rubber ball hit too hard by a racket.

"I told you this would happen," she screamed as the hallway started to curve.

As she followed the curve, the space widened until she was no longer in a hallway but a room.

She bounced against the far wall, spun around and pressed her back against it. The hallway vanished. She was in a room with no entrances. No exits. No discernible source of light, although all the surfaces had that unearthly white glow.

"This is your Place now," someone said. Not Jack. But familiar. She should know that voice.

The whirring made her look up, just as the blinking red light fixed its baleful glare on her.

Moja jerked awake, rolling to the side as if to duck away from whatever the drone was about to shoot at her. Laser beam? A miniature cannon ball?

But there was nothing in her cabin. Just her breath. Night insects chirped. The eerie call of a bush baby, answered by another.

Moja blinked into the darkness. The absoluteness of it reminded her of where she really was. Home. Or as close to home as she would ever get.

She gazed into that darkness, unafraid. It was full of life. A kinder life. Not the frenetic breed found in the city, or the oppressive gossip of a small town. The forest was as crowded as the largest metropolis, and as intimate as the littlest village. There was a community for everyone, a home without needing to become something she wasn't.

She chuckled, her voice raspy. "Look who's waxing poetic."

She reached for her watch and hit the small light. Five o'clock. Another hour before the predawn light touched the horizon, and an additional half hour before any of that light reached into the forest, penetrating the thick leaves and underbrush.

She lay back, staring up at the ceiling. Something rustled in the thickly woven straw. It wasn't big enough to disturb her. Probably a mouse.

"You're being paranoid."

Jack's voice, as clear as the last time they spoke. A familiar ache started in her throat and worked its way down.

"No. Not going there." She pushed herself upright and switched on the solar-powered lamp.

A warm yellow glow — a slice of the sun's rays suddenly filling the room.

She started to hurry, even though there was nothing to hurry toward. Life in the park had its own pace. Rushing around wasn't a part of it. But she couldn't sit here, waiting for the sun to rise, or for Ojil to heat up the skillet and make their breakfast.

Imagining Ojil cooking reminded her of the years when he and her father worked together. She spent her summer vacations with them, following them around the park. Ojil had called her a bush baby. He'd warned Father they'd lose her to the jungle if he didn't take care and send her to the city.

Father had shrugged. "Nothing wrong with getting lost in the jungle. As long as you know how to find yourself."

Ojil had nodded as if he understood. Moja was still trying to understand.

By the time the first hint of light tapped at the edges of darkness, Moja had finished her breakfast. She paced in front of the compound's gate. Shouldering her rifle, she broke yet another protocol. She left the compound on her own.

"It's a big park," Father had told her. "Lots of wildlife.

Especially the wild part. You don't go out alone. No one does. Even the lions go out together. And the elephants, the biggest animals on land. Do you see them walking around alone?"

"Some elephants do," Moja said, easing the gate closed behind her.

If she waited for Ojil, he'd want to do the security checks, call in with HQ, and a whole other list of procedures, not to mention a leisurely breakfast while reading the news. Father had always joked about Ojil's inability to be ready any time before midmorning.

She couldn't wait that long. Nor did she want to deal with any questions or knowing glances or — worst of all — sympathy. He tried to hide it from her whenever she looked up, but she knew it was there. Sympathy, bordering on pity. He knew she hadn't come home entirely willingly. It certainly wasn't a career advancement.

Nothing wrong with getting lost in the jungle. As long as you know how to find yourself.

Maybe Ojil suspected she wouldn't be able to find herself. Worse yet, she didn't really want to. Maybe that was why he didn't want her wandering around alone.

She found Baby Moja near the salt lick. A small herd of elephants, all females, were also there. They ignored her presence. No one had taught them to fear humans.

"Let's hope you never learn fear," she whispered.

The matriarch splashed her trunk in the watering hole, then began the journey back into the jungle for the day's work of foraging for food.

Baby Moja watched them go, then leaned against a tree to scratch his hide.

"I knew you'd remember me."

Baby Moja trumpeted and waved his trunk, then held it up for a high five.

Moja obliged. "You don't just have good memories. You elephants are also more trustworthy. Why can't humans be more like elephants?"

The albino snorted water from his trunk, splashing her face.

"That's disgusting."

He ambled past her and into the jungle, following a well-worn trail. Despite the elephant's size, his thick feet plopped softly against the ground.

She let him go ahead several meters before following. In the dawn's mottled light, his hide appeared as pale as ivory. But as the sun strengthened, it would look more like a pinkish brown. Not exactly the glowing white people pictured when she told them about the white albino. But pale enough to cause him trouble with the sun. He was also easy to find if a poacher decided albino hide was worth a few coins.

"Not on my watch," she promised.

Moja paused and pressed her hand against the trunk of a tree, closing her eyes. Remembering.

She was sitting next to Jack. They were in a café, offline. In those early days, their interactions had all been in the physical world, in person. Close. Intimate. They were laughing, taking a break from developing the greatest app ever, from creating a new world, or perhaps reshaping the old one.

She shook herself out of the memory, but another immediately followed. Because with every positive memory of Jack, there was always that other one, the one where he betrayed her.

She shouted at him as she left the meeting room. Her eyes teared up, causing the walls to glow silver, blurry at the edges. A mixture of sympathy and scorn in the faces that watched her leave.

Humans really sucked.

A trumpet yanked Moja out of her memories, and she pushed away from the tree, jogging after the elephant, wishing she could leave the memories as easily as she'd left hAPPening.

Baby Moja had stopped walking. For a moment, she imagined he'd stopped so she could catch up. A silly idea, but she was still disappointed when she saw he'd found a new toy.

The disappointment shifted into something else when she saw what he was playing with.

A crumpled up cigarette box.

She waited until the elephant became bored of it. After he continued his stroll into the jungle, she picked up the trash. An empty box of Smolders. The same brand Jack loved to smoke.

She turned it over, as if expecting to see the mystery of the litter written on the back.

"How did you get here?"

The park wasn't well known. Certainly it lacked the international fame of the Maasai Mara. The more intrepid tourists who made the journey to Uhuru were always accompanied by a guide. And no way would any of the rangers allow someone to toss their garbage. Sure, it was just cardboard, and it would've decomposed quick enough. But it still didn't belong on pristine land.

She folded it, and stuffed it into a jacket pocket. She was about to follow Baby Moja when an unnatural glint caught her eye. Stooping down, she picked up a piece of metal.

"Now what is a tourist doing with a broken drill bit?" she murmured.

The crackle of her walkie-talkie almost made her drop

the bit. Exhaling heavily, she pocketed the bit, and clicked the talk button. "I'm okay."

"Moja," Ojil huffed.

"I'm not far. So please don't lecture me—"

"Something's happened."

"I'm sure something has, somewhere in the world."

Ojil gasped, then wheezed, "Oh! I'm not joking. Get back now. Quickly."

Moja raced back to the office, thoughts thumping as loudly as her heart. What if Ojil was injured? He hadn't sounded hurt, but he was one of those stoic sorts. He'd once been gored by an enraged water buffalo. The whole time she and Father were attending to his torn thigh, he'd been telling jokes to distract and entertain them.

She burst into the office, slamming a hip against her desk. "What's wrong? Are you okay?"

Ojil didn't answer, scrolling through the notifications on his Doodad.

"Are you kidding me?" Moja asked.

"Hmmm …"

"You made it sound like an emergency."

"If you had a Doodad instead of that antique, you'd already know."

"It can't be an emergency if it's in there."

Ojil didn't answer, just patted the chair next to him. She slumped in it and glared at his device.

"I just joined Metals & Mud—"

"Congratulations. Still not an emergency."

"It's a Place focusing on resource extraction. My Placer recommended it. You know what that is, right? A Placer—"

"Yes. I know what a Placer is. I may not have a Doodad or a hAPPn account, but I haven't been living under a rock, either."

"Could've fooled me. Look at this."

Reluctantly, she glanced at the Doodad. Ojil fished out an article from the Place's news stream. It was an info-post — a lengthy advertisement written as if it wasn't promoting a product or service. Paid for by a company called e-Trax.

"Okay. So?"

Ojil scrolled down to a map of Kenya. It displayed recently discovered deposits of a rare earth metal called EA-L029. "Look where they found it."

He jabbed a finger at the map, causing it to explode across the screen, magnified around Nairobi.

Moja waved his hand away and resized the map.

"Look," he repeated.

Moja stared at the map, where the outline of the EA-L029 deposit glowed in bright blue. The deposit was under Uhuru National Park.

"You see?"

Moja nodded, her throat clenching, the pain moving downward, to the pit where she stuffed unwanted memories and difficult questions.

"There's no mention of the park."

Ojil tapped the map again. "Hmmm. It's like we don't even exist."

Chapter Ten

JAMAAL TRIED to ignore the insistent *bing* on his Doodad as he sat in his digital office the next day.

"Serves him right for being such a conspiracy theorist," he muttered.

Bing, Bing, bing, bing!

A three-dimensional notification popped up in front of him in the shape of a wolf dressed in a business suit. "Little pig, little pig, let me come in," it said in Abe's voice.

Jamaal sent a permission link and Abe popped into view. "You're an idiot. You know that, right?"

"Need I remind you I wasn't the one who had to resort to studying rocks for a living?" Abe patted the holster hovering at his side. A cartoon gun peeked out and blinked up at Jamaal.

"What the heck is that?" Jamaal asked.

"What does it look like?"

"A pet gun?"

"It's not just any old pet gun. It's a smoking gun."

As if on cue, the gun wiggled out of the holster. Using its bullet-shaped limbs, it scrambled onto Abe's shoulder. It then pulled a Smolders out of the air and inserted it into its nozzle. *Puff, puff, blow.* A column of pink smoke rings floated up, and drifted around Jamaal's head where they changed into laughing emojis.

"That's weird," Jamaal said.

"So says the grown man who has a pet rock."

"Pet rocks have been around forever."

"So have smoking guns."

"Don't listen to him, Rocky," Jamaal told the pet rock squatting in a corner of his office.

The pet rock knocked its head against the wall in response.

"That's not normal," Abe said, gesturing to the rock.

"What do you want?"

Abe shrugged. "I couldn't find the article. Someone removed it from the stream."

Jamaal grinned. "All is forgiven."

"That doesn't change what I saw."

"I guess it was fished out for containing fake news or something."

"No. They would've labeled it as misleading or inaccurate. But no one removes info-posts, Jamaal."

"Sure they do. hAPPening is pretty strict about what it allows into hAPPn. There's some kinda review system and—"

"Algorithms. They've installed smart algorithms. That's not the same as a review process."

Jamaal rubbed his temples and stared at the core samples on his desk. "How are you my best friend?"

"Who said I was your friend?"

"Again: what do you want, Abe?"

Abe looked around.

So did Jamaal. He preferred to work online rather than offline. His basement room was comfortable, but not nearly as interesting as his digital office. His department had given him a budget to decorate as he saw fit, and he'd used every cybercoin provided.

One wall kept shifting into different rock formations. Another showed the sedimentary layers of a cliff with the complete skeleton of a winged dinosaur embedded in its face. The floor was black granite. The high ceiling boasted several stalactites covered in shimmering films of oily blues and greens.

Mama-i didn't allow pets in the house, but in here? There were no valuable Persian carpets to soil. His pet rock — a round piece of quartz with six legs and two bulging, onyx eyes — rubbed up against his legs like a cat.

"Forget about the article," Abe said.

"Forgotten."

"I found something else that might be even more informative."

"The location of a new tie shop?"

"Amusing." Abe stared at the pet rock. "What madness made me you buy one of those?"

"It's cute."

"Really?"

"It's all I could afford at the time."

"Yet you paid for an upgrade. Typical."

"No, I didn't."

"I can see the signature stamp, same as you can, Jamaal. It was updated this morning. According to the signature, the upgrade includes a bark function. Why would you want a barking rock?"

Jamaal let his eyes unfocus enough to read the signature stamp embedded in his pet's code. "You're right."

"As if there was any doubt."

Jamaal snapped his fingers. "Make a noise, Rocky."

The pet rock spun in a circle and barked. It sounded like gravel being mixed in a blender.

"I swear I didn't order that," Jamaal said and studied Rocky for any other upgrades.

"I should hope not. It would be a colossal waste of cybercoins, and you already threw enough away on the basic version."

Jamaal scratched Rocky's rough back. "What did you find, Abe?"

"A map."

"You get lost easily, do you?"

"I found it in the Green Defense Fund's Place."

"You're a member of … Why would you associate with a bunch of green necks? Fanatics, all of them."

"Not all green necks are terrible, you know."

Jamaal snorted. "Please. They're always doing sit-ins at the first sign of anything that looks like real work. The proposed mine in Northern Alberta? Shut down. Because someone saw what *might* be a new variety of dung beetle or whatever. Who cares? But they *always* do. It's ridiculous."

"If you'd just let me finish—"

"e-Trax has an excellent environmental record. That mine we did in Colombia? Everyone living near it said the same thing. The quality of drinking water actually improved after e-Trax rehabilitated the land. And all the trees were replanted, and then some."

"Yes, Jamaal. e-Trax is great. Long live our CEO. That's why we work here."

"Glad we agree." Jamaal pulled his floating monitor closer. "Nice chat. Some of us have work to—"

A notification *binged*. He pulled it up on his Doodad and groaned. His supervisor, Ms. Chan, had sent him an invite for a private meeting that afternoon.

"Talk about weird," Jamaal muttered.

Ms. Chan never invited him for anything except the obligatory Monday morning meeting. That suited him just fine. She was always on his case about being late. Was it his fault his mom's cat needed to be fed twice a day?

"Are you listening to me?" Abe asked.

Jamaal looked up at him. "What? No. I mean, I don't understand why you're a member of an environmental Place. And I thought you were already at your limit? Geeks Rule. Legalicious, and what's the other one?"

"Dragon Racing. Those are my personal Places. Green Defense Fund isn't personal. It's part of my job to keep informed about possible legal challenges. And do you know the best way to do that, my soft-brained cousin?"

Jamaal shrugged. "Plant a virus in their software?"

"Close. Be embedded in the enemy camp, so to speak. e-Trax paid for me to have access to Green Defense Fund, because they are the Place most likely to file a lawsuit over an environmental issue."

"Huh. Four Places. Who woulda figured?"

Abe looked smug. "Money buys everything, including membership to the truth."

"If this is another conspiracy theory—"

"I promise you. It's not."

Jamaal hesitated. Another notification appeared on his Doodad. It buzzed up his forearm. He looked at the screen covering his inner arm. Ms. Chan had sent him a PM. First an invite. And now a private message?

"All I ask is that you give me three minutes of your precious time," Abe said. "I can send you a one-time invite to visit their Place."

Another notification. A link to Ms. Chan's digital office. Wow, she really wanted to speak to him. What could possibly be so urgent?

"Are you in, or not?" Abe asked.

"Only three minutes?"

"I wouldn't want to impose any more than that on your precious time."

"Yeah, sure. Whatever. Let's get this over with. But if it's another disappearing article, I don't wanna hear another thing about it, okay?"

"You have my word. I've sent you the link." Abe popped out just as Jamaal's Doodad binged again.

"Placer, on," Jamaal intoned.

"Hello, Jamaal. How may I assist you?" Sarah asked.

"Open Abe's invite link."

"Connecting to the link sent by Badi-u-llah Yazdani."

His office with its fossils, stalactites and pet rock disappeared. Instead, he popped into a Place that appeared to inhabit the middle of a forest. Giant redwoods towered above him. Grateful he'd worn an S-Suit that morning, he stroked the heavily textured bark.

Motion above his head made him look up. Fairies with glowing wings flittered in between branches, creating a constantly moving string of lights.

"Over here," Abe said.

Jamaal joined him next to a particularly large tree. A screen was embedded into the bark around eye level.

"Tell me you see it?" Abe prompted.

Jamaal shushed him and studied the image on-screen, a map entitled Kenya Wildlife Service: National Parks.

Scrolling text along one side of the map caught his attention. The fencing of the country's youngest national park had been completed a few months ago. It was part of a ten-year project to prevent elephants from destroying crops in nearby villages.

Jamaal looked at his forearm. "Sarah, retrieve the e-Trax map of the near-surface Lucy deposit."

"Map retrieved."

As she spoke, a map crystallized across his skin. He zoomed in, studying the outline of the deposit. He then glanced up at the screen on the redwood. The Kenya Wildlife Service's map showed a large national park in the same zone as the Lucy deposit.

"What did I tell you?" Abe gestured to the screen.

"It doesn't mean what you think." Jamaal wiped the map off of his Doodad. "What's the source of this map? For all we know, Green Defense Fund created it to look official."

"Why don't you fly over there and find out for yourself? You're supposed to be the geologist. So go do some geology."

A notification binged on his Doodad before he could argue. A red exclamation mark floated up and hovered in front of him. "Guess it really is urgent."

"What is?"

"It's from my supervisor. She's moved up our private meeting. It's in an hour."

"So?"

"Nothing. Except …" Jamaal frowned, re-reading the invite. "Head of Legal's been added to the invite link, as well. Fog. Double fog—"

"Relax. I'm sure it's just a routine …" Abe matched Jamaal's frown with one of his own. "Legal is going to be there?"

"Yeah, Abe. *Head* of Legal! Mr. Smeidt is on the invite. She's never invited me to her office before. And now I get an invite to meet her *and* Legal?" He looked at Abe, something sick squirming in his stomach. "What if she fogging knows I'm here?"

"Why would she or my boss care if you were?"

"You mean … you think it's possible? That they know?"

"Possible but not probable. It's not illegal to visit other Places." But Abe didn't look convinced, either.

"I'm seriously fogged up. And it's your fault."

"Relax. Blame me, if you need to."

"Oh, I intend to. I can't be here. Ms. Chan'll kill me. Or worse, fire me."

"You need to re-evaluate your priorities."

"Whatever." Jamaal popped back into his office before Abe could infect him with any more conspiracy garbage. He prayed Ms. Chan didn't know where he'd been, but knew he wasn't that lucky.

Chapter Eleven

URGENT, quick meet. No time to delay.

"This better be quick." Eva clicked on Jack's invite link, which took her to his high-level, private fish tank office.

Privacy was a commodity like everything in hAPPn. Most members were satisfied with the minimum protections required by law. Their personal data wouldn't be sold except in an aggregated, impersonal form. That didn't mean conversations and other sensitive data were immune from spying. Nor were locations kept secret, or posts anonymous.

Members who wanted more privacy could rent a high-level room for any duration of time. Such rooms had multiple levels of encryption, the kind only found around bank vaults and national security data. Per-minute pricing wasn't cheap.

But owning a private room like Jack's fish tank? That required a healthy cybercoin account in the realm of multimillionaires or large companies, and a successful application to hAPPening's board. Privacy was otherwise an illusion.

Eva's gaze twitched around the glass office. Why would Jack invite her into this room? The CEO's regular meeting room had a sufficient level of encryption to protect against almost any intrusion or eavesdropping. What was this really about?

She reduced her avatar's responsiveness to sixty percent. Much lower, and she'd look stiff and uninterested. She took deep breaths and settled her features into a semblance of calm. Not an easy task in the fish tank.

She'd always found the design for Jack's private sanctuary unsettling: a glass box submerged inside a tropical ocean. The walls, floor and ceiling were thick glass. A coral reef crowded with life exploded with color under the floor.

A swarm of bright orange fish flitted past one wall, reminding her of Theo's fingers stained with orange paint. Splashes of sunset against the darker ocean currents.

"Hope I wasn't interrupting anything?" Jack asked from behind the glass desk.

"Actually, we're about to have dinner." She focused on the fish. As one, they darted in and out of the coral city.

"Of course. Family time. This won't take long."

She drew a deep breath and met his gaze.

Jack was a fit, handsome man whose offline appearance nearly matched his avatar. But unless he'd been working out a lot lately, he'd definitely augmented his arms. They looked more muscular under his jacket than she remembered. And who knew what augments he'd snuck under his avatar's skin when designing it.

A trumpeting distracted her. A baby elephant stood in one corner, waving its trunk at her and stomping on the glass floor. It was beautifully designed, with more detail than most digital pets were given. She magnified her eyesight until she could see the individual hairs on the animal's back, and the long, thick lashes framing its large eyes.

Jack had spared no expense on this one.

"What happened to the flying horse?" she asked.

"That one's just for show."

"Your elephant looks like one of the first-generation pets. Hand-designed."

Jack stroked the elephant's head, then stared down at his desk. "Good eye. It's one of the first."

"I'm surprised you haven't upgraded it. You know, into a golden version. Or one with wings."

Jack chuckled. "No, I couldn't. It was a gift from ..." His voice hitched. "A friend."

"I didn't tag you for sentimental."

"We all have our weaknesses."

Eva nodded, wondering if the *friend* was one of his.

"You remember e-Trax?"

She kept her mouth shut while she compiled a neutral response. e-Trax had recently become one of the company's most important clients. She nodded again, not even trying for words.

Jack tapped his fingers along the glass desk. She'd seen him do the same thing offline on the few occasions they'd met outside of hAPPn.

"They came back to me. They're really happy, by the way. And grateful. Always good to have grateful clients, don't you think?"

She glanced at the wall behind him. A large shark glided by, floating over the coral reef, one eye focused on the fish tank.

"Grateful is good, I suppose. Is this going to be much longer, Jack?"

"Not at all." Jack paused. "The e-Trax CEO submitted a recent advertising request to me directly. We have an understanding between us, you see. Strong relationships, Eva. That's the foundation of any business. Strong relationships."

She nodded, keeping quiet. The shark drifted overhead, disturbing the watery light. Its shadow flowed over them.

"Thing is, this request? It needs to be handled with a certain degree of …" He mimed bouncing balls, like a juggler. "Discretion."

Eva was glad she'd lowered her avatar's responsiveness. Offline, her body squirmed at the implication. A few weeks ago, Jack had asked her for a small favor. And now … "I see."

"And as you were so helpful the last time. I mean, you did a great job." He stopped his imaginary juggling, and showed his empty hands as if expecting her to fill in the conversational void.

The shark circled around the room. An octopus jetted in front of the toothy snout.

"I mean, what company wouldn't be happy with that? Proprietary information on hAPPn demographics doesn't come cheap, you know." He chuckled.

Eva stared past her boss and watched the octopus. It slid into its den before the shark could do any more than bump against one of its tentacles. Other fish darted around the coral reef's canyons and through its valleys, searching for escape.

Selling highly aggregated demographic information was a normal part of business. Data mining was a multi-billion-dollar business. hAPPn was a convenient platform with which to do it. The fact that people had fun in it, found their perfect-fit communities, and were able to engage in 3D meetings and classrooms? Those services were a bonus. And one that also provided hAPPening with other income streams. All legal, all above board.

Data mining wasn't something hAPPening discussed publicly, but it definitely wasn't a secret. But this? It had been different ...

It had felt like such a tiny favor at the time. A case study, really. A small, practical test of hAPPening's powerful, information-gathering algorithms. That was how Jack had described it. Test the company's ability to collect individualized details on the membership of a certain Place.

And then share it with a third party.

"It's not like we're giving them people's home address and bank account details," Jack had told her after she'd conducted the test. "Just some basic information so e-Trax can be more targeted in their messaging. Provide better products to their clients. That sort of thing."

Such a tiny favor when he'd first proposed the test, and one she now regretted giving him. It sat inside her like a splinter, poking at a crack in her armor she hadn't known existed. After she'd completed the assignment, he'd winked at her whenever they met. Like they were co-conspirators, or members of a revolution, one she didn't want to be a part of.

"There we are," Jack concluded. "Happy client."

"That's great," Eva said.

A swarm of angelfish flitted underneath the floor, the tips of their fins grazing the glass. Why hadn't they designed the room to sit on the ocean floor? Why suspend it with glass on all sides? A fish tank within a fish tank.

"Sure is. Which is why I need your help."

Just a small favor. Tiny, really. Inconsequential. I'd be grateful forever.

Eva cleared her throat, even though her avatar had no

need to do so. "I'm sure Advert would be thrilled to get such a large assignment."

Jack chuckled and did his imaginary juggling act again. "Sure they would. But you know."

She waited for him to continue. The shark disappeared under the tank, gliding close to the ocean floor before disappearing behind her.

"You might've heard the news. About a rather significant find. A large deposit of a rare earth metal."

She shook her head and frowned. "Geology isn't in my wheelhouse."

"Of course not. Me, neither. Bunch of rock diggers. But as a Chief, you need to know what's going on across hAPPn in various Places, including … no, *especially* in Places we're not interested in. Good thing we Chiefs can visit all of them anonymously." He laughed.

The shark reappeared at the edge of her vision, circling the school of angelfish. Did sharks eat angelfish? They were so tiny.

Jack tapped his desk. "Thing is, Lucy—"

"Who's Lucy?"

"The rare earth metal. It's called something else. Some code, a serial number. I don't know. Doesn't matter. The kids are calling it Lucy for short. I think it—"

"Isn't Lucy the name of the oldest humanoid skeleton found in East Africa?"

Jack snapped his fingers. "That's why it sounded familiar! See, you do know something about geology."

"That's anthropology."

"Same thing. Digging through the dirt for old stuff. Fossils are basically rocks, right? Anyway, e-Trax has laid claim to this deposit in East Africa. It's near-surface, so it's cheaper to mine. In a wasteland area. It's the perfect material for eco-friendly power plants. Transform cities, blah, blah, blah. You get the picture."

"Okay." She glanced at the small digital clock floating in a corner of her vision. Any minute, Theo was going to check in on her, make sure she hadn't forgotten dinner.

"It's all great news for e-Trax. One problem. You know how those green necks are."

Her hands twitched, and she stared at Jack. Is that what people called Rossi, now that she'd joined an environmental Place? Would they label her a green neck? A radical, antidevelopment extremist?

"There's always some group of green necks hanging around a mining project." Jack waved a hand at the coral, as if the fish might be secret pro-green extremists plotting against them. "And these environmentalists automatically freak out whenever they hear about mining. Especially strip mining. Crappy name, if you ask me. Someone really wasn't thinking about the public relations angle when they came up with that terminology. Right?"

He paused, and Eva nodded. Rossi was probably sitting at the table right now, eyes glued to her Doodad, arguing with Theo about the no-screen rule and puppies. But at least she showed up to meals on time.

"Anyway. Green necks will be green necks. So e-Trax wants to toss a few info-posts into the news streams of various Places."

"That's their right."

"Exactly. It's all above board. These particular posts are written by independent experts. Purely educational. A proactive approach, cutting off the protests before they happen, so to speak."

"I'm sure Marsha will do a great job over at Advert." Eva wondered how much longer this would take. She'd already been here longer than five minutes. Theo hadn't messaged her yet, but he shouldn't have to.

"Of course. She's a professional. Usually. But the thing is, I was hoping you could handle it. Personally, discreetly. Danielle, the e-Trax CEO—"

"I know who it is."

He laughed. "Right. Of course you know Danielle. You were such a terrific help the last time. And Danielle's eternally grateful. Always good to have appreciative clients. Remember that, Eva. It'll help you go a long way in this industry. Anyway, she asked me to make sure this was handled directly by myself and you."

"Advert is better set up for this." *Because it's their job.*

"Theoretically. But you know Marsha. She hates me, and I don't think she's a big fan of yours, either. Right? She applied for your job. Not that I'd ever approve of her being my right-hand woman."

Eva stared rigidly over Jack's shoulder. A giant manta ray glided over the wall, and across the coral reef.

"Thing is, Marsha knows this is a big deal, and she'd probably take this as an opportunity to make me look bad. Besides, you know she's a member of one of those uptight, green neck Places?"

Eva allowed some of her surprise to shift across her avatar's face. "No, I didn't. She never struck me as the type to care about anything."

"Except revenge, am I right? What a fogger. Anyway."

Eva frowned at Jack's use of a term he claimed to despise.

"You know how difficult Marsha can be. Do me a solid, and help out. I know it's not in your job description, but I won't forget this. Neither will Danielle."

Eva hesitated. She knew very well how difficult Marsha could be. More like hostile and aggressive. They'd both worked product development together in the early days. Eva had led her team to create a critical Placer upgrade, winning praise from their Chief in the process. It hadn't seemed like a big deal at the time, but Marsha was definitely one to hold grudges. She'd been snippy with Eva ever since. Now Marsha had lost the bid for the second-most powerful job in hAPPening. Who knew how she'd treat Jack's request?

"Educational info-posts?"

Jack grinned as if she'd already agreed. "Exactly. People need to understand what Lucy really is. And I don't mean that gorgeous set of bones."

"I've never worked in advertising before."

He waved a hand dismissively. "You know hAPPn as well as anyone else, and probably better than Marsha. Am I right? Of course I am. You've been involved in a lot of product development. As Chief, you have the ability to see across multiple Places. You're the perfect person for this. You don't need Marsha's team helping you out."

Eva nodded. This assignment was nothing like the unfortunate favor he'd asked of her before. It was a bigger request, but it wasn't quite so on the edge of breaking company policy. At least with this favor, she'd be educating people, sharing facts.

Still, she studied Jack, searching for any hint that this was anything other than what it sounded like. He met her gaze with twinkling eyes. He was by nature jovial and flirtatious. He kept his cool even when he was upset, played nice, laughed a lot. It was impossible to read him.

"Is that it?"

"Why? Oh, right. Dinnertime." He glanced away. The shark drifted around them again. "The animation in this Place is crazy great, isn't it? I love coming here. It's perfect for meditation. You're welcome to use it, you know. If things get out of hand, and you need a break. Or a private moment. Anytime."

"Right."

He tapped his fingers against the glass desk. "Speaking of time, you have a family dinner. See you tomorrow."

Ding!

She flicked her forearm over to read Theo's message scrolling across her Doodad.

Dinner's ready. You know. That thing humans have to do once in a while. Eat food.

"Eva?"

She glanced at Jack. "Right. Tomorrow."

Only when she used the invite link to return to her welcome arch did Eva realize what had been off about him. He hadn't flirted with her once in that conversation. Not that she was complaining, but it was weird.

Chapter Twelve

It's like we don't even exist.

Moja stared at the map. The bright blue oval lazily encircled the deposit, obliterating the borders of their park with a careless sweep of a digital pen.

"They won't really mine here," Ojil said, interrupting the chaos clanging around her heart.

She shook her head. "Of course not. They can't. It must be an editing error."

Moja knew it wasn't even as she said it. She fished out the broken drill bit, held it up, then dropped it on Ojil's desk. It clinked against the surface, and rolled back and forth, the second hand on a ticking bomb.

Ojil's wrinkles deepened as he frowned. "In the park?"

"Along with this trash." She tossed the empty Smolders box into the burn pile, then pulled Ojil's Doodad toward her.

"Me, I only have the 2D version," Ojil said. "But it's easier to use if you don't know hAPPn. Let me show you."

But Moja was already navigating through Metals &

Mud, searching for similar articles. Ojil pulled his hand back, and watched her, his eyebrows rising.

Ignoring his surprise and unasked question, she swam through the news stream. All the information about the rare earth metal deposit was from the same source — e-Trax. The articles were little more than extensive advertising thinly disguised as scientific conversation.

"Easy to use?" Ojil asked.

"Sure. They seem pretty confident the mining project is going ahead. Too confident."

"KWS won't allow it." Ojil's voice lilted upward in a question infiltrated by a nervous edge.

"Of course not." Moja wished she sounded more confident. "Why has no one mentioned the park?"

"Hmmm."

"Like we don't exist."

Ojil cleared his throat and shifted in his chair.

Moja scanned the discussion generated from the info-post. One conversation stream discussed the exciting potential to upgrade energy storage technology. Supporters elaborated on the social, economic and environmental impacts of having smaller, cleaner, cheaper power sources.

"Seems Lucy's popular," Moja said.

"Lucy?"

"Nickname for the metal."

"Strange choice of name."

"People are pretty excited, regardless of the name. Assuming even half of what they're saying about the metal is true."

"But our park."

"They're not going to …" Moja stopped as she reached another conversation stream outlining how much safer strip mines were.

No risk of cave-ins, poisonous gas, or depression from

long days in the darkness. And since the Lucy deposit was in a designated wasteland, there was no environmental consequence.

As a bonus, e-Trax had promised to rehabilitate the land after each strip was finished. As one enthusiastic member of Metals & Mud commented, it was a win-win.

Except for one minor detail. This wasn't a wasteland. How could e-Trax think it was?

Ojil coughed, and Moja blinked. For a moment, she'd forgotten where she was. She almost expected to look up and see her old office, with Jack leaning in the doorway, grinning at her, a cup of coffee in hand.

"They're not going to what?" Ojil asked.

"To mine in the park, of course," Moja said, trying to ignore the latest comment from an e-Trax employee. She slid the Doodad across the desk, toward him.

"Is that what they're saying?" Ojil nodded at his device.

Moja looked around the office, avoiding his gaze. It had only been a day, but the KWS compound already felt like home. "They don't know what they're saying."

"Oh?"

"Some crazy person said e-Trax has already received unofficial approval."

"Hmmm."

Silence. Moja stared at the Doodad between them, her hands trembling. She wanted to jump into hAPPn, scream the truth until the online world echoed with it.

Her gaze drifted up to meet Ojil's. She hated the weariness she saw, the acceptance of an injustice rolling toward them as implacably as a bulldozer.

Unofficial approval.

If true, it was only a matter of time. She saw it in Ojil's eyes. He didn't need to say it. They were both thinking the same thing. Kenya routinely made Transparency International's annually updated list of the most corrupt countries.

Uhuru National Park was a minor park, little known, tucked in a corner away from the main tourist route. It received very few visitors compared to the larger, more famous parks.

Was it really too difficult to believe payments had exchanged hands, and eyes became blind as an economically insignificant parcel of land was obliterated? Especially when the benefits extended far beyond e-Trax shareholders.

"Make a comment in the conversation stream," Moja said.

"Which stream? And what?"

She tapped the one about global benefits. "Mention there's a national park in this area, protecting an important rainforest."

Ojil hesitated, then added a comment. Moja watched the conversation stream explode a minute later.

Radical green neck scum.

Fake news! e-Trax has excellent eco record.

Where do u live? Under a rock?

Get real, or get out.

I know a guy who knows a guy who knows how to plant a virus in avatars.

Read the proof, green neck. Designated wasteland certificate included in above info post.

Safer for minors, increased access to affordable energy, greening wasteland. It's a golden project. What's your prob?

Ojil paled as the abuse and accusations piled on top of each other. His hands shook as he logged out and closed hAPPn. "Maybe we should go back to work."

"We might not have anywhere to work if we don't do something."

"KWS will stop it."

"KWS doesn't have a lot of power in government. Not compared to some ministries."

"Greenpeace, then. United Nations."

"It'll be too little, too late." Moja leaned forward, tapping the Doodad. "If they're already getting approvals—"

"Unofficial ones."

"The prequel to official ones."

"They won't."

"You don't know that."

Ojil slid the Doodad away from Moja, not meeting her gaze. "Us, we have work. We need to walk the fence line in Section Nine. Make sure one of the old tuskers hasn't punched another hole."

"And what about the mine?"

"*Proposed* mine. It has to go through many steps for approval. It won't make it to—"

"But if it does?"

"Me, I'm too old for a fight," he said and huffed a laugh. His voice sounded scratchy, and Moja could hear the trembling from his hands echo in the words.

"Since when? You're a park ranger. You're never too old for a fight."

"Oh! I'm about to retire. But you. You're young. Strong." He glanced at his Doodad. "You think they'll kick me out of my Place?"

Moja forced a smile. "It's okay, Ojil. Wait a few days, and your fellow members will move on to something else. They'll forget all about your green neck comments."

He chuckled, then coughed. "Okay. Tea before we head out?"

Moja stood, her legs as restless as her spirit. "Maybe later."

"Are you sure?"

Ojil's words summoned a memory of another elder. "Are you sure?" Indra Patel had asked.

"Of course. I'm a god in there. We all are." She'd glanced at Patel, then Jack. "And gods have no limits."

"There are always limits," Patel had warned.

"Ha! I laugh at limits."

"Be careful, Moja. Being god is a bigger burden than you can imagine."

Memories trailed after her as she hurried out of the office and strode toward her cabin.

But I'm no longer a god, she thought, slamming the door and collapsing onto her bed.

She stared up at the thatch ceiling, listening for any sounds of the creature who'd been there the night before. A heavy silence filled the space, untouched by the calls of birds and monkeys in the forest around her.

We were all gods in there.

The three of them. Creating one of history's wealthiest companies, and a brand new world. Despite Patel's warning, she and Jack had become intoxicated. With the power. The creative freedom. The godlike status.

As she lay on the bed, staring into the layers of thatch, another memory drifted over her, like a Doodad showing the latest episode of a soap opera that never stopped running.

"We have to have stricter regulations," she'd yelled at Jack during one of their design meetings. It seemed they'd been arguing more lately.

Jack had scoffed. "What happened to no limits?"

"A mistake."

"You can't control everything."

"But we have to try. Those loopholes are big enough to drive an elephant herd through."

Patel had intervened, as he did whenever the arguments escalated into a shouting match between Moja and Jack. "Does everything have to be either right or wrong, yes or no?"

"Yes!" she'd stated, glaring at Jack.

"And there it is. The caveman brain asserting itself."

Distracted, Moja had turned to Patel. "The what?"

"Human beings are essentially still cavemen. Or cavewomen."

Moja schooled her expression, wondering if she should be insulted, intrigued or impatient.

Patel's smile widened, and Moja had the uncomfortable sense he saw through her mask.

"The part of our brain that controls our emotional responses, that dictates how we respond to danger or perceptions of danger. It hasn't evolved. The amygdala is a caveman's brain. It treats a traffic jam with the same chemical reaction as a saber-tooth tiger attacking us. Its questions are binary in nature. Is this berry safe to eat, or poisonous? Will the tiger attack me, or run away? Will I survive the winter, or starve?"

Patel paused to pick up the white, three-headed elephant statue, and ran a thumb over its back. "As you can imagine, this doesn't work so well in the twenty-first century. The yes-or-no, right-or-wrong approach is not just primitive. It's misleading, potentially dangerous, and certainly divisive."

"I guess."

He eyed her. "Look around. People have become increasingly hostile to anyone on the other end of a question. But it's not humanity's fault entirely."

Feeling like she was in school, Moja supplied the

answer, ignoring Jack's gloating expression. "It's the caveman brain."

Patel smiled, beaming at her like a teacher proud of the student who has finally understood. "Modern reality is far more complex, the answers nuanced, more sophisticated. Yet seldom do we allow ourselves time to explore those subtleties."

"And what exactly does this have to do with the loopholes in hAPPn?"

Patel shrugged an elegant gesture. "Perhaps nothing. Or perhaps everything."

"How very binary of you."

A pause, then the three laughed. Crisis averted, but not forever. The argument slunk away, a defeated hyena lurking in the shadows, biding its time.

Moja shook away the memory. Her legs twitched, and she glanced at the door. Her elephant was somewhere out there, wandering through the forest shadows. She could find him easily, even without the tracking chip in his ear. She knew where he liked to stay when the sun was at its harshest.

She tugged the necklace over her head, then bounced a small key in her palm. She stared at the bedside table, at the locked drawer.

"Do you dare?" she whispered.

She had to know. So yes. A binary response to a simple question. But lurking behind it was a nuanced reality.

She stretched over, opened the locked drawer, and stared at the contents. Specifically the device that was a must-have for countless members of hAPPn. When had she last used it?

The day Jack had betrayed her. The day she'd abandoned her post as a god within hAPPn.

She pulled out the Doodad and a bandwidth booster.

She studied the Doodad before turning the booster on. She retrieved a set of wraparound Shaids, slipped them on, and glared at the pop-up warning:

Is life hAPPning without you?

"Seriously Jack? Talk about overkill."

Is life hAPPning without you?

"Sure is."

Before opening her welcome arch, Moja obscured the location beacon of her signature stamp. She also checked the walls surrounding her digital heart, just in case a virus tried latching onto it.

"If only all hearts could have walls," she said and opened a private room. She sent the invite before she could change her mind.

A minute passed.

Would he accept her call? Did he want to see her again? Maybe he was offline, notifications turned off. Maybe, like her, he had left the world of hAPPn behind in his memories, and had retreated into retirement.

Just as she was about to cancel the invite and return to her jungle, Indra Patel appeared in the room.

He smiled. "I was wondering when God might call me."

Chapter Thirteen

"I'M SO FOGGED." Jamaal glanced around his office. "Ms. Chan knows I've been visiting green necks. She's gonna fire me. Maybe sue me."

His pet rock squatted in one corner. If it had been a real cat or dog, he would've worried the creature was about to crap on his floor.

Rocky's jaw creaked open to a series of gravelly barks.

"Hey, you're supposed to be quiet. That's why I bought you instead of a digital dog. That and your price."

Rocky whined, spun in a circle, and collapsed on the floor, panting. All of the dog-like behavior hadn't been part of the basic model, and he definitely hadn't requested or paid for any upgrades.

"Weird."

Bing!

Jamaal jumped, his breath hitching into a hiccup, making his throat ache. His heart sped up. He glanced at his Doodad, holding his breath. It was Abe, but that didn't help his breathing even out.

Jamaal summoned his digital *do not disturb* animation. A rock troll about the size of his hand popped into the room.

"Rock troll. Inform all visitors I do not wish to be disturbed for one hour."

"Do not disturb," the rock troll intoned in a creaky voice. "Do not disturb." The little creature marched around the room.

Anyone who *binged* Jamaal with a call or message would receive the animated rock troll as a response. If Jamaal had been a Level 1 Advanced member of Geo Rocks, he could've asked for a rock troll that would also take messages. But in order to move up from his current Level 3 Intermediary membership, he had to invite another twenty more people to join hAPPn, pay for a membership upgrade, or have a gazillion interactions in the Place.

Jamaal didn't think he knew another twenty people. He'd invited and re-invited everyone he knew, as well as his mom's Persian cooking club, and his offline backgammon club. He could always buy his way to the next level, but only if he kissed his bubble bike goodbye.

He sighed, hoping the rock troll would be enough to give him some privacy. The meeting was an hour away, and he planned to be the good little employee. Recover from the mess Abe had pulled him into.

He was making good progress with a rock sample analysis when the rock troll reappeared.

"Intruder," it moaned just as Abe appeared in the room.

"Didn't you see my rock troll?" Jamaal grumbled and waved the animation away.

Abe shrugged. "You're going to need a serious upgrade if you want to keep visitors away."

"I don't have time for this, Abe. Ms. Chan's on to me. She must've seen me log into your stupid environmental

Place. I have to get some work done. Discover a diamond deposit in the parking lot, or something."

"Relax. I figured out what you can do. Worst case scenario, you tell her you were investigating the Place with me."

"Yeah, about that." Jamaal twirled his chair around and tilted it back. "There's a logical explanation for … you know."

"The map?"

"Yeah. The map. It's wrong, Abe. It's out of date. Or … more likely, those green necks edited it to make it look like there's a park when there's only wasteland. To mess with us. That's what they're doing. Fogging up our bonus."

"Really?"

"Yeah."

"They faked a map. Look who's into conspiracy theories now. It sounds like a lot of effort."

Jamaal nodded, starting to feel better. "Yeah. That's it. That's what they did."

"Ey, baba!" Abe said.

"Don't *ey, baba* me. You sound nothing like my mom. And fake news is a serious issue these days. I mean, you heard Mama-i. She thinks Eco-War Now are heroes. Which makes their leader Eco Warrior the modern-day Robin Hood. Even though everyone knows they're gangsters. They were behind the destruction of all of those monuments."

"If you say so."

Another notification binged. Jamaal glanced at it. "Fog it! Meeting's started. Why didn't I hear the alarm?"

"Did you set one?"

"Of course I … Just my luck, and all of it bad. The one time she takes interest in me outside of team meetings, and I'm up to no good."

"You're exaggerating the situation. Everything's good apart from your pet rock and your horrific wardrobe."

"Whatever. Gotta go. And stop inviting me to strange Places."

Before Abe could say anything else to confuse him, Jamaal clicked the invite link.

The rock walls around him dissolved, and he popped into a modern office decorated with glass and steel. One wall was a window with a stunning view of Vancouver's North Shore. Ms. Chan sat behind her stainless steel desk. Standing next to her was the head of Legal, Mr. Denzel Smeidt.

So much bad luck.

"What happened?" Ms. Chan asked, fingering a brass letter opener with a sharp point. "Did you get lost this time? Or did the cat distract you?"

"No, I—"

"What were you doing in Green Defense Fund's Place?" She jabbed the letter opener toward him.

"Um … Nothing."

As usual, Ms. Chan was wearing her mood digitalizer. Jamaal stared at his supervisor's angel and devil duo on her shoulders. The angel was yawning, almost asleep. But the devil was scowling and giving Jamaal the bird.

He tried not to audibly gulp. Back home in his mother's basement, he was sweating like he'd just run a marathon, which he would never do. Because why? At least his avatar didn't sweat as much. But he knew it could still look nervous.

"You're related to Badi-u-llah Yazdani, aren't you?" Mr. Smeidt asked, not looking up from his in-built Doodad.

"Yeah. Unfortunately. He's my cousin."

The hAPPening

Wouldn't they already know that? And why was Abe's boss here?

Jamaal couldn't recall the guy's name. Maybe he once knew it, but his brain was having a meltdown. His heart was stomping across his ribs so fast and hard, he could feel bones bruising.

He almost hoped he was having a heart attack. Because that would be way easier to handle than whatever this was. An investigation? Interrogation? Inquisition, more like it. There were pills for heart issues, right? But no pill could cure all his trouble.

"Why were you with him, Mr. Shirazi?"

"He wanted to show me his work." It sounded like a question, so Jamaal answered, "I mean, yeah. He wanted to show me ... some stuff."

"Mr. Yazdani already logged in this morning to review the news stream in Green Defense Fund." The guy kept studying his forearm. "Once a day is the minimum and the maximum number of visits required. I can't imagine why he would go again, and there's even less reason for him to take you. Unless you're looking for another Place to join? Is that what's happening here, Mr. Shirazi?"

Pools of sweat formed under his armpits offline, and his avatar wasn't doing much better. "No. Not at all. He ... um, he just found something he thought might interest me."

"What could possibly interest you in a Place frequented by environmental extremists?" Ms. Chan scratched the letter opener against her palm.

"Nothing. Nothing at all. Turned out to be a joke. One big, not very funny joke. On me."

"Nothing, indeed," said Mr. Smeidt. "Let's keep it that way going forward, shall we, Mr. Shirazi? It's a sensitive time for e-Trax, what with the EA-L029 deposit and all. You understand."

The man still wasn't looking at anyone. His fingers drifted up and down his Doodad as he scrolled through whatever lawyer bosses scrolled through when interrogating innocent geologists. For all Jamaal knew, his and Abe's transgressions were listed in alphabetical order on the guy's forearm. In Abe's case, that would be a long list.

"Absolutely, sir. Ms. Chan."

Ms. Chan nodded at Jamaal. "Remember, Mr. Shirazi, *focus*. Now's not the time for distractions. I have a meeting with the CEO in a few minutes. She wants to make sure everyone is focused on this new deposit, on the project application. So are we, Jamaal? Are we focused?"

"Yes, sir. I mean, ma'am. That's me. Focused. No doubt about it. Totally focused. Work first, second and only work."

She stared at him, her hand curled around the letter opener. Even though they were inside a digital environment, he had to remind himself she couldn't really hurt him. He wouldn't die, even if she decided to stab him. Still, Jamaal had to force himself not to twitch or giggle nervously or any of the other indications that he was freaking out.

"I expect your full focus on this, Mr. Shirazi."

"And you have it. One hundred and ten percent."

"This is a big deal. A really, really big deal. For the company. For the world. For us. Are we clear?"

"Clear as glass. I mean, assuming the glass isn't colored or foggy or—"

"It's not just those extra bonuses on the line." Ms. Chan waved the sharp letter opener between them. "Once this announcement goes viral — and it will — our stocks are going to be like meteors. Not the type that crash to earth, either. Meteors that shoot across the sky and keep going. That's what we want, right, Mr. Shirazi?"

"Definitely. Meteors. Not the crashing kind. No doubt about it."

"Focus. And next time, reply to your notifications."

"For sure—"

But she'd already disconnected the invite, sending him back into his office.

Jamaal slouched in his chair. What had Abe been thinking? "Placer, call Abe."

"Calling Abe."

He must've been waiting for the call, because Abe's face filled the screen immediately, floating in front of Jamaal. "Look who's still alive. What did they want?"

"You're gonna get us both fired. They wanted to know what we were doing, and I told them it was just a joke. A joke I don't want to be part of. You hear me, Abe? If you want to lose your job and get sued for breaking an NDA, you do it by yourself."

He hung up before his cousin could extract anything from him. Determined to focus — because conspiracy theories and outdated maps weren't his job — he opened another floating screen and began picking out the top items from his to-do list. The Lucy deposit was number one, two and three. Because focus.

Bing.

"What, Abe?" Jamaal snapped.

"Are you still employed here?"

"You're a real fogger, you know that?"

"No one made up that map, Jamaal."

"We're not discussing this."

"Aren't you the least bit curious?"

"Nope. Because you know what happens to the curious cat?"

"It catches the worm?"

"Stop mixing metaphors, and get back to your job. You do still have a job, don't you, Abe?"

"They couldn't manage without me. Now, I may not be a rock digger, but I suspect the location of a proposed mine is somewhat important information for you geologists. Run a check on the map. That's all I'm asking. It's part of your job to verify deposits, isn't it?"

Jamaal hung up before he could tell Abe where to shove his conspiracies, then stared blankly at his to-do list. Rocky crawled up to him, its little pebble feet clacking against the black granite tiles.

"This is so fogged up, you know that?" He glanced at the digital clock floating on the ceiling above his desk. "Fine. I guess a quick search won't hurt anyone. Sarah."

"Yes, Jamaal."

"Enter Geo Rocks."

"Entering Geo Rocks."

His office dissolved into the large, public cavern of Geo Rocks. At the far end of the cavern, a group of school kids followed a guide around the sedimentary rock exhibit.

He skipped the tour and entered the members-only cave, which led into another cavern. Rocks of all types, colors and textures decorated every surface. Chairs and tables were made of delicately carved marble. Gold flecks lit up the ceiling. Bioluminescent creatures floated along the walls, illuminating the smaller caves tucked along the edges of the main space. Trees had slate bark, emerald leaves, and various gems for fruit.

"Do you wish to access the news stream, Jamaal?" Sarah asked.

"Nope. I'm not here to admire the landscape."

He opened up a search portal, and did a quick search into the geological formations of Kenya. A familiar map popped into view, with the newly discovered Lucy deposit bolded in bright green.

Jamaal then did a search for national parks of Kenya. Another map superimposed itself, indicating there were twenty-three national parks, and another four marine national parks.

He discounted the marine parks, and studied the remaining twenty-three. None of them were anywhere near the Lucy deposit.

He glanced around, half-expecting to see Ms. Chan pop into the cavern, pinning him with an accusatory glare. A few members were strolling along the edges of the cavern. A small group of researchers were tucked into a side cave, comparing notes and arguing over theories. On the other side of the cavern, a couple were dipping in the news stream. No one was paying him any attention.

"There's nothing wrong with what you're doing," he told himself with a quivering voice. "Just doing your job. Verifying the location. That's all."

Stone leaves cracked against each other as a breeze rustled the branches.

He called up another search for any national parks created in areas designated as wastelands, or reclassified as a wasteland. Nothing. A big, fat zero.

Jamaal grinned, the gurgling in his stomach easing away. He'd been right. Not that he'd had any doubts. But now he had his own proof. He could tell his cousin the truth, and hopefully kill the conspiracies and fake news.

"Not so smart now, are you?" he whispered.

He glanced around again. Not that anyone in Geo Rocks could see his private search, unless they specifically looked for it.

And why would anyone do that?

He could conduct an anonymous search. That way, no one could look into his activities.

But an anonymous search required some serious cyber-coin. It wouldn't give him anything different from what he'd just found. There were no maps showing a national park in the Lucy zone. No articles. No references to support Abe's suspicions.

He tossed a question into the Geo Rocks news stream, just in case, then mirrored it in his Metals & Mud Place.

Heard a rumor. New Lucy deposit not in designated wasteland but national park. Thoughts?

The news streams in both Places overflowed with replies in seconds.

Rumors by green neck extremists.

Who told you this crap? Economic terrorists.

Stop spreading fake news!!! Underneath that comment was a digital flamethrower directed at him.

He quickly replied to the flamethrower, just in case the person upgraded it to something nastier. *Not my fake news. Didn't believe it anyways. Just confirming.*

Deep fakes, green necks killing us, someone else posted, and included a 3D noose that swung over Jamaal's head before being swept away by the current.

Before anyone else could attack him, Jamaal drowned his original question and the related comments at the bottom of the stream, closing the thread to any additional responses.

He looked up and down the cavern. A few members had popped inside, but no one was close enough to engage him directly in conversation. Nor did they look his way, make threatening gestures, or give any indication they cared about anything he had to say or ask. It was bad enough reading and hearing people's comments in the stream, along with their unpleasant emojis. But

The hAPPening

having to face someone's avatar? See their disgust at his stupidity?

"Last time I listen to a lawyer," he muttered.

Satisfied he'd done his job, Jamaal left the members-only cavern. The school group had moved on to the metamorphic rock exhibit. His personal favorite.

He exited the Place and returned to his office. Abe was crazy. Obsessed with conspiracy theories, following every hint of anything that smacked of treason to the company. Even when they were kids, his cousin had relished having fun at Jamaal's expense.

Well, this was about as fun as a cave-in or a gas leak at a mine, and just as dangerous.

He dictated a quick message to Abe, then settled down to work.

Bing!

"Abe, if that's you, I'm not answering," Jamaal said, his glare fixed on his floating screen. "In fact, I'm gonna ignore everything you—"

"It's not Abe, Jamaal," Sarah said.

Liquid mercury filled his stomach. If not Abe, then maybe Ms. Chan? What could she want? Had she found his search? Doubted his loyalties?

"I'm gonna lose my job," he whispered to his pet rock. "That's it. She knows. She …"

Rocky barked.

"You're right. Maybe it's not her. Maybe she's clueless … I mean, not clueless. Super smart, but she didn't see my search. Doesn't care."

He turned over his forearm, peaked at the Doodad, and almost sobbed. Not Ms. Chan.

"Ha! Told you. She really doesn't care about me. Thank the hAPPn gods!"

Rocky whined.

Jamaal's smile faded as he studied the notification's signature stamp alerting him that he'd received a private message on a highly secured channel from an anonymous source. No location info.

"Weird," Jamaal said.

Not because it wasn't possible. But because it was so rare. He'd never received anything like this. And whoever had sent him the message had spent some serious cybercoin to encrypt it.

Jamaal glanced around his office. "Abe, is this your idea of payback? Or a joke? Because it's stupid and not funny."

Rocky turned in a circle, its pebble feet clacking against the tiles.

When Abe didn't materialize, Jamaal returned to his Doodad. "Not Ms. Chan. Not Abe."

His finger hovered over the notification. To open, or not to open.

"Grow some curiosity," Abe had told him.

When had curiosity brought anything but trouble?

Rocky plunked onto the ground and fell asleep. Its snores sounded like a soft stone breaking underfoot.

Jamaal's finger twitched. The notification binged again, reminding him of its presence.

"Oh, why not?" Figuring he needed a break after all the morning excitement, he clicked the message.

Four words popped into view, floating in front of him just long enough to read the message before it disintegrated into white dust.

We need to meet.

Chapter Fourteen

Dinner was the usual drama. Theo and Rossi argued about environmental activism, the appropriate use of Placers to spy on children, and the need for a real dog. Eva kept thinking about Jack's little favors.

Note to future self, she thought as Rossi informed them why dogs were better than people. *Stick to my job description.*

After dinner, Eva wandered into Theo's art studio where he was touching up his current masterpiece.

"I think it's finished." She nodded at the canvas.

Theo dabbed a corner. "It's better I massacre a painting than a relationship."

"This is hardly a massacre."

"Are dogs really better than people?"

Eva shrugged. "She didn't mean it."

"Don't be so sure."

"What's it like to work completely offline?"

"You work offline," he said.

"No. I sometimes take my work offline and sit in my physical office. It's still digital. Most of my work is online by nature. But yours …"

She gestured to a finished portrait. A fiery orange and red sunset contrasted with the pale blue tint in an elderly man's hair.

"Messy," he said and picked up a flattened tube of paint. "And I do some work online."

"Digitalizing your paintings doesn't count."

"If you say so." His tone was light as he tossed a brush on the workbench, but Eva could see the tension in his neck.

"She still loves you, even if you aren't a dog," Eva said.

"So you say." He squeezed the tube, pummeling it with his fingers, leaving tiny crescents on its metallic surface.

"What did that tube ever do to you?" she asked.

"It ran out of paint."

Eva stared at the workbench, restraining an urge to organize the bank of brushes scattered across its surface. If it had been hers, the brushes would've been laid out in order of size. The tubes of paint would be collected in buckets, one color group per bucket.

"You're both really messy," she said.

"At least we have that in common. Did you receive the notification from Rossi's Placer?"

Eva reached for the Doodad in her back pocket. "I heard it but was in a meeting. Was it urgent? I was going to look at it later."

"Not urgent, exactly."

Eva chewed on her lower lip and wished they were online where she could dial down her avatar's responsiveness. "What happened this time?"

"Her Placer used Rossi's current interests and her recent geography essay to suggest a second Place to join."

Eva's tension exhaled out of her. "That's great. You wanted her to try out new Places."

Theo scratched his scalp, then tugged on his hair. "It's a Place called Eco-Kids. Another environmental group."

"Good for her."

"Is it, though?" He frowned, and Eva wondered what she'd done wrong this time.

"Are they planning a revolution?" she joked.

"Shouldn't Rossi be expanding on her interests at this age, not narrowing them down? I mean, two Places for environmental activism. What are we raising, a green neck?"

She laughed. "I didn't know you were so snobby."

"No, but she's only twelve."

Eva clicked on the notification. A 2D rendering of the Eco-Kids Place filled her Doodad's screen. "It has a 10+ kid-friendly rating, which means it's designed for kids. No adults allowed."

She scrolled through the images, then dipped into the news stream. "Nothing radical." She paused when the title of a post caught her eye. *Vancouver-based mining company hits payload: rare earth metal discovered in East Africa.*

Another post drifted into view: *e-Trax to strip mine wildlife.*

"It's a wasteland," she muttered.

"What is?" Theo asked.

"Nothing. It looks fine to me, Theo."

"You don't think she should try out new things?"

"Honestly, if this is the worst she does, she's not doing too badly at all. At least she cares about something important."

"I still think she should have other interests." His jaw slid to one side, then the other.

Eva sighed and raised her hands in surrender. "Fine. Although I don't think it's a big deal."

Theo led the way upstairs, arms swinging like he was in a street artists' marching band.

Rossi was sprawled across her bed, Shaids on, a wide smile the only part of her face Eva could see.

"Knock, knock." Theo marched into the room.

"Placer, interrupt Rossi Taylor's current interaction and bring her offline," Eva spoke into her Doodad.

"Summoning Rossi Taylor," the Placer said.

Rossi shrieked and ripped off her Shaids. The smile sunk into her fury. "What the fog!"

"Language," Theo said.

"It's not even a real swear," Rossi said.

"We heard you joined a new Place," Eva said, forcing a bright cheer to her tone she didn't feel. Judging by Theo's jaw, he wasn't feeling it, either.

"I have to get back to Fluffy," Rossi said. "Thanks to you, I've dropped down to fourth place. I haven't spent enough time with her."

"Fluffy can wait a few more minutes," Theo said. "About your new Place."

Rossi rolled her eyes.

"Roll those any harder, and they might fall out," Theo said.

Rossi snorted a laugh, then seemed to remember she was furious at her parents for interrupting her dog preparation session. "Whatever. It's a cool Place."

"We're sure it is." Theo glanced at Eva. "And we'd like to see you try out something that provides a different perspective on issues."

"Like what? A pro-logging Place? 'Cause that would *so* be cool. Listening to people justify ripping out old trees."

"Not exactly," Theo said.

"You don't get it," Rossi huffed.

Eva covered her smile. "I'm pretty sure I said the same thing to my parents back in the day."

"You mean like, before there was dirt? Yeah, I get it, Mom. Except you guys are part of the problem. You don't do anything about it. And you don't even support me when I try to do something."

"Of course we support you. It's just that ..." Eva frowned at Theo. Why were they having this conversation?

"Don't you think one environmental Place is enough?" Theo said.

Rossi threw up her arms. "If you don't like it, you can always override my membership. It's like Big Brother. I don't have any freedom."

"Actually, kiddo, I think you have quite a lot."

"It's fine, Rossi." Eva shook her head at Theo. "You want to stay in these two Places, and that's okay with us. All we're asking is you consider a membership in something different for your third Place."

"Are we done?" Rossi asked, juggling her Shaids.

The motion reminded Eva of Jack. She glanced down at the floor, half-expecting to see a shark swimming beneath them. "Sure. We're done. Green Teens looks like a fun Place. And Eco-Kids, as well."

Theo cleared his throat, his mouth a flat line.

"What?" Eva asked. "It's not like she joined Eco-War Now."

"I should hope not. That Place is a hive of radicals."

"It is not," Rossi said. "They're awesome."

"Not really, Rossi," Eva said. "They've been involved in some pretty violent forms of protests, and—"

"Oh, please," Rossi said.

Theo nodded. "Your mom's right. Their last two protests ended with property damage, acts of vandalism, spray painting their logo on public buildings, street fights with the police—"

"That's not true! Total propaganda. That's not what happened."

"And you know that how?" Theo asked.

"Same way you know. I watch the news."

"We're clearly watching very different stations," Theo said.

"Yeah. You're watching the dinosaur news streams. Did you know Eco Warrior won a Greenpeace Award last year? And that Eco-War Now supports three food banks?"

"I hadn't heard that," Eva said.

"They get blamed for everything." Rossi glared at her Doodad. "But all they did was put up some posters and wave placards. The police attacked them."

"I highly doubt that," Theo said.

"You know what? It doesn't actually matter," Eva cut in. "No one is joining Eco-War Now, so it's irrelevant."

Rossi fiddled with her Shaids. "So I can keep my two Places?"

"Fine," Theo said. "But I want to see something different for your third Place, kiddo."

"That's so—" Rossi tugged at her sweatshirt, dragging the bright orange hood down her forehead.

"Unfair?" Theo offered.

"Unconstitutional."

Eva snorted, then coughed to hide her laugh.

Theo smiled, the knot on his forehead smoothing out. "Unconstitutional, eh? Well, that's a new one."

"You're limiting freedom of association," Rossi said. "And expression."

"You're a minor," Theo said. "It's my right as your parent to limit your freedom."

"Whatever. Fluffy needs me." Rossi yanked on her Shaids and flopped back onto her bed.

Theo started brainstorming on their way downstairs, thinking out loud about the possible Places they could encourage Rossi to join. Eva nodded and hummed between his pauses, but she was thinking about the article in Eco-Kids.

It was exactly the sort of false facts e-Trax was trying to proactively stop.

Feeling better about Jack's request, Eva made a mental note to widen her search. She needed to drop the e-Trax info-posts into more Places.

Strip mining wildlife. As if!

Chapter Fifteen

I WAS WONDERING when God might call me.

Moja was already drowning in memories.

"No gods here," she said.

Indra Patel's soft wrinkles deepened with his smile. "Glad to hear it. Being God—"

"Is a bigger burden than I can imagine," she finished. "I remember." She smiled. It was going to be okay. Patel always had the answers, a reassuring confidence infusing every word and gesture.

His expression shifted into intelligent observation, reminding her why her mentor had been such a successful businessman. He was as shrewd about his investments as he was about the people he worked with, and he never made choices based solely on sentimentality. She couldn't have created hAPPn without him.

Dark eyes flicked across Moja, studying her unspoken words, the tilt of her head, the tightness around her eyes and mouth.

Moja forced herself not to squirm or hide. This was why she'd contacted him after two years of silence, after all. His wisdom. His observations. Her thoughts were too crowded with the undergrowth of fear and anger to see the view. He on the other hand missed nothing.

"Uncle ..." She paused at the awkwardness in the word.

"I'm glad you still think of me that way."

"Of course," Moja said, although there was nothing *of course* about it. "No matter what happened, you'll always be like family to me."

Patel nodded. "A strange family that doesn't keep in contact. We tried to find you."

"I ..." She shrugged. "I've been offline."

"For two years?" He punctuated the question with a disbelieving cough.

"It's possible, you know. To live entirely offline."

Another cough.

"Asthma?"

He nodded. "It's not as bad as it used to be."

"Good to hear."

Trying to be discrete, Moja peered through his avatar's surface appearance and studied its digital signature stamp embedded on one edge.

Patel's silver tiger sniffed from within the nest of code. If she wanted to, she could read the signature for his physical location and recent activities—

"Still in Seattle," he murmured. "Or close enough."

She looked away, wondering why she'd bothered. Did it matter where he was?

"I like your choice of rooms," he said.

"It was always my favorite."

Patel made a show of admiring the virtual private room she'd created. An exact copy of his study, in recognition of all that had transpired there. The three gods of

The hAPPening

hAPPn clustered around his antique wooden desk. Plotting and planning, designing and shaping their world.

One wall was lined with bookshelves. Another wall included a large window looking out at a carefully tended garden. The room was warm, cozy, full of memories of an innocent, naïve time in her life. When she'd believed she could create a new world free of old vices.

"Moja," Patel said, his voice a verbal embrace.

She nodded and blinked away tears before they could betray her. Patel was like Ojil in some ways. Both men had adopted her as *family* when her father had been killed by poachers.

"You were always there for me."

Patel shrugged, as if being the ground upon which Moja had stood was an insignificant feat. "As you were for me."

"I've missed this ... Us."

"As have I. The three of us were quite the team, weren't we? Do you know almost everything in hAPPn *still* contains our stamps embedded in the code? It's remarkable, really."

"I suppose."

She avoided his gaze by looking out the window. She'd recreated a sunny day. The garden seemed a chaos of color, but every flower and shrub was exactly where Patel had designed it to be.

"The room of eternal summer," Jack had called it when he'd seen the virtual version the first time. He made it sound like a bad thing.

What's wrong with sunshine every day? No one wants to live in winter.

She finally met Patel's gaze. He didn't look like a software genius, or an astute investor. He reminded her of the elderly couple who'd lived next door to her childhood home. They'd sit in their matching rocking chairs all day, watching life hurry around them with mild curiosity, waving their walking sticks whenever they saw a neighbor.

Not that Patel used a rocking chair or a walking aid. The man exuded vitality despite his age. But he'd definitely softened around the edges since the first time they'd met.

"Two years," Patel whispered. "A difficult time. How—"

"What's done is done. That's not why I'm here."

He sat behind his antique desk and gestured for her to take a seat. Just like old times. His expression remained thoughtful, unperturbed as she told him about the info-post she'd read in the Metals & Mud Place. About the unofficial approval to strip mine the Lucy deposit, and the map showing only wasteland instead of a rainforest. She blurted it out in a series of breathless sentences, reluctant to give reality to this disaster with her words, but fearing it was already too late.

When she finished, she slouched back in the chair. Silence flittered around the room like a trapped butterfly.

Patel steepled his hands. "It seems your fears have come to pass."

Moja blinked misery out of her eyes and stared at the old desk. It was at least two hundred years old, historic even before they'd sketched out the beginning of an online revolution.

"I was naïve to think I could put in measures to avoid this." She winced at the surrender in her voice.

"We did what we could. But for the determined with deep pockets, everything is open for manipulation, especially the truth."

Her head sunk forward. She stared at a carpet even older than the desk.

"What now, Moja?"

She straightened, lifted her chin. "e-Trax is feeding members false information. Is hAPPening aware of this? Or have they started selling space for the highest bid, regardless of the truth? What happened to vetting of paid info-posts?"

She met Patel's calm gaze with her frustration, and he let her marinate.

"Why are you calling me?"

"Don't you care?"

"Perhaps I should ask you the same. You wanted nothing more to do with hAPPening. That's what you told everyone. You walked away from us. From me! Have you changed your mind?"

Her arms twitched, her hands clenched. The movements created tremors of confusion across her face before she could rein in her responsiveness.

"No. I'm sorry, but no. They betrayed me. *He* betrayed me. There's no going back."

"Ah, yes. There it is. The caveman brain strikes again. Right versus wrong. Yes or no. You still haven't escaped it."

"That's not fair—"

"Am I wrong?"

"Yes. Maybe." She hesitated. "I'm not sure."

Patel's eyebrows rose in an elegant set of twin arches. "Then?"

"You're the only one I can talk to about this. Who else can understand? Who else can I trust?"

A smile touched his thin lips. "Of course. We are two fellow digital exiles. How can I help?"

"I want more information about e-Trax and their info-post. What are they really up to? Do they know about the park? Or are they being fed bad data? And hAPPening. Do *they* know?"

"Why don't you ask Jack?"

She clamped her mouth shut, her silence louder than the heavy thudding of her heart.

"I see," Patel said after a moment.

"Sometimes reality does fall into a yes or no, right or wrong, binary response."

"And sometimes it doesn't. Moja, have you thoroughly investigated the situation? Have you stepped back from the trees to see the forest?"

"The forest is an old-growth jungle, home to endangered species. So yes, I have."

"Step back again. Why is this deposit so important? Is it only greed that motivates the search for Lucy? Or is there more to it?"

Moja paused, trying not to grit her teeth. He was trying to help her. Probably. "This is one of those times I wish you'd agree without …" She struggled to find a word matching her frustration.

"Providing you with alternative perspectives? Broadening your vision? Increasing your tolerance of other worldviews?" With each question, his smile widened, the twinkle in his eyes deepened.

"Without compromise."

He tutted. "Come now, Moja. I never compromise on what's important."

"Neither do I."

Silence. She let it linger, a fragile bubble drifting between them.

"Very well," Patel finally said. "I'll look into the matter, ask around. Keep in mind I left hAPPening around the same time you did."

"But you still have your contacts and influence."

He laughed. "True. I only crossed the bridge. I didn't burn it behind me."

"Some bridges need to be burned."

"As long as the fire doesn't follow after us." Patel waggled his head side to side in the way that had always made her smile.

"Be careful of the fire, Moja." He stopped his head-waggling and shook a finger. "If you're right, things could get ... messy. You know that."

"I know. I'm safe over here."

He snorted. "If you believe that, you don't appreciate the ways of the world. No one is safe anywhere, especially if what you said about the deposit is true."

"A slice of doom and gloom, brought to you courtesy of Mr. Indra Patel."

"You're laughing at me. I'm serious. I wish you'd come home."

"I *am* home."

"I mean your other home. Here. With me. I wish we could sit across the kitchen table, drink tea and talk."

"You mean argue."

"I'm too old to argue now. Besides, those weren't arguments. They were heated discussions. We always gained something from them, no?"

"Hmmm. A headache."

"You be careful. Okay, Moja? I'm worried for you."

"I'm fine."

"If you say so. But some things aren't worth the risk."

"And some things are."

"Are you sure?"

"How can you say that? My father died protecting the park."

"And do you think he wants his daughter to do so, as well?"

She looked out the window at the garden. Sunlight bounced across the bobbing heads of flowers.

Patel sighed. "I see. Have you heard any news about Prime Placer? It seems the myth is larger than life."

"Not interested. And thanks."

"For what?"

"For ... well, for everything."

He tilted his head in the barest of nods. "You should come over for a cup of tea one of these days. It's been too long. Nothing beats an offline face-to-face."

"Maybe someday. I'm a bit too far to drop in for tea."

His eyebrows lifted higher. "So you went back to *that* home? To Kenya?"

"To Uhuru, yes."

"Good. I'm happy for you, Moja. You deserve some peace after everything. I'll message you with any results I find. Let's not let another two years pass before we meet again."

She mumbled vague and empty promises to stay in touch. Patel popped out of the room, retreating to his world, leaving her alone. She was about to leave when something glimmered in her peripheral vision.

She narrowed her eyes. The glimmer solidified.

"A tracer program," she whispered.

Someone was trying to track her physical location.

"Increase wall fifty percent," Moja ordered.

Her firewall flared into view, creating a circle of flames around her.

Tentacles from the tracer program reacted to the motion, and stretched toward her. The firewall hissed and crackled, scorching the tentacles.

"Copy object," she said.

A white cube appeared in her hand. She stretched it until it was large enough to capture the tracer, then threw it.

The cube surrounded the tracer, pulsed, sizzled, and

bounced back to her. A copy of the tracer was tucked inside, isolated, securely locked so it could do no damage.

She snatched it out of the air, compressed it with both hands, and stuffed it into a pocket.

"Log out."

Patel's study dissolved, and she was at her welcome arch, the cube floating under the archway.

"Aren't you a pretty thing? Now, who sent you, and why?"

Before she could analyze the file, a heavy-handed knock startled her. Blearily, she pulled off her Shaids, rubbed her eyes. She was in a cabin at the edge of a forest. A world away from Patel's study.

"Moja? You ready?" Ojil asked.

"Just a minute." She stowed the Doodad and Shaids in the drawer, locked it.

As she hurried out of the cottage to rejoin Ojil, a question gnawed at the peace Patel thought she'd found.

Had she logged out in time, before the tracer program had located her? And why would anyone want to find her?

Chapter Sixteen

JAMAAL BLINKED at the empty space, the message still visible on the back of his eyelids. The shower of white dust continued for a few moments after the message disintegrated.

We need to meet.

Who was *we*? And who paid a ridiculous amount of cybercoin to send an anonymous message along a highly secured channel?

Just in case he was mistaken — because since when did things like this happen to a guy like him? — he studied the notification, searching for the signature stamp.

Every post and message, every interaction and movement in a news stream, basically *everything* in hAPPn had a digital signature stamp.

The stamp was a combination of the personal signature of the activity's source (usually a hAPPn member), the zip code for both sender and receiver, time, date, and a specific serial number for the activity.

hAPPening kept track of every member's interactions inside its app using these stamps. Active members received points. The amount depended on the interaction's complexity and quality.

Jamaal had already exchanged some of his points for cybercoin to purchase Rocky. Other points had gone to increasing the level of his membership. He was now saving up for something bigger and more expensive: one of the flying bubble bikes that also went underwater.

Point was, everything had a digital stamp.

But this message? There was no stamp. No serial number specific to the activity. No signature from the sender. No location or time details. Nothing. Total anonymity, something nearly impossible inside hAPPn.

Jamaal rubbed his forehead, tempted to log out, toss his Shaids onto the bed, and hike up the stairs to find out what Mama-i was cooking for lunch. Because this day was getting a little too exciting for him. And not in a good way.

Rocky rubbed up against his leg, then opened its toothless mouth for a snack.

"Not now."

Clacking in irritation, the critter sat on its haunches and clicked its front paws together. The little pebble feet clattered in tune with its bark.

"Bad rock. Go lie down."

Rocky growled.

"I just fed you this morning," Jamaal grumbled and looked for the box of treats. "You don't actually *need* food. You know that, right? You can survive just fine on digital air."

Rocky turned in a circle and barked repeatedly. It sounded like gravel in a concrete mixer.

"Placer, we've run out of pebble treats."

Sarah appeared next to the desk. She had changed into a fitted business suit. "Would you like me to order more snacks, Jamaal?"

"Not really, but Rocky does. Order one box of pet rock snacks."

"Ordering one box. Permission to debit your account by two cybercoins."

Jamaal sighed. When he'd purchased Rocky, he'd assumed the little guy would require zero maintenance and a matching expense. What business did a rock have demanding to be fed?

"Sure. Debit account."

"Debiting account two cybercoins. One box of pet rock snack food has arrived."

A blue box with flashing, neon pink writing popped onto his virtual desk.

He reached over, opened it up and poured out two snacks. They looked like gravel. "This is it for the day, okay, Rocky?"

The pet rock blinked its black pebble eyes at him and snapped up the treats. A contented rumble filled the office.

"Glad someone's enjoying this. What a waste. Now I have two less cybercoins for my bubble bike. Happy?"

Rocky lay down, and panted. Jamaal tossed another treat into the pet rock's open mouth.

Bing

New notification, same anonymous details. Hesitantly, he opened the message, expecting to see the same words glowing white in the air around him. *We need to meet.*

Instead, a giant silver stopwatch appeared, covering the wall in front of him. Its long arm pointed at the number sixty.

"Abe, if this is you fogging with me ..." he muttered.

But this wasn't his style. Abe was flashy, in-your-face. He wanted to be there to execute the joke, so he could gloat and laugh. Orchestrating a trick and not being there to enjoy the results? Nope.

Crunch!

Jamaal jumped as Rocky munched on the gravel treat. "Finish it, already!"

Rocky swallowed, snapped its mouth shut, and stared silently at the box.

With a loud *bzzz*, the stopwatch began counting down the seconds. *Fifty-nine … Fifty-eight …*

"Sarah, remove the stopwatch," he whispered, his throat tight. What happened when the sixty seconds were finished?

"Please repeat the request," Sarah said.

"Remove …" He paused and cleared his throat. "Remove it. Now."

"Please specify what needs to be removed."

Fifty seconds.

"The stopwatch. Remove the fogging stopwatch!"

"Please specify the location of the stopwatch."

"That one! The one on my wall. Can't you see it? It's right there. It's …"

Forty-one seconds.

"I am unable to identify a stopwatch on your wall. Please try again."

"Oh, fog it."

An invite link appeared beneath the stopwatch. It was for an anonymous, private room.

Another rarity. Or rather, another expensive commodity. Jamaal had the *perception* of privacy in his digital office, but it wasn't nearly private enough. Anyone from upper management — including Ms. Chan — could enter the office of any lower-level employee without asking for permission. And he was pretty sure they could overhear conversations he had in here, if they cared enough to bother. Not that they would. Why would they?

Thirty seconds.

But an anonymous, private room was guaranteed privacy. No one could enter without an invite. And no one could locate it from outside. It had no traceable existence.

Twenty-five seconds.

"And then what?" he shouted at the stopwatch.

"Please repeat your request."

"Not you, Sarah!"

The invite link began to blink in time with the stopwatch's hand. Would it self-destruct at the end of sixty seconds, like something out of a Mission Impossible movie?

Twenty seconds.

"What's the worst that can happen?" he asked, staring at the first invite he'd ever received from an anonymous location. "Oh, I know. Your avatar's heart can be infected by a virus, and who wants to go through that hassle? Antivirus treatments are nasty."

Not to mention they cost a decent amount of cybercoin. Worse, he could lose his heart. An antivirus treatment often required a forced reset. His avatar would be rebooted, sending him back to Level 1 Basic membership in all his Places.

It was a rare occurrence. hAPPn had excellent antivirus systems set up. But it still happened. And no one wanted to deal with that nightmare.

But what if this was Ms. Chan, testing him, seeing if he was fit to move up the ladder? Maybe this was the opportunity he'd been working so hard for … Okay, maybe not working *hard*, but definitely hoping for. A promotion.

The invite link blinked neon white as the stopwatch ticked down to ten final seconds.

Or better yet, Ms. Chan was being replaced. Or he was being moved to another division with a kinder, more understanding boss. He could definitely live without Ms. Chan always breathing down his neck.

Besides, the timing was unusual.

Five seconds.

"Placer, accept invite."

"Accepting invite," Sarah intoned.

An alarm blared. The stopwatch exploded. His office disintegrated.

No time to panic. He popped into a room without doors or windows, or any furniture. Every empty surface glowed white.

He twirled around, trying to figure out which way was up. Was he standing on the ceiling? One of the walls? Did it matter? He jumped up and down a few times.

"Gravity still works, then," he said.

But nothing else seemed to. He glanced at his Doodad. No notifications. Or anything at all. His Doodad was dead.

He tapped his forearm. The blank screen sank under his skin.

"What the ... Sarah?"

Silence.

A depth of nothingness he wasn't used to. The pure aural vacuum of deep space. A gaping void filled only with white light. Not the, *I'm going to Heaven* kind of light. More like the kind of light an invading alien army might use to obliterate a planet or something.

"Placer. Respond."

Nothing.

Jamaal tapped on his forearm, trying to summon the Doodad from below his skin. He pressed hard enough to leave indents in his arm.

"Oh, this is bad. This is ... I fogging knew I shouldn't have clicked on that link. The link. Where is it?"

He looked around for the invite link. It should be here,

floating at the edge of his vision. That was how these things worked. You clicked on an invite. It took you to some other Place or meeting room. But the invite link stayed with you, waiting to take you back to wherever you came from. One click in. One click out. Simple. Safe. Foolproof.

But there was nothing here. No exits. No link to pull him out of the room. Only solid, glowing white walls.

So, officially time to panic.

Chapter Seventeen

Eva could almost feel the boredom growing like mold across her brain.

Meetings should last no more than ten minutes. There was a direct relationship between the length of time scheduled, and the amount of hot air and useless trivia filling up the time.

Like this meeting. The one Jack requested with the top management of Growth. He'd insisted on half an hour, then arrived late with his baby elephant.

"Who brings their digital pet to a meeting?" she said under her breath.

The elephant waved at her as it plodded to a corner of the room.

"I'll keep this quick." Jack held out his hands, doing his juggling mime. "I know you all have a lot of work to do. And if you don't, then you really should."

Restrained laughter, followed by restless silence.

"On the one hand, great job on the growth rate." He snapped his fingers, and a blue ball bounced on one hand.

"Within a few short years, we've gone from zero to 3.7 billion members and counting."

The numbers puffed into existence on the ball, which he tossed toward the ceiling. It disintegrated in a shower of gold coins.

"Stellar. Absolutely stellar. Can't complain. However …"

Eva glanced at the table. Of course Jack was going to complain.

"Let's be honest. 3.7 billion members doesn't equate to 3.7 billion *members*. They're not all engaging with their Places. Not nearly as much as we want them to, right? That's right. hAPPn is so much more than a lowly social platform. It's where we work, shop, order our next meal, do our banking, learn, get entertained, get informed."

Eva glanced around the room. Her team was nodding politely, but they'd all heard this spiel before. It was the basic promo for hAPPening's single most successful product.

"Remember, folks, time equals revenue. The more time members spend being users, the better our advertisers, online shops, and services will do. And that means …" He widened his arms and awaited their response.

"More revenue," came an assembly of tepid replies.

"That's right! More revenue. So we need to up the ante. We need more time spent in hAPPn. Am I right? You bet I am. Any questions?"

Eva prayed no one would be stupid enough to actually ask a question. Fortunately, her team was anything but stupid. It was comprised of the brightest, hardest working, most ambitious employees in hAPPening. None of them wanted to be in this meeting longer than absolutely required, and proved it with their silence.

"Excellent. Now. Membership. We've been talking

about this a lot, and the topic will keep coming up until the problem is solved. After an exponential growth for the past few years, it's leveling out. Sure, we have almost forty percent of the global population signed up as members. Let's call that an 'excellent start.' We need more members, and we need the members we have to be using hAPPn only slightly less than they're breathing."

He glanced around the room, tapped his fingers against the meeting table. Eva wondered why there was a meeting table at all. It wasn't like their avatars needed to sit or write things down or even hold anything. They didn't drink coffee or tea. There were no snacks to munch on. If they needed to make notes, they could send a request to their Placers to transcribe the meeting, just as hers was doing right now.

She'd asked Jack once. Why bother with furniture?

"It's all about the visuals," Jack had said. "Perception. Visuals. That's the new reality, Eva. That's what hAPPening actually sells. Everything else is window-dressing."

Or maybe the table was a prop for Jack. He needed something to tap, to make a noise to complement his voice.

"Folks, industry experts say the saturation point is closer to *sixty* percent. Personally, I think we can push it higher than that. After all, this is hAPPn, where everything happens. Anyone old enough to hold a Doodad should be in here. So there's still plenty of room to grow. No pressure." He chuckled.

"You heard the boss," Eva said, interrupting whatever else Jack was about to spew out. "Room to grow. I just opened a new document where we can dump ideas. We'll reconvene tomorrow. Thanks so much to our CEO for … the inspiration."

Her team took the cue, and almost simultaneously popped out of the room and back to their offices.

Jack said, "You're going to do great. By the way, I sent you the first info-post for our friend."

She nodded, not sure if she should say anything.

"Click the link."

And then he was gone.

"Invite link received by CEO Jackson Rustle," said her Placer in that unflappably calm voice she sometimes envied. "Accept invite?"

Eva exhaled heavily and rubbed at her forehead, her hand brushing against her Shaids. The avatar remained standing, arms hanging by her side. Jack didn't feel the meeting room was private enough, not that they were doing anything wrong. Irregular, yes. But illegal? Absolutely not. So what now?

"Fine. Accept invite."

"Accepting invite."

Water gushed around her, and she was back inside the fish tank, floating above a coral jungle, the shark a distant shadow. Colorful fish swarmed in and out of view, playing with the currents.

"Just so we're clear." Jack studied his glass desk as if its gleaming surface held the meaning of life.

"Clear about what?"

"These info-posts, like the one I just sent you? They can't be linked to e-Trax's advertising account."

Eva stared at the floor. A pair of striped eels slithered through the water. "That's …"

"Unorthodox?"

She looked up. "Inappropriate. These are advertisements at the end of the day."

"Info-posts. Written by independent experts."

"So they say. It's one thing to bypass Advert. But to

delink the posts from e-Trax's account seems ..." She hesitated.

"Like I said, unorthodox. If e-Trax drops them in the streams using their hAPPening account, the posts won't look too expert and objective, now will they? You know how folks are these days. They won't believe the articles are factual or independent of e-Trax influence."

"Are they?"

Jack stared at her unblinking. "Are they what?"

"Objective. Independent. Factual."

"Of course. That's the whole point, isn't it? Make sure we preemptively share the truth before e-Trax is attacked for a perfectly acceptable, environmentally friendly mining project."

Eva's avatar remained still while offline her body tensed. So this was what happened when you did a little favor, followed by a slightly bigger favor. Jack could use whatever logic, but it boiled down to the same thing. He wanted her to disguise the info-posts so they weren't linked to e-Trax.

"And how do I go about doing that?"

Jack waved a hand vaguely at a leatherback turtle swimming by. "Post them through private accounts, of course. Use our bot members. They should still be active, right?"

Eva nodded. In the early days of hAPPn when membership was still low, hAPPening had designed highly interactive bots to populate the Places. The bots helped human members feel they were joining an active Place.

Over time, as more humans signed up, bots became decommissioned. However, a few were left in each Place so hAPPening could run tests, or drop public relation messaging it wanted or sometimes needed all the members to read.

"Yes. They're still active."

Jack beamed and held up his hands in a hallelujah. "There you go! Problem solved. Drop the info-posts through our friendly bots. No one will be the wiser."

"No. They won't."

"Great."

"Yes. Great. Great for e-Trax."

"Sure is," Jack said and tipped his head at her. "It's great for us, too, Eva. Don't worry. I made sure Danielle knew this wasn't standard procedure. She understands."

Eva nodded, but fingers of memory were twisting around each other. He'd said the same thing the last time he'd needed a little favor, when he asked her to give e-Trax proprietary information on hAPPn demographics. Not in an aggregated form, either. Personalized, detailed information. The kind that should never have left hAPPening's workPlace.

She spoke without meaning to. "You said that before."

Jack blinked, but quickly recovered. "Sure. But that was part of this. It's the same favor. All connected to the current project I have with e-Trax. It's a one-off in the big scheme of things."

"I see."

"I knew you would. So, the info-posts. Dropped by the end of the day?"

"Sure, Jack."

"That's my girl."

"No. I'm not, really. And this is the last time?" She didn't mean to make it sound like a question.

Jack winked, his flirty smile back on, and closed the invite, sending Eva back to her office.

Chapter Eighteen

Section 9 was infamous for elephant damage. Park rangers had woven electric fencing between the regular fence. Elephants still managed to occasionally break through and wander into farms. Crops were a tantalizing treat for the giant mammals. A herd could wreak havoc within a short period of time.

Walking the fence line was one of the less interesting tasks of being a park ranger. But Moja was too absorbed in her questions about the tracer program to be bored.

"Shilling for your thoughts," Ojil said.

"They're worth more than that."

"Oh! Me, I'm not paid enough. How about a bag of peanuts?" He dug into a pocket and pulled out a package.

Moja glanced upward. The sun's rays prickled against her skin, reassuring her this world still existed, even if a part of it was being threatened. "Throw in a cup of tea, and you have yourself a deal."

Chuckling, Ojil led her to the shade of a thorn tree. A couple hundred meters away, a small herd of elephants grazed alongside zebra and a solitary giraffe.

"This place is heaven," Moja said.

Ojil pulled out a thermos. "Hmmm. Your dad also said that. Because of him, we have this park."

Moja tensed, her shoulders hunching at the mention of her father. If Ojil noticed, he kept quiet. She avoided his gaze — just in case he looked a bit too closely — and stared at the forest on the other side of the open field. A landscape of memories with a soundtrack of bird songs, and the slosh of tea pouring into cups.

"A good man," Ojil said. "Thomas knew the importance of things. Knew he had to protect what was important."

Moja crunched loudly on a handful of peanuts.

"I was there," he said.

She swallowed the half-chewed snack, swishing down the jagged bits with a mouthful of tea.

"He died as he lived. Brave. Determined. Stubborn as a water buffalo. The creator of this place."

Moja glanced sharply at him, but Ojil wasn't looking at her. He was studying the tree-filled horizon.

"We can talk here," he said. "You and me. It's safe."

No one is safe anywhere.

Moja shook her head. "It's done. Nothing to talk about."

A warm, heavy hand settled on her shoulder. "You sure?"

She shifted away from Ojil's touch. "Sure. Of course."

Ojil hummed in response, his disbelief weaving between the sound. "Have you grieved?"

She shrugged, stretched out her legs, digging the heels of her boots into the grassy soil. "Was it …" She bit off the end of the question. Did she really want to know? Would it help her?

"He didn't feel a thing. It was quick. A blessing, maybe. We caught the poacher. Me, a few of the other rangers."

She nodded, and didn't tell Ojil she already knew. She'd followed the story closely, even as she withdrew from everything. Jack. Patel. hAPPn. Her family. Ojil.

Have you grieved?

In her own way. A silent, lonely way.

"I was there, you know," Ojil said again. "I should've seen them. Should've stopped them. Warned him."

Moja pursed her lips tightly, holding back whatever might try to leak out of her. Tears? Anger? Guilt?

"But it's no one's fault," Ojil continued. He was still staring at the forest. "Nobody knows their time until it arrives. Nobody can stop it. And maybe it was the best death for him. Protecting this park."

She slurped at her tea, wishing he'd stop.

"He was proud of you, your father. Always talking about you. Just like me. I'm proud of you."

Moja's lips began to tremble, fighting to open up, to allow the growing noise inside to burst out. And what did the noise want to say? What darkness threatened to spew, covering them both with an emotional oil spill?

"It's okay. The tears," Ojil said. "Them, they don't make you weak. They wash out pain. Clean the eyes and the soul."

Moja hardened her expression, glared at the closest elephant. As if it was the poor beast's fault her father decided to stand between the herds and the poachers. Maybe it was.

"I should've been here."

The words snuck out before she realized they were there, lurking in her heart's shadows, waiting for a moment of weakness to creep out and taint the air around her.

Ojil sighed. "Oh, it wouldn't have changed a thing."

He was probably right. Just like Patel was right. Between the two of them, they'd helped fill the void left by her father's murder. Both of them always there when she needed them, even as she pushed them away.

Be careful, Moja. Being God is a bigger burden than you can imagine.

"Not a thing," Ojil said. "That's the truth. You know what truth is?"

She shook her head.

"Truth is like sunlight."

"It burns?"

"It warms your soul. Chases away shadows. Makes good things grow. Without it, there's mold and decay, despair and hate. Stay in the light, Moja."

"If I can find it."

"It's all around us. Sunlight doesn't stop. It's us who hide from it."

"Right."

She studied the elephants as they meandered closer, unconcerned by the presence of two humans. She wished they weren't so comfortable. She wished they would stampede away from them, away from the sight and stench of humanity.

"Hypothetical question," Moja said.

"The answer is yes, there's always more tea."

A laugh spluttered out of her. She turned to face him, leaning one shoulder against the tree trunk. "Let's say you have the key to open a box."

"Hmmm. Which box?"

"A hypothetical one."

"Oh! That one."

"Right. Inside the box is a cure for a disease, but opening the box means you die. Would you? Do you open the box?"

Ojil's wrinkles softened as he smiled. His skin crinkled at the corners of his dark, calm eyes and around his generous mouth, reminding her of Patel.

"If the cure can save my children, or another's child?" He nodded. "I'd take that key, and open the box. What choice do I really have?"

Chapter Nineteen

JAMAAL SPUN AROUND, searching the empty, glowing white room for the invite link, his ticket out of this trap.

"It's supposed to be here. *Right here*," he mumbled, glancing over his shoulder, above his head.

Nothing.

"Sarah. You there? Placer. Respond!"

Silence.

His hands formed fists. Screaming, he banged them against the walls, hoping he'd come across a door, a window, an invisible link. *Something.*

Irrational, but rationality had left the building the moment the stopwatch had appeared.

"Let me out! This is illegal, you know. Locking someone's avatar up. It's like ... kidnapping. It *is* kidnapping!"

He paused, his heavy breathing the only noise. The room seemed smaller, as if the white, glowing walls were closing in. Or the space was being filled by his terror, squeezing out the air.

Avatars don't need to breathe.

But that thought didn't soothe his sense of suffocation.

"Hello? Abe? If this is your idea of a joke, it sucks worse than the time you forged papers to convince me I was adopted."

No response. He tapped at his forearm, but his Doodad was gone, covered with his avatar's light brown skin.

"This can't be happening. I have deadlines. Important deadlines!"

"They can wait."

Jamaal twirled around at the sound of a garbled, robotic voice. He crouched, preparing to do … something. Probably scream and have a nervous breakdown. Of all the days he'd decided to wear an S-Suit, it had to be the day a faceless villain kidnapped him. Would they torture him?

"Please don't hurt me," he begged. "I can't handle pain. I'd have to log out without my avatar, and start all over."

"Then stop bruising my walls."

"Right." Jamaal loosened his fists, shook out his hands, focused on breathing. "Sorry."

A translucent avatar appeared in front of him. Its edges were indistinct, a shimmering cascade of white flecks. Almost like a snow blizzard isolated to a single locus. The constantly swirling particles formed the vague outline of a human. An unusual avatar, meaning *expensive*.

Seeing his host made him feel better. Not much, but enough that he could talk without his teeth chattering in terror. It wasn't a logical reaction. For all he knew, this person was a serial killer who lured their victims into an anonymous room by promising the impossible.

"Can't be. No axe or chainsaws," he whispered.

"Excuse me?"

"I'm asking if this is your room? Because I really want to leave. Now. Please. If it's all the same."

"You want to leave."

"Yeah."

"Are you sure?"

"Yeah." Jamaal nodded emphatically. "Real sure."

"If you're so sure, why did you open the invite?"

"Curiosity. Stupid curiosity. Like a really dumb cat. Won't be doing that again. You're not a virus, are you?"

"Some call me that."

"Fog. Why me? Why?"

"Don't worry."

"Easy for you to say. You're not trapped in ... where are we?"

"Do you know who I am, Jamaal?"

Jamaal crossed his arms tightly, bouncing from side to side. *Keep them talking. As long as they're talking, they aren't killing me. Talk, and there's hope. Right?*

"No. Not a virus, you say? So who are you?"

"Good to see you have some curiosity left."

"Nope." Jamaal held up a hand. "Absolutely none. No curiosity. I don't want to know. Just ... let me go home. I haven't seen you. Don't know what you really look like. Don't know your name. Don't want to know. We're good. I won't tell anyone—"

"I'm Prime Placer."

"Fog it! I told you I don't want to ... wait. Prime Placer? As in *Prime* Placer?"

The blurry head nodded.

"I've been kidnapped by Prime Placer. A myth. The thing that doesn't exist. Maybe work stress has finally broken my brain. Except I don't work hard enough to be stressed. Must be Abe. I knew it. Fun's up, Abe." Jamaal looked around, waiting for his cousin to pop into the room. "Really funny."

"Abe's not here. I'm not a myth, although I appreciate the sentiment. I stopped existing. But I'm back now."

"Good for you. Wow. Look at the time. It's been great chatting, you insane, imaginary person. But I really want to work right now, and those are words I thought I'd never say. So if you don't mind …" He waved vaguely over his head.

"You have a choice, Jamaal."

"I choose option B. Especially if option B means going back to my office. Ms. Chan is right. Focus on the work."

"Forget about Ms. Chan."

"Wish I could. Really, I do. Except I'm pretty sure Ms. Chan thinks I performed an act of treason. Is it even possible to commit treason against your employer? Because if it is, that's what she thinks I did. But I didn't. It's all Abe's fault. Oh. I bet you're working for her. That's what this is. For the record, I love my job. It's all I think about. I miss it so much right now. Are we done?"

Some part of Jamaal's brain realized he was babbling. The other part was too busy panicking to care.

The white, blurry humanoid stared at him. At least, he thought that's what it was doing. But the avatar had no eyes, or any indication of a face. And yet everything about it made him feel watched. Studied. Intellectually dissected.

This was the last time he'd ever open an anonymous link. How stupid was he? On a scale of one to ten — ten being as dumb as a broomstick — Jamaal was easily a hundred. He'd be lucky to escape with his avatar intact.

He might lose everything if he had to reboot it, including Rocky. Sure, the pet rock was just a rock, and not even a real rock. A digital rock. But the thing had legs and eyes, and it liked to be fed gravel as a snack. He couldn't let the little thing die because he clicked on a virus-loaded link.

"You have a choice," said the blur.

"So you told me."

"You can decide to stay blind, and be complicit in one of the biggest disasters of the decade. Or you can bid farewell to everything you think you know, and discover the one thing you don't."

"What will I know?" Jamaal asked against his better judgment.

"The truth. The absolute, unadulterated, unfiltered, pure truth."

Jamaal stared at Prime Placer or whoever this was. And it stared back.

"Is this a joke?" he finally asked. "The truth? I already know the truth, and it's irrelevant. I've got a lot to do today. And playing mind games isn't on my list."

"Blind obedience, or truth. What will it be?"

He'd had enough of this scam. "I'm going with blindness."

"You ... you'll what?" Prime Placer's avatar had no facial expressions, but there was something about the tilt of its head that suggested surprise.

"I choose to stay blind. Ignorance is underrated. A little goes a long way. Now if you don't mind ... Goodbye?"

Jamaal glanced at his Doodad, but it was still invisible. And when calling out for *his* Placer, he got no response.

"You're not the least bit curious about what I have to tell you?"

"Nope. Not at all. You see where curiosity got me? In trouble. That's what it did. Life is good. Whatever you have to say, it's not going to help me one bit."

"I see."

Jamaal looked around for the link to appear. "Anytime now."

The walls remained solid, empty of doors and links. Fear gave way to a hint of anger.

Who did this person think they were?

He searched for the other avatar's signature stamp. Nothing. Just a splotch of static where the stamp should be. That wasn't even possible, was it? Didn't hAPPn's terms of use — not to mention the actual law — require everything and everyone to have a stamp?

"Fine. I'll release you—"

"'Bout time."

"If you answer one question."

"You fogging kidding me?"

"No. I'm not."

Jamaal could feel a headache forming in his body offline. He was tempted to yank off the Shaids and be free. Who needed this hassle? But he might lose his avatar if he didn't log out correctly. This Prime Placer or whoever they were could snatch the avatar and block him from reentering.

What would he do then? The process to replace a mirror avatar was convoluted, messy, and expensive.

"Fine. What's your question? Not that I have a choice."

"We all have choices, Jamaal."

"Sure. Whatever. So?"

"This morning, you performed a search for information on Kenya's national parks."

Jamaal's heartbeat jolted upward. Ms. Chan was behind this whole thing. It had to be her. What else had she discovered?

"How ..." His voice hitched. "How did you know?"

"Does it matter?"

"Yeah. It fogging well does. That was a private search."

"A private search in a public Place?"

"It wasn't public. I was in the membership-only section."

"You were standing in the members-only lobby of Geo Rocks, open to all members. Definitely not a private space."

Jamaal knew his avatar couldn't have a heart attack or stop breathing. But it sure felt like he was about to pass out or die. "How'd you—"

"What if I gave you the file from an on-the-ground assessment of the proposed mining area?"

"I already have one."

"Another one. From another source. Would you look at it?"

Jamaal willed his avatar not to flinch or rub his mouth or—

Fog it. That was exactly what he was doing.

He pushed his arms down, let them hang by his sides. Maybe he should forcibly pull out of hAPPn, yank off the Shaids, be done with it.

Sure, he'd lose a few days' work. Maybe have to start from scratch with his cybercoin account and everything else. So what? At least he'd be alive. Because the way he was feeling, he was pretty sure he was having some kind of a nervous breakdown, or a heart attack. Possibly both.

Maybe he was already dead.

Prime Placer watched him, silently awaiting his decision as if they had all the time in the world. No deadline, no lengthy to-do list, no supervisor breathing down their neck, dumping more work on them.

Well, not everyone has that luxury, crazy Placer.

What if this was Ms. Chan in disguise? e-Trax HR policies required everyone to use a mirror avatar. Mods and add-ons were only allowed in gaming Places. But this was a private room — an *anonymous* private room — which meant Ms. Chan could put on any avatar she wished.

What if e-Trax was setting him up because they knew Abe had found fake news about the deposit? What if they were testing his loyalty?

It sounded nuts, even in his own mind, but he wouldn't put it past them. It was totally something Ms. Chan would do. She loved mind games. Almost as much as she loved tormenting subordinates.

Jamaal would lose his job if they suspected him of working for the other side, for the green necks. He'd also lose his robust benefits, and any chance of getting a comparable job in the industry.

Some people complained about the day job as if it were a prison sentence. He actually enjoyed his work. Everything apart from his supervisor, and he didn't have to deal with her too often.

But if it seemed like he might be working against e-Trax, his career would be tanked. His reputation ruined in a community that was small enough to hear all the gory details. And never mind the lawsuit he could face for breaking his NDA.

He was glad his physical body was in the cool basement. Even still, his T-shirt was plastered against his chest and under his armpits. Any more sweat and he might die of dehydration, just like the foggers who couldn't give up their online addictions. A painful irony.

Jamaal tugged at his shirt, pulling it away from his damp skin. All this introspection was gnawing away at his nerves.

He froze as a new idea came to him.

What if he agreed to do whatever this weirdo asked of him?

Once he escaped and returned to the normal world, he

could always alert e-Trax and Ms. Chan about an anonymous hack trying to sabotage their work. He'd score way more brownie points than he'd risk losing.

Maybe he'd even get a raise. Or a promotion! And if that promotion moved him onto another team, all the better.

His search results would be the same as this fake Prime Placer's ground assessment, because truth was truth. Why would two searches have different results?

"Okay. I'll take a look," he finally said, breaking the silence. "One look. And you'll let me go, soon as I finish. No strings. Deal?"

"Of course." A trace of laughter trickled into the words.

Jamaal tensed, waiting for a trick, or for the floor to disappear from under him, opening to an abyss teeming with avatar-devouring viruses.

Instead, images filled the room and swirled around him.

"Fog."

"Do you see now?" Prime Placer asked.

"Yeah. I should've gone with option B."

Chapter Twenty

"Post ready for drop." The Placer paused, almost as if sensing Eva's hesitation. "Proceed to drop?"

That was the question.

Eva wasn't sure how much the question was actually worth. Based on Jack's determination to assist e-Trax and its CEO, she figured it had to be substantially more than her salary. Probably more than her current mortgage.

She stared at the info-post, dark pixels against a silver background floating in front of her.

To drop, or not to drop? That was the question.

She glanced around her workPlace office. Her table, which she didn't need, was made of mahogany with a reddish sheen to it. The floor tiles were blood garnet, just like the archway of her welcome arch. The walls shimmered with a silver glow. A mahogany door was to her right. A large bay window to her left, overlooking the Washington Bay islands. A flock of birds fluttered across the skyline.

The image accurately mirrored the view she would've had if she were in a physical building perched on the edge of the bay, but heightened for better clarity and interest. Whales didn't permanently inhabit the bay, especially not narwhales. The tusked whales preferred the icy arctic waters.

It didn't matter in here. Whenever she glanced out her digital window, a narwhale reared out of the water, showed off its long horn, and arched its back in greeting before plunging into the depths.

Who cared if it wasn't realistic? Reality was overrated. She loved seeing the whale. One of the perks of working online. Reality could become hyperreality. And what was more hyperreal than a unicorn whale outside her office?

"Post is ready to drop," her Placer said. "Proceed to drop?"

Eva sighed and scanned the article again. It mentioned everything Jack had already told her: the newly discovered rare earth metal would revolutionize power generation and battery technology; the deposit was in a designated wasteland area; no animals would be harmed during production. Not a single tree uprooted.

And after the mining operation was finished, the strips would be rehabilitated. The expert projected that within ten years, a large swathe of green growth would inhabit what was currently a big nothingness. Win, win.

But still she hesitated.

She'd never given her Placer an avatar, yet Eva could almost feel someone standing over her shoulder, awaiting her order. No one had to breathe online, but she still inhaled deeply. She rubbed the back of her neck, erasing the hint of a breath brushing her skin.

Why didn't e-Trax want to go through the normal procedures? Sure, Marsha was difficult. Obnoxious. Overly ambitious. Not particularly friendly. But she was a professional. Eva would admit that much about the Chief of

Advert. She did her job well, and Eva had a hard time imagining she'd let personal beliefs get in the way.

Marsha and her team would only flag an advertisement or info-post if it promoted hate speech, messed with elections, or funded terrorists. That sort of thing. She might recommend amendments, but she wouldn't deny e-Trax's request to post educational material. So what was the big deal?

"This is why I'll never do anyone a favor again," Eva muttered.

"Please clarify your request."

"Cross-reference the bot account list with e-Trax's preferred Places document. Create shortlist of mutual Places. Drop the info-posts in resulting shortlist."

"Dropping info-posts via bot accounts to highlighted Places," the Placer said, emotionless. It didn't have a care in the world because it didn't care about anything.

Sometimes, she wished she could program herself not to care.

"Last time, Jack. No more favors."

"Info-posts dropped," the Placer said. "Additional requests?"

"Mozart's Requiem."

Music weaved around her, drowned out her heart's heavy thud with melancholy chords. It vied with the scenery for dramatic genius.

She breathed into the waves of sound lapping against the shores of her mind and erasing the footsteps of doubt.

"Open schedule."

The silver screen opened to the left of her vision. No more meetings scheduled for the day. What a relief.

"Incoming invite."

"From whom?" Eva asked her Placer as she opened the ideas document. Her team had already started brainstorming suggestions for the next membership drive. A few weren't half bad.

"Source unknown."

Eva frowned and glanced up at the ceiling. Blue sky. A soft puffy cloud drifted over her. "How can the source be unknown?"

"Synonyms for unknown. Unrevealed. Hidden. Secret. Anonymous—"

"Stop. Placer, trace invite to source."

A second passed. Then another. In Placer time, a second was a minute. "Source unknown."

"Check location beacon in stamp signature."

"Location beacon not present. Stamp signature not present."

"That's not possible."

As Chief, she was close to a minor god in hAPPn. There were few Places she couldn't enter. Nothing was hidden from her, except the secrets held within a human heart.

Certainly there was no such thing as an anonymous invite. Without a source? Not possible.

"Pull up invite. Display."

The day's schedule transformed into a link.

"There has to be a source," Eva muttered as she searched the invite using decrypting software only available to hAPPening's upper management.

Nothing.

A message appeared underneath the link.

I know about e-Trax. Come find me.

At the end of the sentence stood a white, three-headed, animated elephant. It lifted its trunks, and squirted water in her direction. She instinctively flinched from the 3D spray of droplets. Moisture settled against her skin.

She stared at the elephant icon. Jack could be a joker,

but he would never have selected a three-headed animal. His favorite icon was the flying unicorn, a miniature version of one of his pets built into his signature stamp. Eva knew only one person who could even use the three-headed elephant.

"But they're ..." she whispered.

"Instructions," the Placer said.

"No instructions."

She tried another direction, probing the message for a signature stamp. Everything, everyone, every interaction, every word and picture dropped into hAPPn had a signature stamp.

But this message had nothing. No stamp. No signature. No indication of who had sent it, or from where, apart from the three-headed elephant. The symbol of a myth, a legend, an impossibility.

The little elephant waved its trunks, then seemed to fall asleep.

"What do you think you know?" Eva asked and sent the reply.

No one could possibly know what she'd done. Not even another Chief could track her digital footprints. She'd been careful, using high level encryption when engaging with the bot accounts.

Was this a coincidence? Some random stranger decided to contact her now, of all times, just like that? And how did they know to contact her specifically?

Theo believed everything happened for a reason. She wasn't as convinced. His logic implied a higher power, an intelligence in creation, one that silently observed while hiding behind the folds of the universe.

An automated notification appeared. "Message failed."

Eva snorted. The last time she'd ever received a message like that was in the bad old days of email. But hAPPening's message system was several levels more advanced. Even a minor mistake in an address would be solved by the highly developed algorithms churning in the background. Spam was unheard of, and lost messages even more so.

But there it was. Message failed. Her Placer was right. There was no source to reply to, which was impossible. Because *someone* had sent her an invite, and the *someone* was *somewhere*.

There was nothing threatening in the words. She still felt something tighten around her neck. An invisible noose.

The white elephant. Three heads. A mythological creature, much like the person who once used it as part of their personal signature stamp.

"But you're dead," she whispered to the message again. "Dead, or permanently offline. Pretty much the same thing these days. So who resurrected you, and why?"

The elephant blinked awake, then trotted out of the message toward her. It hopped onto her shoulder, then tapped its trunks against her temple.

"Unbelievable," Eva said.

More than unbelievable. The small elephant's actions indicated an almost unheard-of talent in animation and software programming.

She'd never met Prime Placer in person. No one had, apart from Indra Patel, the original angel investor of hAPPening, and he was a recluse. A ridiculously wealthy, eccentric recluse that retired a couple of years ago.

Prime Placer had disappeared about the same time, like a ghost, leaving no trace of its passage. They had an almost mythological status, especially within the company. Newer employees, as well as a lot of the members of hAPPn, assumed Prime Placer was an urban legend, the creation myth to explain the miracle of

The hAPPening

hAPPn. But Eva knew there were no miracles, only unexplainable genius.

"Is that who sent you?" she asked the elephant, brushing it onto her hand. "Is Prime Placer responsible for this little miracle?"

The elephant trumpeted, then bounced back into the message and tugged on the invite link.

She smiled at its antics. It wouldn't hurt to find out — her avatar had the highest level of security encryptions, after all. Even if the invite source was a hacker trying to break into the company, they wouldn't stand much of a chance. Eva could retreat faster than they could work.

"Placer, open invite link."

"Warning. Unknown source. Do you wish to proceed?"

"Yes."

"Accepting invite."

Her desk began to melt, pixelating into a whirlwind that tore a hole through hAPPn. Her office disintegrated piece by piece, falling into the swirling chaos.

The whirlwind yanked her down a long, white, undulating tunnel. Shadows of online reality played on its surface. The tunnel ended in a white room without doors or windows.

She glanced around, looking for the invite link that should be hovering beside her. The portal back to her office.

But the link was gone. There were no doors or windows, no access points for her exit. It wasn't a private room someone was renting, either. She could tell by the digital infrastructure shimmering inside the walls. This Place was fully anonymous.

It officially didn't exist.

It must've cost the owner a fortune.

"Thank you for coming."

Eva turned as an avatar appeared in the far corner. A blizzard of glowing white pixels created the vague outline of a human. Genderless. Faceless. Motion within stillness.

She asked her Placer to scan the strange avatar's code for a signature stamp, but there was none. That should be impossible. Every avatar had a signature stamp. Except for this one.

"Your elephant was persuasive. Prime Placer, I assume?"

The pixelated blizzard tilted its head.

Eva pursed her lips. "You have five minutes."

Prime Placer chuckled. "I suspect you'll want to stay longer."

"And why is that?"

"Because I know what e-Trax and your CEO are really doing," they said. "And it's not at all what you think."

Chapter Twenty-One

MOJA FINGERED the black leather strip around her neck. She pulled out its length from under her shirt for the second time that day. A small key dangled on the end.

Memories whispered around the room.

Of course I'm sure. I'm a god in here. We all are.

Be careful, Moja. Being God is a bigger burden than you can imagine.

No one is safe anywhere.

Do you open the box?

Moja stood in front of her bedside table, staring at the locked drawer. Inside was the paraphernalia connected to her past. The box with a secret to cure a disease.

But the box required sacrifice.

Bits of peanuts caught between her teeth kept scratching at her tongue. She wiggled them loose, thinking of Ojil pouring them into her hand as they sat under the shade of the thorn tree.

"Inside the box is a cure for a disease, but opening the box means you die. Would you? Do you open the box?" Moja had asked him.

Ojil replied with no hesitation, a steel rod of conviction giving strength to his words. "If the cure can save my children, or another's child? I take that key, and open the box. What choice do I really have?"

Moja sighed and brushed her fingers across the bedside table. "If only all of us could be so brave."

It wasn't just courage. Moja knew Ojil well enough to understand how he thought. His life was only as meaningful as the impact it had on the lives of those around him. He and Father had worked together for decades, dedicated to protecting the last wild spaces for their children, and others yet to be born. Father had died in service to that cause.

But was it worth it?

An error on a map, a bribe in the right pocket, and all he'd sacrificed for would be devoured by a bulldozer's metal teeth. Stripping away the top layer of living earth, leaving behind dead rock and empty soil.

Be careful of the fire, Moja.

She rubbed her face, and felt the grit of the day grating against her skin. She really needed a shower, then sleep. That's what she should do. Forget about boxes and keys, cures and diseases. She'd left hAPPening — was practically exiled — so this was their problem now.

Except it wasn't.

Because if no one corrected that map, or reversed the approval ... if plans proceeded, then her home, and the home of Baby Moja and the other elephants, would be stripped from the planet.

Then where would they go?

Moja sank onto the edge of her bed as she toyed with the key, murmuring "That isn't your life anymore," even as her hand drifted toward the locked drawer.

The key trembled in her grip.

The hAPPening

Why had Jack allowed this to happen? Did he even know? Or care? Surely, he didn't hate her this much.

She grasped the key in both hands, its small teeth digging into her palm.

Maybe Patel had found an answer, relieving her of the need to continue. Maybe it had all been a mistake, and the deposit was in another part of Kenya. Not here. Not in a national park or other protected area. Or there was no unofficial approval leading inexorably toward the permits.

A thin ray of hope. Would it betray or save her?

Moja pushed the key in the lock, then turned it before she could change her mind.

She slid the drawer open and stared at the tools of her past life. She had avoided using them for two years now, and yet she'd opened this drawer twice in the last few hours.

Her fingers fluttered over the contents. Wraparound Shaids. A Doodad. A portable bandwidth booster, allowing her to enter the 3D mode.

Assuming she even wanted to use hAPPn.

"I really don't," she said.

But her moan was a lie. Her pulse fluttered. With fear? Excitement? Was there a difference?

Entering the hAPPn version of Patel's study earlier that day had reminded Moja of the addictive thrill waiting for her online. All she needed was her S-Suit, and she'd slip back into the skin of a digital god, a creator of worlds and weaver of dreams.

"We saw where that led us," she said.

What choice do I really have?

Ojil was right. There was no going back now. Knowing the truth didn't make it any easier to swallow.

Her hands trembled as she turned on the Doodad and

the booster, laid them next to her on the bed, then donned the wraparound Shaids.

Unlike most members of hAPPn, Moja didn't need a Placer to guide or assist her. She, Jack and Patel. A trinity of gods in the world, its creatures made in their likeness.

Was that why everything was going so wrong?

She sent out an invite, then noticed a 3D message waiting for her from Patel. She opened the invite and he appeared in front of her, his features strained.

"Moja, stay out of hAPPn. Keep a low profile, remain hidden. Something's gone terribly wrong. I'm working on the problem. I can't say anything more. Just stay away. And stay safe. I'll be in touch soon."

"Good, old uncle Patel," Moja said to herself before recording a quick reply. "I'm safe where I am. Don't worry. Worst thing that can happen is we run out of tea. Ha-ha. I'll wait to hear from you. Thanks so much for checking."

Her rapid pulse settled into a soft hum. Opening the box hadn't been too bad, after all. She logged off but set an alert for any messages from Patel.

For the first time since reading about the Lucy deposit, Moja felt at home again. At peace in a world that didn't require false gods to run it.

Her last thought as she drifted off to sleep was about Patel. He'd find a way to solve the problem, and put the park back on the map. This was all a mistake. A silly clerical error. He'd set everything right in no time.

Moja woke up tense, expectant. Blinking past dreams and memories, she looked at the window facing east. Darkness fluttered behind the thin curtain.

She remained still, searching for the sound that had woken her. Except it wasn't a sound, but the absence of any. A tropical forest was never truly silent, unless something disturbed the natural ebb and flow of its inhabitants.

Moja rolled softly off her bed, pulled on a jacket and reached for her boots. Maybe it was Baby Moja, coming to investigate. He was more comfortable around humans than the other elephants. He was probably looking for a treat now that she was back.

Yes. That was it. The elephant's presence had startled the resident bush babies, owls and night insects.

Her mind was comfortable with the logic. But her body had its own ideas. Tense, she eased the door open, then closed it just as carefully. She didn't want to startle the elephant, after all.

Assuming it's just an elephant.

"Don't be ridiculous," she murmured to the night.

Moja was just experiencing a bit of paranoia prompted by Patel's message. There was nothing out there except the wildlife, and she would stay safe so long as she stayed inside the compound.

They were too far from town for her to worry about crime. No robber in his right mind — or even in his wrong one — would venture into the jungle at night. And what would they steal from a couple of park rangers? Even their rifles were antiques, dating back to almost World War II.

My rifle.

Moja softly cursed her negligence. She'd left her rifle in the cabin. Not that she'd need it to check on Baby Moja. She searched the darkness outside the fence for glimpses of a pale pinkish brown hide.

But the elephant wasn't anywhere near her cabin. Maybe he was at the front gate. Sniffing around. Detecting her tracks from earlier in the day.

She folded her arms to pin her jacket closed, then followed the fence toward the compound's entrance. A single bulb at one corner of the gate cast an anemic puddle of light. Still no sign of an albino elephant moping around.

Something was wrong about the silence. Baby Moja could move with surprising quiet, but not with an absence of sound. He snuffled, chomped, trumpeted. She should be able to hear a soft puffing as he blew air out of his trunk. Or the muffled crunch of damp leaves under his feet.

Instead she heard nothing. Not a flicker of color or sound. Should she call his name? Return to her cabin to get the rifle?

A shadow stirred, darker than the starlight-tinged shadows she was used to.

"Ojil?" His name came out softly, too much for anyone other than Moja to hear.

She opened her mouth to try again, but something about the man-shaped shadow made her stop.

Ojil was a big, hulking guy. He looked like a grizzly, but was really more like a teddy bear. Unless he needed to stop a poacher. Then the gentle giant vanished with the snap of his rifle's safety clicking off.

The shadow prowling at the edge of the compound was slim, shorter. Definitely male, but not especially large.

"Ojil," Moja whispered, reaching for the walkie that wasn't there.

The shadow slipped through the gate.

She squinted her eyes. Had she only imagined it? Was it a ghost who floated through the fencing and electrified wires?

Keeping to her side of the dimly lit compound, Moja slinked closer, close enough to see the gate was open. The padlock was still intact, but the chain-link had been broken.

So not a ghost.

The shadow slunk toward the center of the compound,

to the covered picnic table. What was he going to do? Have a late-night snack?

The shadow paused next to the table and Moja realized his goal. He dragged something across the surface, metal scratching against wood. The broken drone. Their proof of illegal activity.

Moja shouted — no words, just a guttural bellow.

Startled, the shadow dropped the drone, then cursed and started to hop, clutching a foot.

"This is private property! Trespassers can and will be prosecuted."

Let Ojil hear her. But knowing the old man, he was sleeping deeply, with rumbling snores filling his cabin.

The shadow stooped, picked up the drone, and ran toward the open gate.

"Stop, or … or I'll shoot!"

She regretted the words the second they left her.

The shadow paused, reached under his jacket, and made a sound.

The sound of the safety sliding back on a gun.

Chapter Twenty-Two

"Option B," Jamaal muttered. "Why didn't I go with ignorance? Nothing wrong with that, is there? But no, I had to say yes. Curiosity is a curse."

Prime Placer — or whoever they really were — remained silent. The flurry of white particles gusted in and out of a vaguely humanoid shape.

"This is so not good."

Jamaal shook his head, staring at the 3D images floating around the glowing white room.

He zoomed in to pick out the details, especially the signature stamps. There was no mistaking the location beacons. They matched the coordinates of the near-surface Lucy deposit.

He waved one of the images closer. "Where did you get these from?"

"From the site of the proposed strip mine. You do know what strip mining does to a tropical forest, don't you, Jamaal?"

"Of course I do. I'm a geologist. But this ... this wasn't part of the survey file."

"No. It wasn't."

The image he'd summoned hovered in front of him. He walked into it.

The white room disappeared.

Jamaal was surrounded by a lush tropical forest. Moisture dribbled off of the large leaves hanging close to his head. Long, ropey vines connected thick-trunked trees.

He couldn't feel the heat or humidity — this was only an image, not a touch-rendered, S-Suit-compatible replication — but he could tell from the vegetation he was probably close to the equator. He'd be a pool of sweat and a collection of mosquito bites if he visited the location.

He craned his neck back. The sky was obscured by thick clusters of leaves and multicolored flowers, some in shapes he'd never imagined. A bird with bright yellow wings stared down at him, permanently frozen. Jamaal was almost tempted to reach out and stroke its feathers. He could see every tiny detail.

He pushed the image away. It bobbed around before joining the others in a gently revolving carousel with him at the center. The other images kept orbiting him, creeping closer, the circle tightening.

Jamaal felt like he was at the center of a wheeling swarm of buzzards.

"What does strip mining do to a place like this, Jamaal?" Prime Placer asked.

Another image caught his eye. "Elephants? You've got to be kidding. There're elephants there?"

The unusual avatar floated toward the image of elephants and pushed it toward him.

"No, thanks, I'd rather—"

Too late. Jamaal was in another section of the forest, near a small lake so blue, it felt like a chunk of sky had fallen to the ground. A small herd of elephants clustered along one edge, drinking. A baby elephant had waded part of the way in and was playing with another baby. Spray from their water fight hung around them. The image was detailed enough for Jamaal to see the individual drops suspended in midair.

"What would happen if they mine this area, Jamaal?" Prime Placer's voice echoed around him in the image, almost mocking.

He pushed the image away, and spun around, trying to reorient himself.

"Strip mining ..." He paused and licked his lips, even though his avatar suffered no dryness. Offline, his physical lips crackled under his tongue. "Strip mining would remove everything on the surface, including the soil for the first several meters at least."

"Does this look like a designated wasteland?"

"No. But ... There must be a mistake."

"Check the stamp on the images, Jamaal. They have the coordinates embedded in them."

"I know. I already checked. They're wrong. They have to be ..."

Another image floated in front of him, almost teasing. A pair of parrots sat on the branch. Bright green except for their yellow chests. Heavy rain blurred their feathers.

"An endangered species," Prime Placer said.

"No. No, no, no. They're not there."

"What would happen to them if the rainforest was removed, and replaced by a strip mine?"

Jamaal kept his mouth shut. Because of course these creatures couldn't coexist with a mine. Especially not a strip mine. As for e-Trax's promise to rehabilitate the area? It would take centuries to approach the current level of vegetative growth and biodiversity. Assuming anything survived to repopulate the mining zone.

Assuming this wasn't an elaborate hoax.

"Are you thinking what I'm thinking, Jamaal?"

"This is so fogged up."

"I'm thinking strip mining in an old growth forest would permanently destroy its biodiversity."

"We'll rehabilitate—"

"I'm sure you will. Too bad many of these unique species won't be around to enjoy it."

Jamaal looked away from the parrots, the elephants, the blue lake. It didn't help. He was surrounded by images that made a lie of e-Trax's claim.

The carousel sped up. One after another, 3D images collided against him, briefly submerging him in a forest that wasn't supposed to exist before careening away.

"What do you think, Jamaal?"

His vision blurred as he lurched back and forth, trying to flee the visual bombardment. But there was no escaping the truth.

"Look at the location beacons, Jamaal."

Images spun around the room, plastering the white walls. Green leaves hid the ceiling. Vines, roots and ferns covered the floor.

Dizzy, Jamaal collapsed to his knees. His stomach clenched. Bile scorched his throat. He squeezed his eyes shut, but images continued to pulse against his eyelids.

Whimpering, he stared at the vines coiling around his wrists. Rough bark scratched at his skin.

"The truth, Jamaal. That's all I want."

Gasping, he searched for Prime Placer, but there was only a green blur.

"The truth—"

"They can't mine in here," he screamed.

The images vanished. Vines and ferns disintegrated

into glowing white pixels, creating a sensation of solidity beneath him.

"My thoughts exactly."

Jamaal wiped at his damp face. Tears, sweat or rain?

Not real. It's not real.

Shaking, he stood up. Real or not, he was as wet as if he'd been inside the tropical forest during a storm. He pressed a hand against a wall, leaned against its reassuring presence.

"Jamaal—"

"e-Trax would never do this."

Prime Placer sighed. "Such misplaced faith."

He turned to glare at the pixelated avatar. "Those images have to be from some another location. And I don't care what the stamp says. Someone's messed with the location beacons. It's the only explanation."

"It's *one* explanation."

Jamaal shook his head. "We had independent, objective, third-party experts assess our claim. There're plenty of info-posts in hAPPn about Lucy and the near-surface deposits. Just read them. None of them mention elephants or endangered parrots or … old trees."

"I'm very aware of those posts."

"And that's that. This." He waved a hand at the walls, praying the circling images wouldn't return. "Not real. The CEO of e-Trax wouldn't agree to mining inside a forest. She wouldn't stake her entire career and the company's fortunes on a false claim. The stock value would be destroyed if …"

His voice faded into a whisper.

Prime Placer nodded. "If what, Jamaal?"

"Where's the link out of here?"

"What if those info-posts are … let's say *inaccurate*?"

"Inaccurate? As in they're mistaking a designated

wasteland for a forest?"

"Something like that."

"It's ridiculous. It's not a mistake. It's a cover-up." As soon as the words left his mouth, he snapped his jaw shut. *A cover-up?*

"I know about Abe's map," Prime Placer said. "And the article he found."

"How?" Jamaal instinctively wiped his hand across his forehead.

He knew avatars couldn't sweat; they were nothing more than digital mirrors, sophisticated code. His online responses were a combination of his active imagination and his S-Suit mirroring his physical reactions onto his avatar. None of this was real, not *really* real.

Jamaal was starting to suspect he'd fallen down the proverbial rabbit hole into an alternative dimension where none of the usual laws existed.

Large windows appeared along the walls. The view was the same, putting them in the middle of a forest that couldn't possibly exist.

The vaguely humanoid avatar gestured to the windows. "This is a national park, Jamaal. And it's been removed from the map e-Trax is using. Search for the truth."

Jamaal shook his head. "It's not possible."

"Everything is possible. Kenya has twenty-four national parks, but your company map shows twenty-three."

"Won't people notice if a mining company moves into a park?"

"The damage will be done by the time enough people realize what's going on."

"Then tell someone who can do something! Show them your images. *If* they're real." He paused. "Why haven't you publicized this already?"

"A very clever master hacker with enough time and

cybercoin can interfere with parts of the stamp. Too much interference will leave digital tracks. But a small amount, such as a tweak of the location beacon ... Almost undetectable. Did you know that?"

"These are fakes, then!"

"No. But you know what e-Trax will do?"

"No."

"They'll hire a master hacker to explain how the beacons can be altered. The testimony will spread enough doubt to make sure everyone becomes suspicious of everything, including the truth."

"So—"

"I need solid proof. Something showing e-Trax's manipulation of the facts."

"You want me to betray my company?"

"It's not really yours. Now is it, Jamaal?"

"Why are you doing this to me?"

He inhaled deeply. His lungs weren't working the way they were supposed to. He became acutely aware of existing in two places at once, both inside and outside hAPPn. Jamaal was standing in a digitally created room somewhere inside an app while sitting in his comfy but sweat-soaked chair in his mother's basement.

But he couldn't breathe in either place.

"I have to ... let me go ... I need to ..."

Jamaal bent over, gripped his knees, even though that wasn't going to help him.

"Do you know the words engraved on every welcome arch?"

"Here for truth," Jamaal mumbled.

"No, Jamaal. Originally, the words were *search* for truth. That's what you need to do. Search."

Prime Placer snapped their fingers, and the walls disintegrated.

Chapter Twenty-Three

"Because I know what e-Trax and your CEO are really doing. And it's not at all what you think."

Eva studied the swirling, pixilated avatar claiming to be Prime Placer. There was no signature stamp in a world where everything had one. Either they wanted to hide their true identity, or their current location in the physical world, or both. But why?

The anonymous avatar filled the silence with an outlandish tale. Of a conspiracy as impossible as flying horses and fish tank offices. It belonged to one of the 3D games, or an interactive thriller novel.

Except she hadn't signed up for a game or an online story. Her thoughts disintegrated into swirling fragments of sentences and concepts, all of which finally coalesced into three words.

"That's not possible," Eva finally said.

"Which part?"

"Pretty much all of it. You're accusing my boss and his ... *our* client of changing the map of a country."

"That's correct."

"And they're knowingly planning on erasing the borders of a national park, threatening endangered species, and strip mining a rainforest."

"Again, correct."

"Jack would never ..." Could she swear on oath that Jack was above such antics?

"No, he probably wouldn't. At least, not knowingly. But he is involved nonetheless."

"If it's true—"

"It is."

"Why hasn't the Kenyan government responded?"

"For the same reason no one else has. Truth is fragmented. Facts scattered into useless snippets across a vast terrain."

"You're saying the government will allow a strip mining operation in its national park?"

"I'm saying most of the government won't know it's even happening until it's too late."

"But they've almost finished approving the mining permits—"

"For a designated wasteland."

"That's ..." Eva wrestled with language, trying to wrangle the right word from a mind crowded with them.

"Preposterous?"

"Impossible!"

"So you keep saying."

"It's not just the info-posts they've given me to drop. I've read enough about the company and this particular deposit to know it's a win-win. Easily accessible, safe for miners, environmentally friendly—"

"Yes. A perfect project except for one problem. The deposit isn't in a wasteland area."

"So *you* keep saying." Eva resisted the urge to slide off of her chair and pace her physical office.

She'd made that mistake once while wearing Shaids. It didn't end well. She was limping for a few days afterward. Still, the urge to pace remained, so she directed her avatar to wander the room.

"Why don't you show me your signature stamp?" Eva asked.

"How is that relevant?"

"A sign of good faith."

"Will that make you a believer?"

She shrugged. "It would go a long way to reassuring me you are who you say you are."

"It won't solve your dilemma, Eva. Your client is trying to convince everyone who matters to allow them to mine in a sensitive, protected area. That's not your problem. But they're using hAPPn to push their false narrative across every Place that matters to the project. And that *is* your problem. Particularly when you're directly assisting them."

Eva narrowed her eyes and scanned the code around her. Still no signature stamp. As a Chief, she had access to all code, even for private rooms. But this room, and the white avatar? It was as if they existed in an alternate dimension of hAPPn, one in which traceability didn't exist. Where her high-level software was powerless.

She lifted her hand, rubbed the inside of her forearm. Smooth skin, no Doodad; another impossibility.

"We've met before, you know," Prime Placer said. "Online, and offline."

Eva dropped her arm and stared at the blurry face. "I think I'd remember you."

"Of course I didn't look like this. I was always impressed with your loyalty and discretion. But I fear both are misplaced in this situation. Misplaced, and manipulated."

Eva clenched her fists. How did they know she'd been

the one to drop the info-posts? Worse than that, worse than the implied judgment, was her own suspicion, creeping through the emotional sludge churned up by recent events. A traitorous feeling that maybe Prime Placer was telling her the truth.

"I don't entirely blame Jack for this, either."

"Why?" Eva asked.

"I have my reasons. They're irrelevant right now."

"Then what is relevant?" She loosened her fists. But that did nothing to the acidic churn in her stomach, or the bile sloshing up her throat, like a nightmare about to be unleashed.

If even some of what Prime Placer had told her was true …

But that was impossible.

"I need your help."

"You?" Eva had to make sure. "If you're really the all-powerful creator of hAPPn, how can I help you?"

A hint of a smile flickered across the impermanent face. "The firewall and various layers of encryption protecting hAPPening's workPlace are the strongest and most advanced in the world. They've also undergone numerous upgrades since I worked there. Any attempt at hacking into the company would trigger alarms and trip-wires, temporarily shutting the system down until the hack could be mended. I can't risk it."

"What do you need from me?"

"Evidence. Anything giving me more than my theories to share with the world."

"No one shares anything with the world anymore. They only share with their Places. Their perfect-fit communities."

"You mean intellectual ghettos. Don't worry about how I'll share it. I first need something to share. Solid proof."

Eva looked up at the ceiling, half-expecting to see either a blue sky or a shark's belly. There was nothing, only more white, an emptiness unnerving her more than the ocean life swirling around Jack's fish tank office. "I'll think about it."

"Fair enough."

Before she could request the invite link to appear, the private room erupted into a cascade of white static. Eva blinked against the glare.

Then she opened her eyes and found herself back in the office. The three-headed elephant waved at her right before the message vanished.

Eva twisted her forearm around. Her Doodad was back. Its records showed she hadn't left her office.

"Placer …" Her voice squeaked. She cleared her throat. "Return to welcome arch."

"Opening welcome arch."

As soon as her avatar was on the platform in front of the garnet archway, Eva logged out. She didn't hear her Placer acknowledge the command.

She yanked off the Shaids, standing fast enough to send her chair crashing on the wooden floor.

Theo called from outside her door a moment later. "Eva?"

"I'm fine," she gasped. "I'm fine. I—"

Her stomach heaved. She stumbled into her office bathroom and vomited. Nothing came out but scorching bile. Shaking, she dragged herself up by the counter, and splashed her flushed face.

When her breathing had settled into a soft wheeze, Eva stared at her reflection.

Pasty skin, sticky with guilty sweat.

What had she and Jack done?

Chapter Twenty-Four

THE *SNICK* of the gun's safety was loud against the watchful night. Moja froze, a gasp her only reaction.

An explosion shattered the quiet.

The shot went wide, pinging off of the office building's metal roof. Moja's legs finally got ahead of her baffled mind.

She ducked behind the ancient Land Rover, cursing yet again for leaving her rifle in the cabin.

"Moja?"

"Ojil, be careful." Her strangled voice was still too loud.

A second gunshot, this time from behind her — Ojil, shooting into the air.

Moja waited, praying, hoping the sound of a rifle would scare the interloper away. An adventurous thief, trying out his luck? A poacher who'd confused the KWS compound for … for what? Why would a poacher come anywhere near them?

Wrapping her arms around her bent legs, Moja searched the shadows for her uncle.

"Stay there, Moja," Ojil called, squatting at the edge of his cabin.

He fired another shot, this time over the shadows around the gate.

Her heart stuttered, teeth clacking together.

When the shooting subsided, and there was quiet, Ojil whispered, "Moja, you there?"

"Barely."

Ojil's hum floated through the solid air, reassuring her everything would be okay. She wasn't sure she believed it.

Ojil left the safety of the cabin before she could warn him. He ran toward her, hunched over, and reached the Land Rover without getting killed.

Moja tugged him to the ground. "You crazy, old man?"

"Sometimes."

They stayed crouched behind the vehicle, waiting. Ojil eased his gun around a tire and fired off a couple more shots.

Silence.

Moja broke it. "He took the drone."

"Hmmm."

"Think he's gone?" she whispered through chattering teeth.

In all the years she'd shadowed Father and Ojil, Moja had never witnessed anyone using a gun. Sure, they all knew how to use one. It was part of their training as rangers. But this? A gun battle?

She'd always imagined herself fighting off poachers. Shooting the weapons right out of their hands. Heroically sweeping them up in a raid at their bases of operation. Saving wildlife from being chopped up, their body parts and babies sold to the highest bidder.

This didn't feel heroic. It didn't even feel like they'd won.

A large hand wrapped around her upper arm. She tilted her head back, staring into Ojil's eyes. If he was scared, he didn't show it. Or maybe his fear was hidden by the shadows around them. Calm reassurance met her gaze, reflecting the light from one of the fence's security lamps.

"I didn't train for this," she said.

"Nobody really does. Wait here."

"Wait, why? Ojil, don't."

But he was already stalking toward the main gate, keeping low, avoiding the few lights shining down from the fence.

He ducked behind a water tank, a box of supplies, a bush, a tree, then dashed across open ground to the front gate.

Then she lost sight of him.

Stupid. Stupid, brave man ...

"He's gone," Ojil called out. "Probably just a poacher."

"That's one dumb poacher."

"Hmmm."

Would a poacher break into a KWS compound to collect a drone? It was a risky move, even if the drone had their fingerprints. Everyone knew the rangers were armed. There was an unspoken understanding: a poacher who dared try his luck in a national park was fair game. Poachers usually went out of their way to avoid the rangers, not shoot at them in their own compounds.

Moja scurried into her cabin, snagged her rifle, and ran after Ojil, who was scouting the area.

"Found a casing." He held up a small metal cylinder.

"Too small."

Ojil nodded and pocketed the casing. "Handgun."

"Poachers don't use handguns."

Ojil continued his search. Looking for tracks, or some

indication of who the shooter had been. If he was still there.

"Strange, isn't it?" Ojil said.

Moja kept quiet. Was this because of the tracer program? Had it found her location before she'd strengthened her firewall?

But the shooter had arrived within hours, and who around here had the resources or motivation to create a tracer?

Maybe the two weren't connected. A coincidence, then? That also felt wrong. Either way, Patel was right to be concerned. Maybe she wasn't as safe here as she'd always believed.

Moja scanned the shadows, tensing in anticipation of another shot. The security light above the gate didn't penetrate the forest. But it made them visible, enough for someone hiding in the nearby undergrowth to have a good line of sight.

"We shouldn't be out here."

"Hmmm."

"Ojil, you hear? This isn't safe …"

No one is safe anywhere.

"Let's call for backup," she said.

"Backup?"

Moja grimaced. He was right. No one would be coming to help them until well after sunrise. "HQ should know. We're not going to find anything. He's gone."

"Hmmm." Still studying the ground, he returned to the gate and gestured for Moja to go inside. "I'll call the other stations." He glanced at her sideways, as if waiting for her to reply. When she didn't, he added, "Get some rest. We'll have another look tomorrow."

She nodded, numb, her hands shaking. Moja was

pretty sure she knew what they would find. Nothing. Or at least nothing useful.

Going back to sleep was impossible, but she didn't argue with Ojil. She stretched out on the bed, stared up at the thatch ceiling, her lantern set low.

She'd turned on the light to reassure herself she was alone. Instead, it accentuated the shadows, highlighting pockets of darkness where someone could be lurking, waiting for her to close her eyes before launching another attack on her.

Do you open the box?

What if Moja opened the box with the promised cure, but instead she released the disease?

She rolled onto one side, then tossed around onto the other.

Moja, stay out of hAPPn. Keep a low profile, remain hidden. Something's wrong.

No one is safe anywhere.

Patel's words whispered in her ear. She was good at that, at hiding, at disappearing. She could find a new sanctuary, retreat into a deeper level of obscurity than the one she'd created here.

Then who would take care of Baby Moja and the other animals in the park? And what about the park rangers who'd dedicated their lives, who might very well lose them? Yes, she could disappear, but no one else could. She'd lose Ojil, Baby Moja, the park.

Keep a low profile, remain hidden.

Or Moja could come out of hiding, pick up the mantle she'd discarded, and right the wrongs she left like litter on the road behind her. She'd risk her privacy, possibly her life. And for what?

"It's only a stupid map," she muttered, waiting for some sign, even the rustle of the little creature living in the thatch. But there were only shadows interwoven with fragments of light.

Was it worth it?

I take that key, Ojil whispered in her other ear, *and open the box. What choice do I really have?*

What if the map hadn't been a mistake? What if e-Trax knew?

She gave up on the pretense of sleep, rolled out of bed, and stared at the locked drawer. What was inside, salvation or damnation?

This time, it didn't take her as long to use the key. She logged in, and stood in her welcome arch. She pulled the glowing cube toward her. The copy of the tracer program pulsed inside, curled into a ball of tentacles and thwarted ambition.

"Let's find out who sent you." She expanded the cube until it was big enough to enter.

Tentacles slashed at Moja as she entered, but they were harmless here.

She pushed herself into the tracer program. Weaving her way through the code, she started dissecting the tracer from the inside.

"Whoever set you loose has serious clout," she murmured while studying a twinkling cluster of elegant code. "You are one lethal beast. Beautiful, though."

Tracers were expensive and extremely difficult to acquire, due to ever-tightening privacy laws. Clients needed court permission to even apply for one, then a permit to release it in hAPPn.

But this tracer was different. She couldn't find the permit in the signature stamp, because it didn't have one.

"Everything has a stamp," she huffed, increasing the speed of her work.

Her breathing became frantic and hoarse as she flicked

through line after line, searching for the signature. Scattering discarded bits in a pile around her, she tugged at the heart of the tracer.

There it was. The signature, embedded in an algorithm fitted inside a digital snake. She caught a glimpse of the time stamp.

It was created two years ago.

She reached for it, but the stamp evaded her, slithering through the debris of broken code. Moja chased it until she finally cornered it, then tossed a net. "Got you!"

The thing exploded, covering her with snippets of code. The force of the blast tossed Moja out of the cube and into her welcome arch.

Gasping, she yanked off her Shaids and waited for her eyes to adjust, for her lungs to catch up with her.

"Who creates an exploding signature?" she asked the silence.

Odder still, the tracer had been built around the time she was kicked off the board. It had been designed to detect her reentry into hAPPn. She'd triggered it the first time she'd logged in.

Who would go through the trouble and expense? Why would anyone want to know the exact moment she returned?

She lay down, listening to the creature rustling in the thatch overhead. A land of shadows making a home for her thoughts.

"Truth is like sunlight," she whispered Ojil's words. "It warms your soul. Makes good things grow. Stay in the light."

She waited for the sun to spear the shadows. Watched as they withered before the force of its rays.

When her cabin was filled with the warmth of a new

day, she rose. She pulled on her Shaids, logged into hAPPn, and recorded a message for Patel.

Moja spoke clearly. He needed to believe she was serious in ending her exile, in joining him. Together, they could stop whatever this was, save the park, and maybe themselves.

"Prime Placer has returned. It's time to chase away some shadows. See you soon."

Before releasing the message, Moja added her signature stamp: a three-headed albino elephant.

Chapter Twenty-Five

S*earch for truth.*

Prime Placer's voice whispered around him as the anonymous private room dissolved into a storm of glowing white pixels.

When the blizzard cleared, Jamaal straightened and twirled around. He was in one of e-Trax's public rooms, the Map Room. A favorite with the geologists.

The walls, floor and ceiling were papered with maps. Maps that detailed the world's transport networks. Forests. Fresh water sources. Topography. Known deposits of various minerals. Suspected deposits. Every kind of geology-related map for every region and sub-region could be found here.

And of all the maps he could be looking at, Jamaal was standing in front of a floating map of Kenya's national parks.

He stepped closer. There was no protected area anywhere near the proposed mining zone.

"Ha! Prime Placer's wrong, so wrong. Knew it. I ..."

Jamaal slapped a hand over his mouth. He was

babbling like a crazy person, crazy like a certain pixelated avatar. He did a quick check to make sure no one was near him. The last thing he needed was to be called in for a psych test.

He wasn't crazy. Prime Placer or whoever, *they* were the crazy person. Jamaal was a totally normal guy with a pet rock and a great job.

But a quick search wouldn't hurt …

"Placer, search for Kenyan national parks."

"Searching for Kenyan national parks," Sarah said, materializing next to him. Her voice didn't soothe him the way it usually did. "Results obtained. Would you like to see them, Jamaal?"

"Yes, of course, I want to see them. That's why I asked you to do the search."

"Displaying search results."

A screen appeared to one side of the map. A list of twenty-three national parks scrolled in front of him, matching details on the map. Twenty-three parks, none of which were in any danger of being mined.

He glanced around again. No one else was within hearing range. "Sarah?"

"Yes, Jamaal."

He wiped at his trembling lips. "This is crazy. Crazy, crazy—"

"Searching for crazy—"

"No! Cancel search."

Silence.

"Sarah, how much …" He cleared his throat, looked over his shoulder, and started again in a whisper. "How much does an anonymous search cost?"

"An anonymous search costs twenty-five cybercoins."

Jamaal gasped. A private search only cost two. How

could anyone justify charging *twenty-five*? Anonymity shouldn't cost much more than privacy.

"Would you like to commission an anonymous search, Jamaal?"

"Not really."

He'd never used an anonymous search before. Very few people ever did. Why bother? The searches inside his workPlace, Geo Rocks, Metals & Mud, *and* Geeks Rule were sufficient for everything he ever needed.

Until now.

Because what if Prime Placer had told him the truth? Crazy as that whole falling-down-the-rabbit-hole experience had been, what if …

"I'm blaming this on Abe," he muttered.

Abe and his incessant curiosity. His obsession with conspiracies. Questioning everything, especially authority. When they were kids, Abe had been the one to get them in trouble. Sure, he also managed to get them out of it … usually. And if not? He'd leave Jamaal holding the empty cookie jar, or the results of whatever mischief he'd gotten them into.

This was one of those times. For all he knew, maybe Abe arranged for his kidnapping and the appearance of Prime Placer.

Probably not. It wasn't Abe's style, but still. His cousin was one of those who believed in the urban legend of Prime Placer. Jamaal was agnostic. More importantly, he was happy. Or at least satisfied. He liked his job. He liked his mom. Heck, he even liked his pet rock! What did he have to gain from all of this exploration and questioning and doing secret searches?

Nothing. Nothing at all, except maybe unemployment. A lecture from Ms. Chan, at the very least. Possibly a lawsuit or jail sentence, and who needed that headache?

"Not worth it," he said.

"I don't understand the request, Jamaal. Please repeat. Would you like to commission an anonymous search? It costs twenty-five cybercoins."

"Is it, though? Is it really anonymous? I mean, I have to withdraw the fee. That transaction can't be erased from my account. And while it's not rock shattering, anyone who's looking for that sort of thing could find it." He smacked his forehead. "But why would they? I'm talking like Abe."

"Calling Abe," Sarah intoned.

"No! I mean, cancel call."

"Canceling call to Abe."

"I mean I *sound* like him. With his conspiracy theories and his questioning and … *Arg!* Who would bother looking at my account? Who cares what kind of searches I do?"

Sarah said nothing. She stood by his side, like a model pretending to be an airline steward.

"Why would anyone bother? Nobody. Exactly." He began pacing around the floating map of Kenya.

On the other hand, he'd be questioned about the unusual withdrawal if things went wrong.

But what could go wrong? It was just a search, really. One that temporarily removed any connection his search engine had with his Places and workPlace. The search would troll well beyond his regular Places, exploring the wider body of knowledge out there in the online universe.

Unusual, yes. Illegal? No! Of course not. Not even e-Trax and their ironclad nondisclosures could trap him into feeling guilty.

"I'm gonna be sick," Jamaal groaned.

His breathing was doing that marathon sprinting thing again, and his heart didn't feel healthy. This was why he didn't jog. He got enough exercise going up and down the stairs from the basement to the kitchen and back again.

But running outside for fun? Who needed to strain his lungs that badly?

"It has to be anonymous, right?" He stared at Sarah, but she simply gazed back at him with a bland expression. "That's why they charge so much, right? Because it's anonymous. They strip all of the stamps from my interactions during the anonymous search. That's what happens, you know."

Silence.

"Placer, send me to my office."

"Return to office."

The Map Room disappeared, and Jamaal was sitting in his digital office. It wasn't any more private than the Map Room. But the illusion of being alone helped settle his breathing into something that didn't sound like a heart attack in process.

"Placer."

Sarah appeared next to his desk, hands loosely clasped in front of her. "Yes, Jamaal."

"Initiate anonymous search. Debit twenty-five cybercoins." His voice snagged in a sob at the end.

Twenty-five cybercoins! He could kiss his bubble bike goodbye. Jamaal almost envied Sarah and her total lack of emotional response.

"Debiting account twenty-five cybercoins. Initiating anonymous search. Questions for search?"

"How many national parks does Kenya have? What's their location. When was the newest park established. And locations of any Lucy ... I mean, EA-L029 deposits."

That should be enough to prove both Abe and the crazy Prime Placer imitator he hired that they were wrong.

"Initiating search."

Seconds passed. This was an anonymous search, which

would naturally require more time. It was searching across a far broader area than his Places.

"How much longer?"

"Forty-seven seconds," she said.

Jamaal watched the clock on his ceiling.

"Compiling search results," Sarah said.

"Display results."

"Displaying results."

A silvery screen floated in front of him at eye level. His questions were listed along with the search-generated responses.

Number of national parks in Kenya: Twenty-three.
Newest park: established twenty-seven years, three months ago.
Locations of parks: see map.
Locations of EA-L029 deposits: see map.

A map appeared when he scrolled down. National parks were shaded in green. Lucy deposits were yellow diagonal lines. Yellow and green never touched.

Jamaal puffed out a breath, a smile lifting his cheeks. "Told you."

"Do you wish me to display the search result from the aberrant source?" Sarah asked.

"Aberrant?"

"Definition. A departure from—"

"I know what it *means*. What's the aberrant source?"

"A non-digitalized map referenced on a Kenya Wildlife Service website. Site last updated four years, one month ago."

"Non-digitalized …"

"A photo of the map. The map can't be verified."

"Because it's a photo. The signature stamp is for the photo, not the map."

"Yes."

Jamaal's smile twitched at the corners. "Display."

"Cleaning data—"

"No. Don't clean it. Just display what you found from the aberrant source."

A photo of a map appeared. Unlike the first one, there was no shading to indicate any mineral deposits. More importantly, there was an additional green zone.

Jamaal didn't have to look at the e-Trax map to know the new green zone was located in the same area as the recently discovered, near-surface Lucy deposit. A sentence appeared under the map.

Number of national parks in Kenya: Twenty-four.

Chapter Twenty-Six

EVA IGNORED the stream of notifications on her Doodad. At least two were from Jack, thanking her for her great job in dropping the info-posts with infinite discretion …

Discretion. What had Prime Placer said? That her loyalty and discretion had been manipulated.

Ding!

Another message from Jack. *Info-posts moving like a virus! Super job.*

"Great. I've released a virus," she muttered, denying his enthusiasm a reply.

He was right. When she checked the stats, she saw the info-posts were appearing in additional news streams as media sources shared them, and members commented. Each interaction added more legitimacy to claims that were possibly misleading, or worse, lies.

And she had been instrumental in helping e-Trax spread its narrative.

She slid her Doodad onto her desk and leaned back. The chair creaked, a comforting sound. A reminder she was back in the physical world where things weren't as tidy as in hAPPn.

Had she really been in the same room as the legendary Prime Placer?

Another alert distracted her. Not the normal *Ding*, but a miniature elephant's trumpet, a soft *twoot!*

Eva eyed her Doodad, waiting for something to jump out and spray water. But she was offline. Nothing like that happened in the physical world.

Twoot!

She kept her hands on her lap. She hadn't changed her sound settings. How could anyone force a trumpet into the notification alert?

Twoot!

"You're not going to give up, are you?"

Twoot! Twoot!

Exhaling loudly to cover another *twoot!*, Eva picked up her Doodad and opened the notification.

Since it's so important to you, here's my stamp.

The anonymous message was accompanied by the partial code for a signature stamp. It excluded geographical information, and the Place from which the sender had written the message. But it did have the personal verification.

Eva rubbed her fingers together. "Placer, open stamp."

Every member had a unique stamp which acted like a personal identification number. It wasn't necessarily a number. It could be a word, an image, a color, a sound. In this case, it was a white, three-headed elephant.

Eva covered her mouth. There was no forging or mistaking it. No other member of hAPPn could have a stamp that even vaguely resembled this. Unless …

She shut off her Doodad and pushed it away from her. "If you're clever enough to figure out I dropped the info-posts, then maybe you're clever enough to forge that stamp."

The screen stared blankly at the ceiling. No trumpets. No digital elephants waving at her.

Eva paced her office, rubbing her lower back. "Who are you really? What are you after? Motivation's everything."

She stopped in front of the large window and looked at the view. She waited for a narwhale to leap out of the depths, but of course it didn't. Narwhales lived in the Arctic, not along the Washington coastline.

She knew the company history well enough to know the app's creation story. Three god-like inventors had said, "Let there be code," and so it was. It definitely took longer than seven days, but the result was Biblical. An entire world ready to be populated by whatever the human mind could imagine, and then some more.

One of those gods had vanished, leaving behind only a myth and the memory of a powerful name. How many creations in hAPPn had the brand of the three-headed elephant embedded in their code? Enough for Eva to know the myth had been real.

Another god had descended into the role of CEO. She could go to Jack. He'd know if this was a fake.

"No. Not him. Not yet," she said to herself.

And the third god ... Not vanished exactly, but he'd abandoned his creation for a well-deserved rest, a prolonged seventh day.

He would've known Prime Placer very well. At least enough to be able to confirm the stamp's code and its source. But Mr. Indra Patel redefined *reclusive*. An angel investor, a brilliant programmer and the first to support hAPPn, he'd retired from the business world and was notoriously difficult to locate or contact, maybe even impossible.

Rumor had it he'd left Seattle for someplace more private. Finding his new home was only the first obstacle. For all she knew, he had a small army of security agents, drones and automated alarm systems to preserve his desire for privacy.

Then again, Eva was now a Chief. And that came with unique perks and benefits, not all of which were written up in the contracts.

She glanced at the time. It was close to midnight. Theo and Rossi were both asleep by now. The house had the deep quiet which could only be felt late in the night. How long had she been online?

And I worry about Rossi using hAPPn too much.

Rubbing her eyes, she wandered into the hallway. The ground floor was dark apart from a couple of floor lamps.

Midnight. The hAPPening workPlace should be deserted.

She paused at the bottom of the staircase and glanced up, as if she could see through floors and doors into the rooms of her sleeping family. Pure silence echoed from above, reminding her of when Rossi was still a baby. Eva would tiptoe into her child's room and watch her sleep. It was the only time their daughter was ever truly quiet. She'd been a loud, rambunctious toddler who'd evolved into a recalcitrant teenager.

Just a phase.

Hoping it was true, Eva retreated to her office, settled into her chair and slid on the Shaids.

"Log in. Access menu. Enter workPlace."

Her Placer moved through the commands, and Eva found herself in the hAPPening lobby — a grandiose monument to all things modern. A cathedral of glass, steel and space-age technology to worship at the altar of human ingenuity.

As glorious as it all was, Eva wasn't interested in the exaggerated displays of robotic engineering and advanced artificial intelligence that hAPPening boasted would be their next frontier. Summoning her menu, she selected Human Resources, then Members Database.

She had no reason to go to HR, never mind the database which contained details of every member of hAPPn. But if there was a way to track Indra Patel, it was there. And she had to know the truth. She had to know if she was being manipulated by yet another mind, or if Prime Placer was the real deal.

She glanced around. The room representing Database was empty, but that didn't mean much here. It was one of the drawbacks: even if Eva thought she was alone, someone could always appear out of nowhere, and with little or no warning. No footsteps on the tiles, light-switch clicking, or door creaking open. Just a soft *pop*, then company. Only private rooms were immune from this nuisance.

"Make it quick," she muttered out loud.

The user-facing portion of Database was little more than a walk-in closet with a large screen set into the wall. This provided the interface to a vast storage system behind it, containing the informational equivalent of the diamond fields of South Africa. A seemingly never-ending trove of wealth. Layers of data, most of which was only accessible here. And precisely because it was so valuable, it was off limits to everyone except for Chiefs and the CEO.

Even with her new credentials, Eva couldn't access it from outside. She could request aggregated data, highly generalized and not particularly useful in this case. But she needed Patel's current signature stamp with the location beacon intact, pinpointing his geological position.

"Request search, Indra Patel. Late seventies."

Search results began scrolling across a floating screen. Patel's previous residence in a wealthy Seattle neighborhood showed up. But he wasn't there anymore.

"Refine search. Former investor of hAPPening. Current shareholder."

She continued to feed more parameters, narrowing the search. There were still several possibilities by the time everything she knew about the eccentric investor was loaded into the appropriate fields.

"Download search results into my account. Clear search from Database screen."

The forearm dinged. *Success.*

A soft *pop*, then Jack was standing beside her.

Eva gasped.

He did a double take, then quickly recovered. "Fancy meeting you here, after hours."

"Right."

He stared at her. She instinctively shifted, hiding her forearm from view. It was stupid, in hindsight. He couldn't see what was there, but he could clearly note her retreat.

"I didn't expect to find you here. Ever." His easygoing smile hardened around the edges. It looked about to shatter. Eva imagined a mouth full of jagged shark teeth.

"I'm looking for key influencers," she gushed. "You know."

His eyebrows tilted upward. His mouth flattened.

"People who can share the e-Trax info-posts with others. To increase believability."

He nodded. "Smart. Really smart." It didn't sound like a compliment.

His avatar shimmered around the edges. Bits of static

speared through him. It reminded her of the one time she'd gone camping with the family. She had to use an outdated portable bandwidth booster to attend a meeting while Theo and Rossi went fishing.

But why would Jack need a booster? Like most cities, Seattle had no digital dead zones. Every resident had access to sufficient bandwidth to log onto even the data-intensive, 3D version of hAPPn. hAPPening had its own system in case the public service ever faltered.

The static sparkled across his chest like miniature lightning bolts trapped in his jacket, then vanished.

Eva glanced past Jack at her link. It floated midway between floor and ceiling, visible only to her. Her exit out of this mess. She itched with the need to push him aside and tap the link to her office.

What would Eva say if she wasn't sneaking around and doing something that was borderline against company policy? "And you? Out for an evening stroll?"

He chuckled. "I have a meeting with Danielle. You know."

"Good. Really good."

"She wanted to discuss the info-posts. She sends you her greetings, by the way."

Eva smiled. It felt like her mouth was about to snap off her stiff face. "Glad she's happy."

The link bobbed closer to her, almost within reach.

Jack glanced at Database's giant screen, then back at her. "Anyway, I saw you were here. Thought I'd pop in. See how things are going."

"Great. It's all great."

"That's great."

They stared at each other a moment too long.

"Was that a …?" Eva made a show of glancing at her

Doodad. "Yup. Theo. Wondering what I'm doing at this time of night. See you tomorrow."

"Wouldn't miss it."

She reached for the link, desperate to escape the awkwardness. Almost there. A small step, and she'd log off, slip into bed, and—

"One more thing," Jack said.

Eva forced herself to look at him, at the wariness in his eyes that belied his smile. "Yes?"

"You take care, Eva. You're working too hard. I'd hate to lose our newest Chief. None of us want that, now do we?"

She held his gaze while tapping the link. "No, sir. We certainly don't."

Chapter Twenty-Seven

MOJA GLANCED OVER HER SHOULDER, compulsively checking to make sure the door was locked. She ignored the *ping* on her old cell phone, knowing it was Ojil, checking up on her. Again.

He'd sent her three or four messages a day since she'd left the park.

Checking u r okay. When r u coming back?

She'd packed her bag the morning after the shootout with the drone thief. Packing had been easy. Ignoring Ojil's confusion, not so much. He deserved an explanation, but each answer would only generate more questions, each needing more time.

Time was a rapidly depleting resource. She felt each minute falling before the savage teeth of unseen bulldozers. The battle to save the park wouldn't be fought here, but in another world. She needed secure access to hAPPn without the risk of interruptions or data failure, and that wasn't possible with a bandwidth booster.

"Have you requested another ranger yet?" she'd asked instead of answering his questions.

Ojil stared at her bag, bouncing the Land Rover keys. "Why?"

"You can't manage on your own. And I don't know when I'm coming back."

"You don't need to go. That poacher, he won't be coming back." He'd said it like he knew this as a fact, but his forehead crinkled and suggested otherwise.

"It wasn't a poacher."

Ojil didn't challenge her, because what kind of poacher uses a handgun? Or steals a drone? Or breaks into a Kenya Wildlife Service compound inhabited by armed rangers?

"I'll deal with it. If he does come back, which he won't," Ojil said, patting her shoulder. "Don't be scared."

"I'm not scared."

"Hmmm."

Moja didn't argue. Of course she was afraid. Being shot at wasn't like in the movies. It wasn't an event that began and ended in one scene. She still felt the echo of gunshots in her heartbeat, heard it when a door slammed, or a branch snapped. It clung to her, armpit sweat that wouldn't dry.

"I'm worried about *you*," she said.

"Oh! Me, I'll be fine."

"Father said the same thing." She closed her mouth before she tainted the air with more of her fear. Fear for Ojil, for Baby Moja, and for all the other inhabitants of the park.

"I'll ask for a temp."

"Good."

"You'll be back soon." It sounded almost like a question.

"As soon as I can," she'd promised. "It's for the best."

Ojil grunted. It had been a quiet ride to Uhuru Town's bus depot. Followed by a lonely ride to Nairobi.

The hAPPening

Moja dropped her bag next to the battered metal desk, and double-checked the door, making sure the lock was engaged. This was Nairobi, after all. Reliable bandwidth, yes. Along with crime and insecurity.

She crossed the room to the window facing Kenyatta Avenue. This was the other problem with Nairobi. The noise. She'd forgotten how loud people were. Muted honking drummed against the thick glass. A constant reminder she was in the center of a city growing increasingly loud and chaotic.

Since arriving, she'd been spending her days at internet cafés. She selected the ones with private rooms which were rented by the hour for deep dives into hAPPn.

She never stayed longer than a few hours, despite her high level of encryption. She used different routes and varying locations, sometimes going into a neighboring town.

Try tracking me now, she thought while pulling down the noise-muffling shutters.

The lack of predictably in her routine combined with her security systems should make it difficult for anyone to find her. Even if they could break through the multiple layers of firewall she'd established around her online presence. Those alone blocked just about anyone from finding her.

But the person who'd designed the tracking program wasn't just *anyone*. There were very few people with the skills to create such a sophisticated tracker, so Moja was taking no chances.

Turning off her cell phone, she settled into the body-hugging chair and prepared to enter hAPPn. This time, she'd be reaching out to the one person she'd vowed to never see again.

Her hands shook as she slid on the Shaids. She took a

minute, inhaled deeply, held her breath for a count of four, then exhaled slowly, visualizing the tension leaving along with her breath.

"It's time."

But still she hesitated, waiting for some sign. Seconds ticked by, grains of sand dribbling one by one through an hourglass made of her fluttering breath. As the sand collected at the bottom, she rehearsed what to say. But each attempt felt more unbalanced, less in line with what she needed to do, and more an emotional response.

Either Jack had no clue what was going on — unlikely — or he was knee-deep in exactly the sort of activities she'd warned them about. He'd sold out.

Either-or. The caveman's brain.

Moja huffed a laugh at Patel's words. He'd always been obsessed about the human brain, the either-or mentality, its inability to evolve past the Stone Age. Or so he said. Then again, he was a rare example of a highly evolved being.

"Okay, caveman brain," she muttered and turned on her Doodad. "Time to face a few dinosaurs."

Or in this case, CEO Jackson Rustle.

Even thinking his name … Her mind snarled, but the rest of Moja betrayed her. Why else would her stomach clench, but her heart beat faster?

Let's give him a chance. We'll hear him out. Listen to his side of the story.

Assuming there was anything to tell.

She logged in and stood before her welcome arch. Unlike almost every other member of hAPPn, Moja didn't have a Placer. She didn't need one. Neither did Jack or Patel. They were the gods of this world. And no one else had a menu like hers.

On the surface, it was simple. A few options presented on a glowing, silvery screen floating next to her right hand.

But Moja could quickly dive deeper with a few clicks. She had access to all the layers of hAPPn, an ability to enter the members-only areas of any Place without an invite or membership. And that was something no one else could do, not even her fellow gods.

"How's that for a primitive brain, Patel," she whispered.

She'd secretly designed back doors during the early days in order to study the platform. Make improvements. Catch the bugs before they grew big enough to devour essential infrastructure.

She'd always intended to close those doors, to put herself on an equal footing with her co-creators. But somehow, the opportunity never availed itself. She quit after getting booted off the board, and thus forgot all about the doors.

Until someone tried to shoot her and destroy her home.

Today's dive wasn't deep. She wouldn't need the back doors. She sent the invite, and waited as a fisherman waits for his rod to twitch. The baited message was simple, non-emotional. Binary if she was being honest.

Meet me, or don't. One chance only.

The words didn't scream out her pain, the hurt flaring every time she remembered the day it all ended. How Jack had stood at the head of the board's table, unable to meet her gaze. His fingers tapped a death march against the digitally created jade surface.

Moja pulled up the link and entered her private room. She was now tucked deep inside hAPPn, with more layers of protection than pretty much any other location online. It wasn't just private. It was anonymous, and officially didn't exist.

More seconds tiptoed around her.

Would he accept her invite? Ignore it? Maybe he wasn't online—

She scoffed. Jack was *always* online. He had his Doodad by his side even when he logged off to eat, notifications streaming across its screen. He would've seen the invite.

Maybe he didn't want to see her.

She glanced around the room. She'd recreated Patel's study, the place they'd spent so much time in together. Every detail, down to the small, white, three-headed statue. Its jeweled eyes glinted in the soft lighting.

"Hello," she whispered to the miniature elephant.

A buzz tingled in her hands, right before Jack popped into the room. He was using a mirror image avatar. The exact likeness made everything worse.

She'd been expecting rage, anger, hurt. But this? The axe of memory chopped her defenses with a single swing, leaving behind a stump of sticky emotion. She choked on an overwhelming need to toss the past into a strong box, lock it, lose the key, and fling herself into his arms.

She lowered her avatar's responsiveness, turning it into a statue of herself.

The corner of Jack's mouth twitched, and he blinked several times. He'd never bothered creating a responsiveness sub-program for his avatar. Nor had he taken Patel's meditation lessons seriously. He'd try for a few seconds, then huff impatiently and tell them to hurry up. No time for calm or relaxation.

Being together in the same space distorted time, slowed it down, reversed it. Each second adopted a physical presence, collecting on the desk between them, strengthening the barrier in a way no firewall ever could.

He gazed around, studying everything but her. "The room of eternal summer."

"I like sunshine."

"Of course." He rocked back on his heels. "This is a surprise."

"A pleasant one?"

He shrugged, his gaze flicking up and down as he took in her appearance. "It's been a while."

She said nothing, keeping her expression neutral. She wouldn't let him see the shredded contents of her soul.

"How's Baby Moja?"

"Big."

He looked away. His smile quickly wilted. "Good memories in here."

Moja pulled at her prepared speech, but the words drifted away, dandelion seeds on a breeze.

He cleared his throat, shuffled side to side, stuffed his hands into his pockets.

"Memories," she said. "Yes. That's all this room really is."

He nodded, finally looked up and met her gaze. She wasn't sure what she'd expected to see in his eyes. Triumph? Disdain? Instead, there was a hollowness, one suggesting a sorrow almost as deep as hers. "Moja, I'm—"

"We need to talk," she blurted before he could say anything that might soften her resolve. She didn't want to hear an apology. She was here for the future, not their past.

He snapped his mouth shut and nodded, his hollow look sliding under a mask of his own creation. "Of course."

Moja stared at him, mental claws easing out, wanting to shred that artificial visage, rip it up until his heart lay in tatters before her. "Do you know—"

"I'm sorry, Moja," he gushed, the mask disintegrating before her, the hollowness also gone, leaving only sorrow and something else, something she didn't dare look at. "I'm sorry about what … well, you know."

"Really? What do I know? That you went behind my back? Turned the others against me? You had me removed from the board, kicked me out of my own company. *Our* company."

"No." He shook his head. "That's not what happened."

"It was a bloody coup, Jack! You're *sorry*? You're two years too late for that."

"I didn't have you removed." His voice remained level, as if he were the reasonable one. "It wasn't my decision, although I didn't disagree. You were pushing too many restrictions. We were building a world where everything and anything can happen. *No limits.*"

"And see where that's led us?"

He lifted his arms, then let them fall. "And here we go, the same old argument. You created something magnificent, then wanted to slow it down with all these red lights—"

"Red lights stop accidents. That's why we use them."

"Too many, and you don't move at all. You trim the world into some distorted, insignificant version of its true potential."

"I wanted to protect the members who aren't gods!" Her words blasted across the desk, each one a verbal bullet.

But none hit their mark.

Jack shook his head, mouth turning down in disappointment. "*This* is why we had to remove you."

She straightened up, surprised she'd been hunched over. She rested her hands on the antique desk Patel loved so much.

What had happened to her calm? Her detachment, her ability to distance her avatar from her body's responses?

She inhaled deeply, exhaled with attention. But this time, it didn't work. Her entire body quivered.

"This was a mistake," she muttered, reaching for the link to take her out of this room, away from him.

"Wait," Jack said and stepped toward her. "Didn't we agree to keep business as business, and nothing to do with us?" He gestured with one hand between the two of them.

"We were stupid. Naïve. It was never just business. The app, this world, we created it together. It was as much a part of our relationship as ..." Moja clenched her teeth before the words could betray her. "It doesn't matter anymore. It's done. That's not why I'm here."

Jack sighed, his shoulders curled inward as if whatever had held him up was leaking out of him.

"You're right. It *was* our creation. But hAPPn is no longer yours, Moja. Even if you were instrumental in its design. Things have changed. You haven't."

"Yes, they have. For the worse. I created all of this for people to interact with the truth, to meet each other in a space that mirrored reality, but was free of its limitations."

He barked a laugh, his mask back in place. "That's rich, coming from someone who wanted to impose more limits."

"To prevent what's now happening. I assume you've heard about e-Trax?" Moja studied his expression, searching for a response. A reaction to tell her if he was complicit, or ignorant, and to hell with Patel's caveman brain theory. Because sometimes, reality did fall into a yes-or-no, right-or-wrong category.

And sometimes it doesn't.

Jack frowned. "Of course. They're one of our bigger clients. Why?"

"Their info-posts are wrong."

"Really. You invited me for this?"

"It's important."

"And you're mistaken. Those posts are independently

created. Why would e-Trax need to lie? Especially when the truth would be so simple to discover. They have a reputation to protect."

"I live in what they're calling a designated wasteland."

Her head jerked back when he smiled.

"That's gotta suck, Moja. Maybe you want to move back to Seattle, then?"

"It's not a joke!"

"Sure sounds like one."

"They're going to destroy my home, Jack. It's a forest, not a wasteland."

"If you say so."

"Did you set up a tracer program? One targeting me?"

"Why would I do that? Those are hard to implement, and I have other things to do." His expression softened, and he took another step toward her. "Moja, if I'd known where you'd gone, I would've followed you. Begged you to come home. But you made it very difficult for anyone to find you. You also made it clear you didn't want to be found."

One of her hands gripped the edge of the desk. Her S-Suit allowed her fingertips to feel the rough grain. But she knew it was only a digital fabrication. Same as his response.

Why would he want to chase after her, when he was the reason she'd left in the first place?

"Did you hire someone to shoot me?"

She knew Jack well enough to see that his reaction wasn't a lie. His jaw dropped, bright blue eyes bugging out at her. "What?"

"Nothing. Forget I asked."

Another step. He pressed against the other side of the desk. A meter of old wood separated them. "Someone's shooting at you? Where are you right now, Moja?"

"It was nothing. A poacher, probably." She bit her tongue at the admission.

"I don't understand why you went back to Kenya Wildlife Service. It's an odd place for the world's most brilliant software and games designer to end up."

"It's a perfect place for me."

"Sure. That's why someone's shooting at you. Come home, Moja. Please. Let's talk about this, face to—"

"I am home, Jack."

He rubbed his chin, closed his mouth, then nodded once. "Be careful, Moja."

"Do you know what's going on? Of course you do. You're the CEO. You know everything that happens."

"Not about the shooting."

"So you knew? About e-Trax, and the park?"

He shook his head. "No."

"Nothing at all?"

He hesitated. "There's nothing to discuss."

"You don't seem too sure about that."

He shrugged. "You know how complicated things can get."

"No. I think they're pretty straightforward."

"That's always been your problem. You think everything is so clean and easy. Always clear cut. But that's not reality, Moja. It never has been."

"Educate me."

"It's way above your pay grade. Especially now."

"So you *do* know something. What are you going to do with whatever it is?"

He looked at his hands, then tapped on the desk.

"Nothing," Moja spat. "Isn't that right, Jack? Don't want to appear paranoid, do you?"

"That's not fair."

"Neither is losing my job. My *life*."

He shook his head, rapped his knuckles on the desk, then backed up a step. "Let's meet. Offline. Where we can talk. I mean, *really* talk."

"We've talked enough. Goodbye, Jack."

She cut the connection, but not before she saw his mask dissolve to give her a glimpse of his despair.

Chapter Twenty-Eight

NUMBER of national parks in Kenya: Twenty-four.

The sentence glowed from the screen like an accusation.

"It's not possible," Jamaal said for at least the third time, still staring at the photo of the Kenya Wildlife Service map. Or more specifically, at the twenty-fourth green blotch disfiguring the otherwise perfectly acceptable map. "How could no one else have found this version of the map?"

"Searching," Sarah said. "Others have found this photo."

"Let me guess."

"Okay."

"Eco-War Now?"

"Yes, as well as Green Defense Fund, Eco-Kids …" Sarah listed several other environmental Places, but Jamaal wasn't listening.

Twenty-three national parks were located at appropriate distances from any possible deposit of Lucy. But the twenty-fourth? The youngest, the one the relevant authorities hadn't bothered to register in a digital map with a signature stamp and location beacons? That park — a rainforest with elephants! — occupied the same space as the near-surface Lucy deposit.

Which of course was impossible ... e-Trax had made it abundantly clear the exciting new mining project would occur on designated wasteland. And after the mining was finished, the wasteland would be transformed into a beautiful new ecosystem. A win-win. That's what their CEO had said. Everyone was a winner with this project, and that was a fact.

Except the twenty-fourth green blotch on the aberrant map suggested an alternative fact, destroying any hope of that extra, year-end bonus.

"It can't be," Jamaal muttered. "Please let it be a mistake. Or I picked up on one of those green neck, fake news maps. That's possible, right?"

"Anonymous search will soon time out," Sarah said. "Repeat request."

"What are the environmental Places doing with the map photo?"

"They're sharing it with each other."

"Yeah, 'cause that's gonna help them. Why not with anyone else?"

"They can only share with Places in which they are members."

Bing

Without thinking, he tapped on his forearm.

The ugly head of his cyborg nemesis popped into view. It said, "Message from Crazy Eyed Cyborg: Can't wait to smear you across the battlefield like the condiment you are, Jam Boy. See you in Hell's Fury!"

The cyborg's hand appeared and made a rude gesture

with its bladed fingers. Then the message exploded in a shower of blood-red drops.

"Nice, except jam's not a condiment!"

"Would you like me to save the anonymous search results, Jamaal?"

"Yeah, sure."

"Please repeat. Would you like to—"

"Yes. Save the search results."

"Saving search results."

"Can you do it quietly?" Jamaal rubbed his temples.

"Shall I turn on silent mode?"

"You can turn on shut up mode."

"Please clarify the request."

"Fog it." He logged out of his office and appeared under his welcome arch.

Prime Placer and Abe had been right.

"Who cares?" He glared at his menu. "That country's halfway around the world. The benefits of Lucy outweigh the loss of one small, insignificant, obscure, unknown national park. Right?"

"Would you like me to conduct a search?"

"No. Unless you want to search for my mind, because I think I lost it."

"Opening search request. Search for—"

"Cancel search. You'd think they would've programmed Placers to understand sarcasm."

"Sarcasm. The use of irony to mock or convey contempt."

"Yeah. That sounds about right."

Jamaal's limbs and head were heavy and weak, drained by the search even though his body was sagging in a comfortable chair. His eyes burned. He knew his brain couldn't *literally* explode, but it felt like it was one search away from doing just that.

He glanced up at the top section of his archway. *Here For Truth.* The words carved deep silver lines into the stone.

He'd always thought of the statement as a promise. Truth was inside hAPPn, as abundant and obvious as blood and gore in Hell's Fury.

Sure, there were conspiracies. Half-baked notions. Ignorance. Prejudice. Hate. Stupidity. All the deficiencies of human society. But also all its greatness. Creativity. Compassion. Bravery. Facts. Statistics. Scientific studies. Glimpses of reality. Truth.

A search within hAPPn should produce the same truth everywhere and for everyone, regardless of what Places a member had joined. Truth was one, wasn't it?

No longer a promise, the silver words looked like a mocking question, taunting him.

Here for truth? Ha-ha, sucker!

Prime Placer's words tickled his memory. *Search for truth.*

Jamaal wiped his face. His skin was cold, clammy. "Placer, open search. What was the original statement on the welcome arch of every hAPPn member?"

"Opening search."

Seconds ticked by.

More seconds.

Then an entire minute.

The anonymous search had been faster.

"Sarah?"

"Opening search."

Jamaal glanced around, even though there wasn't much to see in the welcome arch. Just his floating menu, a circular pedestal upon which his avatar stood, and the large archway.

"Sarah, respond."

Silence.

"Great. I broke my Placer. Who does that?"

"Opening search. How to break a Placer. Results. Placers cannot be broken, although they can be infected by a virus. To avoid this, hAPPening recommends that members do not open any attachments from unknown sources."

"Sarah, what about my previous request?"

"Loading anonymous search results."

"No. Placer, what was the original statement on the welcome arch?"

"Arch. A curved, symmetrical structure spanning an opening, and—"

"Cancel search." He glared at the arch. *Here For Truth.* Was he, though?

Or was he here for the convenient, perceived truth his Places fed him?

"Log off."

"Logging off."

In the cool basement of his mother's home, Jamaal yanked off the Shaids and stared at his screen. A 2D version of his welcome arch filled the view, waiting for him to return. Words in red neon occasionally flashed across his arch.

Is life hAPPning without you?

He picked up his Doodad, scanning over the long list of notifications. Some from his Places. Updates, headlines from the news streams. A reminder about the next session of Hell's Fury.

Ms. Chan wanted to know if he'd finished his analysis of the recent core samples.

Mama-i asked what he wanted for dinner.

Abe had shared a few memes.

The rock troll marched across the bottom of the screen, holding aloft a *do not disturb* placard. A protest of one, a vain attempt to protect his endangered work time.

Jamaal watched the rock troll march back and forth. Its little arms and legs pumped tirelessly, never questioning its limited, tightly programed existence.

"Of course not. It's a piece of software."

Leaving the rock troll to its work, Jamaal decided to work offline. He downloaded the geological report he was preparing, and spent the next few hours mechanically going through it. Editing and cleaning it up. Inserting charts to impress Ms. Chan.

But the entire time he kept wondering: *here for truth, or search for it?*

Chapter Twenty-Nine

I'D HATE to lose our newest Chief...

Jack's words followed Eva as she logged out and slid her Shaids off. She rubbed at her temples, the bridge of her nose, the back of her neck. Everything hurt, as if she'd been doing physical acrobatics rather than mental ones.

It doesn't mean anything.

He was just concerned about her. The last Chief had burned out, a workaholic to the end. The resulting health issues had forced his early retirement. Jack was simply looking out for—

"For me?" Eva scoffed. "Since when does Jack look out for anyone but himself?"

Harsh words, but there was truth to them. Jack was world-class at his job, one of the best. Surprisingly skillful at motivating his staff and getting the press to believe in miracles. He listened to employee feedback, and gave his workers whatever they needed to do their very best work.

But Eva was under no illusions. At the end of the day, if there was a choice to make, Jack would be the first one in the lifeboat.

You take care, Eva. You're working too hard.

It took time to recruit a Chief, and she was perfectly suited for the role. Same for at least a dozen other people, including Marsha. Replacing her would lead to a slight drop in productivity. Hardly the end of hAPPening. Eva couldn't remember Jack ever making that comment to anyone before.

I'd hate to lose our newest Chief…

A threat? A warning?

"What have you gotten yourself into?" she murmured, still talking to herself as she spun in her chair and looked out at the night view.

It was long past sunset, but she could still recall the intense colors blushing across the skyline, reflected perfectly against the still waters. A beautiful view. But at what cost?

Rather than disturb Theo, she curled up on the two-seater, dragged a blanket over her head, and slept.

Dreams twisted around memory. She was back at Database, doing searches for Eva Taylor.

"No results," her Placer said.

"What do you mean, no results?"

"Eva Taylor doesn't exist. There is no member called Eva Taylor."

"I'm right here. Perform search. Eva Taylor."

"There's no—"

Something gripped her shoulder, jolting her out of sleep. "Eva?"

Eva blinked into fuzzy shadows. She tugged off the blanket and stared at Theo. "What?"

He held up his hands. "You want to sleep more?"

"Did I even sleep?"

"You okay?"

The hAPPening

"Yes. Fine. What time is it?"

"That time when humans tend to ingest their first shot of calories. Otherwise known as breakfast."

"Right. That thing."

"That thing."

"Give me a minute."

She waited until Theo's footsteps retreated into silence before going to the bathroom and washing her face. She then checked her Doodad. The search results were there. She hadn't dreamed that part. Which meant Jack had told her to be careful.

Rossi and Theo were already arguing by the time she reached the kitchen.

"You know the rules, kiddo," Theo said, his tone light, the forehead knot tight. "No Shaids at the table. We should be fully present."

"For what?" Rossi said. "I need a break."

"Yes, you do. A break from an imaginary world."

Eva glanced at Theo. *Imaginary* world? hAPPn was as real as anything.

"Whatever," Rossi grumbled and tossed her Shaids next to her plate.

"Thank you."

"It's not imaginary, you know." Rossi pushed her plate away.

"It's not the real world, either. Is it, Eva?"

"And what's reality?" Eva asked.

"I'm not hungry," Rossi said. "And I have to study. I have a test in an hour."

Before Theo could say anything, Eva nodded. "Then off you go."

Rossi didn't wait for a second invitation to leave.

Theo lifted his mug, staring at the steam as if it held

the palette for his next creation. "It doesn't hurt her to sit with us for a few minutes."

"I think we could all use the break."

Silence. If they'd been in hAPPn, the digital mood cloud she'd given Theo last year for his birthday would've turned dark gray streaked with lightning bolts. She glanced up. No clouds. Only the ceiling.

"You worked late last night," he said.

"Something I had to finish."

"How'd it go?"

She shrugged. "Fine."

As fine as a stroll through hell, or through one of the versions found in some of the Christian Places. What if her suspicions were wrong, and she was mentally accusing Jack of a crime he hadn't committed? And chasing after an elderly man who wanted to be left alone to enjoy his retirement?

Worse, what if she was right?

Or rather, what if Prime Placer's suspicions were right? Those suspicions had now sunk into Eva's thoughts. A cancer devouring her peace of mind, molecule by molecule, cell by cell.

"I finished the commission," Theo offered.

Eva focused on Theo, on mirroring his attempt at a conversation. "The one with all the sunsets?"

He smiled. "The one with all the sunsets. They want me to digitalize it, as well."

"That's fantastic!"

"Of course. I listened to you. All of your many reminders about value addition."

She held up her mug. "Exactly. Limited digital editions multiply the value of the original by several fold—"

"Without the work," he finished. "Lesson noted, Chief."

The conversation shifted into more agreeable territory. But Eva couldn't stop wondering what she'd find if she visited Patel.

Chapter Thirty

A PRIVATE ISLAND.

"Of course," Eva murmured as she stared at the map. "Of course he lives on his own island."

By the end of the day, Eva knew she wanted answers enough to intrude on an old man's retirement. She'd retreated to her office after dinner and resumed her search for Indra Patel, using the results from Database.

Soon she had identified the retired investor, and his most likely location. A private island, a forty-minute boat ride off the coast. Close enough he could visit the mainland for groceries and an occasional night out. But far enough away to avoid all but the most determined visitor.

She magnified the map, staring at the brown blotch in the water. The unnamed island was small enough to stay invisible on most maps, and was listed under a company name. He'd gone to great lengths and expense to secure his privacy. What right did she have to invade it?

I'd hate to lose our newest Chief...

"Yeah, I think he needs a visitor," she said aloud.

She asked her Placer to book a FASTr to the port, and

a FASTr-H2O to take her on a two-hour sunset tour. She paused outside of Theo's workshop on her way out. The door was closed. Soft music wiggled out from around the edges. He was humming as he worked on another masterpiece.

She reached for the doorknob, then hesitated. He'd want to know where she was going, and why. But what if this was all a crazy game, set up by some delusional lunatic posing as Prime Placer? Theo would question her, and probably insist on coming. Or at least try to convince her to call Patel rather than visit him.

There were two problems with what was a reasonable suggestion. Unbelievably, Patel had no phone number. The guy had redefined *going offline*. He was still officially a member of hAPPn, although he hadn't accessed the app since retiring, so far as she could tell. So she doubted he'd see an invite to meet her, either.

But more importantly, Eva wanted to see him physically, to watch his reactions when she asked the questions. It was too easy to hide behind an avatar, to limit its reaction to dangerous questions.

She pulled back from the door, and quietly tiptoed out of the house.

Her FASTr-H2O was waiting at the dock of a sailing club. The speedboat's driver was a young man who looked like he spent more time in hAPPn than engaging in the physical world.

Great. I'm catching a ride with a fogger.

"We waitin' for anyone?" he asked.

"No. Just me."

"A romantic sunset tour, by yourself?"

"I'm in love with sunsets."

"Respect, lady. Okay, then. Welcome to Cruisin' Moonlight Tours. Blaire's the name. Romance's the game. Binoculars next to you. Life jacket under your seat. Blanket in that basket. It does get frosty out—"

"Blaire, let's skip the tour, shall we? I've sent you a location."

He checked his Doodad. "Huh. You sure you wanna go there?"

"Absolutely. Why?"

He shrugged, and pushed away from the dock. "Nothin' interesting there."

"I only wish that were true."

The boat cut through growing shadows, the engine growling to itself. Reds and oranges stained the distant water, a giant artist's careless brushstroke spilling across the landscape.

As they approached the private island, Eva reached for the binoculars and peered at their destination.

Blaire was right. Nothing about the forest-covered lump sparked interest. No lights. No building. No dock. Only a small strip of pebble-covered beach tucked under the trees' boughs. It looked about as inviting as the dark ocean swelling around them.

Did the old recluse live in a cave?

"You sure?" Blaire asked.

"Not even close."

"What?"

"Can you take me to the beach?"

"Sure, lady."

He steered them to the shore, cutting the engine a few meters away. The speedboat bobbed like a cork lost at sea, waiting for the current to push it onto land. Wind whispered unintelligible secrets in the silence. Small waves sloshed against the hull, and stones grumbled underneath.

"Now what?" Blaire asked.

Good question. Is anyone even home?

"Wait here," she said.

"Yup." He pulled out a set of Shaids and collapsed onto a bench.

Sunlight had leached from the sky, leaving stars like glitter tossed across a canvas by a petulant child.

Eva climbed the beach's slight slope using the light from her Doodad to avoid pieces of driftwood. Damp rocks twisted underfoot. She checked her current location, confirming she was on the correct island. No mistake, unless this whole trip was a big one. But if this was Indra Patel's island, the place lacked security.

She immediately corrected the thought: it lacked *visible* security. Surely someone wealthy enough to buy an island would have installed security systems, and hired at least one security officer to monitor them?

Yet there was no sign of any security.

Didn't he have any? Then again, how many people could really find him?

She had access to hAPPening's Database — arguably the most comprehensive in the world — and still had to dig through layers of junk to find him.

But this wasn't the middle of the ocean. It was close enough to the mainland for weekend sailors to drift by. At least a few might be curious to explore the forested island.

Eva reached the forest edge and saw the first indication of habitation: an electric fence.

Gotcha.

She muted her Doodad, not wanting to be interrupted by Theo demanding to know where she was, and why she'd gone onto the water at this time of day. Or Jack asking for an impromptu meeting to discuss another favor.

Starting at one end of the beach, she followed the fence, walking slowly, just in case armed guards were approaching her.

But there was nothing. No sound of anyone who might want to stop her. No indication anyone was around who cared about her presence.

At the other end of the beach was a gate hidden in the forest's shade. A motion-activated spotlight flashed on from a nearby tree. Underneath was a camera. A small red light blinked at Eva. As if the electric fence and locked gate weren't warning enough, a sign silently declared, *Private property. Trespassers will be prosecuted.*

And there he is.

She shook the gate. It rattled, but didn't open. A few metal bars separated her from the path on the other side. Solar-powered garden lights bubbled upward as the path ascended the forested slope.

Now what?

Bzzz.

The gate's locking mechanism snapped open.

Eva glanced up at the camera, at the red, blinking light. *Guess someone's home, after all.*

She followed the path to a clearing. The dimly lit cottage in the middle of the forested island looked nothing like the home of a wealthy man. More like something from a fairytale.

Hopefully not a Grimm's fairytale. Those stories tended to end up with someone being cooked in an oven.

The front door creaked open.

"Great, because that's not creepy," Eva whispered and leaned into the shadows.

A man's silhouette appeared in the doorway. They stared at each other across the clearing.

"Are you going to come in?" His voice was especially sharp in the silence. "We'll both catch a cold at this rate."

A cool, damp breeze brushed across Eva's neck, and the leaves shivered around her. Or was she shivering? She approached the cottage, keeping to the path lined with globules of light. Pebbles and dried leaves crunched with every step.

She stopped a few paces from the door and studied her host. She'd been expecting a stooped, frail man. Instead, Indra Patel stood upright without support, his hooked nose softened by his gentle smile and twinkling eyes.

She opened her mouth. Nothing. What did you say when you trespassed on a person's island, invading their expensive privacy?

"Eva Taylor, I presume?" Patel's subtle accent hinted at England rather than India.

It seemed the evening was destined for surprises. She nodded, unsure what to say.

"How delightful. Someone as bright as you was bound to find me eventually." Patel looked over her shoulder, frowning as he searched the night.

"My FASTr driver's at the beach. I came alone, if that's what you're looking for."

Patel startled, blinking at her as if he wasn't quite sure what she said. "Oh. Oh, no! That's not … it doesn't matter. In you come. Quick, now. You weren't followed, were you?"

"No. At least, I don't think so."

"Let's hope that's true, Eva Taylor, for both our sakes."

Chapter Thirty-One

MOJA LOGGED OFF, half-expecting to see Jack in the internet café's private room. She glanced around, but nothing was there apart from the chair and a small desk. She was still alone.

A small sound escaped her. Relief? Disappointment?
Definitely relief.
She scrubbed her hands down her face. Fatigue left grit in her eyes, dried out her skin. How many hours had she spent in hAPPn this week? It felt like too many. Once upon a time, she would've been happy to spend entire days lost in that world, only resurfacing to grab a quick bite and take a short nap. She'd been a borderline fogger. But now?

I've been gone too long. Too long, and not long enough.

She packed up her bag, reviewing the conversation with Jack.

Come back home. Let's talk. Offline.

Moja shoved her Shaids into the bag. Good thing hAPPening designed their products to withstand everything except being run over by a truck.

What had Jack wanted to tell her offline? Would it've

made any difference? Or was he trying to get in her head again?

Moja added her Doodad into the bag, then rubbed her shoulders. Good thing she didn't have a mood digitalizer, especially the version with a shoulder angel and devil pair. The way her mood was swinging back and forth, the shoulder duo would've gone buggy for sure.

The mood digitalizer had been a popular hit, probably still was. Except she wasn't in hAPPn. And the devil's voice was her own.

What if Jack meant it? What if he actually missed her, and wanted to see her in person, offline? In the physical world where you had to do things for yourself without a Placer to serve you, without avatar enhancements or responsiveness-dampening software.

She hurried out of the internet café, determined to abandon her doubts. She focused her thoughts on the people who might be able to help her, if she could convince them.

Patel had promised to contact her when he had more information. And Jamaal seemed to be coming around. But she really needed Eva on board. That woman was hard to read, almost as if she too had a subprogram to control her avatar's responsiveness. As if her avatar was as much a mask as Moja's was.

Moja exited onto Kenyatta Avenue, glancing around. She didn't expect the poacher, or whoever the thief was, to try shooting at her here. Best case scenario, he'd only shot at her because she'd threatened him.

But Moja couldn't afford any risks. She wandered around downtown Nairobi, ducking down side roads, entering small shopping complexes from one side, exiting through the other. Just in case anyone was following her.

You're being paranoid.

Her own thoughts reflected one of the last exchanges she'd had with Jack before his betrayal:

"You're being paranoid, Moja. You wanted hAPPn to be free. And now you want to impose limits?"

"Some limits protect us. Without them, it's a jungle."

"Survival of the fittest works for me."

"Who said you're the fittest?"

Jack had scoffed while Patel kept quiet. But his silence said enough. He sided with Jack on this one.

Better paranoid than dead, Moja thought as she zigzagged across the city. She took a FASTr part of the way, then caught another FASTr in the opposite direction, and finally an unmarked taxi she flagged down on a quieter street. It wasn't a guarantee she'd be left alone, but it would take a lot more resources than a tracer program to follow her now.

She walked the last several blocks before turning into a side alley where she opened a small door in the wall at the back of her grandmother's compound. For the umpteenth time, she was glad she'd made her anonymity a condition for working with Indra Patel, and eventually as the CEO for hAPPening.

No one apart from Patel and Jack had ever met her in person, knew her real name, where she was from, or even her gender. And that was working out very nicely for her. Especially since Nyanya refused to move out of the home that had been hers for several decades. Even when Moja had offered to buy her a larger house in one of the wealthier neighborhoods on the outskirts of Nairobi.

"Why do I want to move at my old age?" Nyanya grumbled each time Moja had made the offer. "Enough talk. Eat your food, girl."

Moja closed the metal door behind her and leaned against the rough stone wall. The garden was a miniature jungle, large trees and vines competing with each other for sunlight. Tucked in the middle of the chaos was a small, colonial-era house. Moja's second home. She'd stayed here while attending secondary school, only going back to Uhuru for the holidays.

It was like the jungle in one other sense — completely offline. Nyanya didn't believe in the internet, or rather didn't believe it should be a part of day-to-day life. She often referred to it as the devil's domain.

"Bah! Why do I want to waste my time in a make-believe world?" Nyanya had demanded when Moja once suggested she sign up for Wifi. "Devil's domain. That's what it is. You do your schoolwork like how we did it back in my day. Paper. Pencil—"

"Pencil?" Moja had laughed. "Nyanya, no one uses pencils anymore."

"And that's just one of the things wrong with the world these days."

Moja smiled, grateful her granny was a stubborn old woman. Moja's anonymous identity, combined with Nyanya's refusal to join the twenty-first century, conspired to create the perfect safe place.

Careful, she reminded herself. *You thought the national park was safe. But someone still found you there.*

Pushing away from the wall, Moja weaved her way around the trees and bushes, and quickly glided into the house.

"That you, Moja?" Nyanya's croaking voice welcomed her home.

"Either me, or Santa Claus."

"That supposed to be funny?" Nyanya hobbled into the kitchen. She'd recently bruised her hip while climbing a step ladder to reach plates on a high shelf. When Moja lectured her against climbing on anything, Nyanya retorted, "If I can't get my own cup and saucer, then shoot me and bury me quick."

"How's the hip?" Moja asked.

"Good enough. Where you been off to now?"

Moja shook her head. "No need to worry."

"Bah. That only makes me worry more. Now, girl, I don't mean to pry—"

"Which means you really do."

"Enough of that. You been here almost a week. And you haven't told me why you quit *another* good job. They not pay enough?"

"The pay was fine, Nyanya."

"Then what? Thought you liked workin' at the park."

Moja slouched at the kitchen table, studying the wooden surface. It looked almost as old as Patel's desk, but more family-aged than expensive antique. "Because I had to."

"How're you managin' without a job now?"

"That's the one thing I don't have to worry about."

"Girl, every human's got to worry about that. You gettin' stranger by the year, and that's not natural." Nyanya put on the kettle, still muttering to herself about her strange grandchild.

"I'm fine, Nyanya. Really."

When it came to savings, that was definitely the truth. She'd done well during her time at hAPPening. Of course, she'd sold off all her shares the day she quit. She didn't need to work anymore. She had to, or go crazy, but she didn't *need* the income.

"Come to think of it, you were a strange child. Always bringin' strays home. That time you brought a pregnant goat into the house. Remember what I told you then? About not gettin' pregnant?"

"You scarred me for life, Nyanya."

"Remember why?"

"So I could finish my education, start my career—"

"I'm regrettin' it now."

Moja smirked. There were two things Nyanya liked to nag her about: her lack of appetite, and her lack of children.

"And what about all those unopened letters? I see you avoidin' them." Nyanya turned a wagging finger her way. "You deal with them. They're clutterin' up my counter. You hear me, girl?"

Moja glanced at the kitchen counter. Next to the fruit bowl was a basket filled with unopened letters. All of them addressed to her. All of them from Jack.

He'd written to her after she left hAPPening. And he sent them to the only address he had for her, a post office box. Nyanya had been collecting them for nearly two years now.

Physical letters. Talk about strange.

Then again, she'd blocked his calls, listed his emails as spam, refused his messages. But a physical letter?

Moja glared at the letters. "I'll deal with them."

"You been sayin' that all week. Now you take them, and you deal with them *now*." Nyanya picked up the basket and tossed it onto the table. A few of the letters scattered across the surface.

"You're incorrigible," Moja said.

"And you're gonna get busy with those letters."

Moja scooped up the basket, marched to her small bedroom, and tossed the unopened letters into a drawer. She'd deal with them later.

First, she had a park to save.

Chapter Thirty-Two

"SEARCH FOR TRUTH. EASY. SEARCH FOR …" Jamaal stopped pacing the basement. "Where? I can't do an anonymous search every time. Not at twenty-five cybercoins a search."

Bing!

He ignored the message from Ms. Chan.

Good thing about being offline was a message couldn't materialize into a 3D projection. And what could she possibly want — he'd already sent her the report.

Jamaal glanced around the room, hoping for inspiration. The basement was one large area, a bed in one corner, his office set up in the other. A small kitchenette against the wall. Everything he needed, in one place. It couldn't get much better than—

"Focus. Focus on the map." He resumed pacing.

Prime Placer — and he was starting to believe the mysterious avatar really was Prime Placer — had told him to search for truth.

But what was he supposed to do with it? Become a whistleblower? Leak the information?

The truth would be more believable coming from inside e-Trax than from some mythological being with a handful of images of parrots and elephants.

It would also mean the end of everything except his room in the basement.

"What would Abe do?" he whispered, ignoring another *bing* from his Doodad. "He'd probably tell me to get a lawyer. Not that he'd believe … Or maybe he would."

He reached for his Doodad, then paused. "Maybe I need a new Place. New Place, fresh ideas, different information … But I like my Places."

He spun slowly on the spot, studying the walls. They were plastered with geology maps and photos of various rock formations. According to Abe, these pinups were the reason Jamaal would be single and living in his mother's basement forever.

"An environmental Place. That's what I need. The green necks …" He gulped. "They can't all be bad, and maybe they can help. They're good at this stuff. Protesting. Causing problems. Trying to protect endangered dung beetles and stuff. But …"

But Ms. Chan might find out. She was a member of Geo Rocks. She was able to see his profile updates, including a change in membership. If she bothered to look. Which she wouldn't. Would she? She didn't care about him enough to track his status.

Did she?

"Why me?" he wheezed. "Option B. Shoulda …"

He rubbed a hand over his heart, which felt like it was convulsing. He stared up at the ceiling, a white expanse of blank space.

It reminded him of the anonymous private room.

"Oh, I don't feel good," he moaned, slouching over.

Everyone in Geo Department was a member of Geo

Rocks. He'd never considered that before. Never thought of his co-workers' presence in one of his Places as intrusive or weird. When he'd signed the stack of digital documents attached to his contract, one of them gave e-Trax permission to enroll him as a member of Geo Rocks.

It hadn't seemed like a big deal at the time. e-Trax wanted all of their geologists to be members of a reputable, geology-related Place. No problem if his fellow members — including e-Trax's upper management — could see what other Places he joined. Of course they'd want to know if an employee was a member of a Place owned by the competition. And who wanted a geologist who hung out with green necks, those pesky bums who campaigned against the whole mining industry?

It had made perfect sense, especially when he was focused on the company shares he'd receive, plus the bonuses and benefits.

But now?

"It's not like she's watching everyone's status updates," he said. "I'm not that important." He started to sweat even though the basement was cool.

Search for truth.

Harder than it sounded.

He picked up his Doodad. The rock troll was still marching.

"Okay. Here's what we'll do. I have to have something to tell them in case they ask. Valid excuse. Why would a geologist sign up for an environmental Place? Why—"

His Doodad binged.

He shrieked and tossed the device up as if it had zapped him. Cursing under his breath, he almost dropped it as he fumbled to catch it.

Maybe it was Ms. Chan. She might be a mind reader.

"Don't be stupid," he said when he saw it was from Abe.

Lunch in the kitchen? Half an hour.

"Sure. Sounds good."

What could he tell Ms. Chan if she saw his membership change and asked what he was doing?

"I was worried about my mom," he said, wincing. "Sure, Jamaal. You're worried about your mom, so you joined an environmental Place to keep an eye on her? Yeah, that's not weird at all. She'll send you to a psychiatrist, for sure, if she doesn't fire you."

The Doodad binged again.

"Does this thing ever stop?" He tossed it onto his chair like dirty laundry into a basket. "Focus. That's what Ms. Chan always tells you. I joined an environmental Place to … practice my debate skills! Much better."

Except why did he need to practice debating? It wasn't like he was in Legal, and needed to practice his skills at defending the company against lawsuits. Or in PR, or in any position requiring him to engage with anyone important.

"How about it was a mistake? I meant to switch from Metals & Mud to Brown Gold, but my Placer misheard me and moved me to an environmental Place."

Dumb and dumber.

"Forget it." He collapsed into his chair, yanked on his Shaids. Red letters scrolled across his view.

Is life hAPPning without you?

He hesitated. He'd never thought about the question before, at least not deeply. What was the implication? Life without hAPPn wasn't happening?

"Doesn't matter. Focus. Log in," he ordered.

His welcome arch appeared before him. Reassuringly solid blocks made of the same ancient, hand-carved stone from Castle Caligula in Hell's Fury. A perfect replica of the castle's entrance, a regular reminder of his vow to find the Caligula Medallion, defeat his nemesis, and survive Hell's Fury.

He stared at the top of the archway, at words he'd assumed were a poetic statement, but were now clearly a lie. *Here For Truth.*

"Placer, request application to a new Place."

Sarah popped into view under the archway. "You are currently at your limit for the number of personal Places you can join."

"Cancel membership to Metals & Mud."

"Are you sure?"

"Not really, but yes. Go ahead."

"Canceling membership to Metals & Mud. Based on your current interests and activities in hAPPn, I recommend a Place that studies mineral deposits in sedimentary rock. Three such Places—"

"No, Sarah. Find me an environmental Place." He squeaked at the end, and almost canceled the request.

Sarah paused. Only a microsecond, but for an artificial intelligence that was the equivalent of several minutes in a human mind. "You are requesting membership in an environmental Place. Confirm."

Just say no, Jamaal thought. *Say no. Take the sedimentary rock Place. No red flags there. All cool. Just—*

"Are there any with a peaceful history? No riots. Or arrests. That kinda thing."

"Yes."

"Confirm. Request environmental Place."

The words slithered out like the treacherous snakes they were. Jamaal slapped a hand over his mouth as soon as he'd said them. It was too late. He'd committed to the move.

His personalized menu glowed bright silver as a new Place — Green Table — was added, replacing the recently deleted Metals & Mud.

"Congratulations, Jamaal. Your application for membership at Green Table has been accepted." Sarah's microsecond hesitation was now a thing of the past. She was all business. "Do you wish to visit your new Place?"

"Not really."

"Shall I allow notifications—"

"Yes, of course I want to visit my new Place," Jamaal blurted out.

"Opening—"

Bing!

A little devil appeared in front of him. Ms. Chan's mood digitalizer. The shoulder devil did a hectic little jig while holding up a card with an invite link to a meeting.

"Oh," Jamaal groaned. "I'm so fogged up."

"Do you wish to accept the invite from Ms. Chan?"

"How did she find out so fast?"

"Clarify the question."

"Me changing Places."

"As a co-member of Geo Rocks, Ms. Chan can see all your significant status updates in the news—"

"You ever heard of a hypothetical question?"

"Hypothetical. Based on—"

"I know what it is! I can't believe she pays attention to my updates."

"She might not. As your supervisor, she has the authority to request reports on your memberships."

"That's even worse."

"She can also sign up for alerts."

"Alerts."

"Alerts inform a supervisor if an employee changes

Places, or any activity the employer considers suspect or against the interests of the company."

"She can get those?"

"Yes, if she wishes. In addition, you set your updates for automatic release into the streams for any and all activity."

"Because I don't do much of anything, so I figured any news is cause for excitement."

"Shall I propose an alternate time for the meeting?"

"How about five minutes after never?"

"Please clarify request."

Jamaal sighed. "You definitely need a sarcasm upgrade. Accept the call."

"You need to be inside hAPPn in order to accept the call," Sarah said, unfazed by his looming disaster.

"Enter private office."

A second after Jamaal landed in his online chair, Ms. Chan appeared in front of him. The angel and the devil on her shoulders were both studying him with matching looks of disappointment. Rocky barked, then hid under his desk.

"Two times in one day," Jamaal said and tried for a confident chuckle. It came out sounding like a cat being strangled.

"Lucky you." Ms. Chan's shoulder devil rolled its eyes and stuck out its tongue.

"Sure is my lucky day."

"What're you working on, Mr. Shirazi?"

"A report. Analysis. You know, same old, same old."

"Do tell."

"I'll send it to you by this evening so you can read it."

"I'm sure it'll be scintillating. What else is new, Mr. Shirazi?"

"Nothing ... much."

"I noticed you joined a new Place. Interesting choice."

"Really? Nothing interesting—"

"Green Table. You need a little bit of activism to spice up your life?"

"Green Table?" His voice squeaked. He forced a grin, hoping it didn't look like he felt, like he was about to throw up. "I … It's my mother. She's insane."

Ms. Chan's eyebrows rose.

"I mean … my *Placer*. My Placer needs a serious software update. I think she caught a virus or something. She must've misheard me. I wanted to join *Stone* Table."

"Stone Table." Ms. Chan's eyebrows almost disappeared into her hairline, matching her shoulder devil's incredulous expression.

"Yep. Stone Table. You know, where all the stoners hang out and talk about …" He mentally searched for a topic a group called Stone Table might discuss.

"Stones?" Ms. Chan suggested.

"Sure. Stones. I'll get right on it and correct that mistake. Because it was a mistake. *Big* one. Who'd wanna join a group called Green Table? So lame."

Jamaal waited for Ms. Chan to pop out of his office, go harass someone else. Pluck the wings off of defenseless baby birds. Whatever she did when she wasn't silently accusing him of treason.

Ms. Chan didn't move.

"Right. Fix that mistake. Placer?"

"Yes, Jamaal," Sarah said as she appeared next to Ms. Chan.

"I thought I joined Stone Table. Please remove my membership from that other Place. What was it? Green something …"

"Green Table," Sarah said.

"Right. That one. Not what I ordered."

"You wish to cancel your membership with—"

"Yes, Sarah. That's what I want to do. So please. Just cancel the membership. It was a mistake. And update your software while you're at it."

If Sarah had been human ... Jamaal thanked the internet gods she wasn't. He could imagine what a human PA would've said and done. At the very least, a snarky comment about his inability to make a decision.

"Canceling membership. Membership canceled. Will that be all, Jamaal?"

Ms. Chan smirked at him. "Yes, Jamaal. Will that be all?"

"Absolutely. That's it. Nothing more."

Ms. Chan and Sarah disappeared in unison.

"Log out," Jamaal whispered.

As soon as his welcome arch replaced his office walls, he pulled off his Shaids. His shirt stuck to his back, and he was pretty sure he was about to throw up.

Just in case, he grabbed the small garbage can next to his desk. He'd never used it before. All paper was online, and he ate in the kitchen. But his mom had insisted an office should have one, along with the stapler and a set of pens, none of which he used.

"Yay, Mama-i," Jamaal mumbled, staring at the bottom of the empty container.

Why had Ms. Chan reacted to his change in membership so fast? Sarah had mentioned something about creepy, intrusive alerts. Was that a thing? Supervisors monitoring their staff? Wasn't that against some human right or labor law or ...

"Maybe she just happened to be inside the Geo Rocks Place when my status update appeared."

He silently repeated the words, testing them for any trace of hope. It was possible, but it was late morning, and

Ms. Chan wasn't the slacker type. The only time she ever visited Geo Rocks was outside of work hours. So unless it was a huge coincidence, and not the result of a monitoring system tracking his every activity …

"Oh, I really hope it was a coincidence," Jamaal mumbled and hung his head between his knees.

It didn't help the stomach, but it allowed his sweaty back to dry.

He glanced at his Doodad. Lunch was a few minutes away, and he had no interest in going back online. Abe was in Legal. Maybe he had a few answers to the growing list of questions.

Top of the list: Was e-Trax really monitoring their employees? Did they know about his conversation with Prime Placer?

And most important: *how much trouble was he in?*

Chapter Thirty-Three

Indra Patel led Eva into a cozy study. Physical books lined one wall. A fire crackled in a large, stone fireplace. There wasn't a screen or Doodad or any indication of the modern world apart from a few table and floor lamps. A small brown-and-white dog gnawed at something.

"You're not scared of dogs, are you?" Patel asked. "Raj is friendly enough."

"I'm sure it's fine, thanks. Why did you ask if I've been followed?"

"People in our positions shouldn't be surprised if the competition becomes a bit too ... let's say *entrepreneurial*. I'd rather they not find me. Tea?" He indicated a tray on the low coffee table. Two cups.

"Were you expecting company? I'm sorry to interrupt—"

"No interruption. Not at all. When you rented your speedboat, you had to input likely destinations into the system. I receive an alert any time someone plans on boating near my home. Congratulations on your new position, by the way."

Eva sat on the edge of a plush armchair, and stared at the dog. The little beast growled at her until she looked away.

Patel held up a spoon. "Milk? Sugar?"

"Neither. Thanks."

"I suspect you'll need a cup or two. It's rather pleasant in summer. But it can get quite chilly at night. Don't you agree?"

"I suppose so."

"And there I go, rambling on about the weather. I'm sure you didn't come all this way for such nonsense. Drink up. You'll feel as right as rain in no time."

Patel sunk onto the sofa across from her, not looking like a man who'd received an unexpected — and possibly unwelcome — visitor. He scratched the mutt under its muzzle, smacked his lips, stirred his tea.

Eva wrapped both hands around her cup, her numb fingers burning in the sudden heat. The warm fire relaxed her shoulders as much as the tea and Patel's easy manners.

She glanced up, staring through the steam at Patel. He was wearing an embroidered housecoat. Maybe he'd been on his way to bed. Older people slept early, didn't they? She'd disturbed his evening routine. Yet he acted like her host, sipping his tea and humming contentedly.

"You're not upset I showed up out of the blue?"

"Not at all." He set his cup on a side table. "I don't receive many visitors these days."

"I suppose you wouldn't."

"By design. Raj and I are more than happy to be left alone. But occasionally, I do appreciate the rule breaker who makes it through walls of secrecy to find me."

"You don't have any security?" It came out as a question. She hastily added, "Apart from the electric fence and camera. I expected a guard or …"

Patel chuckled. "There's no need for that. No one's coming to bother me. Few people know I'm here. Who cares about a small cottage tucked away on a no-name island? Although lately I've been thinking of a change in scenery, or a security system. One of the two, possibly both."

"Why?"

He waved a hand, flicking her concern into the fire. "It's probably nothing. An old friend recently reached out, having stirred up the proverbial hornet's nest. Or a land mine. Yes, that might be a more appropriate metaphor. It's raised all sorts of issues."

"Is that why you asked if I was followed?"

"One reason, certainly. You know, maybe I should move back to the mainland. I seem more aware of my mortality these days. Morbid, I know. My asthma acts up at times. I left the big city for better air, but it seems even the trees are against me. Being out here, alone with a dog, might not be the best scenario for a man of advanced years and declining health. Wouldn't you agree?"

She hummed, not sure how they got to mortality so fast. She searched the room for a way to redirect the conversation. "I'm surprised you live in such a small place. I expected a mansion."

"This is sufficient. You know, Ms. Taylor, I came to this country as an IT worker. Do you know what the problem with that scenario is?"

"No."

"I needed a work visa. I was dependent on others to agree to my presence here. At one point, I was denied a renewal and had a handful of days to pack up my life and leave. I couldn't go to England for the same reason. No visa. And returning to Delhi was out of the question. My asthma doesn't agree with the pollution. Do you know what I learned?"

Eva shook her head.

"One way to be independent of others' approval is to be successful. *Very* successful. No one's going to kick you out of a country if you employ thousands of its citizens."

"So you were motivated by financial reward?"

Patel laughed softly. "Hardly. Financial success was a means to a greater end: the ability to explore the far reaches of technological innovation without worrying about displacement or pesky immigration officials. That has always been my goal. Not mansions or a downtown office with a view."

"Just a private island."

"For health reasons."

"I guess that makes sense."

Time tiptoed around the room, each second almost audible in the crackle of flames, the crunch of dog's teeth around whatever it was chewing. She expected Patel to interrogate her, but he seemed content to sit in silence, sipping his tea, and occasionally nodding at her.

"I really didn't mean to intrude—"

"My dear, not to worry," he said. "I'm quite happy you did. Truly, I am. But I suspect you have a question or two."

She set her cup down and pulled out her Doodad. "I do. What do you know of Prime Placer?"

Patel sighed, and smiled wistfully at the fire. "The question really is what *don't* I know. We were the founders of hAPPening, and the creators of hAPPn, you know."

"I did."

"Ah, yes. Prime Placer, Jack and I. Quite the trio, we were. Jack might not look the part now, but once upon a time, he was a fine programmer."

"I've heard the rumor."

"A five-star team. To create a world together!" He sighed again. "We were like gods. Then Jack left the design side of the business to become a politician. Because that's what his job is, really. You're going to become one, too, Ms. Taylor. Don't shudder like that. It's true. Prime Placer was always on a different path from us. The true idealist. I miss that. We don't have enough idealism in the world."

Eva thought of Rossi's heated lecture about their lack of environmental activism. "Oh, I don't think it's entirely dead, either."

"That's good to hear."

Eva nodded, trying to frame her next question. It felt like an accusation however she worded it. Instead, she tipped her head toward an ivory statue on the side table next to Patel's chair. "Interesting."

Patel picked it up. "Beautiful, isn't it?"

"To be honest, I've never seen a three-headed elephant outside of hAPPn."

He chuckled. "This isn't any ordinary three-headed elephant."

"I don't imagine any elephant that has three heads is."

"An excellent observation, Ms. Taylor. White elephants are considered good omens in Hinduism. This one represents the mount of the gods. It's also the king of all elephants. It's why Prime Placer selected the image for her personal stamp."

"Her?"

"Oh, my. I wasn't supposed to say that. But now it's done. The tiger's out of the bag, you might say. Yes, Prime Placer is a woman. Please keep that detail to yourself. She protects her privacy more fiercely than I do."

"Of course." But Eva wasn't thinking about privacy and gender. "And Jack?"

Patel chuckled and set the statue down on the side

table. "He's very much like a Jack Russell, you know." He snapped his fingers at the little white-and-brown dog wrestling with a rawhide bone. "They're a tough little breed, but willful. Very difficult to train. You have to keep them on a tight leash. Otherwise, they'll run amok and dig holes under the fences. Being on an island, I don't have to worry about that."

He reached down and scratched the dog behind its ears. The dog thumped its stubby tail in appreciation but didn't let go of the bone.

"We used to tease Jack a lot. But he was a good lad. Still is. Such a pity what happened between him and …" He shook his head and stared into his tea.

"Between who?"

"Him and Prime Placer. For a while, I had hopes for them. Yes, I know. An old man, meddling in the romantic interests of the young. It's genetic, though. My grandmother was a famous matchmaker in our town. She'd always say she had a ninety-eight percent success rate, and the two percent failures were drunkards or villains. I was her one failure who was neither. She gave up on me after my parents sent me to England."

First health. Now marriage. Eva smiled, nodded and watched the dog shake its head viciously. She marveled that its neck didn't snap.

"If you don't mind me saying, you look a little worn out," Patel said. "You need to take better care of yourself. Slow down a bit. I say this with only the best intentions. You must think of me as an uncle."

Eva met the old man's gaze. It was kindly, and she could imagine calling him Uncle Patel. "It's something Prime Placer told me. About a possible misuse of hAPPn."

"Huh. Yes, she always did have that concern."

The hAPPening

Eva's head jerked back. "Really? And what did you think of it?"

"Every technology has its vulnerabilities and potential for misuse. Coal plants fueled the world while polluting the air. Not that hAPPn is at the same level, of course. However ..."

He held up a knobby finger. The thick veins crisscrossed the top of his hand like worms pulsing through the earth. But his hand didn't shake. "The potential for abuse doesn't mean we don't go forward. We simply try to patch any possible holes."

She continued to stare at his hand. Firm. Not a trace of doubt in his voice, or in his gestures.

"The three of you talked about this before, then," she guessed.

"Oh, did we talk! And argued, and occasionally fought about it. I don't blame her. Not at all. We did our best to create the systems, policies, algorithms to prevent the worst abuse. But humans are humans, and someone will always find a loophole. That's why other humans must always be on the alert. Plugging those holes. Tightening the loops. The point is, we don't give up on technology because of a few malcontents."

His last sentence came out sharp, a hidden memory clinging to the end of each word.

"She wanted to close down hAPPn?"

He shrugged. "She wanted to create more limits. And we did, to a great extent. But it wasn't enough to satisfy her. That's ultimately why she left. Me, Jack, hAPPening. She left everything but the memory of a legend. And she was legendary. The most talented software developer I've ever met, and I've met a number of them. Financed more than a few."

The pause ballooned between them. The crackle of flames lapping at charred wood filled the bubble.

"That must've been difficult," Eva offered.

"What was?"

"Her departure. If she was so important—"

"We had systems in place to compensate."

Eva cleared her throat, turned on her Doodad, and pulled up the signature stamp she'd received from Prime Placer. "I was recently contacted by someone claiming to be Prime Placer."

Finally, Patel looked surprised. His gray eyebrows, bushy with age, crawled up his forehead like fat caterpillars. "My, my. Prime Placer? That's ... well, I'm impressed."

"This is the signature stamp. Would you be able to confirm if it's really her?"

"Of course." Patel pulled out a set of eyeglasses and took her Doodad. He studied the stamp, expanding it, contracting it, peering into the code. He then nodded and handed it back to her. "Oh, yes, Ms. Taylor. That is indeed hers. The three-headed white elephant? No one else has that in hAPPn. She made sure of it. And the detailing in the code ... Well, there is no mistaking her style."

Eva stared at the signature stamp, at the three-headed elephant waving its trunks at her. "I can't believe it."

"Belief is a powerful force, isn't it? We believe something is true, and it becomes true. Or we believe it's false, and its reality ceases to hold power over us. Belief is everything. Everyone has it. So what do you believe, Ms. Taylor?"

Eva glanced up at Patel. His eyes reflected his wide smile. "I believe I've taken enough of your time."

"Nonsense!" He clapped his hands and laughed. "I

find this conversation immensely enjoyable. Tell me more. What has my dear white elephant told you? How is she?"

Eva hesitated. "Fine. She's fine."

"Good to hear."

A piece of wood popped in the heat of the fire. The dog growled at it.

"Are you still in contact with Jack?" Eva asked.

"Not really."

"Do you trust him? I mean, to do the right thing?"

"In what context?"

"You're familiar with the Lucy find?"

"Ah, yes. EA-L029. The metal that will save us, or so the faithful would have us believe. Don't look so surprised. I'm retired, not braindead. I like to keep abreast of research and innovation, particularly when it promises a technological revolution."

"And Lucy will?"

"Undoubtedly."

"Jack asked me to drop info-posts without going through Advert, and without using e-Trax's advertising account. It feels wrong."

Patel laughed and tapped the small elephant statue. "That sounds like Jack. He always did think a little differently. Perhaps there's more to this dilemma than you've considered. I've known Jack for a number of years. He's not one to engage in dodgy behavior."

"I hope not. But what if the info-posts are misleading?"

"What if they're not? Perhaps the e-Trax information on EA-L029 has a basis in reality, albeit a slanted perspective."

Eva frowned. "Prime Placer believes the deposit's in a rainforest, not a wasteland."

"Problematic if true, but there are always sacrifices on the road to progress."

"You're saying it's justified?"

"Think of it another way. Air pollution accounts for more than seven million premature deaths every year. Let's say we knew of a device that could save those people. Would you use it?"

"Of course."

"At any cost?"

"I—"

"Do you have asthma?"

"No."

"I do. Air pollution makes it almost unbearable. But I'm lucky. I can afford the latest medicines. The best doctors. A private island away from city smog. Most sufferers cannot."

Eva sunk back in the chair, unable to look away from the intensity in Patel's eyes.

"Lucy seems to be the key to the next leap in energy generation. With it, we can create portable power stations to electrify a town. Imagine! Cheap, clean energy for everyone, without any air pollution. No more coal burning. We can also do away with the messy business of radioactive waste. Electric vehicles have long been limited by the price of the batteries. With Lucy, affordable batteries the size of an apricot can power a bus. No more diesel fumes."

Eva said nothing. How long had she been here? Would Blaire leave without her?

"Prime Placer is worried about one forest. I'm worried about one planet. Humanity can now completely eliminate the need for fossil fuels, for flooding valleys behind hydroelectric dams, for digging holes for spent nuclear fuel. Imagine the countless human and animal lives saved, the natural areas protected from oil drilling and spills. Perhaps sacrificing one forest might be justified, in the grand scheme of things."

"Sounds like you're a believer, then."

"Maybe I am."

"So you think we should go ahead with e-Trax's info-posts?"

Patel clapped his hands. "I might be the wrong person to ask, but yes. I've made my money by sparking technological revolutions. I see the costs *and* the benefits. Maybe it's wrong to hide the truth about the location, but I can appreciate why they might want to do it. To ignore the existence of one forest when there is an entire planet to save."

"I understand. Thank you, again."

"Of course. What will you do?"

"I … I'm not sure."

"Be careful, Ms. Taylor."

She blinked at him.

Patel chuckled. "I don't mean to be dramatic, but if what you say is true — and I have no reason to doubt you — some people won't be happy with your meddling. Watch your back."

Chapter Thirty-Four

ANOTHER DAY. Another private room in one of a string of nameless internet cafés.

But this time, Moja felt almost hopeful about her self-appointed mission. She reflected on her progress as she left the café. Patel still hadn't contacted her, but Jamaal and Eva were turning out to be helpful. Maybe even allies.

She didn't know if it was enough, but at least it was a start. Once she had enough evidence, she'd be able to recruit more powerful forces. Organizations that could take legal action against e-Trax, organize protests, have their members tie themselves to trees. Whatever it took.

Even the city's chaotic rhythm seemed to have settled down into a familiar pulse. The blaring horns were no longer quite so jarring.

She avoided meeting anyone's gaze in case she became ensnared in a conversation as she weaved around the informal stalls cluttering the sidewalks. Old books. Secondhand clothes. Newspapers with secondhand news reading like soap operas on repeat.

An ancient diesel bus careened around the corner,

belching thick gray smog. Moja coughed the contamination out of her lungs. A smaller bus — a minivan with seatbelts for ten but holding at least fifteen passengers — choked out another toxic cloud.

And this is why we need electric vehicles.

Electric vehicles, powered by new-generation batteries which required new-generation materials. Materials like the rare earth metal, Lucy. The most accessible deposit of which rested a few meters under the surface of her national park.

She frowned at the treacherous direction her thoughts had taken her. There were other Lucy deposits. Deep ones, more expensive to reach but none under a rainforest. Let e-Trax mine those, and leave her park alone.

Patel's warning whispered through the fumes: *Beware the binary thinking of the caveman brain.*

"The great curse of the modern age," he lectured her and Jack until they'd rolled their eyes and begged him to stop. But he never did. At least, not for long.

"Reality is like a diamond," he'd say.

"Expensive?" Jack had asked.

"Good for drilling through hard rock?" Moja had added, smirking at Patel's mock outrage.

"No, my thickheaded masterminds. It's multifaceted." He'd then grab whatever was at hand, usually the three-headed elephant statue. "From one angle, you see one facet, a two-dimensional plane. But swivel it around even slightly, like so. And see! A new angle reveals itself with another element of reality inscribed on its surface."

As he spoke, he turned the elephant so they could see the different details. "Only when you've identified all of the facets can you truly appreciate the complexity and multiplicity of truths inherent within its structure. Forget about yes or no, right or wrong, square or circle. All of them inhabit the same creation at the same time. Open your minds, my dimwitted, young geniuses."

Inevitably, the conversation ended when Jack got flip, or Moja excused herself to make another pot of tea. But Patel would always circle back, prodding, poking, pushing them to think wider, deeper, broader.

But sometimes wrong is just wrong, she thought.

A horn blared.

Moja jumped backward, barely avoiding the front end of another overpacked minivan. The driver didn't even look at her, while the young conductor smirked and shouted at her to pay attention.

He was right. She'd been wandering down the same road, keeping to a straight line, paying no mind to her surroundings. Usually, she zigged and zagged several times on her way to Nyanya's.

She glanced around, instinctively searching for anything that seemed out of place. For anyone who seemed more interested in her than they should be.

Something about a motorcycle caught her attention. It shouldn't have. Motorcycles were common in Nairobi. Traffic being the disaster that it was, more and more people chose to use one of the motorcycle taxis. They slalomed between cars at precarious speed, disregarding all traffic laws.

It took her a few moments to figure out what bothered her. The motorcycle wasn't speeding. It wasn't even cruising. It was rolling along at walking speed. Her speed.

The rider — a man — was wearing a black helmet with an opaque visor. She couldn't see his face. The lack of visibility and his unnaturally slow speed made her skin prickle.

A coincidence. He's looking for his next customer.

But Moja was barely convincing herself.

She rolled her shoulders and lengthened her stride, starting to zigzag and swerve, randomizing her pattern as much as her human brain could.

She ducked into a shopping center, losing sight of the motorcycle and the heavy traffic.

The tension in her shoulders faded with every new block. She was just about to wave down a taxi when a flicker of black made her glance to one side.

The motorcycle was back.

Rolling down the street.

Matching her speed.

Her heart stuttered, and she froze. Was this the shooter? Was he sent by whoever had created the tracer program?

Coincidence, she argued. *That's all it is. City center's a small piece of real estate. And look! The helmet. It isn't black. It's blue. It's just the stress. Keep breathing. It's okay.*

Her body didn't agree with her mind.

Moja was running across the street before she'd formulated a plan, dodging cars.

She dashed into a shop. Exited through the storeroom into a narrow alley. Sprinted down the alley. Leaped over a pile of stinking garbage. A rat squealed as she landed near it.

Keep running. Don't look back. Don't slow down.

A few blocks more, and she summoned a FASTr. She changed vehicles several times, zigzagging away from Nyanya's house before finally circling around the city and back.

She exited the vehicle several streets later, and jogged the rest of the way home, compulsively checking around her.

But there was no motorcycle trailing behind her. No thief clicking off the safety.

She staggered through the garden gate, and collapsed against the wall. Only then did Moja pay attention to herself. Her limbs were quivering, breath escaping her lips in heavy, rasping gasps.

Her mind twirled in a frenzy of thoughts.

It's okay, she reassured herself. *It's safe. It's—*

No one is safe anywhere.

She brushed her shoulders, almost expecting to find the angel and demon mood digitalizers. But those only existed in hAPPn, not outside in the physical world.

She waited until her breathing was steady, a soft huff of air in and out. She wiped a sleeve across her face, pushed away from the wall, and slowly approached the house.

Her gaze got snagged on something that shouldn't be there by the door. A pair of men's shoes.

"No," she wheezed. "Nyanya. Nyanya!"

She ran into the kitchen, her heart louder than her thoughts.

"'Bout time. What's all the fuss?"

Moja screeched, and spun around.

Nyanya stood in the doorway, her face puckered like a dehydrated apple.

Moja collapsed into a chair. "Nyanya, don't sneak up on me like that."

She snorted and waved her walking stick. "How can I sneak around with this? You goin' deaf?"

Moja clasped her hands together, willing them to stop quivering.

"You look a mess, girl. What's gotten into you?"

Moja shook her head. "It's fine. It's all ..." She stared at the tray on the kitchen table. Teapot. Three cups.

Nyanya nodded. "Clean up, girl. You got a visitor."

"I do?" Moja froze. "No one knows I'm here. Did you—"

"Me, I'm old, but not stupid. I don't tell just anyone."

"But you told someone."

"Bah. It's good to have guests."

"Who …" Moja stopped. Only two people knew she was in Kenya, and one of them would never make the long trip. The other had until now respected her privacy, apart from a flurry of letters.

So what had changed?

"Jack," she huffed, using his name like a curse.

"Now, you go easy on that boy," Nyanya warned.

But Moja was already striding into the living room. Fuming. Ready to rain verbal fire and brimstone.

Jack was sitting on the edge of a plush chair. He jumped up, eyes wide, dark shadows underneath them. "Moja—"

"Really, Jack?"

"I'm sorry. I—"

"I told you I never wanted to see you again. Last time I checked, *never* doesn't have an expiry date. Now does it?"

"No, but—"

"How did you find me?"

"I knew you were working in Uhuru. Bandwidth is terrible there, by the way. And portable boosters don't quite cut it." He chuckled. The laugh withered under her glare. "Ojil told me you were in Nairobi, and gave me Nyanya's address."

"Of course he did. Meddling old fool. And you just had to come here, into my home."

"Nice place, by the way."

"How did you know I was in Uhuru?"

"I … um …"

"*You* created the tracer."

"What ... no! I know how much that park means to you, so I figured you'd head there. I made a few calls, and—"

"It doesn't matter. Why did you bother? Never mind. Not interested. You can go now."

"Manners, girl!" Nyanya shouted from the kitchen.

"Stop eavesdropping! Fine. Please can you leave, right now?"

Jack held up his hands. "Hear me out."

"Why should I? What's the emergency this time? Couldn't figure out how to screw over someone else?"

He had the decency to flinch, but he didn't back down. "Nothing like that. Or maybe worse."

"Now, now, children," Nyanya said as she hobbled into the living room. "Who's gonna help me with the tea tray?"

Jack hurried into the kitchen. He avoided Moja's gaze, so she directed her glare at Nyanya. "I can't believe you let him in the house."

She shrugged. "You expect me to leave the boy on the roadside?"

"Ideally, yes."

"Bah. He came a long way to see you. Least we can do is give him tea."

Jack appeared in the doorway, tea tray in hand. He glanced to Nyanya on one side, then at Moja. "Where—"

"On the coffee table, Jack," Moja said. "Where do you think?"

"Moja," Nyanya said, clucking her tongue. "This is what happens when you raise a girl in the jungle. Wilder than the wildlife. Named after an elephant. Very fitting."

Moja was tempted to retreat. Let Nyanya entertain Jack, then send him on his way. She could stay in her room.

But curiosity tickled a corner of her mind. Jack wasn't

the type to chase after people. He'd respected her privacy all this time. And now he was here.

"Why? Why now?" Moja selected a high-back chair. The stiffness of the backrest matched the stiffness in her shoulders. It was also the tallest chair in the room, and she made sure Jack felt it.

"Like I said, some things need to be said face-to-face."

Moja opened her mouth, but Nyanya interjected. "Isn't this nice? The two of you, together. Tea, young man?"

"No, thanks."

"Sugar? Milk? Both, of course."

Jack reluctantly took the cup. If Moja hadn't been so furious, she would've laughed. There was no getting around Nyanya once she'd decided on something. But that didn't mean Moja wasn't mad at her.

"Moja, it's lovely havin' visitors, isn't it?" Nyanya slid a cup toward Moja.

"Positively brilliant."

"Me and Jack, we've only met on a video call. Remember, Moja? You took me to a funny cafe that didn't serve tea. What kinda cafe doesn't have tea?"

"The internet kind."

"Never could understand why you young people like that internet stuff so much. This is much better, sittin' around a table together. Cookie?" She held up a plate. Store-bought. Because Nyanya couldn't bake to save her life.

"Ah, well …" Jack glanced between the women.

Moja smirked. "Say yes."

"I'd love one." He picked up a cookie.

Moja slurped loudly at her tea. She glared at a point over Jack's head. She was still trying to decide if she should push away the curiosity and ignore his presence, or interrogate him on it.

"She never read any of your letters." Nyanya nodded at Jack. "I think it's lovely. Writin' a letter on paper. Mailin' it. Very classy. Now me, I'd have read them all and stuck them in an album. But her?" She hissed. "My granddaughter prefers elephants to people. You know that about her, right?"

"Yes, I—"

Moja slammed her cup on the saucer. "Why are you here, Jack?"

He cleared his throat. "You really didn't read my letters?"

"Why would I?"

"But you kept them."

"No. My granny did. I'd have used them for fire starter."

He nodded, staring at the coffee table, at the plate of store-bought cookies.

"And she quit another job," Nyanya added to her list of complaints. "Can't keep a job. Can't keep a man. How am I gonna get great-grandchildren at this rate? Bah! If your father could see this."

She clucked and hummed, frowning at Moja as if the lack of offspring was an epic disaster. "You, you're young, but not *that* young. You keep waitin', and before you know it." She made a disgusted noise, then smiled at Jack. "Nice trip here?"

"Not bad. A bit of jet lag—"

"So save yourself the lack of sleep and go back."

"Raised with the wild animals," Nyanya muttered. "Maybe raised *by* them."

"Thing is, I'm not sure I can," Jack said, finally meeting Moja's gaze.

"Sure, you can. I'll call you a FASTr. Take you straight

to the airport. There should be an evening flight back to the US."

Jack shook his head.

"Or are you here to apologize?"

Jack sat back in his chair, his expression tightening.

"You know, say sorry."

"I—"

"You're not sure where to start, right?"

"Girl—"

"Not now, Nyanya. How about this, Jack. You can apologize for kicking me off the board of my own company. Or maybe that's too much for you? We'll start small. You can explain to me why you're allowing e-Trax to drop info-posts with an altered map of Kenya."

"I know, that's—"

"Or maybe you can apologize for showing up here uninvited, then leave."

"I get it. You're mad—"

"No, not mad. That would imply I care enough about what you have to say."

"Oh, she's good and mad," Nyanya said.

"It wasn't my decision to kick you off the board."

"You didn't protest."

"We can't all disappear when things get tough," he snapped, leaning forward. "And maybe you should read my letters instead of sticking your head in the sand."

"Oh, that's rich. I'm sticking my head in the sand? I'm out here in the real world, Jack. Where are you?"

"Right here with you. Trying to explain."

"You're doing a pretty crappy job. Why don't you tell me what was in the letters? Executive summary version, please. Go ahead. Blow my mind, shake my world. Come on, Jack."

He hesitated, glanced at Nyanya, then at the floor. "It's better we discuss this in private."

"Oh, privacy," Nyanya said and nodded. "Me, I can leave—"

"You're staying." Moja stood. "Jack lost his right to a private meeting with me two years ago."

"Afraid of what I might say?"

She huffed. "There's nothing you can say that'll change what you did."

"You're right. But—"

"Great. We agree."

"Are you afraid of being alone with me? Of having to actually listen to the truth for once?"

"The truth? You want to know about truth, Jack?"

"I wanna know why you two are shoutin'," Nyanya said.

"Here's the truth. You're a backstabbing bastard. You show up uninvited. And it's time for you to leave."

"The manners of a warthog," Nyanya mumbled.

Jack stood, nodded at Nyanya, then marched to the door. Moja followed him to the front gate and opened it, waiting for him to walk through.

Before she could slam it, he leaned in, laid a hand on her arm, and said, "Read my letters. I'll be at the Kapinski for the next two days. Read them, and after that, if you're still determined to hate me, I'll accept it."

"Then get ready to accept it." Moja kicked the gate shut.

"You want the truth, don't you? Read all of them."

"I think I've had enough truth out of you to last me …" Her voice crackled, and she ground the end of her sentence into muted syllables. What was the point?

"Call me." He banged on the gate. "At the Kapinski. Please, Moja. The letters. They'll explain everything."

"Your actions have explained enough."

She sagged against the gate, waiting until a door slammed, and the FASTr drove away.

Then she sagged to the ground, covered her face, and wept herself empty.

Chapter Thirty-Five

JAMAAL WAITED until Mama-i had retreated to the kitchen before saying anything. "I think they're on to me," he mumbled.

Abe held up a kebab. "I did warn you about the possibility of bed lice when—"

"Not that. *Them*."

"Who's on to you, and about what?"

Jamaal glanced over Abe's shoulder at the kitchen. His mom was pulling more kebabs from the oven. "Them. My supervisor. Possibly our CEO. Maybe even higher. Who knows? I think they have me under surveillance."

Abe set down his fork, tugged at his tie, and sighed. "I suspected this day would come."

"Which day?"

"The day you officially lost your mind. Jamaal, I love you like a cousin—"

"Because you *are* my cousin."

"Precisely. Why would anyone be interested in anything you do or say?"

"Um, thanks?"

"Unless …"

"Unless what, Abe?"

"Have you been visiting porn sites at work?"

"Which sites?" Mama-i asked as she heaved a large platter onto the table.

"Nothing," Jamaal said.

"I think your son's into porn, auntie."

"I am *not*. It's just … I tried to join Green Table."

"Is that code for porn?" Mama-i asked. "It's okay. I'll still love you as my son—"

"Because I am."

"But if it's porn—"

"Mama-i! No. It's not porn. Abe, keep quiet."

Abe smirked. "I'm a lawyer. I talk for a living. Why would you sign up to an environmental Place?"

"You joined an environmental Place?" Mama-i clapped her hands as she returned to the kitchen. "Good for you. At least it's not porn."

Jamaal lowered his voice. "It was a mistake. I canceled the membership right after I joined."

"Again, why?"

"I just told you. It was a mistake."

"I mean why did you join in the first place?"

"To get feedback on something I found."

"So did you?"

"No, I didn't have time."

"Then why did you cancel it?"

"Because Ms. Chan called me about it."

Abe whistled. "I see. You should've thought of that before, or consulted me. The way you behave sometimes … It's almost as if you forget you have a lawyer in the family."

"Why would I—"

"A coworker of mine lost her job for poking around in undesirable Places."

"Why didn't you tell me this before?"

Abe leaned forward. "I didn't think you'd be foolish enough to join an environmental Place. You know how geologists are about green necks."

"I knew this was a bad idea. Such a bad idea." Jamaal pushed his plate away.

"I do concur. Ms. Chan is probably cyber-stalking you as we speak."

"I knew I should've ignored it."

"Ignored what?" Abe asked.

"Nothing."

"You gave her a believable excuse for your momentary lapse in judgment, I assume?"

Jamaal nodded, staring at his untouched food. His stomach clenched at the thought of eating.

"Then don't worry about it. My coworker was reckless, not to mention the Place she selected was so off the grid as to be in an alternate dimension. Who signs up for …" He hesitated and glanced at the kitchen doorway. "You get the picture. It'll be fine."

"What will?" Mama-i asked as she sat.

"Your son," Abe said. "He doesn't need a lobotomy after all."

The sounds of munching and cutlery clinking filled the silence. Jamaal could feel Mama-i watching him, probably preparing her interrogation about his loss of appetite. He poked at the food, moved it around, took a few bites.

"If you want my legal opinion—" Abe said.

"Not really."

"What were you hoping to find?"

"You started this, Abe," Jamaal said and held up his

fork. "With your conspiracy theories about maps and national parks."

Abe smiled. "You found something, didn't you?"

"More like something found me."

"So you *do* possess a smidgen of curiosity, after all. That's a relief. I always wondered how we could be related, with you as dull as a butter knife."

"Thanks."

"What are you planning to do next?"

"As little as possible."

"Typical. What did you find?"

Jamaal glanced at his Doodad. "Turn them off."

"That's code for …?"

"Turn off your devices."

"I see. Done. Now—"

"What if I told you I met Prime Placer?"

Abe laced his fingers together, and stared at Jamaal. Studied him for a moment. "You're quite serious?"

"Unfortunately."

"Did you check the signature stamp?"

"Not visible. That shouldn't be possible, should it?"

Abe shook his head. "It's illegal. Are you certain—"

"I may lack curiosity, but I'm not blind or stupid. I know how to check for a stamp. It was blurred over."

Abe rested his chin on his clasped hands, and stared at the large bowl of stew. Jamaal glanced at Mama-i. She was also staring at the bowl.

"Is it so impossible?" She reached for the ladle and poured stew for both of them. "Why is it so difficult to believe?"

"That little thing called the law, auntie."

Jamaal frowned at Abe. "I think it's a trap."

"Now who's spouting off conspiracy theories," Abe said. "What if it really is Prime Placer?"

"If it reached out to you, maybe there's a reason," Mama-i said.

"Yeah, to get fired, then sued, maybe thrown into jail."

"What did they want?" Abe leaned forward, his eyes glittering.

Jamaal shrugged. "Same as you. They were asking about the park, and the Lucy deposit, and how maybe things weren't what they seemed. Turns out there's a rainforest over the deposit."

Abe smacked both hands on the table. "I knew it."

"Yeah, congratulations."

"What else?"

Jamaal shook his head and focused on eating. Blindness versus truth, Prime Placer had said. The problem was, he no longer had a choice. Now he could see things he hadn't before, and that disturbed him. He couldn't go back to *not* seeing them. The anonymous search had destroyed any possibility Prime Placer had lied to him.

But now what?

"How much trouble could we get into?" he asked softly.

Abe huffed a laugh. "That depends. How much digging do you plan on doing? As the lawyer in the family, I'd recommend extreme caution *and* discretion. Digging up dirt tends to reveal skeletons and other messy, decomposing items."

"Noted. I'm not sure. Proof that e-Trax doesn't know where its claim really is, maybe?"

"What if it does know?"

Jamaal opened his mouth. Nothing came out.

"I see," Abe said. "Congrats on your well-thought-out plan."

"I didn't think I'd get this far."

"Clearly not. Imagine we proceed with your *plan*, and

find evidence against e-Trax. What will we do with it? People stay in their Places. They only read or watch information from co-members or media sources that have regular access to their Places. For argument's sake, let's say you uncover a nefarious plot to deceive the world—"

Jamaal groaned and held his head.

"And in the process of sharing this plot, you ruin our lives and obliterate our professional options. Why would anyone really care?"

Jamaal rubbed his face and wished he was back in Hell's Fury battling with Crazy Eyed Cyborg while wearing his S-Suit. Because that would be way less painful than this conversation. "Why did you ever tell me about the map and the article?"

Abe shrugged. "I wanted to see your reaction."

"Seriously?"

"And I wanted to make sure my employer was on legally sound footing, so I can defend them if they aren't. As for blowing the whistle? I know it sounds heroic, but are you sure that's what you want to do?"

"I didn't say anything about whistles."

"Why else do you continue on your quest for truth?"

Jamaal gulped. Both Mama-i and Abe were staring at him, as if they actually expected him to have an answer that made sense.

"Maybe it's nothing. Let's just focus on getting the information. Facts first. Decision later."

"Organized procrastination," Abe said. "I appreciate that. But let's be clear. The only reason I'm assisting you in this madcap misadventure is to make sure you don't land in prison. Or worse, land me in prison. Auntie, if anyone asks, you were in the kitchen this whole time."

"I was?"

"Absolutely. So what's the plan, my dear cousin?"

"How much access do you have to documents in Legal?" Jamaal asked.

Abe leaned back and brushed invisible particles off of his suit jacket. "You can't be serious."

"I think I may be. At least, I'm thinking about it. So?"

Abe chuckled. "You're either going to make us heroes, or get us arrested."

Chapter Thirty-Six

Eva GNAWED at the memory of Patel's answers as she jogged to the beach. His warning to watch her back twisted the shadows into menacing forms.

Jack, what have you got me into?

She opened the gate and the camera's red light blinked at her.

Stones clicked against each other under her hurried steps. Waves swished across the stony beach, and sloshed against the boat. Moonlight cast a silver glow over the water. Dark shapes lurched against the skyline, a scattering of islands like black pearls from a broken necklace.

Blaire was stretched out on the bench, no doubt too busy in hAPPn to care how long she'd been away. She opened her mouth to shout at him, but the words thickened in her throat, strangling the yelp that wanted to wiggle through.

She was not alone on the beach.

A new sound slid in between the waves and her steps. She glanced behind her. The fairy lights twinkled along the empty path. Nothing there.

She scanned the shore. Stones. A clump of seaweed waiting for the tide to sweep it into a cold embrace. Pieces of driftwood.

Bzzzz.

Bees at this time of night?

Eva rubbed an ear, turned slowly on the spot. A glimmer of light reflected off of silver. She squinted at the far end of the beach. Something was moving through the trees.

Patel's words surged around her.

You weren't followed, were you?

Lately I've been thinking of a security system ...

Be careful, Ms. Taylor ...

Watch your back.

"Blaire?"

But of course that wasn't him. He was in the speedboat, plugged into hAPPn, oblivious. She could die on the beach, a few meters away, and he wouldn't notice until his battery died.

"Not happening," she whispered, but the words did nothing to motivate her frozen limbs.

Leaves rustled. The silver globe edged into view, hovering in a slice of moonlight. It was a security drone. But Patel didn't have a security system. He said he was *thinking* of getting one.

A green light blinked from the contraption underneath the drone. Camera or gun?

Eva stumbled down the beach. It seemed larger. Had the tide receded? Why was there a drone?

Some people won't be happy with your meddling.

"Blaire," Eva gasped.

Watch your back.

She glanced over her shoulder. The drone had cleared

the trees and descended to head level. It was following her. Green light blinking.

"Start the engine."

Her shoes splashed into the waves, summer's heat forgotten in the ocean's cold current.

Bzzzz.

"Blaire, you fogger!" she screamed, water sloshing up her legs. "Wake up!"

Be careful, Ms. Taylor.

Eva clambered into the boat, skidded to her knees, dug her nails into Blaire's arm.

"What the ... Lady, what?" he spluttered, yanked off his Shaids, rubbed his bleary eyes.

"Engine. Now."

"You finished here?"

"Go!"

"Okay." He slid into the driver's chair, muttering, "Crazy lady."

The engine coughed awake, startling the silence, sending the vessel scuttling toward the shadowy islands surrounding them. The speedboat puttered away from the beach.

Please be a camera, please be a camera. She glanced behind her. Whimpered involuntarily.

The drone was matching their speed.

It hovered a few feet above the water, the camera or whatever angling toward the boat. Green light blinking. Who used a drone to stalk an employee of a social media app? Jack? Danielle from e-Trax?

Eva huddled in the seat next to Blaire, searching for lights on the mainland. "Can't this thing go any faster?"

"Lady, it's built for romantic moonlight cruises. You know. Cruising around the bay. If you're cold, there's a blanket under the bench."

She twisted in her seat, peered over the back, keeping low. The drone was gone.

When they reached the club, Blaire helped her onto the dock. "Lady, you're still shaking."

"Low blood sugar."

"You need to get out more. Too much hAPPn ain't good for the nerves, you know?"

"I'll keep that in mind." She hurried down the dock, her shoulders tensing.

"Thanks for choosing Cruisin' Moonlight Tours," Blaire called after her. "Hope you enjoyed the cruise."

She only stopped shivering when she was safely tucked into the back seat of a FASTr. Patel had given her a lot to think about. Too bad that new information cowered in the shadow of the threat awaiting her at the beach. Someone had tried to intimidate her with a drone.

Had it been personal? Had that thing followed her to Indra Patel's island? Was he safe? He'd warned her. She'd thought the worst that could happen was being fired. She hadn't imagined the worst was actually being fired upon by a weapon-carrying drone.

Don't be dramatic. It was probably just a camera.

But who was behind that camera, and why? Drones were mindless, not sightless. Someone had been on the other end, guiding the drone to follow her.

She pulled out her Doodad — the screen was covered in notifications — with shaking hands. She left the device on mute, and focused on deep breaths.

Deep breaths, and *not* screaming. Her FASTr driver had close to a five-star rating, but she doubted he'd be able to concentrate if she melted into hysteria in the backseat. It'd be just her luck: he'd swerve into a tree, and then what? All she wanted was to get home, collapse on the living room sofa, and scream into a pillow.

She only made it as far as the front door. She slammed it shut, leaned against it, and slapped both hands over her mouth to throttle the horror.

"Rossi?" Theo called from upstairs.

Eva dragged her hands down her face, as if she could wipe away the shaking limbs, the frazzled nerves, Patel's soft voice warning her to be careful. If she'd been in hAPPn, she'd have reduced her avatar's responsiveness to twenty percent. It would've turned her avatar into nothing more than a human-looking robot, but no one would hear the terror trembling at the edge of her words.

You're not in hAPPn. And Theo can't know. Not yet. I have to get them out of here.

But where? And what excuse could she give them? A drone chased her off a beach? Maybe some kid was playing around with their birthday present, having fun at her expense. Or maybe Patel had already purchased a security system, and—

"Eva, is that you?" Bare feet slapped against the hardwood floors, pausing at the top of the stairs. Theo flicked on the light, then *slap, slap, slap*. He hurried down.

Her eyes squinted against the brightness, grateful for the sudden change. She exhaled the chaos in her stomach and found a smile as Theo came into view.

"Is Rossi with you?" Theo asked.

Eva rubbed her eyes. Her lids scratched against her eyeballs. Granules of salt and sweat pressed into her skin. "No. Why?"

"She's not here."

His words stretched between them, each syllable distorted by the waves created from the evening's events. Eva dropped her hands, feeling nothing at the words, as if she'd somehow dimmed her responsiveness to outside stimuli. "Who isn't here?"

Theo frowned, approaching her slowly as if she were a wild creature he'd found trapped in the house. "Rossi. I've looked everywhere. She's not answering my calls, or returning my messages. I thought she went out with you."

What if the drone hadn't been a kid's prank, or Patel's newest acquisition, recently let out of the box to roam the island? What if it had followed her there, and another one had found Rossi?

Eva bit her knuckles and stared at a memory.

Be careful, Ms. Taylor. Watch your back.

"What's going on?" Theo asked.

A reasonable question, but it struck her as funny, almost ridiculous. She hiccuped a laugh, followed by another. Then she started sobbing.

"Eva."

She slapped her cheek, then the other. "Have you checked her Places?"

"You think they're having an offline event at this time of night?"

Eva glanced at her Doodad and unmuted it. Half of the notifications were from Theo. "It's not that late."

"It's late for a twelve-year-old on a school night." Theo stared at Eva as if unsure of which was the bigger emergency: Rossi's disappearance, or his wife's strange behavior.

She nodded, straightened up. *Focus.* "Did you check home security footage?"

"She left an hour ago. See?" He showed her a still of the footage. Rossi in her orange hoodie and black jeans, opening the back door.

"Placer, log into Green Teens."

"I already checked."

"Doesn't hurt."

He started pacing.

The hAPPening

She performed a quick scan on the most recent posts and activities. Nothing, except for an online collage about beautiful spaces the members wanted to protect. Eco-Kids was doing a fundraiser to plant more trees in a nearby park. No mention of any offline event.

Theo stopped in front of her. "I called her classmates. Nothing."

The drone, Patel's warnings, all sunk into a fresh and visceral horror. Eva nearly stopped breathing.

Where was her daughter?

"Placer, read private messages to Rossi Taylor from members of Green Teens and Eco-Kids. Override privacy protocols."

Her Placer soundlessly pulled up recent messages Rossi had received from fellow members. Eva scanned through the subject lines.

Fundraising appeal — have you donated yet?
Collage color options.
Invade the space.
I love your dog!
Space is filling up.
Theme preferences, survey results.
Take the survey for favorite green spaces.
Fill the space—

"What space?" Theo interrupted her recitation of subject lines.

She scrolled up and opened one of the messages mentioning space. "You've got to be kidding," Eva said, handed Theo her Doodad, and collapsed against the front door.

"Eco Warrior? As in—"

"Read to the end," Eva said.

There was a moment when Theo said nothing. Just

stood next to her and read. Eva waited for him — *prayed* for him — to tell her she'd misread the message.

Instead, he asked, "How did a prominent leading member of Eco-War Now get into a Place designated for teenagers?"

"I don't know. It shouldn't be possible. The safeguards—"

"Cleary aren't working, Eva." He clicked on the video link.

A man in a full face mask appeared. "This is a call for action. It's time to invade the spaces of tree-chopping politicians and their capitalist cronies. Online protests are for the weak. They get ignored. We need real protests for real action. You want to make things happen? Thursday night, in front of City Conference Center. That's where life's happening."

"City Confer—"

"That's tonight." Theo was already reaching for his keys.

Robotically, Eva slid her Doodad into her pocket. "And Rossi confirmed she's attending."

Chapter Thirty-Seven

READ MY LETTERS. You want the truth, don't you? Read all of them. They'll explain everything.

Jack's words poked at Moja long after he'd left. Each one a jagged tooth chewing at her heart.

She remained seated by the gate until the tears subsided. And then a bit longer until the cold trickled against her skin, slipping into her muscles enough to stiffen them.

He'd done it again.

Moja had thought she'd moved on, created a new life, returned to her old world. And then he'd invaded it, carrying a suitcase of memories he'd unpacked in her home. Not all of them bad. She rubbed her arm where he'd touched her. Her skin still tingled.

Memories.

"Liar."

There wasn't a lot of energy in her curses, not as much as there should be. Because he deserved it. He was jet lagged and tired, was he? She'd been exhausted for the past two years, every bit of energy expended in recovering, moving on. He had the audacity to come back, pry open her life, throw in his lies and—

"Moja?" Nyanya's voice was soft, almost frail.

Moja scoffed. Nyanya played the frail old lady card when it suited her. Like now, probably.

"Coming!" She dragged herself into an upright position. By the time she reached the front door, Nyanya was in full lecture mode.

"That the way you treat all your men friends? No wonder you're still single. It's like you ate sour pudding for breakfast."

"Nyanya, I really—"

"You're really sorry?"

"No."

"You should be. Sorry. Ashamed. Me, I'm embarrassed for you. What kind of nonsense is this? I know I raised your father better. I should never've let you spend so much time in that park. Raised by animals, you were."

"He deserved it."

"Who? Your father?"

"Really, Nyanya?"

Nyanya huffed and gestured for her to come inside. "That boy, he likes you plenty enough."

"Plenty enough for what?" Moja already regretted the question. There was only one possible response when it came to Nyanya.

"To get married! Or at least give me some children to spoil. What's so wrong with that?"

"Pretty much everything."

"Bah. Young people these days."

"You don't know what he did," Moja said, and then added, "and no, I don't want to talk about it."

"Good. Because you talk too much. Go after him. Apologize—"

"Apologize? Me?"

"You see anyone else in here? My eyesight's bad, but I'm not blind."

Moja had lived long enough with Nyanya to know a few things. Like, there was no winning an argument. The old woman could talk her way in and out of any situation. Even when the police tried to arrest her the time they caught her driving her neighbor's uninsured car.

When the officer had asked for her license, she'd huffed, wagging a finger at him. "Me, I'm too old for a license. And you're too young to be harassin' your elder. Does your mama know how you treat a grandmama?"

Moja held up her hands. "I give up."

"I don't understand," Nyanya said. "Remember that time you made me join you two on one of those video call things?"

"Biggest mistake ever."

"I thought you two were gonna tell me some big news."

"Guess you thought wrong."

Nyanya studied her, that knowing look a little too sharp for Moja's comfort. "I still think there's big news between you."

"You're right, Nyanya. But it's not the good kind. I'm going to bed."

"Good. A good night's sleep might put some sense into that thick brain of yours."

"Love you, too."

"Bah."

Moja closed the door, and stared at the empty basket where Nyanya had stored the letters. Now tucked away in a drawer. Taunting her with their unread words. Pleading to be opened.

Not interested.

She tried not to wince at the obvious lie. Of course she

was interested. Interested to prove that nothing Jack had to say could change the past.

You want the truth, don't you? Read all of them.

It wasn't his words that snagged her attention. It was his expression. Desperate. Lost. Not like Jack at all.

Patel had been the voice of reason. He'd rein in their enthusiasm, reminding them of the business reality. Moja had been the idealist, the visionary. And Jack ... he'd been an engine of boundless confidence, prepared to run full throttle into the new world of their creation. They balanced each other. A great team, the three of them. Once upon a time.

So what happened? She stared at the drawer, visualizing the stack of letters hidden away.

What had he been trying to tell her? Maybe she should've stepped outside for a few minutes, to hear him out. Even if she couldn't trust him. Even if there was *no way* he could tell her anything new, or anything to win her over. At least she could say she'd given him every chance in the world, and he still screwed up.

Unbelievable. She yanked open the drawer. "Un-bloody-believable. He's not even here, and he's managed to irritate me."

But curiosity won over pride. She prayed it wasn't the type that led to a fall. She was still nursing her wounds from the last crash.

Jack had picked at those scabs by appearing in her living room.

She stacked the letters in the order they were written, then yanked opened the first one. Her eyes widened as she read what he'd written — *by hand*.

A handwritten letter, in this day and age. Nyanya was right. It was romantic. Not that it mattered anymore. But still, he'd taken the time, the effort, knowing she was unreachable by her own choice.

She scanned the contents, then read slowly.

He missed her. Wanted her to come back. He'd quit his job, if that would convince her. He was sorry. Not about her removal from the board, of course. It was the best option for the company. But he was sorry it had pushed her out of hAPPening, pushed her away from him.

The second letter repeated the message, same as the third. Different words with increasing desperation and hopelessness.

Come home, Moja.
I'm sorry.
Let's start over.
Just the two of us.
We don't need hAPPening.
As long as we're together.
Too late, Jack.

She tossed the fourth letter to the floor, but there was no heat in her words. No certainty. The worm of doubt had burrowed its way in between her rage and her determination. And that should've pissed her off. She should be even angrier at him. Instead, she felt angry at herself.

What a conniving bastard.

He really was, even when he wasn't being conniving. Because she knew Jack well enough to know he didn't apologize very easily. She could count on one hand the number of times he'd ever apologized unconditionally.

His apologies usually started with "I'm sorry," immediately followed by "but …" and a sharp rationalization for his behavior. An indirect way of saying he didn't actually have to be sorry. But this series of letters? This was one of those few unconditional, wholehearted apologies.

The most recent letter shifted in theme, its tone anxious. He seemed to have accepted her lack of interest in reconciliation. Instead, he started off with an acknowledgment.

I think you're right, she read. *About the dangers. About the need for more limits, the right kind. Not the limits the board has imposed on the number of Places members can join. People love being part of a community, of connecting deeply. But I'm starting to see how this can be abused, just like you said it would be.*

She curled up on the bed, her gaze fixed on his words.

We always said we'd avoid the problems other social media platforms have. We'd be a home of truth. Of connection. Of community. But we're failing, Moja. I wish you were here. I wish you'd reach out to me and tell me what to do. Because I'm really not sure how to handle this. I know you want nothing to do with me, but for the good of hAPPn, and the world, please contact me. Jack.

Moja's hand shook as she turned the page. There was more writing, scrawled, messy, as if Jack had added these words in a great hurry.

She inhaled noisily, wondering what new revelations Jack could possibly provide.

And did she really want to know? She'd left all this behind for a reason. Well, a few reasons. And with each letter, her resolve to never look back was being eroded even more.

Moja kept reading.

Forgive me, but I have to do this. The very thing we promised never to do. They'll hurt you if I don't, and I can't let that happen. I can't let them find you. I could never live with what would happen if I did. Remember the process we created for paid info-posts? I'm skipping it. Even if they distort the truth. I can't give you more details. But if our investor friend asks where you are, don't tell him. Moja, for your own sake, don't tell anyone *where you are.* Especially him. *Stay hidden. Stay safe.*

Moja stared at the message. Reread it. Investor friend? There was only one person who fit that description.

But surely Jack was mistaken.

She had nothing to fear from Patel.

Don't tell anyone where you are. Stay hidden. Stay safe.

"Oh, Jack," she whispered. "What have we done?"

Chapter Thirty-Eight

"My dear cousin, you do realize this might be the high point of your miserable existence, assuming you really are interacting with Prime Placer?"

"Sure, Abe," Jamaal said as he finished drafting a vaguely worded message. "I've always wanted to get arrested for industrial espionage."

Abe leaned over his shoulder. "Your grammar is atrocious."

"Oh, well. Sending now." Jamaal's hand hovered above the Doodad.

"Are you going to send it, or—"

Jamaal spun his chair around, the message unsent. "You really think we can get arrested?"

"We can always get arrested. That's the easy part."

"Not helping."

"We'll be fine. You worry too much. You've received an anonymous invite."

Jamaal squinted at the link. "So have you. But I didn't send the message. How did they know—"

"Prime Placer knows everything." Abe rubbed his hands. "Saddle up, boy. We're going in."

"I thought lawyers are supposed to be law-abiding."

"That's a misconception. We're law-*acknowledging*. In addition, we haven't broken any laws. At least, not yet. And in conclusion, lawyers know the legal system well enough to help their clients *around* the laws without actually breaking any. Have you ever heard of loopholes?"

"We're going to get fired, aren't we?"

"Probably, but I have a contingency plan."

"Oh, goody."

"We'll hire someone to write our story, then sell it for a small fortune. I'll also sue e-Trax on your behalf."

"I feel so much better."

Jamaal waited for Abe to log in, then joined him in the freakishly white, anonymous private room. The humanoid-shaped blizzard of white pixels was already there.

Abe whistled. "You weren't kidding, Jamaal. The signature stamp's a smudge."

"Way to be discreet," Jamaal muttered.

"What did you find, Jamaal?" Prime Placer asked.

"Let your legal counsel answer that," Abe said. "He didn't find anything that's concrete enough to hold up in a court of law."

"What about the court of public opinion?"

"That court is full of jokers, clowns and naked emperors. Public opinion may not be enough to stop the project, unless that opinion is almost universally shared with votes and money attached to it."

"What do you think we need, then?"

"Proof no one can doubt," Abe said. "Physical proof, preferably."

"We're thinking of looking in Legal," Jamaal said.

"Allegedly," Abe added.

"Operation Blow Whistle," Jamaal said.

"We can neither confirm nor deny the plan," Abe said. "It officially doesn't exist. You didn't hear that from us."

Prime Placer seemed to glance between them, although it was hard to tell where they were actually looking. The face was a blurry haze of moving white particles. "I need commitment. Because if you do this ..." The words hovered above them, dangling unspoken suggestions into the silence.

"Let's say hypothetically we find solid evidence of wrongdoing, then what?" Abe asked.

"If you find the evidence, I can drop it everywhere."

"Everywhere?" Abe repeated. "As in all the news streams in every Place?"

"Yes."

Jamaal snorted. "hAPPn has some of the world's best security. No hacker has ever been able to take down even a small section of a wall between Places, never mind move between them and drop anything they want."

"Did you like Rocky's update?" Prime Placer asked.

"Rocky?" Abe asked.

"My pet rock."

"Right! I tend not to remember the names of rocks, no matter how many legs they might have. I can't believe we're related."

"Makes two of us." Jamaal waved at Abe to be quiet. "What about Rocky?"

There was a hint of a smile before it disappeared in a flurry of glowing white speckles. "Were you expecting an update? Did you receive an invoice? A notification from the producer about an available upgrade?"

Jamaal hesitated. "No. Which is kinda weird. I mean ..." He pointed at the white avatar. "How'd you know about the update?"

"You're welcome."

"Fine. You can hack into a pet rock," Jamaal said. "Whoopee. If you're such a master hacker, why can't you find the files? Or whatever the evidence is. I mean, it's not like e-Trax keeps anything offline these days."

"Actually, it does," Abe said.

"Seriously? I thought only my mom does that."

"And the legal department of pretty much every company big enough to have shareholders. We have some offline storage capacity in the downtown office."

"There's that," the Prime Placer said. "In addition, the e-Trax workPlace's encryption is an order of magnitude more complex than the one between Places. I'll set off an alarm if I slip up or trigger a digital tripwire."

Abe looked convinced. Then again, his cousin was built for trouble. And that's exactly what this smelled like.

"So you can access multiple Places?" Jamaal asked. "Prove it."

"Name seven Places you want to visit. And I'll take you to each of them."

"My three Places. And my mom's Place, Persians for Peace. And that new environmental Place I tried to join. Green Table."

"And one of my Places," Abe added. "Law for Lawyers. But not Legalicious—"

"Why not?" Jamaal asked.

Abe snickered. "I'd invite you if I could, but it's strictly members only, if you know what I mean."

"You know my mom's rules."

Abe held up his hands. "It's purely innocent. Lawyers find the law delicious and luscious. Get your mind out of the gutter."

"Sure, Abe."

"Are you ready?" Prime Placer asked.

"We were born ready. Right, Jamaal?"

"Option B."

The room exploded, enveloping them in a blizzard of glowing white pixels that sparkled as they brushed against his skin before solidifying into the central cavern of Geo Rocks.

Jamaal took in the marble furniture, the bioluminescent creatures on the walls, the gold flecks shining down from the ceiling, then checked his Doodad. "We're really here."

"It's not too shabby for a mob of rock diggers," Abe said.

"Wait 'til you see—"

The cavern dissolved into gold and silver dust, revealing the main bio-dome for Geeks Rule. It looked like something from a sci-fi movie mixed with a 3D game. All stainless steel and glass, neon colors and laser guns. Light bled from behind the walls.

A robot approached them, and asked in a mechanical voice, "May I take your order?"

"Maybe another time," Prime Placer's bodiless voice said.

Stainless steel melted into the green leaves and tropical flowers of a digital jungle.

"This must be Green Table," Jamaal said. "They focus on tropical environments."

The world became a green blur that solidified into a large room with hardwood floors, expensive-looking furniture and a giant stone fireplace with a roaring fire inside. Two of the walls were covered in bookshelves.

"Welcome to Law for Lawyers. Smell the knowledge." Abe inhaled dramatically.

"And you call me a geek," Jamaal said.

Persians for Peace looked like they'd stepped into an

Arabian Nights story, complete with a bazaar, camels, and a flying carpet that zipped overhead before disappearing into a palace.

"Proof enough?" Prime Placer asked.

Abe checked his forearm. "She wasn't kidding. Look at your location history."

Jamaal didn't bother checking. "Fine. We believe you."

The Middle Eastern marketplace dissolved into the glowing white walls of the private room.

"Now what?" Jamaal asked.

"Find anything that incriminates e-Trax, or at the very least proves they've been misled. Then give it to me. I'll take care of the rest." Two coins popped into existence in front of them. "You may need these."

"Do my eyes deceive?" Abe snatched the coins out of the air and whistled. "Is this an incognocoin?"

"They'll buy you ten minutes of complete anonymity in any location within hAPPn."

"That must've cost you a fortune," Abe said.

"Make my investment pay off. Find the evidence."

The room dissolved, and Jamaal found himself back in his digital office, incognocoin in hand.

Chapter Thirty-Nine

"What's the news saying?" Theo asked.

Eva gripped the door handle as he took a corner without slowing. She kept jumping from Place to Place, scanning various articles. "The protest's targeting this year's Sustainable Resource Extraction Convention. They're also protesting Eco Warrior's arrest."

"Of course they are. But isn't City Conference closed for the night?"

Eva flicked to another Place. Same news, different slant. "No. Everything's open until midnight. Oh, fog."

"What now?"

"The road, Theo," Eva shouted as they hurtled toward a red light.

Theo slammed on the brakes. "I can't believe she snuck out. What was she thinking?"

"Eco Warrior is there."

"I thought she was arrested."

"Out on bail."

"Typical. Bloody justice system."

Traffic was thin, so they were making good time. But the news was moving faster than they were.

"Eco Warrior's breaking the rules of her bail," Eva said. "Police have started to mobilize. They're cordoning off a three-block radius around the conference center."

The light clicked green. Tires squealed as the car lunged into the intersection.

"I'm grounding her for the rest of her life," Theo said.

"Police chief has requested additional officers to report for duty." Eva flicked through the ongoing conversation between the members of Seattle Police Place. "People are calling the protesters terrorists, Theo."

She closed her eyes, feeling like one of his paint tubes, her insides being squeezed with nowhere to go. She glanced over. Theo's jaw was sliding back and forth. His hands and arms were rigid, and when she touched his forearm, there was no softness in it.

"We have to find her before ..." Theo shook his head, pressed the accelerator.

She nodded, her lips pursed, her trapped doubts fluttering into a web of fearful imaginings. What if they didn't find her? The police were gearing up as if preparing to battle an invading army rather than a loosely coordinated group of unarmed, idealistic citizens. What if the police found Rossi first?

"We'll find her," Theo whispered, as if his words could sweep reality away.

How would they find her? Rossi had left her Doodad at home, and there was no other way to track her. It wasn't like in hAPPn, where children's movements and activities were visible to their parents. Here, in the offline world, she was on her own.

And the offline world was about to get very messy.

Ding! Ding!

She scanned through the media feeds, searching for photos of the protesters. Lots of photos. No sign of Rossi. Notifications scrolled across her Doodad. She'd requested updates from a number of Places.

"What is it?" Theo asked.

"Nothing good."

"Tell me anyway."

"Seattle Police are on war footing. 'Illegal protest ongoing. Prepare for mass arrests.' 'Sending in bomb squad, antiterrorist unit.' 'Leader known as Eco Warrior on site. Proceed with caution.'"

"That it?"

"Eco-War Now is warning its members to prepare for police brutality. Engage in non-violent measures only. Police congregating with gas masks?" Eva put her Doodad down, and stared at the streetlights creating a path through the darkness.

The police had already started cordoning off the area by the time they arrived.

"What if they don't let us through?" Theo grabbed her hand.

"Keep driving," Eva said, pulling up a post from the police chief. "They haven't finished barricading. There's an opening about a block … There!"

Theo swerved into the space behind a bus stop. A police officer shouted at them, but Eva and Theo were already running toward the conference center.

"I'll go to the main exhibition area," Theo said. "You check the plaza."

Eva tugged at his arm, and pulled him into a hug. He was shaking, and it took her a moment to realize she was, too.

"We'll find her," Theo whispered, kissed her cheek, then pulled away. "We will."

Eva nodded. Not because she believed it was inevitable that they would succeed. But because she couldn't allow herself to contemplate anything else.

Chanting grew louder as she jogged toward the crowded plaza. Journalists hovered on the outskirts like vultures around the carcass. Protestors stood inside, restless, a herd about to stampede, but who would be trampled?

Eva maneuvered around the edge of the plaza, searching the crowd for a child. She was wearing her orange hoodie, the color of a fiery sunset. But all the colors here were blues, grays, black, matching the night sky. Placards waved overhead, wooden and cardboard stars against a background of humanity.

"Rossi. Where are you?"

Her voice was devoured by the chanting, words pummeling words, canceling each other out. At least the protesters weren't engaged in vandalism or anything that might appear violent. She hoped they would stay that calm, at least until she found Rossi.

"This is the Seattle Police Department," a voice bellowed over a loudspeaker. "This protest is illegal. Disband immediately, or face legal consequences."

Using this declaration as a cue, the protesters sat, and their chanting grew louder.

Eva pressed against a statue's base, too visible. Across the plaza stood a line of police dressed in riot gear and gas masks. Behind them, more police were positioning a water cannon. The placards and chanting seemed feeble, a candle against a hurricane.

Her Doodad buzzed in her pocket. She pulled it out, praying it was Theo. He'd found their daughter. They could go home, drink a cup of hot chocolate, and forget about this.

"You found her?" she blurted.

"No. And I can't get any closer to the exhibition. The police have blocked access. You?"

"Not yet. Keep looking."

She continued to inch along the edge of the protest, ducking around cameras and reporters eagerly providing on-site, live footage. This was a reporter's dream. Imminent violence, an emotional cocktail of anger, desperation, determination, fear.

She reached the far edge of the plaza, and scanned the seated protesters. Searching for a bright orange hoodie worn by a child who shouldn't be here. Not now. Not with this crowd. But her gaze kept flitting upward to the line of police. It had been reinforced by a second, then a third line. They were now stepping into the plaza, their faces hidden by masks.

Rossi wasn't here.

It took several minutes for Eva's mind to accept what her heart knew. Her daughter wasn't with the protesters. And she wasn't sure if that was better or worse.

Eva clenched a hand over her mouth to hold in the cries, the panic, the sheer desperation. Being chased by a drone had been scary. But this? This wasn't scary. This was leprosy of her soul, a toothy beast devouring the very core of her being, ripping little shreds off of her heart until there was only a puddle of blood left. It yanked the muscle out of her willpower, leaving her trembling, ready to collapse to the ground with only a solitary scream remaining.

"Rossi!" she yelled.

Except it wasn't a yell. It was a shriek that started from the base of her spine and tore out of her, leaving a shattered frame behind.

A few people glanced over at her, mildly curious but too engaged in their own drama to care about hers.

She spun around, almost knocking a camera off of its pedestal. "Rossi, where are you? Where—"

A flash of orange caught her attention. It wasn't among the protesters. It was down a side street that connected the plaza to the main road.

The stores were all closed, windows shuttered. A few street lamps offered stingy puddles of dingy yellow light. A small, feminine shape wearing an orange hoodie was struggling with someone — a large man in a black leather jacket.

Eva stood there, staring in the opposite direction of everyone else, gawking at a mugging, or a kidnapping or … or something that was happening a few dozen feet away. In the shadows between two wells of yellow light. Her daughter. Being attacked. Kidnapped? Worse?

"Move," she whispered, but the air barely brushed against her throat. The word dribbled off of her lips and collapsed at her feet, panting with the effort. Her legs remained immobile, nailed to the ground with pegs of mind-destroying terror.

Rossi pushed against the man as he wrapped his arms around her waist. Laughter tickled at the edges of the chanting crowd.

"Move!" she screamed.

The force of her word broke the spell. She lunged forward. Running. Howling. Preparing to use fists, nails, teeth, feet, her entire being to stop whatever this was.

She was still screaming when she reached the first puddle of light. The man in the black jacket and the young woman in the orange hoodie turned to stare at her. Amused. Curious.

It wasn't Rossi.

The woman in the orange hoodie giggled, whispered something to the man, who laughed.

Eva skidded to a stop, banging her hip hard against a dumpster. Her wordless shout now a labored gasp.

The couple remained in their embrace, kissed, and strolled away from the protest.

Eva studied the side street, searching the shadows and empty shops. But all the light and life were in the plaza.

With the still-sitting protesters, patiently waiting for chaos to descend. They chanted their determination to save the world from the destruction of greed.

With the police as they stood, patiently waiting for the order to move, staring straight ahead with zero emotion, as if they'd dialed their responsiveness down to zero.

Everything blurred. The police softened into three dark gray, furry lines. The crowd was a series of shadowy blobs with only a few squirts of color. A brush of white here. A stroke of pink there. A splash of orange.

Eva's gaze sharpened. "I see her. Theo, I …"

Rossi wasn't wearing her hoodie. She was holding it aloft like a banner, or a piece of sunset captured in her hands.

Eva staggered forward.

The lines of police stepped into the plaza, marching forward. An implacable wave crashing against the shore of an immovable force.

"Rossi. Rossi," Eva sobbed.

Her throat ached, the words raspy as they clawed out of her and burst into the air, mingling with the chant, reaching for her daughter who was always out of reach.

Eva stumbled around the seated protesters, over their outstretched legs. She marched forward until she collapsed next to Rossi.

"Mom?"

"Rossi," Eva whispered and wrapped her arms around her daughter.

"Are you crying?" Rossi's voice snagged at the edge of tears.

"Doesn't matter."

"Mom, I'm sorry. I'm so sorry. I thought my friends would be here. They said they would. But—"

"I know. We need to go," Eva said, preparing for the argument. But this time, she'd end it quickly. She'd drag Rossi out of this mess. Kicking and screaming if she had to, because there was no way—

"Okay," Rossi said, starting to cry. "I didn't know—"

"This is your last warning. Disband now!" The officer's harshness echoed around them.

But Eva was no longer listening. Dry-eyed, she pulled Rossi up, then led her through the seated crowd and out of the plaza.

Holding onto each other, they followed a couple — the man in black, the woman in orange — as the police closed in behind them.

They kept walking, hand in hand, away from the plaza, away from the center of that night's breaking news. A story full of violent hooligans or peaceful demonstrators, depending on which Place you read your news.

Chapter Forty

"Stay cool." Jamaal muttered as he logged in the next morning. "Just stay cool."

"I am unable to alter external temperatures. Would you like me to send a request to the environmental control system in your house, Jamaal?"

"Cancel cooling request," he said and studied his welcome arch. "It's fine, Sarah."

"Canceling request."

"Why don't you take the day off? Just kidding."

Sarah stared at him, silent. The absence of any judgment in her expression felt like a judgment.

Jamaal silently repeated Operation Blow Whistle. The details were woefully few. He'd follow his normal workday routine. Log in. Enter his online cubicle. Enthusiastically start on another report.

Nothing strange here, apart from the enthusiasm. Nope. All good. Focused work.

Until lunchtime …

Most employees honored their lunch hour by logging

off, as per hAPPn's health guidelines. But he and Abe were going to use the incognocoins to enter Legal. They'd do a few searches, hopefully find evidence, copy it, and be out before anyone knew it. Bonus: *they wouldn't have to visit the physical office and risk being identified.*

The entire Operation Blow Whistle was easy, safe and secret, thanks to those magical coins. More importantly, no one would know it was them.

"Ten minutes isn't a long time," Jamaal had complained over breakfast.

"Worlds can change in ten minutes," Abe told him with a grin.

"You talking about your Legalicious Place again?"

Abe waggled his unibrow, then shut up when Mama-i came in from the kitchen with a plate of toast.

"Keep it together, Jam Boy," Jamaal whispered. "Follow the plan. Operation Blow Whistle. Cool name. Super easy. Nothing to it."

He selected his workPlace from the floating menu. The archway glimmered, a silver sheen filling the space inside it. A breath later, he was sitting in his online office. Rocky bounced around him, clacking its mouth, making the new barking noise.

"So much for a quiet pet." He scratched his pet rock on its back.

The little creature flipped over, wagging six legs in the air, an invitation for him to scratch the belly.

"Part of the upgrade, I guess?"

This was weird. Playing with a pet rock. One that now barked and liked to have its belly scratched. As if he'd tripped into an elephant-sized rabbit hole and woke up in an alternate dimension. And not necessarily a nice one.

"You've got this. It's the right thing to do. Isn't it?

The hAPPening

Besides, Abe won't let anything bad happen. He's a pretty good lawyer, you know."

Rocky stared at him, then spun in a circle, yapping.

"Yeah. We'll be fine. No one'll know it was us. In. Out. Incognito. Easy."

Jamaal focused on his report. The one he'd promised to submit the day before. He set up his *do not disturb* rock troll on a timer until lunch. Not that it would stop Ms. Chan if she decided to check up on him, which he was constantly expecting to happen. Good luck had declared war on him a while ago.

He spent the next several hours plucking away at the report. When he figured it must be close to lunchtime, Jamaal glanced up at the floating clock on his ceiling, then groaned.

It had only been thirty-seven minutes.

Please let this day be over.

He redoubled his efforts. There were graphs to build, stats to massage, words to juggle. A few minutes later — or maybe a few hours — a notification from his rock troll alerted him to Ms. Chan's arrival a second before the soft *pop*!

She casually gazed around the room. But there was nothing casual about Ms. Chan. Ever. If casual was a pair of jogging pants and a sweatshirt, she was a polyester suit and a starched, buttoned-up, bleach-white shirt.

She caught him looking at her and smiled. It wasn't a happy smile. More like Mama-i's cat when it caught a small, defenseless creature and dumped the mangled carcass outside his door. An *Aha! Caught you* smile.

"Nice upgrade on the pet rock." She nudged Rocky out of the way. "Are you done with the report?"

"Almost, I—"

"I'm reassigning it to Charlie."

The report vanished from his desk, immediately replaced by another assignment. "We just received these core samples from a location in northern Alaska. Analyze them, and let me know by this afternoon."

She popped out before he could ask why she hadn't had him arrested yet.

Jamaal waited a minute, just in case she returned, then sent a message to Abe. An automated, 3D response in the form of a unicorn pranced across his desk. A smoking gun riding the unicorn sang, "Abe's in a meeting. Abe's in a—"

Jamaal dismissed the unicorn and gun. He called Abe.

"I saw your message. I'm in a—" Abe began.

"She knows," Jamaal whispered. "Ms. Chan. She—"

"She doesn't know. Otherwise, you'd have been fired or arrested already. You were taking too long." But Abe's forehead was creased.

"Yeah. Maybe. That must be it."

"We can still back out."

"Don't tempt me." He picked out the incognocoin from his pocket. "You think these things work?"

"Absolutely. See you at lunch."

Jamaal stared at his new assignment. Why would Ms. Chan take the Lucy file from him, and give him core samples from some rubbish site in northern Alaska? He could tell with one glance it was a useless ore, hardly worth the company's time to study, let alone drill for it.

He held up the incognocoin. It felt solid, heavy for its size. The coin's gold surface twinkled at him. It reminded him of the golden Caligula Medallion in Hell's Fury, the one Crazy Eyed Cyborg always managed to find before his team ever got close.

His fist closed around the coin. "Not this time. Game's on. And there are no rules."

He tucked the coin away, and whistled as he wrote a

scathing report about the Alaskan find. Lots of poetic irony or metaphors or whatever people called fancy writing.

He only stopped whistling after conjuring another possibility: *Prime Placer was part of an elaborate trap, and he was about to pop right into it.*

Chapter Forty-One

Eva could feel Theo's questions bubbling into the silence, but he said nothing. Flashing red lights splashed a discolored stain across his profile as he twisted the wheel. The car pulled out of its parking spot and glided away from the growing mass of police vehicles, riot gear and reporters.

Theo cleared his throat, staring at her and Rossi through the rearview. His mouth opened. She shook her head. His jaw slid to one side, grinding his words into a puff of air, stopping them before they popped the silence. He stared at the empty road stretching before them.

Rossi eventually stopped shivering, and slid away from her mother. She tugged her hood over her head, casting her face in shadows, and huddled on her side of the backseat. Eva stared at their hands, separated by the middle seat. She started to withdraw her arm when Rossi reached over and grabbed her hand.

"Thanks," Rossi whispered.

Eva squeezed her hand. She didn't dare speak in case her voice startled the moment between them, like a branch snapping near a grazing doe.

Theo parked the car in front of their home and they sat for another wordless moment, as if someone had just died or been born. Theo's slamming door shattered the trance.

Eva expected Rossi to retreat to her room. Instead, she joined them in the kitchen, slouching at the counter and fiddling with her sleeve cuffs.

"Hot chocolate?" Eva offered and held up the box of cocoa.

Theo glanced between them. "Are we going to talk about this?"

Eva frowned at him, then focused on mixing the chocolate powder and hot water.

Rossi burst into tears. "I'm sorry."

"That's all very well, but—"

"She won't be doing that again. Will you, Rossi?"

Rossi shook her head, and wiped her nose with her sleeve.

Theo stared at the counter, teeth clicking as he worked his jaw. "Fine. But your mother and I *will* be discussing your consequences. Won't we, Eva?"

"Yes, we will."

"Great. I'm going to check on what's happening out there." He reached the doorway, turned to meet Eva's gaze. He pointed at Rossi, and mouthed, "Talk."

Eva nodded. She pushed the cup of hot chocolate in front of Rossi, then moved around the counter to sit next to her. "I'm proud of you."

Rossi tugged her hoodie partially off her face and stared at Eva as if studying her expression for either a lie or a trap. "Why?"

"Because you did what you thought was right."

"But it wasn't, was it?"

"Why do you say that?"

Rossi shrugged. "It was scary. All these people shouting. The police. I think I was the only kid there."

"You were."

Rossi sniffed at the hot chocolate. "Have you ever been so scared, you can barely breathe?"

"Plenty."

Rossi's eyes slid to the side, and she frowned. "Really?"

"Really. Like tonight. When I couldn't find you …"

Rossi's shoulders hunched even more, as if she was about to fold in on herself and disappear into a black hole created by the dying sun of her heavy heart.

"I think it's great you want to be active in defending the environment. It's not an area I entirely understand, but I'd be up for learning. Maybe we can attend a protest that isn't illegal?"

Rossi smirked. "Where's the fun in that?"

"You're right. What was I thinking? Getting arrested is so much fun."

Rossi rolled her eyes. "Whatever. Green Teens has an exhibit this weekend at the conference center."

Eva held out her hand. "It's a date."

"Yuck. I'm not dating my mom." But Rossi took Eva's hand and shook it. "You mean it?"

"Absolutely."

Rossi tugged the hood off of her head and slurped at her drink. The refrigerator's hum blended into the stillness between them. Chocolate perfume wrapped Eva in a comforting embrace.

Theo returned and sat across from them, hands clutched loosely. They reminded Eva of Mr. Patel's hands. Long fingers, elegant, an artist's tool. But Theo didn't have the thick, wormlike veins pulsing across the surface. Instead, hints of red and yellow paint edged his fingernails.

Impulsively, she reached across and gripped one of his

hands. He glanced at her, eyebrows rising in surprise even as his mouth quirked into a smile.

"Don't get all mushy and kissy-kissy in front of me, please," Rossi grumbled. "There's only so much trauma a kid can handle in one night."

"We'll try to restrain ourselves," Theo said.

"So about that dog," Rossi said.

Eva tensed.

"I've decided I don't want to enter the dog show. You know, the one online."

Theo straightened up. "That's news."

Rossi drained the rest of her drink. "It's just that … it's kind of stupid when you think about it. Getting points for looking after a dog that doesn't actually exist? I think I've got enough to do around here. Like take my mom to a legal protest."

"You okay with that, Chief Growth Engineer?" Theo asked.

"I think I can handle it."

"Cool. 'Cause I'm done here." Rossi pushed away from the counter. "Remember. Legal protest, this Saturday. And *not* a date."

Theo waited until Rossi's footsteps were a fading echo ascending the stairs before asking Eva what was on her mind.

"You were right. About the view."

"I'm always right. What am I right about this time?"

She laughed. "The view from the top isn't all landscapes and sunsets."

Theo cupped his hands and stared at them. Maybe studying the paint-stained lines on his palms. Or visualizing his next piece of art. "You sure?"

"Of course not." She looked around the kitchen. State-

The hAPPening

of-the-art everything. Modern, yet classic. Like the whole house, every tile and tap mortgaged.

"Private schools are probably overrated," Theo mused. "Definitely overpriced."

"We did okay slumming it."

He reached for her hands. She met him halfway.

"The apartment wasn't so bad, was it?"

He laughed. "Oh, it was *bad*. But at least it was ours."

She nodded. "Good to know. But don't pack up just yet."

Theo squeezed her hands. "I have no intention of going anywhere. Do you know why?"

"Because you trust my impeccable judgment?"

"Because whatever we decide to do together, it'll be the right thing."

"I hope that's true this time."

Ding! Another notification on her Doodad, demanding her attention.

She huffed a laugh. "This thing was blowing up all night."

"And yet life still goes on, even outside of hAPPn."

Eva pulled out her Doodad and scanned the most recent notification. A message Rossi had posted on both her Places:

going 2 green teens exhibit Saturday. Bringing parents!!!

Eva smiled. "You know, you may be right."

Chapter Forty-Two

IF OUR INVESTOR friend asks where you are, don't tell him. Don't tell anyone where you are. Especially him. Stay hidden. Stay safe.

Moja reread the letter. Jack was mistaken. Why would Patel threaten her? Or try to blackmail Jack? He was their mentor, a friend. Her adopted uncle.

This can't be right.

She repeated the thought, as if it would become true in the repetition.

Jack had to be confused. He was accusing *Patel*. Maybe they'd been joking around, and Jack had taken it too seriously. Or perhaps he'd misheard.

Unless he was telling the truth.

But, no. Patel was family. He knew how important the national parks were. Not just to her, but to Kenya, and the world. He'd never do that to her.

But he was the only other person who knew where she was. He was one of the few people who had the skill, the resources, the influence to make all of this happen. The longer Moja mulled over the contents of the letters, the less certain she felt about anything.

Moja folded the letters, slid them into a drawer and locked it. Had anyone else seen the contents of those letters? The envelopes didn't look like anyone had tampered with them. Yet another benefit of offline communication.

If Patel was behind whatever this was, he could've easily created the tracer program. Maybe he was keeping tabs on Jack, as well. She fiddled with her phone. To call, or not to call. Her fingers made the decision.

"Kapinski Hotel. How may I help you?"

She should really hang up …

"Hello?"

"Jackson Rustle, please."

Why would Patel do this? It couldn't be about money; his bottom line had always been about technological revolutions.

But at any cost?

"Moja?" Jack's voice was a whisper, as if afraid to startle her into leaving.

"Tell me it's not true."

He said nothing, but his silence said plenty.

"So what did you do about it?" she asked.

"Nothing. What could I do?"

"A lot, Jack. You could've done something."

"He's powerful."

"So are we."

"You don't understand."

"Then enlighten me."

"Things have changed. The system. He's changed some of the code. Made himself *the* god, instead of one of three."

"Gods can die, too."

"Not easily."

"Is that why you're here, Jack? Trying to escape?"

"I'm trying to save you. When you never responded, I figured you either hadn't received my letters, or hadn't read them," he said without accusation or bitterness. It was simply a statement of fact.

"And now what?"

"I …" He gulped. "I really don't know."

"We can stop them."

"Patel—"

"He's just one man."

"He's so much more than that."

"We have to deal with this, Jack. I'll send you an invite to my private room—"

"No. It's not safe enough."

"Patel might be a brilliant developer, but he can't break through *my* walls."

"Are you sure?"

She hesitated.

"Moja, it's serious. If Patel finds out I used a link to visit you—"

"And you don't think he's tracked you here?"

"Why would he? I'm taking a holiday. I haven't gone on leave in a couple of years."

"Hmmm. He might be suspicious at the timing of your holiday."

"I haven't given him any reason. I've cooperated. Done everything he's asked."

"You sure have. I'll be there in half an hour."

The Kapinski was an elegant hotel with a classical design. It also wasn't cheap. Privacy was part of its famed service. Foreign presidents stayed there, according to rumor, their visits unannounced until long after the fact.

That's what you get when you pay premium rates, Moja thought, standing in the lobby entrance and searching for Jack.

Security kept an eye on her until he arrived and waved at the guards to let her in. The grandeur receded into soft blurs of beiges and cream as they stared at each other, a couple of meters and years in between them.

Jack looked away first, then led Moja to a small seating area tucked in a corner behind giant, potted plants. She took the chair with its back to the wall and watched him, waiting for him to start.

He tapped the armrests, studying the plants.

"Jack—"

"You were right. All along, you were right."

She'd waited so long to hear him say those words, to hear him and Patel validate her fears instead of accusing her of paranoia. That hAPPn, her creation, could be manipulated. After all this time, she expected to feel vindicated, triumphant. Instead, she felt empty.

A cold wind filled the void.

A hand brushed over hers, and she glanced up.

"It happens to the best of us," Jack said.

"What does?"

"Reality."

"Oh, that."

"Yeah. That. I just finished a call with one of my Chiefs. I had to lie — make a threat in order to save her. Since when was that part of my job description?"

"Did we do the right thing?"

Jack tightened his grip on her hand. The warmth sunk through the cold, but she still shivered. "You mean, were we right to create hAPPn? Or have we created a monster?"

She waited for the response, hoping he had one. Her hands were now both in his, the warmth spreading to her arms.

"Don't forget all the good things that have happened because of it. It's easy to let the bad news drown us, but also remember the successes, the happy stories, miracles and victories. There's always going to be a few people who abuse the loopholes in every system, but—"

"This is different, Jack. They're using hAPPn to bury the truth, to push ahead a project that will destroy an ecosystem. What else is hAPPn being used for? What will be next? Overthrowing governments?"

"You giving up on me, Moja?"

"No. I came to Nairobi prepared to fight. And that's what I'll do, with or without you. But I've seen what we're up against, Jack. Places becoming more and more polarized. Everyone taking a stand, convinced they're right, and everyone else is wrong. No one's talking anymore. And I wonder … Are we any different? Maybe Patel's right to back this project. Maybe it's for the greater good."

"If that's true, then why do they need the lies?"

"Because people can't handle the truth?"

Jack smirked. "You believe that?"

"I'm not sure."

"He's getting into your head."

"He never left." Moja tugged her hands free, clasped them on her lap.

"They shouldn't have kicked you out."

"You were there, too."

"And I should've said something."

She crossed her arms, the cold returning, a brittleness seeping into her bones with each inhale. "So why didn't you?"

"Because I believed Patel. That's the truth."

"Like sunlight," she whispered.

"What?"

"Something Ojil said. Truth is like sunlight. The world dies without it. So we stay in the light."

"Which means …"

Moja started to laugh. A tentative sound, on the verge of collapse. A newborn giraffe struggling to stand on shaky, awkward legs.

But it refused to fall. The cold evaporated before its warmth, taking the last two years of anger and grief with it.

She reached out, grasped his hands, squeezed them. "It's time to reclaim our company, Jack."

"I'm not sure if I'm relieved or scared."

"Probably both."

"How reassuring. What's the plan?"

She told him what she'd learned from Eva and Jamaal, and what she hoped to receive from them.

"Great. We'll take that to the board—" Jack began.

"We'll need to do more than that. If Patel's achieved this much, he'll block the board's efforts to do anything based on what we give them. Or he'll create more lies and half-truths. We'll have to force the board's hand, make it impossible for them to ignore the facts."

"Okay. How?"

"We'll spread the information as widely as possible, enough to matter, enough to change the conversation around the project."

Jack tapped his fingers on his armchair.

"Nervous, or thinking deeply?" Moja asked, starting to smile.

Jack grinned. "Are you accusing me of being a deep thinker?"

"I'd never dream of it. Then what?"

He sobered. "It'll take a lot of time to visit enough Places to matter. As visitors, we have limited privileges. We won't be able to drop anything into the news streams. And I'm out of touch with the design." He frowned. "At the time, it made sense. But now, in hindsight? Patel discouraged me from participating in the updates and new design languages. He said I needed to focus on being CEO. Maybe he wanted to make sure I couldn't modify the design."

"He always was a strategic thinker."

"And you're out of the loop even more than I am," he continued, his tapping increasing in speed and force. Like he was punishing a set of keyboards for not responding fast enough.

"Jack," Moja said and grabbed his hands again. "There is a way."

"Prime Placer faces the same limitations we all do."

She lifted her eyebrows.

"Don't you?"

She glanced at the plants screening them, then at Jack. "No one else knows this."

"Knows what? Patel knows who you are."

"But he doesn't know that I installed back doors."

"So what …" His eyes widened. "Back doors? Where?"

"Everywhere."

"What about Places created after you left?"

"The doors replicate."

His mouth opened, but nothing came out.

Moja mentally counted off the time. Being speechless didn't fit his personality, but she managed to silence him for a whole nine seconds.

"And those doors are still there?"

She nodded.

And he hooted. "Impressive. Good thing you didn't trust us enough to tell us."

"That's not it. I—"

"Don't worry. It's all good."

Silence settled like a lazy cat basking in a puddle of sunshine. Warm. Comfortable.

"He'll figure it out, you know," Moja said. "Once we open those doors. You'll probably lose your job."

Jack shrugged. "No. I'll quit before they fire me. There'll be other jobs."

"They may come after us. Someone's already shot at me. Or near me. I don't think it was planned, but—"

"You think Patel was trying to kill you?"

"No. He wouldn't go that far."

"You're sure?"

She paused, shrugged.

He breathed deeply and held it for a moment. "How safe are you now?"

"Safe enough."

"I can't convince you to back down now, can I?"

"Do you want to?"

"No. I guess not."

"Exactly. hAPPn is *our* world, Jack. Don't you think it's time we defend it?"

"Don't make me regret this."

"No promises. Are you with me?"

He braided his fingers with hers. "Absolutely. I mean, as long as we get to stay in five-star accommodations. You know I don't like roughing it."

"I'm sure I have a five-star tent lying around."

"I'm good with that. It does have indoor plumbing and room service, right?"

"Don't all tents?"

"They should."

"Ready to conquer the world?"

"Conquer, or destroy?" Jack asked, his mouth crunching downward at the edges.

"Destroy. Or possibly save."

Jack sighed. "Fine, but—"

His Doodad buzzed, and the call icon blinked brightly

enough for Moja to see the glow from her angle. Jack glanced at the screen, then blanched.

"What?" Moja asked.

Wordlessly, Jack lifted up the Doodad and showed her the caller ID.

It was Patel.

Chapter Forty-Three

"You sure you can get me into Legal? I don't have clearance," Jamaal asked after joining Abe in the e-Trax lobby.

Abe nodded. "Yes, and I know. But feel free to ask me again. I'm sure my answer will be different from what it was two minutes ago, half an hour ago, and two hours ago."

Several of Jamaal's colleagues were entering the Games Room. They'd opted for online entertainment over offline lunch. One of them paused when he saw Jamaal in the lobby.

Jamaal pretended not to notice the friendly wave. "Just in case these coins aren't real—"

"They're real."

"But if they don't work for some reason. If we're not incognito, and your boss sees us—"

"I'll tell him it's *Bring your idiot relative to work* day."

"I think I'm gonna be sick."

"If you vomit now, you'll find it all over your lap when you log off."

"Right. Caligula Medallion."

"Excuse me?"

"How do these work?"

"Toss it like a pill and swallow. Your avatar becomes magically invisible. It's an expensive, one-time invisibility cloak."

"Fine. Let's—"

Abe knocked down his arm. "I have to take you to Legal first. Once you swallow the coin, your Doodad disappears so people can't find you. And once your Doodad goes—"

"I can't access your invite," Jamaal finished. "Got it. But if we pop into Legal, and someone sees us before we swallow the coins?"

Abe smiled. "Aren't you glad I already have an excuse made up?"

"Idiot relative day."

"There's hope for you after all. Placer, share invite link to Legal with Jamaal Shirazi. See you on the inside, cousin."

Jamaal had never been in Legal before. There'd never been a reason. He stepped out of the entrance arch, and gawked.

Legal's workPlace made Geo look underfunded. It had been designed like a private library inside a wealthy lord's castle. Antique furniture and carpets dotted the space. Tapestries covered some of the walls on the ground floor. Three levels of balconies circled above him, giving access to side rooms and files. Thick candles floated through the room, casting a mellow glow. A soft, steady *tick-tock* echoed around the room.

"This Place is huge," Jamaal muttered when Abe appeared beside him.

"Ready to pop that coin?" Abe asked.

Jamaal held his in front of his mouth. "On the count of three—"

"Just eat it." Abe swallowed. A second later, he vanished.

Jamaal looked at his Doodad and searched for Abe's location. *This member is offline* came the automated reply.

"Dang. They really do work!"

"Jamaal, eat the coin. Mr. Robard my supervisor just stepped onto the second-level balcony."

Abe's disembodied voice startled Jamaal.

He looked around, seeing nothing.

"You can't see me," Abe said. "That's the point. But you know who can see you? Everyone who looks over here. Maybe it really is idiot relative day."

Motion above nabbed his attention. A gentleman in a pinstriped suit removing a file from the bookshelf. He tucked the file into his Doodad, and began to turn around.

Jamaal chomped on the coin.

Nothing happened.

"Abe. It didn't work."

Mr. Robard finished turning around and looked down at the ground floor.

Jamaal tensed, preparing for a surprised shout, an accusatory look. An interrogation. Maybe a forced visit to HR to explain his presence in Legal.

Nothing.

The supervisor popped out of the second-level balcony, and appeared on the first-level balcony.

"Abe?" Jamaal whispered, then jumped when he saw a translucent man standing right next to him. "Why can I see you?"

"Our incognocoins are synchronized. We have ten minutes. Keep an eye on the ceiling clock."

Jamaal craned his neck. A giant grandfather clock was

suspended horizontally under the arched ceiling several stories above them. The pendulum swung side to side, the source of the soft *tick, tock*.

"Where do we go?" Jamaal asked.

"The location for all our files related to Lucy is on the third-level balcony, the one with the oil painting of a fat, old guy. Nine minutes, twenty seconds. Let's run."

"Aren't there links in this Place to move faster?" Jamaal grumbled, following Abe up a set of metal, corkscrew stairs.

"Not inside here. Manual labor it is."

They reached the oil painting and Abe gestured to three mahogany filing cabinets with brass handles. "You take the left one. I'll start on the right. We'll meet in the middle."

Jamaal started flicking through digital files that appeared as yellow file folders. "What if there's nothing here?"

"There's always something here."

"Survey maps." Jamaal pointed at a folder.

"I don't speak rock."

"e-Trax does its own studies — both remote and on the ground — to detect viable deposits. Survey maps are the end result of those studies. They have all the major land features indicated. Mountains. Water bodies—"

"Forests?"

"Exactly. The Lucy maps are in here."

Tick, tock.

Abe gestured for him to hurry up. Jamaal started to smile as he pulled out the folder. It disintegrated in a shower of yellow confetti.

"Fogger," Jamaal said and yanked back his hand. "Is that supposed to happen?"

"No. You must have hit a tripwire."

"These things are booby-trapped?"

Abe frowned. "It seems a bit peculiar, doesn't it?"

"You think? I could lose a finger, or an arm! You know how expensive it is to replace a whole arm?"

"Why would they booby-trap these files if they're already in a secured location with limited access?"

Jamaal peered into the cabinet and poked at another file.

Tick, tock.

Abe glanced at the ceiling. "Seven minutes left."

"This is crazy."

"Not as crazy as this." Abe waved a folder between them.

Jamaal glanced at the neon green words written across the yellow surface and shrugged. "Share transfers. What's strange about that?"

"Share transfers are processed and filed in Accounts, not in Legal. So why is anything about shares here?" He opened the folder and whistled. "Oh, my. Take a look—"

The folder exploded in a puff of neon green smoke. Abe clutched his hands as if they'd been burned, and stared at the charred remains of the folder smoldering at his feet.

Tick, tock.

Jamaal compulsively looked at the ceiling. Three minutes left. "We should get outta here. Where's the link?" He looked over his shoulder, expecting to see the invite link glowing in preparation for his departure.

"We'll have to walk to the entrance. It's the only way in or out of this room."

Jamaal peered over the balcony rail. The entrance looked far away.

"I suppose this is the end of it," Abe said as they

hurried down the corkscrew. The metal stairs bounced and creaked under their weight.

"Were those the only copies?"

"I doubt it. Legal keeps physical copies of anything important in the downtown office."

"And you have the access card for Legal, right?"

Abe glanced back at him. "Can you hurry it along? We have less than a minute."

"Abe, do you?"

"If you're thinking of trying to find the physical versions of those files? Forget it. We'd need a few hours to sift through everything."

"But we could, couldn't we?"

"Now look who's the troublemaker."

"I mean, if you think it's a bad idea—"

Abe grinned. "I *know* it's a bad idea. I'm impressed and a tad embarrassed you thought of it before I did."

Jamaal started to reply when a strange sizzling sound interrupted him. He glanced at his hands. They were no longer translucent. A tinge of color seeped across them. "Abe?"

"Time to speed this up," Abe said and zoomed ahead. He reached the archway just as his incognocoin expired. "See you at dinner!" he shouted and popped out of the library.

"What are you doing here?" a voice bellowed from above.

Jamaal jumped at the amplified voice, and blurted, "Idiot relative day. Looking for the bathroom!"

He jumped into the archway, and smacked his hand on the invite link, popping out before anyone could question him further.

Chapter Forty-Four

SHE KNEW IT WAS PARANOID, but Eva stared out the window of her offline office for a minute too long, searching for a drone. Nothing but a beautiful view stared back. Maybe whoever had been flying the drone figured she'd received the message.

Oh, yes. She donned her Shaids and logged in. *Message received. Now here's mine.*

She increased her privacy setting to maximum, and used a digital *do not disturb* monkey to take messages. Then she went through the file Jack had originally given her. Everything seemed in order except for one thing: a contract. Wasn't that a requirement?

She thought about calling one of Marsha's minions in Advert. But Marsha would find out, so she sent her a request.

A minute passed. Then another. Right before the request expired, Marsha replied, inviting Eva to enter her office.

"My, my. Ms. Taylor. I didn't expect a visit from you. Ever." Marsha arched her heavily plucked eyebrows.

Eva glanced around the office. Nothing fancy. Very utilitarian decor. An open door indicated anyone could pop in to see her.

"I thought it was about time we chatted," Eva said.

"How you honor the lowly."

"I have a few questions about advertising."

Marsha scoffed and rocked back in her chair. "Why don't you ask your best friend? I'm sure Jack could teach you all sorts of interesting tricks."

"Maybe later. Tell me about Advert's contract process."

"Really, Eva? Now you want to take over my department?"

"I'm visiting all the Chiefs. Trying to understand the bigger picture."

"How's this for a bigger picture? I'll send you the tutorial I give all my new staff."

"Sounds good. How about the summary version right now?"

"Anything specific?"

"Corporate clients."

"What about them?"

"Is there any situation in which they don't require a contract?"

"*Every* advertiser needs a contract, corporate or not. It's hAPPening's policy, not to mention the law."

"Right."

"For small spenders — under ten grand a month — it's a standardized version. They click a button accepting the terms and conditions that none of them bother to read, and they're good to go."

"Big spenders?"

"We tailor the contract to their specifications. The client signs off on it, then I do, then it goes to Accounts."

"I figured as much."

"Anything else I can help you with, *Chief*?"

Eva forced a smile. "I'll let you know."

"You do that."

Eva popped back into her office and went through the file again, slowly. No contract or mention of one. But this wasn't a small spend. And the law required a contract even if the work was a favor.

"What are you up to, Jack?"

An invite link appeared in her bottom left vision, bypassing her *do not disturb* monkey.

Speak of the devil. She clicked the link and popped into his fish tank office. "Funny thing. I was just thinking about you, Jack. You sure you don't have our offices bugged?"

He looked at her, frowned, then chuckled. It sounded forced. "That would be a severe invasion of privacy. How're things going?"

"Great. What's up?"

"Not much. We're on track with the info posts, right? Did you reach out to those influencers you found from Database?"

"Thanks for the reminder." Eva glanced at the baby elephant in the corner. It waved at her.

"Any time." He tapped on his glass table, staring down at the ocean floor.

"By the way, Indra Patel's name came up in conversation yesterday."

Jack sank back in his chair, his expression stony. "Really? Have you ever met him?"

She shrugged. "Should I?"

"It's an experience best avoided. That old man can pick out a winning investment from a mile away, but he's nuts. And possessive. His retirement was the best possible thing for this company. How's Rossi?"

Eva hesitated. "Fine."

He nodded, his attention returning to the glass table. What was he seeing there that she couldn't? Communication from e-Trax's CEO with more instructions for their next quasi-illegal activity?

"Jack, I—"

"You have to watch kids closely, Eva. Really closely. Seems Eco-War Now has found ways to infiltrate child-only Places. A serious security breach. Were you aware of this?"

She swallowed hard. "So I've heard. It's also on my to-do list, to investigate how it happened, and plug up the hole."

"Good. You're lucky the police didn't find Rossi. That would *not* have gone down well. You saw the news this morning? About what happened at the protest last night?"

Eva's avatar didn't suffer from a constriction in its throat, or sudden parchment in its mouth, but Eva did. She stared numbly at Jack. Was he threatening her? Warning her? How did he know Rossi was there?

As if reading her mind, Jack said, "Don't worry. I saw her photo in one of the news streams and removed it. Along with any other photo she was in. I've taken care of everything."

She nodded.

"Timing is everything, Eva. I don't want the board finding out your daughter was involved in an *illegal* demonstration any more than you do. Because what would be the point? I'd hate to lose my best Chief."

"You know how that age is. She's just a kid."

"I agree. But the police take a hard line with illegal protests, especially ones that include eco-terrorists. You know their leader is on trial for destruction of property?"

"I know." Eva stared over Jack's shoulder, her eyes

twitching back and forth. A school of fish floated close to the wall, glistening iridescent green and blue. There was no sign of the shark. "I couldn't find the contract."

"Your new contract? I thought you signed it already."

"No. I mean the contract for e-Trax. You know, for the info-posts. They're corporate clients, so they should have—"

"I've got it handled," Jack said, tapping the glass table. "You don't need to worry about it."

"Glad to hear it. Do you mind sending me a copy? I'd like to have a complete file. Jack? Can you hear me?"

Jack froze and shimmered, as if he didn't have enough bandwidth to support his presence in the online world.

But that didn't make sense. hAPPening had the highest level of connectivity, and it never failed. So why was Jack full of static?

"I'm sorry, I didn't hear that," Jack said when he solidified.

"The e-Trax contract. I want a copy."

"I said I'll take care of it, Eva," he snapped.

She took a step back, her hands instinctively rising in a show of peace.

He exhaled heavily and wiped around his mouth. "Sorry. I'll take care of it." His voice was calmer but still scratchy.

Eva couldn't tell if it was the connectivity, or his voice that was failing. "I understand, Jack. But …"

"Enough!"

Jack blurred around the edges, frozen, his mouth open, his eyebrows bunched together in a scowl.

The entire room became pixilated. The wall behind him shivered, as if about to crack under the ocean's vast pressure. Except there was no real water on the other side.

It was all highly condensed pixels, forming a perfect 3D image that looked more real than the physical world.

Knowing this didn't change Eva's gut reaction. She stumbled backward as a line of static formed a crack across the glass tank.

"Placer?" she whispered.

Nothing. She glanced at her Doodad, checking the description of her location beacon, of the desk's, the fish, the coral. They were all listed as present. But Jack wasn't.

"Jack?"

And then he was back. "—so stop interfering," he shouted, his face flustered. "Lives are on the line. You get it? Lives, Eva. Real lives. Not digital creations like ... like all of this. So back off."

"Jack, where are you? Your signature stamp, the beacon, it's—"

"I'm working out of state. And quite frankly, it's none of your business where I am. Just do your job, Eva. Got it? Do. Your. Job!"

"What's really going on, Jack? Mr. Patel said—"

"Patel? That lunatic? It's all his fault."

"What is?"

The room seized with convulsions again. Chunks of digital glass cascaded around her, while deep cracks flashed across the walls.

The school of fish glitched, disappeared, then reappeared on the other side of the fish tank office. But not outside. They were *inside* the room, floating between her and Jack.

Another glitch, and they were embedded in the floor. Neon pink currents swished overhead.

"Jack," Eva whispered.

"—circumvented proper procedures," his voice shouted, even as his avatar remained frozen and streaked with static. "You're not supposed to drop paid info-posts without the proper screening. It's required by law. It's your digital fingerprints all over this, not mine … sorry … I didn't … Don't worry about it, though. I'll handle it … the contract."

The glitching softened, fading into the neon pink currents. The fish wriggled out of the thick glass. The school swooped down to the coral reef, vanishing into its crags and valleys.

Jack silently mouthed an entire conversation, his face sweaty. His hands juggled an invisible ball at a speed that blurred his arms. His voice caught up at the end. "I'm sorry, Eva. But you have to trust me. Can you do that?"

She forced herself not to gulp, not to blink, not to let anything leak onto her expression. "Of course, Jack."

"Good. Really good." He nodded in time with his words, but he wasn't looking at her. He was studying the surface of the glass desk. "Sorry about all that. My offer still stands."

"Which one?"

"To use this room whenever you need it."

"Sure."

"And don't forget. Meeting of Chiefs. This afternoon. I … will try be there. It's going to be your first one. So don't be late. Or it might be the last. Remember. Timing is everything."

His chuckle crackled as he ended the invite, sending Eva back into her office.

Chapter Forty-Five

JACK'S DOODAD continued to buzz. Patel's name blinked on the screen.

"Were you expecting a call?" Moja whispered, as if Patel was right around the corner. She wouldn't be surprised if he was.

Jack shook his head. "We talk once in a while, but it's always scheduled in advance."

The buzzing intensified, the Doodad desperately working for Jack's attention.

"Don't answer it."

Jack clutched the device in his hands. "I always answer. Especially when he calls. It would be weird if I didn't."

"Weirder than you being in Kenya?"

"I don't know. Maybe?"

"We should go. Message him later that it ran out of batteries."

Jack raised his eyebrows. "Do you not know me? When does my Doodad *ever* run out of batteries? I have backups for my backups, Moja. He'll know—"

"Did you tell him you were traveling?"

"No. But my staff know I'm on leave, although they have no reason to tell him. He wouldn't think of following me, would he?"

The buzzing and blinking ceased, and Moja puffed out her breath. "He'd need contacts in Immigration keeping track for him, and why would they? More important, why would he?"

The Doodad buzzed again. A sour taste filled Moja's mouth as she and Jack stared at the notification.

Incoming caller: Patel. Status: urgent.

"I have to," Jack whispered. But he still waited for her to nod before forcing a smile and connecting. "Patel! What a surprise."

Moja leaned away, just in case Jack had answered in video mode.

"Am I interrupting?" Patel's voice was cheerful, calm.

Moja tore a leaf off a plant and began to shred it. Something about this felt off.

"Nope. Not at all."

"You're offline today." A statement, almost an accusation.

Moja checked the time. It was early morning in Seattle. Patel was expecting Jack to be logged into hAPPn by now, busy at work in his digital office, attending digital meetings. Not almost halfway around the world, ten time zones over.

"I needed a break. I'm taking a holiday offline. It's been a while."

"Where are you?" Patel asked, following a pause.

Jack licked his lips and looked up at Moja, his eyes wide. "Visiting a friend. Would you believe it? I still know a few people who aren't on hAPPn."

Another pause, this time longer, more pointed. Then, "I trust you'll sign them up."

Jack chuckled, a forced sound, not his usual relaxed,

jovial, *all's right with the world, and I'm king of it* chuckle. "Next on my list of things to do. Didn't think I'd need a to-do list while on leave, but—"

"You'll be back online soon, then?"

"As soon as I'm done signing her up."

"Her?"

Jack grimaced. "Yeah. You know. As in a woman."

"So you're finally moving on."

Jack glanced up at her, then away. But not before Moja saw him flinch. "Yeah. Something like that."

"I'm glad to hear it, Jack. It's about time. I'd love to meet her. Although I prefer not to leave the greater Seattle area."

This time when Jack looked up, he didn't look away, but mouthed, "Help!"

Moja made a cutting motion over her throat, then pointed at the Doodad.

"Yeah, will do. I better run. You know, gotta pay attention to the traffic—"

"Traffic? It's looking fairly good, according to *Seattle's* traffic cams."

"Figure of speech. We'll talk later, right?"

"I look forward to it. Let me know when you get back home. That is, back to the office."

"Sure thing." Jack hung up, and slid the Doodad onto the coffee table. As if Patel could climb out of it.

"He knows you're not at home," Moja said.

Jack wiped a hand across his mouth. "Yeah, because I told him I was visiting a friend."

"I mean he *knows*. We have to leave."

"Why do you say that? I have friends offline."

"No, Jack. You don't. You barely have friends *online*."

"Ouch?"

Moja stood, gesturing to Jack. "Time to check out."

"I just checked in."

She looked at the series of wall clocks hanging behind the receptionist counter. "And you have exactly five minutes to check out. I'll wait for you at the entrance."

Moja called a FASTr while waiting for Jack. He was downstairs by the time it arrived.

"Why would he call you?" Moja asked as they settled into the vehicle. "Maybe he had a tracer on you."

"He'd need a court order to do that."

Moja stared at Jack. "He owns a few courts and judges. It's not difficult for him to arrange. How else do you explain it?"

"Freaky coincidence?"

"Really, Jack?"

Jack began to tap his fingers across his thighs. "The old fogger."

Moja ignored his muttering, and studied the traffic. The FASTr driver was doing a decent job of navigating the hectic afternoon rush hour. But they were no match for the motorcycles weaving around vehicles, zipping past them, sometimes swerving in a little too tightly.

No match for the drone, either.

It was floating above the median strip, a couple lanes over. The city council logo marked it as a traffic and security drone. It sent updated traffic information to a public website. Police could request access to its video footage during a criminal investigation.

Nothing strange about the drone. Except it was keeping pace with their vehicle.

Who else had access to its camera?

"Jack," she said, lowering her voice. Not that it would help. She raised her window.

"What if I told him I decided to track you down? I

mean, it's the truth. He'd believe I was still—" He glanced at her, cleared his throat. "Well, he'd believe it."

"Is your Doodad still on?"

"Sure."

"Give it to me."

"Okay, why? Wait … what!"

Moja reached across him and tossed the device out his window.

"What was that for? That was … It has …" Jack twisted in his seat, staring out the back. "Stop the vehicle. I … Oh, no. Not a garbage truck!" He flinched, then slouched forward. "Why—"

"That drone. He's highjacked it."

Jack stared at her. "I can't believe—"

"You can get another one."

"You're being paranoid."

"Better paranoid than dead."

"You think he's watching us? Through a *traffic drone*?"

"It's scanning the vehicles. Sit lower."

"It's measuring the traffic."

"Too slowly."

"It's just a coincidence."

"I don't believe in coincidences."

The drone ducked in front of a minibus, entering the next lane over. Its camera swiveled slowly, studying one car, then the next.

"It's looking for us." She opened his door. "Time for us to bail."

"To what?"

"You still pay the full fare," the FASTr driver shouted and stopped the car as Moja climbed over Jack and jumped out.

"Is this normal around here?" Jack tumbled after her.

"You see anyone complaining? Get down." She dragged him to the ground.

The drone drifted up to their FASTr, peered inside. The camera revolved as it scanned surrounding vehicles' occupants.

Traffic rolled forward.

"Did it see us?" Jack asked.

"Don't know. Follow me. Keep low." She grabbed his hand, and ran against traffic, away from the drone.

"My Doodad," Jack groaned and pointed to a small circle of rubble crunched into the asphalt.

"Stop fussing. It's just a thing," Moja huffed and pulled Jack to the median.

"An important thing. A thing with all my life on it."

"I'll buy you a new life."

Horns blared as they darted across the highway and into the busy labyrinth that was downtown Nairobi.

"Remember what you said about five-star accommodation?" Moja asked when she was pretty sure the drone was no longer following them.

Jack shouldered his bag, glancing behind him more often than Moja. "I'm guessing that's not going to happen."

"Not even close. But I can promise you the most *uncomfortable* night you've had in a while. And maybe, if we're lucky, we won't get shot at. Compromise?"

"Not dying would be great. And then?"

"And then …" Moja checked for any sign of a drone before entering an internet café, one with decent private rooms. "And then, the gloves come off."

Chapter Forty-Six

"Self-destructing files. Secretive share transfers. It seems someone doesn't want anyone knowing about something important to e-Trax," Abe was pacing the basement.

Jamaal leaned back in his chair. "Way to be specific."

"That's all we know. Why else would they blow up their own files?"

"Stop pacing. You're making me nervous."

"That's not all that should make us nervous."

"Is the share transfer something we can use against them?"

"I'm not sure. In itself, it's not illegal."

"But don't you think the timing is peculiar?"

Abe smirked. "Look at that. Curiosity has finally taken hold in my cousin's Neanderthal brain. One detail — or rather lack thereof — does bother me. They didn't provide any information on who received the shares."

"I'm guessing that's not normal?"

"Definitely not. I only got a glimpse, though. It's possible the details were somewhere else in the file."

"You know what we have to do."

Abe stopped in the middle of the room and shook a finger at Jamaal. "You're crazy, cousin. I've suspected it for a while. Who voluntarily decides to be a rock digger? But this … This is a whole new level of insanity. I'm not saying I'm *unwilling* to engage in shenanigans. You should see what we do at Legalicious …"

"No, thanks."

"But breaking into an actual, offline office—"

"Whoa." Jamaal lurched upward, his chair rattling against his desk. "Who said anything about *breaking* in? You have the access card for Legal, right? So it's not breaking anything."

"No, apart from a few company regulations. There's no incognocoin when you go offline, Jamaal. If a security guard or supervisor just happens to be strolling by when we're rummaging through files we have no business—"

"You work in Legal. What files can possibly be off limit for you?"

"Plenty, although I appreciate your confidence. The filing room is technically off limits to junior staff."

Jamaal leaned against his desk. "Search for truth."

"Poetic, however—"

"Why do we play Hell's Fury so much?"

"Because it's fun. Because we can legally kill each other without actually killing anyone, so we don't go to jail for embarking on a mass murder spree. Because it's a fictional, online game, as opposed to that little thing I like to call *reality*. Perhaps you've heard of it, the world that exists outside of hAPPn?"

"Exactly. The world that exists *outside*. And part of that world is going to be stripped of a rainforest—"

"Allegedly stripped," Abe said, holding up a finger. "We haven't found definitive proof yet."

"Those files—"

"The exploded ones? Those don't count."

"But you said they're available offline," Jamaal said. "Didn't you?"

"Who's the lawyer around here? I'm supposed to be the one who argues us in and out of trouble."

"Why did you decide on law?"

"To make money."

"Not to defend truth and justice?"

"Those are commodities to be bought and sold. But I see your point. You want to be the hero now."

"I want the truth."

"At any cost?"

"What's the cost of turning our backs on it?"

Abe whistled. "The rock digger has turned to philosophy."

"No one has access to all the facts. That's how they want it."

"Who's they?"

"You know." Jamaal waved a vague hand. "The proverbial *they*. We all quote them and their convincing statements without any proof. But in this case, the *they* is everyone who doesn't want the world to know that a rainforest inside a national park is about to be bulldozed over, stripped of all its biodiversity—"

"Okay, eco-preacher." Abe shook his head. "I can't believe you have both a conscience *and* confidence. When I said you should grow some curiosity, I was thinking along the lines of watching a few documentaries. Reading a book occasionally. Not breaking into—"

"Legally entering."

"The legal department of the company that pays our bills."

"What bills?" Jamaal smirked. "We live with my mom, Abe. She pays the bills."

"Not the ones in Legalicious."

"Gross."

"Fine. You win. Are you ready to go and maybe get arrested, or at the very least fired?"

"At least I have my lawyer with me."

"Only the best."

Jamaal picked up his Doodad. It was early evening, and the stream of notifications had slowed as people logged off from work.

The one from Ms. Chan grabbed his attention.

"Mr. Shirazi, I'm hoping the cat hasn't eaten your homework, or rather, the report I asked you to compile. I'm assuming you're offline and working diligently in order to complete your assignment by midnight."

The message ended. No *thank you*. No *sincerely* or any other of the typical niceties most people used, even if they didn't mean them.

"At least she's not a hypocrite," Jamaal said.

"If we go, you won't have that report finished by midnight," Abe warned.

"You have your key card?"

Abe sighed, pulled out his wallet and fished around for a small, red card. "Here's your passport to a world of trouble."

Jamaal rubbed his hands. "Awesome. Let the game begin."

Chapter Forty-Seven

EVA SAT OFFLINE, staring at her Doodad and the steady stream of notifications.

Ding. A belated congratulation on her new position.

Ding. A bouncing green heart from Rossi.

Ding! A reminder to be on time for the Meeting of Chiefs.

Her Placer updated her schedule as new invites were received. Assistant Growth Engineer wanted to meet tomorrow morning. *Ding.* Dinner reminder from Theo. *Ding.*

Notifications scrolled across the screen, but she stopped seeing them. Instead, she saw the school of fish trapped in the glass. Fragments of reality cascading around her. A shark cruising around the coral reef. Jack glitching.

Blinking away the images, she studied the signature stamp she'd copied before Jack had dismissed her. A part of his stamp had been blocked, his location beacon hidden. He definitely wasn't in Seattle. She'd never experienced such unstable connectivity.

Not that he had to be in the city. Almost all their work was done in hAPPn. But why would he hide his new location? And why had he gone there?

She paced her office, lingering at the large window facing the water.

"Are you sure we can afford it?" Theo had asked as they waited for the real estate agent to arrive with the sales agreement.

She'd stood at this very spot, in front of the floor-to-ceiling window. "This view alone is worth the price."

"We can't eat sunsets and landscapes, Eva."

"No, but we can afford to enjoy them."

Eva shook away the memories, feeling them scatter around her like drops of rapidly evaporating water. Had Jack been threatening her? Or warning her about a danger outside of his control?

There's no contract, is there, Jack?

At least, it wasn't anywhere it was supposed to be. Using her high-level clearance, she'd scanned the files in Accounts and in Legal, but found nothing. There was only one other location where the contract could be. She had the authority to open that door, as she could any door in hAPPening's workPlace. But this one would be her undoing if she was wrong.

Her eyes unfocused, she saw a glimmer of her reflection in the window. A vague, blurry outline.

"Are you ready to risk it all?" she asked her reflection. "If you're wrong, and if Jack finds out, your career is finished. Destroyed."

Her reflection didn't seem to share her concern. Emotionless, it floated outside the window, waiting for her decision.

"But I'm right."

She didn't have much time to make the decision. And

maybe that was for the best. She'd spent weeks wrangling over what color to paint the walls. But this? A decision that could destroy her family's fortunes?

Timing is everything.

Jack had said it twice. Timing of what?

She checked the time. Less than ten minutes before the Meeting of Chiefs. And she couldn't be late. Jack would suspect something was wrong if she was.

"Timing is everything," she whispered, then cleared her throat. "Placer, locate Jack."

"Jack is currently offline."

Perfect timing.

"Placer, count down nine minutes." She was in the seat, sliding Shaids over her eyes, before she'd really formulated the answer to her question.

Are you ready to risk it all?

She didn't dare answer. Because if she had to — if Eva verbalized her decision — she'd probably say no. Instead, she logged in.

"Placer, open private access to Jackson Rustle's file storage."

She popped into a windowless room, every surface covered in gray stone. The filing system was built into the walls. She searched the directory for key words, losing another second with every fresh breath. She had to arrive on time to the meeting. Her first as a Chief. What excuse could she possibly give for showing up late to such an important event?

None.

"Eight minutes," her Placer intoned.

She pulled files out of the digital storage and floated them in front of her, scanning them. Anything that mentioned e-Trax …

"Seven minutes."

... Lucy ...

"Six minutes."

Or Kenya. But she found nothing new, nothing Jack hadn't already given her.

"Five minutes."

She swept an arm through the floating files, sending them back to storage. "Unbelievable. There really is no contract. The bastard."

She slowly spun in a circle. What next? Think. *Think* ...

Fish trapped in a glass wall.

A pixelated tank imploding around her.

Static-streaked water swirling inward, then flowing back on itself.

What had Jack been reading on his glass desk?

"Placer, retrieve invite link to Jack's private office."

"Invite link retrieved."

"Open link."

Eva held her breath for the millisecond it took for the link to open. Invites were usually time sensitive. It must have expired by now. No way would Jack send her a link that could be used afterward.

Timing is everything.

"Opening link," her Placer said. "Four minutes."

Eva was inside the glass room. The fish tank was empty. Even the elephant was gone. A dark shadow passed overhead. She looked up. A blurry school of small fish drifted toward the surface, like a storm cloud blown into the horizon. An eel slithered through the water, eyeballing her.

What if Jack was spying on her?

It was too late for questions, or doubts.

She moved around the glass desk to where Jack always stood, and tapped its surface. Several translucent folders appeared, outlined in silver. She shivered and compulsively looked around. Jack might decide to come here before the meeting, and he wouldn't give her any notice. He'd pop inside, and that would be the end.

Why had he given her an invite link without an expiry?

The eel bumped against the glass, its toothy mouth open.

"Three minutes."

"All right," she whispered.

She touched each folder, and requested a summary. Text floated above the desk, providing brief descriptions of the contents. One folder held the documents he'd already given her. The second folder was a more detailed analysis of the information provided by e-Trax.

The third folder had no information on Lucy or the info-posts. Instead, there was a single document providing instructions for a transfer of shares from a company called MIJ Creations to several members of the hAPPening board.

"Placer, copy share transfer file. Search for MIJ Creations' subsidiaries."

"Copying file. Search complete."

A short list of MIJ Creations' subsidiaries scrolled down the left side of her vision.

One name caught her attention: *e-Trax*. The company shares would be worth a small fortune if the mining project succeeded.

"Who owns MIJ Creations? Search."

"Unknown. Two minutes."

"How can it be unknown?"

"Repeat request."

"Placer ... Search for MIJ Creations' Board of Directors. Repeat for all subsidiaries. Cross reference. Extract common members."

"Search complete. Cross reference complete. Extraction complete."

"How many board members in common?"

"One."

"Name."

"Indra Patel."

Chapter Forty-Eight

THE STREETLIGHTS HAD SWITCHED ON, and the traffic had died off by the time Abe and Jamaal caught a FASTr into downtown Vancouver.

They stood side by side outside the main doors leading into a glass-and-steel building, the physical offices of e-Trax.

"We're really going to do this," Abe said.

The evening was pleasantly warm, but not nearly enough to explain the sweat forming under Jamaal's armpits. His breathing hitched, and it took him a moment before he could reply. "Changing your mind?"

"Only if you are."

"I'm not."

"Then as your lawyer, I'm comfortable to proceed. How difficult can it be?"

"Famous last words."

"That's my line."

"Let's get at it, then."

"Also my line."

"So what exactly happens in Legalicious?"

"You're a little too young for that one, Jamaal."

"Whatever."

The security guard gave them a nod as they used their key cards to enter the main lobby. A few people trickled toward the exit. The elevators were all at the ground floor, doors open, waiting. The emptiness of the building sounded loud.

Jamaal had visited the physical office on a few occasions, but normally worked from home like most of his colleagues. Built to accommodate five hundred employees, the building seldom had more than fifty at any one time.

As they exited onto the tenth floor, Jamaal shivered and almost wished they'd bump into someone. Anyone except the supervisor. The empty silence on the top floor was oppressive. The open office layout had a cavernous feel to it, devoid of life apart from a few ferns.

"Sure is creepy at night," Jamaal said.

"Imagine you've just entered the haunted Caligula Castle of Hell's Fury," Abe said.

"Yeah, that's gonna make me feel so much better."

"Who doesn't love the haunted castle?"

"Let's find the files and get out."

"Pretend we're looking for the medallion!"

"Abe. Focus."

Abe led the way through a maze of tables scattered across the open area. Several storerooms, offices and meeting rooms lined one side of the floor.

They stopped at one of the closed doors. There was a security panel on one side.

"Here it is," Abe said. "The dragon's lair where we store the gold."

"I really wish we had an incognocoin."

"If only we were online." Abe shook his head, and held up his access card to the security panel.

"Badi-u-llah Yazdani," a mechanical voice intoned. "Input password."

Abe froze, his card hovering above the panel.

Jamaal nudged him. "Time's ticking. The password."

"I don't know the password."

"What do you mean?"

"I think it's pretty clear what I mean."

"How do you *not* know the password?"

"We never needed one before."

"Before being when?"

"Before I needed to enter this room and steal evidence."

"I mean, do you think they added the password today?"

Abe tapped the card against the panel. "Because of the exploding files? It's possible. Remember I told you the filing room is off limits to junior staff?"

"Abe—"

"I've never gone in here without a senior team member. Now I know why. They have the passwords. Well, this has been fun. Shall we?"

Jamaal grabbed Abe's arm. "Take a guess."

"At the password? No, thanks. What if a few false guesses triggers the alarm? We tried. It's time to go home. Maybe we can catch a round of Hell's Fury after dinner."

Jamaal scowled at the closed door. So close. The files were right there, on the other side. He was sure of it. And once again, his team had to retreat. He kicked at the door.

It eased open a crack.

"Why is the door unlocked?" Abe took a step back and glanced behind them.

"Who cares? Let's go." Jamaal pushed the door open the rest of the way. "Hello?"

No response.

"I don't like this," Abe said, still lingering outside the room. "Someone didn't close the door properly. That's against security protocol."

"You wanna stand around and talk, or do you wanna get in there and grab the files?"

"I was thinking of running to the emergency exit and leaving, but collecting the files first also sounds like a good plan."

The filing room was nothing like Legal's online library. For a start, the filing cabinets weren't made of mahogany and surrounded by oil paintings. They were regular stainless steel cabinets, lined up against a bare wall, one after the other. Handwritten placards identified the contents inside each drawer.

The overhead light wasn't from the soft glow of countless floating candles. A couple of fluorescent tubes glared at him, stinging at his eyes.

"Here it is," Abe whispered.

They stared at the filing cabinet. There were five drawers, each one labeled EA-L029.

"I'll search the top two, you look at the bottom three," Abe said.

"I'm taller. I should go on top."

Abe grinned. "Maybe you would fit into Legalicious."

"That's not what I … Forget it." Jamaal pulled out the bottom drawer and begin rifling through the folders.

There were copies of reports describing the deposit. Analysis of the core samples. Contracts with exploration companies. Future contracts — already signed — for supplying Lucy to power plants and battery manufacturers.

"They're really optimistic," Jamaal said.

"Found something." Abe pulled out a vanilla folder. "It's an order to transfer shares."

"To whom?"

The hAPPening

"That makes no sense," Abe said.

Jamaal stopped flipping through the folders when he saw the one labeled Maps. He had to remind himself he was offline where paper didn't self-destruct. He still hesitated before reaching in and pulling out a folded map.

"The shares were transferred to several anonymous members of the hAPPening board," Abe said. "But they never declared the transfer publicly."

"Do they have to?" Jamaal unfolded the map.

"Absolutely. Especially given the size of the transfer, and the value of the shares. I expected them to try and bribe the Kenyan government. But why would they pay off the board of hAPPening? Who are they trying to buy?"

Jamaal stood up and laid the map of Kenya on top of the cabinets. "Here it is. e-Trax's original survey map."

They stared at the map. The company logo was stamped in one corner. A menu key on the other described the meaning of the symbols. Triangles were mountains. Squiggly lines, rivers. Another symbol inside green shading indicated forests. Yellow stars were deposits.

Jamaal tapped the location of the near-surface Lucy deposit in case Abe didn't see it. A cluster of yellow stars huddled inside a larger blotch of green shading.

"A forest?" Abe pulled out his Doodad, taking images of the map and sharing transfer documents.

Jamaal pulled the map closer, a finger gliding under three tiny words as he said them out loud. "Uhuru National Park."

"So they knew all along. I told you I saw a map."

"Congratulations."

"The big question is what do we do with all of this?"

"Looks like I forgot to close the door," a voice called out from somewhere on the floor. "Give me a minute."

Jamaal jumped around, staring at the doorway. "Abe—"

Abe whispered, "It's Mr. Robard. This is bad."

"Who—"

"My supervisor. He's here!"

Chapter Forty-Nine

Footsteps approached the filing room's open door. The room Jamaal and Abe weren't supposed to be in. The room with information that could save or destroy.

The big question is what do we do with all of this?

"If my supervisor finds us here …" Abe's voice shook. "What do we tell him? Think. Think…"

Jamaal glanced around, but there was no place to hide. The room had a few dozen filing cabinets pressed up against the walls, and a square table in the middle. No closets. No exits. Not even a window.

Nothing. No Placer to call upon for a link back to his office. No incognocoin. Only trouble marching toward them.

Offline officially sucked.

Jamaal stuffed the map back into its folder. Ignoring Abe's frantic gesturing, he replaced the share transfer file and closed the cabinet drawers.

"Why don't you head down? I'll join you in a minute," Mr. Robard said.

Someone grunted, and a second set of footsteps thudded away from the filing room, toward the elevator bank.

A bald man in a pinstriped suit appeared in the threshold. He looked older and less robust than his avatar. He leaned in, reached for the doorknob, then glanced up and frowned.

"Excuse me?" Mr. Robard said.

"I should hope so." Jamaal stepped in front of Abe. "You're Mr. Robard, I presume."

"What are you doing?" Abe whispered.

The supervisor frowned. "And you are?"

"Your lucky day, that's who I am." Jamaal swaggered toward the stunned supervisor. Impressive, since he could normally barely handle a stride. "That's right, Mr. Robard. Your lucky day. You know who I am?"

"No." Mr. Robard blinked, trying to keep up with the conversation. "That's why I asked—"

"It's too late for that, Mr. Robard. Your colleague here has been very helpful. A little too helpful."

"Jamaal," Abe hissed.

"I'm calling security." Mr. Robard took a step back.

"An excellent idea. If you don't, I sure will. I work with Prime Security Consulting. We conduct security audits."

"Security audits?" Abe stuttered.

"That's right. And you, sir." Jamaal jabbed a finger toward Mr. Robard, causing the man to take yet another step back. "You and this department are under a security audit. One you are clearly failing."

"We are?"

"This room, Mr. Robard." Jamaal twirled a finger above his head. "This room is filled with sensitive documents. Information you don't want anyone having access to. Am I right?"

Mr. Robard had stopped blinking rapidly, now starting to realize where the conversation was going. "Yes. It's our secured filing center."

"Then do you mind telling me why the door to a secured location with sensitive documentation was left unlocked *and open*, Mr. Robard?"

"It was—"

"Yes, sir. It was. But I should first inform you that anything you say can and will be used in the security audit report. The one I'll be compiling and submitting to your upper management."

His Adam's apple bobbed sporadically. "But I was right around the corner—"

"I see. So you knew it was unlocked and open?"

Mr. Robard licked his lips. "I was bringing ... I mean ... well, you see—"

"Listen, Mr. Robard." Jamaal leaned toward the quivering man. "I get it. You thought you'd pop around the corner to grab something. A pen, maybe? A cup of coffee, perhaps? And then you started chatting with a colleague. And instead of the few seconds to get your pen, a whole minute ticked by. After that bit of pleasantry, you come around the corner and *BAM!*"

Jamaal clapped his hands loudly.

Mr. Robard stumbled outside of the room.

"You walk in here, and find two agents engaging in industrial espionage." He gestured to Abe, who frantically shook his head.

"Yes, I can see how this must look," Mr. Robard stuttered.

"It looks terrible, Mr. Robard. Thoroughly terrible. That's how it looks. Now, between you and me? I understand these things happen. So I'm giving you a pass this time. But in the future?"

Mr. Robard exhaled in relief. "Of course. Closed, locked and secured. Even if I'm only stepping out for a moment."

"Good man. And you should really thank your colleague here. He's been most helpful. Mr. Shirazi? Would you mind taking me out now?"

Abe forced a smile. "Of course. Right this way, Mr. Prime."

Jamaal practiced his swagger as he headed toward the elevator bank.

Mr. Robard mumbled something to Abe.

Abe mumbled a reply and ran after Jamaal.

"Not a word," Jamaal said under his breath.

Abe summoned the elevator with his key card. They entered in silence. The doors swished shut, and the elevator began its descent.

Abe erupted in laughter with an edge of hysteria. "You almost sounded like a lawyer back there, all that fast talking and hot air."

"Learned from the best," Jamaal said, sagging against the wall.

"You're welcome. You know they can figure out who Mr. Prime really is, based on our key cards?"

"But will they? I mean, we haven't actually broken any laws."

"Apart from the NDA, you mean."

"Oh. That."

"Yes. That. Now what's your plan?"

"Contact Prime Placer, hand the evidence over, and forget all about this."

"Really? I was under the impression you were starting to enjoy this unmasked vigilante experience."

"I'll save it for Hell's Fury." Jamaal grinned. "'Cause

next round, I'm gonna kick that cyborg's ass, and find the medallion."

"Roger that."

Chapter Fifty

JACK WAS BREATHING HEAVILY when they approached the internet café's manager to request a private room. The drone hadn't followed them as they ran through the city, but Moja kept her back to the window, just in case it floated past the window.

The manager was a bespectacled young man who struggled to extract himself from his online game in order to serve them. He looked surprised when they requested a private room for the night. "You know there's hotels for that?"

"You always ask so many questions?" Jack asked, leaning uncomfortably close to him.

"No. Your money. Have a nice night." He slid the key across the counter, and pulled on his Shaids.

The room looked like all the other rooms Moja had been in that week. Cramped. Empty apart from a chair and a small desk.

"You sure it's safe here?" Jack asked as Moja set up her Doodad, and positioned the chair to a comfortable angle.

"It has one of the best firewalls available. Not enough

to keep out Patel if he managed to track us this far. But I have a few tricks I can use."

Jack began to pace the room, tapping on his thighs. "He knows I'm here. He knows you're here. How long before he figures out where we are? I mean, that drone! How many others are around the city?"

Moja shrugged, ignoring the heavy lump coagulating in her stomach.

"Brilliant." Jack continued to pace the room. "A genius psychopath is tracking us down—"

"He's not a psychopath," Moja said as she retrieved her Shaids. "And if he is, he's one of the nicer ones."

"Really? You're joking at a time like this?"

"Keep an ear out." She pointed to the door. "I won't be able to pay attention. I need you to make sure nothing strange goes on while I'm inside."

"Strange? As in being followed by a drone? Or getting shot at by a thief?"

"Exactly."

Jack kneeled next to her, gripping her hand. "You're sure about this?"

She met his gaze, controlling her features. Imagining she was her avatar, and she'd decreased its responsiveness to minimal. "Absolutely. We can do this. And then he'll have no reason to come after us."

"Apart from revenge."

"Not his style. He'll move on to his next project."

Jack peered into her eyes, scouring Moja's soul for any hint of doubt or fear. For a moment, she wondered what might've happened if she'd never left. If she'd accepted the board's decision, forgave Jack, and stayed at her job.

You might not've learned about the park being under attack, she reminded herself. *And it's too late for what-if's.*

"It's going to be fine."

"Good luck." He pushed away from her, and shuffled backward to the door, his gaze fixed on hers. "Remember. Keep it quick. Don't assume you're safe in there. Because God knows we're not safe out here."

She waited for Jack to leave. For the *snick* of the door's lock to engage, the sound filling the emptiness.

Deep breath in. Heavy exhale.

Then she slid on the wraparound Shaids and set a timer for ten minutes. She could last for at least that long, even against a head-on attack by Patel.

Probably.

She sent two invites to her private room, then logged in.

She picked up the presence of a tracer program the moment she entered hAPPn. This time, she'd come prepared.

"Evasive program, engage."

It was as if she'd swallowed an incognocoin. Moja became a ghost. She still didn't have much time. Her entrance into hAPPn had triggered the new tracer program. She might be invisible, but Patel knew she was inside. He'd continue to refine his programs until they were able to track her ghost, and tear it apart.

She checked the invites she'd sent out. Jamaal had accepted his. He was waiting in her private room when she arrived. He looked even more nervous than Jack.

"I think e-Trax is going to figure out it was me," he said when her pixelated avatar popped into the room.

"It's okay, Jamaal. We're almost finished."

"Good. 'Cause I'm done. I'll be lucky if I keep my job."

"Really? You think it's luck to have that job? What if I gave you another one?"

Jamaal's avatar was one hundred percent responsive

with his physical body. A sheen of sweat lined his forehead. Streaks dribbled down his cheeks, forming ever-widening stains under his armpits. "Maybe. After all this, I'm up for a career change."

"I suspect you might be."

Without another word, he transferred the scans of the documents he and Abe had found, then vanished from the room.

Eight minutes.

Another tracer program — stronger, more sophisticated — sniffed at the edges of her private room.

She launched a secondary image of herself. A ghost of a ghost, leaking into the infrastructure of hAPPn. It appeared in another Place, and the tracer program dashed toward the decoy.

Seven minutes.

No response from Eva. She sent another invite to the Chief. Then a reminder, followed by a persistent notification binging on her Doodad until she replied.

"I do have a life, you know," Eva said as she popped into the blinding white room.

"Good to know. What do you have for me?"

Eva had developed her own responsiveness subprogram. It was impressive, and Moja admired the detailing.

Right now, Eva's avatar was only at thirty percent responsiveness. She looked cool, calm and in control. But for all Moja knew, Eva was having a small breakdown at home. She'd certainly earned the right.

"Your assistance is greatly appreciated," Moja said as Eva transferred another set of documents to her. "I do have a favor to ask."

"Another one?"

"To be fair, I haven't asked much from you. Only that you do your job."

Eva pursed her lips. "Fair enough. What do you want?"

"Check your messages when you get offline." Before Eva could ask for more information, Moja pushed her out of the room.

Five minutes and counting.

Moja exited her private room, and immediately detected a third tracer. It was practically invisible, a ghost like her. She only knew it was there because she'd been looking for it.

The most sophisticated, least visible tracer she'd ever seen. And it had Patel's signature all over it. As if he wanted her to know he was onto her, that he was going to find her.

"Gloves off," Moja said, summoning an antivirus boxing glove.

The blurry swirl of glowing white pixels disappeared, and she stepped into full view right before she punched the tracer program with the glove. The tracer disintegrated into fractions of code.

"Find that, Patel," Moja said.

Four minutes.

She flung the boxing glove toward her private room, pausing long enough to watch the walls collapse. A fountain appeared in its place, each drop carrying the message, *Too late, tiger.*

Something wrapped around her as she turned to leave. An octopus virus, each tentacle reinforced with small claws instead of suckers, and thick cords of code visible only to her. Tucked within the code were images of a three-headed elephant being devoured by a silver tiger.

"Damn you, Patel," Moja muttered as the virus sunk its beak into her heart.

Chapter Fifty-One

Moja had a fraction of a second to check the walls around her digital heart before Patel's octopus virus attacked.

It wrapped its claw-lined tentacles around her, trapping her arms and legs. Its digital beak slashed at her chest, exposing her heart before it bit into it. One of the walls began to crumble under its brute force attack.

Her hands twirled. Lines of code flowed through Moja's fingers, filling the space around her. Reinforcing the walls around her heart, stabbing the virus with spears of light.

But like Patel, the octopus was unrelenting, uncompromising, determined. Two new tentacles grew back for every one she destroyed.

Jack was right, Moja thought as she weaved another wall, only to see it crumble, disintegrating into glowing, white pixels. *hAPPn has changed, evolved. I've been out too long. But Patel* ...

She'd always known he was a brilliant strategist and a capable software developer. But until now, she hadn't realized just how good he was.

Gritting her teeth, she launched another spear, damaging a tentacle that had almost reached her heart. She glared at Patel's signature stamp, the silver tiger. He was good, one of the best.

But she was Prime Placer.

She gave up on direct attacks. They only made the octopus stronger. Instead, she attacked the infrastructure around them.

Moja opened her mouth, and released a horde of code in the form of fist-sized robotic mosquitoes. The swarm flew around her, an undulating wall of metallic insects and nylon-lace wings.

Thousands of moving targets bombarded the digital world around them. The beams and girders. The ground. The sky.

Everything in their immediate vicinity.

They plunged their needle-like probes into the very lifeblood of the air, and sucked the light out of every pixel.

Distracted, the octopus lashed out at the swarm, tentacles whipping at the mosquitos in a frenzied blur. For each one it destroyed, three more appeared.

"Things I learned in the jungle," Moja shouted as she wiggled free.

The virus made one last effort. It burst into a wall of bright silver flames.

The fire crackled at the mosquitoes, singed their nylon wings, melted their bodies. The mosquitos fell toward the virus from all directions, a shrinking globe of burning metal.

The virus tried to pull back the heat. Too late. A metal cage made of the mosquitos' melted bodies encased it, creating a globular statue.

It settled to the bottom of the half-destroyed space.

"Have fun getting out of that," Moja said.

The hAPPening

She retrieved the documents Eva and Jamaal had given her, and sent out a command. Every back door throughout hAPPn opened. The package of information began to multiply, each copy designed to release an explosion of truth.

Glowing white worms floated everywhere around her, devouring the packages as quickly as they were created.

Full of facts, the worms buried themselves into the fabric of hAPPn. They wiggled their way through the coded infrastructure of the online world, instinctively sniffing out the open doors.

Within a matter of seconds, the worms appeared in multiple Places across the app.

Their mission almost accomplished, the worms created cocoons to protect themselves from the antivirus and antiworm softwares launched against them.

A few minutes after that, the cocoons split open in a cascade of glowing pixels.

Luminescent butterflies flew out and up through countless Places, navigating the news streams, dodging nets set out to trap them. They flew until they reached the ground level accessible to all members.

And there, written across the delicate surface of their giant wings, the full story unfolded in audio, video and text. Every thought and action, every option and opinion. Right *and* wrong, pros *and* cons. No version of the truth left behind.

The butterflies clung to the top of the news streams. And there they remained, despite all efforts to remove them. Everyone's story exposed.

As Moja retreated from the world she'd recreated, the thousands of beating butterfly wings created an informational earthquake.

Streaming across the top edge of the wings were three

words. The ones Moja had initially engraved on everyone's welcome arch at the beginning of creation. The words that had been eroded by time and neglect.

Copies of those three words fluttered throughout hAPPn and settled onto their new homes at the top of every archway. Members of hAPPn saw the words shine brightly every time they logged in.

Search For Truth.

A reminder. And a warning.

Chapter Fifty-Two

EVA KEPT her Doodad off the entire ride home. Sure, she had a couple dozen messages and a few invites to respond to. But those could wait. Especially now. Especially after the Meeting of Chiefs.

It can all wait, she thought and sighed loudly.

The FASTr driver looked at her in the rearview mirror. "Sorry, ma'am?"

"Nothing." And then on a whim, she directed him to take the longer, more scenic route.

His expression suggested he didn't care one way or the other, as long as she paid the bill.

It was worth the price. It gave her more time to think. Time to ponder the implications of everything she'd done. Time for her to visualize what might happen when she arrived home, and opened the cardboard box on her lap.

Indra Patel. Who would've guessed? The wily investor, playing the part of a reclusive, retired man to perfection. Playing them all.

Eva gazed out the window, admiring the view. The glorious summer sunset. Tangerine and crimson splashed across the horizon. As if a petulant child had tossed his paints against the wall making up the sky. Some of it dribbled into the sea.

The view from the top wasn't always landscapes and sunsets. But right now, it definitely was.

She stroked the cardboard box. It wouldn't make everything better, but maybe it would give them a second chance. A new start.

Ding!

Her hand instinctively reached toward the pocket with her Doodad. She stopped before she could withdraw it. She instead shifted her grip, and focused on the cardboard box, the future sitting in her lap. She reflected on the chaos her news *hadn't* created.

Eva had downloaded the proof of Indra Patel's bribe to hAPPening's board, and his connection to e-Trax. She'd then given a copy to Prime Placer. Let Prime Placer deal with the evidence as she saw fit.

Eva focused on cleaning up her digital footprints, and preparing for the other Chiefs' reactions when she told them the truth.

"Meeting has started," her Placer warned.

"Just a minute …"

"You are three minutes late."

Eva rubbed her hands. "Okay. Open link to Meeting of Chiefs." Her office dissolved into the meeting room's silver walls and jade table.

"Looking for a dramatic entry?" Marsha pointedly glanced at the flock of clocks swirling overhead.

"Where's Jack?" Eva asked over the raised murmurings of multiple conversations.

Marsha's disgust turned to confusion. "You really don't know?"

Eva swallowed past the bile rising through her throat. "He's not …" She didn't finish. Would Patel go that far?

"He submitted his resignation an hour ago. And his whereabouts are unknown. He's disengaged his Placer, and his location beacon."

Eva closed her eyes as Marsha's words filtered through the hubbub around her. At least he was safe. But what about her?

"Are you okay?"

Eva looked up at Marsha, and heard the questioning silence. All the Chiefs were watching her. "Sure. Why shouldn't I be?"

"You're next in line."

"I …" Eva lowered her avatar's responsiveness. She still had a job? Or did Marsha mean the next in line to be arrested? "There's something we need to discuss first."

She dropped everything she'd learned about the info-posts into the meeting's stream. She waited for the accusations. The finger-pointing. Because now Marsha had ammunition against her. Even if she'd been the unwitting pawn, Eva had dropped those posts.

Instead, Marsha asked, "What do you want to do, Eva?"

"You don't seem too surprised."

"I had my suspicions."

"You knew about this?"

Marsha shrugged. "The private accounts used to drop e-Trax's info-posts? I knew what they were. I was here when we were using those bots. Same as you. Might be time to shut those down, Pete."

A bespectacled elderly man nodded. "Prime Placer always warned me those were a loophole waiting to happen." He turned to the Chief next to him and began a muted conversation.

Eva glanced around the meeting room. The calm was eerie. Had everyone installed a responsiveness-suppressing algorithm into their avatars? There was no other explanation for the reasonable tones, the soft conversations buzzing around the room. They'd just lost their CEO, learned their angel investor was a crook, and one of their major clients would probably face criminal charges.

Eva lowered her voice, adjusting the setting to private mode so only Marsha could hear her. "Am I missing something?"

Marsha smirked. "Prime Placer reached out before you did. Or at least, the evidence they'd gathered. Including what you just shared. Maybe it pays to be late for a meeting after all."

"I'll keep that in mind. Now what?"

"A few Chiefs wanted to have you court-martialed along with Jack. But based on the evidence, that won't happen. So we'll go after Patel, even though he'll get away with it."

"How?"

"Lawyers."

"Right. Were you one of them?"

"One what?"

"Who wanted to go after me?"

"No. We need a CEO, and that's a role I don't want. So congratulations. Don't screw this one up."

Eva waited for Marsha to finish. Because of course she wanted something. But the Chief of Advert simply watched her.

"And I suppose you'd like to be Chief Growth Engineer?"

Marsha smiled. "See? I knew you'd be a great CEO."

Eva had entered the meeting expecting a showdown with Jack, and the proverbial firing squad from her peers.

The hAPPening

Instead, she'd gained an ally, earned a promotion, and all without any bloodshed. She chuckled, attracting another confused look from the FASTr driver.

The sunset shifted into deeper reds and oranges, like the glow of embers in the fireplace. Eva leaned against the headrest and stared at the road ahead.

"So what are your plans as CEO?" Marsha had asked after the meeting, as Chiefs popped out of the room one by one.

What, indeed?

"I have a few ideas," Eva admitted.

"Let's get together and discuss them," Marsha said. "I have a few ideas of my own. And maybe we can invite Prime Placer while we're at it. They seem to know quite a bit about the inner workings of this world."

Eva had agreed. This didn't make them best friends, but she could certainly use one less enemy. At least for now.

The sunset's paint finally dribbled to the earth and soaked the horizon, leaving a glittery darkness in its wake. Only then did Eva pull out her Doodad. She stared at the list she'd already compiled for her new job. Questions, mostly.

Increase the minimum age of hAPPn membership?

Tighten requirements for paid info-posts?

Build linkages between Places to encourage info sharing — definitely, but how?

How to reverse fragmentation of truth?

Ding!

A message arrived from Prime Placer.

"Congrats on your new job as CEO. You'll do great. Let me know if you run out of ideas. I have a few. A favor: two friends will soon be needing new jobs. They'll serve you well. They may not appear to have the right credentials, but they have something more important: integrity, and a sense of humor."

Eva glanced at the attached profiles: Jamaal Shirazi, a geologist, and Abe Yazdani, a lawyer.

What do I do with a geologist? she wondered, but promised Prime Placer she'd hire them anyway.

Ding!

The new message floated across her screen. The three-headed elephant bounced on top of the words as she read them.

Search for truth. It hides in the intersection between opposing ideas.

"Madam?"

Eva gasped at the intrusion, then coughed to hide her confusion.

The FASTr driver peered at her. "This is the place, right?" He waved vaguely out the side window.

"Thank you."

She approached the house, taking each step with care. The cardboard box made her movements awkward. The weight of its contents shifted, almost unbalancing her.

"Easy does it," she whispered.

Theo had left the light on over the front door. Seeing the warm globe warmed her more than the glorious sunset, or her promotion, or defending the integrity of hAPPn.

Muted voices greeted her as she eased the front door closed. Theo and Rossi were in the dining room. Their laughter wove in between their words, creating an invitation that made the air around her almost glow. She followed it, treading softly, not wanting to disturb them.

They both looked up, their smiles a mirror of each other. Theo's eyebrows rose when he saw the cardboard box, but he kept quiet.

Eva slid the box across the table toward Rossi and slumped down in the seat next to Theo.

"Success?" he asked.

"On so many levels."

"This for me?" Rossi was studying the box.

"Definitely," Eva said.

Rossi poked at the side. "Too big to be a new Doodad."

"Not that you need a new one," Theo said.

"I could use an upgrade."

"Moving on," Eva said.

"Definitely bigger than a new set of Shaids. An S-Suit?" Rossi turned the box around as if searching for a company logo.

"Not even close." Eva leaned against Theo's shoulder. "It isn't designer. And it definitely isn't digital. But it's kind of sweet in a messy way, very fluffy, and looking for a home."

Rossi chewed on her lower lip as she fingered the flaps on the top of the box. "It's not a flowerpot, is it? You know I really don't do well with flowers."

"That's quite a statement for an environmentalist," Eva teased. "No, it's not a flower."

Rossi stood, her chair sliding across the hardwood floor. Gingerly, as if suspecting a trick or a trap, she pulled the flaps open.

Then jerked backward, squealing as a fluffy head popped out of the box, already whining at her.

"Nice job, Mom," Theo murmured.

Rossi reached inside, wrapping her arms around a wriggling puppy. "You're kidding? This is for real?"

"She definitely isn't robotic," Eva said. "I think it's time. Time we had a little bit of mess and chaos in our lives."

Rossi hugged the puppy and buried her face in its fur.

The little creature licked at her ear, then tried to chew it. "Thanks, guys! This is so much better than Fluffy. I'll take care of her. Feed her. Take her for walks. I promise. You won't regret this."

"I'm pretty sure I will," Eva said. "It's not house trained yet."

Eva's Doodad *dinged* as a notification popped on the screen. Without looking, she took out the Doodad, and turned it off.

Chapter Fifty-Three

"You sure it's safe?"

Moja stared at Baby Moja without answering. The elephant's mottled pink and brown stood out against the backdrop of shadowy greens and flashes of colorful bird feathers. "It is now. Even if he can't blend in. He's too big for—"

Jack snorted. "I wasn't talking about the elephant."

"I know."

He leaned against a tree as comfortable as if he were in his fish tank office inside a shark-infested digital ocean. "So why're you going back in, then?"

"I have to."

"Not really.

Moja reached out and squeezed Jack's hand. "I'll be back soon."

Jack followed her to the Kenya Wildlife Service compound, but didn't enter her cabin. Instead, he joined Ojil at the picnic table.

Ojil glanced at her, eyebrows raised, the hint of a smile on his wrinkled face. She frowned and shook her head.

He laughed, and said in Swahili, "Your granny and me, we're not getting any younger. Neither are you!"

"What's the rush?" she called back. "And don't translate any of this for my friend."

"Oh, a *friend*, is he?"

She slammed the door on Ojil's knowing chuckle, and opened hAPPn. She stepped into her welcome arch, and glanced up at the archway, at the message blinking at her: *Search For Truth.*

"Let them try to cover that up again," she said, and surveyed her kingdom.

Eva had started her new role as CEO of hAPPening. She'd already removed limits on the number of Places a person could join. She'd also tightened the restrictions on paid info-posts. And she and her daughter were having an ongoing conversation about the best ways to train a puppy.

Not a bad start, Moja thought. *Not bad at all.*

Moja glided across the surface of hAPPn, glancing at the chaos her work had produced. But it was a good kind of chaos. The kind that challenged assumptions. Suggested the possibility there were multiple truths in the world.

She checked in on Jamaal. He too was online, settling into his new job at hAPPening. He and his cousin Abe worked directly under Eva as part of a new oversight task force. A golden medallion hung around Jamaal's *do not disturb* rock troll. The troll waved a banner over its square head. *Smear this, Crazy Eyed Cyborg.*

There was a stirring in the code, followed by a *POP!*

"I'm not the villain here, Moja."

She turned around. "Maybe not, but you're not the hero, either."

Patel snorted, then drifted toward her. They were standing at the edge of a cliff, far above the world they'd created. Twinkling lights indicated the location of hAPPn members. Lights blinked in and out, as people moved between worlds. The sight made Moja smile, despite Patel's presence.

"That's caveman brain thinking," he murmured. "There are no heroes or villains."

"But there's truth. A truth you tried to hide."

"Is it a crime to want to lift millions of people from energy poverty, to improve air quality, to save lives? Your actions have set back that agenda by a decade."

"How philosophical of you. But it's not an *either-or* situation. We can do both, you know."

"Not easily. I see more than you do."

Moja held out her hand, and a three-headed elephant appeared on it. Each head faced a different direction, allowing her to see almost all around her.

"You are rather attached to elephants, aren't you?" Patel asked.

"And you're still pretending to be a god."

"Wasn't it you who said we're gods in this world?"

"And you said that's a heavy burden."

"Ah, yes. My clever protégé."

"That was before."

"Before you quit your job?"

Moja shook her head. "Before you orchestrated my replacement as CEO. Before you decided to destroy my home."

"And how many homes will go without electricity because of your decision?"

"We'll find a way. There're always other options."

"Expensive ones."

"Other deposits are out there. Go find them."

"You'll allow that, will you?"

"Of course."

"Is that a promise?"

She glanced at him. "Only if they're really in designated wasteland. Then they're all yours."

Patel nodded and gazed out at the scene. "It's quite a magnificent view from up here."

"I prefer my views with sunsets and elephants. Then again, anything's better than a prison cell."

"I'll walk free, you know."

"You'll walk, Patel, but I'm the one who's free."

"How cliché. The truth will set us free. Is that it?"

"Ignorance is a form of oppression."

"And truth can confuse the uneducated masses."

"Then we'll educate them."

"Not everyone wants to have their eyes opened, Moja."

She smiled. "We don't have to convince everyone of the truth, just enough people. Truth is like sunlight."

"It'll blind you?"

"No. It'll chase away shadows. Warm your soul. Make good things grow. All we need to do is shine the light. Push back the darkness long enough for enough people to see."

"Now who's philosophical?"

She kept quiet, watching the lights twinkle across hAPPn.

"Will we be seeing you again?" Patel asked.

Moja smiled. "Count on it."

What to read next

**Zain Fischer has been trapped
in this examining room forever.
At least it feels that way.**

In this strange cancer clinic, the doctor never comes and the nurse won't answer questions. Zain is lost, wandering endless hallways as she tries to find her way back to Reception, but every door she opens leads to another painful memory of loss and regret.

Get The Last Ten Minutes Today

A Quick Favor

Thank you for reading *The hAPPening*.

If you enjoyed this book, please consider writing a review of it on your favorite bookseller so other readers might enjoy it too. Just a couple of sentences would mean a lot to me.

Thank you!
Vered

About the Author

Vered Ehsani has been a writer since she could hold pen to paper, which is a *lot* longer than she cares to admit. Her work in engineering, environmental management and with the United Nations has taken her around the world. She lives in Kenya with her family and various other animals.

The monkeys in her backyard inspire Vered to create fun, upbeat adventures with a supernatural twist. She enjoys playing with quirky, witty characters who don't quite fit the template for 'normal' despite their best efforts. She's perfectly comfortable exploring the brighter side of human nature.

Are you looking for a mind-refreshing dip into a charming, fanciful world? Then welcome. Sit down with a cup of tea and prepare to be reminded that life can be a delightful place.

Write to vered (vered@sterlingandstone.net) — she loves connecting with her readers!

Also By Vered Ehsani

Society for Paranormals

Miss Knight and the Night in Lagos

Miss Knight and the Ghosts of Tsavo

Miss Knight and the Automaton's Wife

Miss Knight and the Mantis' Revenge

Miss Knight and the Fourth Mandate

Miss Knight and the Nandi's Curse

Miss Knight and the Spider's Web

Miss Knight and the Stones of Nairobi

Miss Knight and the Wedding Killer

Miss Knight and the Throne of Death

Miss Knight and the Poacher's Catch

Miss Knight and the Pyramid's Puzzle

Wavily Witches

Witch Way To Go

Witch Time For Tea

Witch Bat To Swing

Witch Law To Break

Witch Demon to Trust

Witch Bride To Chase

Witch Ghost To Hunt

The Pirates Ahoy Cozy Mysteries

Storm Wavily and the Pirate King
Storm Wavily and the Sea Lord
Storm Wavily and the Lost Treasure
Storm Wavily and the Ghost Town
Storm Wavily and the Secret Society

The Next Evolution

Transition
Convergence
Evolution

Stand Alone Novels

The Christmas Camel
The Last Ten Minutes
the hAPPening

www.ingramcontent.com/pod-product-compliance
Lightning Source LLC
LaVergne TN
LVHW03153506052G
838200LV00056B/4510